THOSE THAT GLOW GOLD

BY MICHELLE MATTESON

ISBN: 979-8-9899085-2-3 (Paperback)
ISBN: 979-8-9899085-0-9 (eBook)

Any references to historical events, real people, or real places are used fictitiously. Names, characters, and places are products of the author's imagination.

Front cover image by Ler (www.twitter.com/bifacialler).

Third printing edition, 2022.

thosethatglowgold.tumblr.com
instagram.com/thosethatglowgold/

FOR MY SON

Never give up on your dreams.

PROLOGUE

It is the mental bonds that are the worst.

Her body is in stasis—of that much, she is confident. Her body will heal; it will not age; it will not wither and rot. She's unsure why the idiot put her body in stasis, allowing her to live. If the situation had been reversed, she would have made sure his body would be a husk so that even if he got out of whatever prison she made—

how could he, she was stronger than him, he would go mad, he would never escape, he would be bound forever, for as long as she wanted

—he would come back to a rotting corpse, to gasp and claw at life only to collapse a moment later, his last seconds on this plane in complete agony. It's what she would have done.

But he must have put all of his energy and effort into constructing her mental prison and didn't want her rotting body to interfere with his magic. She had spent the first few years throwing herself against it, in blind rage and panic. Trying to transport herself away, trying to astral project her spirit out, trying to see the future, just trying to see *something, anything*, that was not the white walls of nothingness that stretched in every direction. She entered some stupor at some point, her mind going numb to protect itself from madness. Was this to be her existence? Nothing as far as she could see. No stimuli? No color? No noise? Just light?

At some point (after decades or centuries, she is not certain), she comes back to herself. And in some moment of clarity, she knows she has to find her way out. And so, she started the endless task of looking for one: a crack, a seam, a door, something. Anything made can be unmade, and she will not let the idiot—

is he dead? she hopes he's dead

—win by giving up and going mad.

So she starts to test the walls of light. She walks along with her hand out—

of course, it is not her hand, it's a non-hand, not a physical one, but it's her hand, her mental hand, an extension of herself, running along her prison

—and she feels for her crack. Her seam. Her door. And some days—

again day is a relative term; it could be years, as far as she knows

—some days, that wall she follows feels like it is only a foot long, and she runs her hand over it, again and again, and some days, oh some days, it feels like it goes on forever. And she walks and walks and walks, hand still out, still feeling, refusing to give up even though it feels like she is walking endlessly.

And finally, finally, after years—

decades, centuries, a millennium, how could she know?

—she finds a crack. A single crack. Where the magic is weakest, either from poor artistry or from time, she doesn't know. It does not matter. When her hand finds the crack, she starts the tedious but vital work of opening up her prison.

And so she rubs, she picks, she pulls, she runs her hand,—

non-hand

—her fingers,—

non-fingers

—at one point, she feels like she uses her teeth,—

non-teeth

—to widen the fracture, make it bigger.

She rubs, she picks, she pulls.
She rubs, she picks, she pulls.
She rubs, she picks, she pulls.
She rubs, and she picks, and she pulls.

It hurts. Sometimes the pain is like a hangnail, and sometimes it's like she has rubbed her fingers to the bone; sometimes, her whole being hurts. But it works, after years—

years, decades, centuries, a millennium, who is counting?

—of work, it's big. Not big enough for her to escape, not enough to locate her physical form, but big enough to get out and walk about in her spiritual state. Not interact with the world, but see it, really see if for the first time in forever—

years, decades, centuries, a millennium, maybe it's only been months, she can hope for months

—and it's more than enough of a reward for her to be happy.

She astral projects herself into the world, searching, grasping, seeing, and is all bright and colorful and dark and warm and cold and loud and quiet. She runs with the animals of the earth; she swims with the creatures of the sea; she flies with the beasts of the air. Sometimes the animals die at her touch, die at her possession of their senses, but what does it matter? She is feeling for the first time in so long. It takes a lot of energy, and even though her time seems short, she returns to her prison to rest—

for years, decades, centuries, a millennium, gods, if she could only tell the time

—and goes out again. Any time out of this prison is time well spent.

She then reaches out to her descendants, which is better than any animal she could find. She can join with them for long periods because of their connection with blood. And she feels their pain, their joy, their hunger, their lust, their love, their anger, their rage. To feel anything is like drinking cold water in a desert, and she gulps it greedily. So what if her presence drives them mad? She needs to feel again. So that when she is forced back to her prison, she has their memories and emotions to sustain her.

But there should be more than four of them; she swears there were more. And her descendants start to dwindle. Four to three to two to only one. After all, they are mortal, killed by famine, war, thirst, sickness, and their fellow man's hand. She panics. What happens when there is none? Will she be forced to possess animals again, with their meager emotions? Will she have to fight the bounds of her prison and escape without her physical form? How long will that take?

years, decades, centuries, a millennium, no, no, no, no, she doesn't want to fight for that long, couldn't fight for that long, damn that man

And when she is about to give up hope, she leaves her prison, perhaps for the last time. She finds the last descendant, and reaches out to her. She is a woman of light and laughter and music and song. She is happy for the light and the laughter and the music and the song. But mostly, she is pleased to see the woman with a baby, a small bundle that she sings to and feeds and rocks to sleep. A baby means another generation she can follow and occupy.

But there is something different about the child. She senses it when she appears to the baby one night, wanting to possess it and feed on its emotions. Even a baby can feel more than she can in her prison. The baby *sees* her, gurgling in delight, even though she presumably only looks like a glowing light ball. It is the first time a descendant has *seen* her, interacted with her. And there is a spark of something there. Something strong.

And she pauses in a moment of lucidity. Maybe she should wait. Let the child live with no interference from her. See if that spark would lead to something, something that could mean freedom for the prisoner.

And so, the prisoner, who had been alive for years—

years, decades, years, centuries, years, a millennium, years on years on years on years

—leaned down to the cooing child. And she said a spell, the first spell she had spoken since she lost her freedom and found herself trapped in that endless jail.

"Grow, little one. Grow and become strong. See if you can take over this world. I'll be waiting to see how you do."

She smiled as the baby made a sound of joy.

"And I'll take over if you are not up to the task."

~ 1 ~

Chrysta woke up with her alarm. She had programmed her phone to play *Morning Mood* for an alert, probably the most cliche song to listen to, but it always put a smile on her face in the mornings, so why not? She stretched and burrowed into the covers. The days were getting shorter and the mornings colder; soon, she wouldn't want to leave the bed at all.

But she did get up and walked over to the heavy curtains to open them. She loved her room for the balcony alone, which gave her a chance to spend a little time outside before she had to get ready for school. She padded out with her phone, letting the music continue as she stretched.

There was the flap of wings, and a raven dropped to the stone railing. She smiled at him as she finished a yawn. "Mornin', Poe," she said.

He gave a squawk and then gracelessly hopped over to her on the railing. She leaned on it as she gave his neck a scratch.

"How are you doing, Poe?"

He gave a louder squawk.

"Oh, really, gonna see the pretty female in the park today?"

Low squawk.

"Just be yourself. She'll like you. Bringing some buttons wouldn't hurt. Want me to find some?"

He clicked his beak together rapidly and closed his eyes as she scratched. Chrysta laughed and then put her head in her hand.

"Lucky bird, getting to go wherever you want," she joked. Her smile died a little. "I think you wouldn't come around if I didn't give you food or shiny stuff."

He looked at her and cocked his head to the side. He suddenly took off, and Chrysta sighed. She loved Poe. She did. She just wished sometimes he wasn't one of her only friends.

After *Morning Mood*, some Mozart started to play, and she closed her eyes and swayed to the music. She heard Poe come back and opened her eyes. He had brought her a large, blue bead, roughly the size of a marble. When she opened her hand, he dropped it into her palm. It was heavy and cold, and she wondered if it was glass. "Oh, Poe," she sighed. "It's lovely; you didn't need to bring this to me." Poe just gave her a squawk and took off.

She went inside. She let her phone continue to play music as she looked for some string. She put the bead on and looked in the mirror. It was beautiful, and it made her smile. That was why she loved the strange bird. Poe always tried to make her feel better.

She dressed and went downstairs. Breakfast with her father was promptly at 7:30 each weekday morning, and her father hated her being late. Chrysta paused on the staircase to take a breath. She entered the first-floor dining room, and he was already there.

Jozef York was an imposing figure, no matter the time of day. Chrysta had only seen him wear suits and ties. Today's selection was dark grey with a red tie and pocket square. His dark brown hair swept back from his forehead, and it had only started to grey at the temples. He was studying some papers laid out on an open newspaper in front of him, his cane leaning on the table. Jozef York walked with a limp but had never told Chrysta why. She waited to his right. "Good morning, father," she stated.

"Good morning," he replied, no warmth in his voice. He slid something from underneath the newspaper. It was an invite to a classmate's Halloween party. "Please give Miss Williams your sincere apologies, but you won't be able to attend."

"Yes, sir," she said, trying not to look disappointed as she took the invite. She didn't like Chloe Williams but hoped her father would let her go. He glanced at her and did a double-take. "What are you wearing?"

For one moment, Chrysta thought he was talking about her uniform, but he reached out and lifted her new necklace. He rolled the bead so the light caught the gold flakes set in the blue.

"I found it," she lied. "I thought it was pretty."

He continued to look at it for a few moments but suddenly pulled it off her neck. She blinked in surprise but bit her lip. She knew from experience that complaining would not get it back. He placed it on the table. "It's gaudy," was his only explanation. She just nodded and sat in her chair at the other end of the table.

Servers wordlessly brought breakfast out—eggs, bacon, and yogurt with fruit. Breakfast, like every meal with her father, was a silent affair.

When done, Chrysta stood with her plate. "May I be excused?" she asked.

"The help will clean up," is all her father said. Chrysta tried not to shift uncomfortably.

"I don't mind cleaning up," she explained.

"Fine," her father said, "take it to the kitchen and get to school."

She nodded and left the dining room. Like every day, she felt a weight lift off her shoulders as soon as she was away from her father. She made sure no one was watching as she took a piece of bacon from the plate.

She grabbed her backpack and violin case in the front hallway and was out the door and in the car. The drive was also silent, so Chrysta watched the world go by from her window. Soon, she would be old enough to move out. No more silent meals with her father, getting to wear what she wanted, going where she wanted. She could get a job, be on her own. Make friends.

The car pulled up to her school, students climbing up the front steps. Chrysta got out without a word to the driver. Most of the people her father employed seemed to be under orders not to talk to her.

She paused once she saw the car pull away. On cue, Poe dropped from the sky and landed on a lion statue flanking the front doors. Girls shrieked and jumped away. Chrysta was surprised to see another bead in his beak, and she held out her hand so he could drop it in there. She let him have a bit of bacon while she inspected it.

"Careful, you will never get rid of him now," said a voice, and Chrysta smiled at her friend, Mary Jackson. She had known Mary for years, and she was the only one of Chrysta's peers not to blame her for her father's controlling behavior. Mary saw the bead in Chrysta's hand and leaned down to take a closer look. "What's that?"

"Don't know," Chrysta confessed. "Poe brought me one of these this morning, but my father took it away." She turned the bead in her hand as she scratched Poe's neck. "I guess he wanted to bring me another one."

"Look, the weirdo has a weird pet." Chrysta winced but tried to keep the annoyance off her face. She turned to see three girls walking up the steps.

"Hey, Chloe," she answered. She tried to hand the blonde girl in front of the group the Halloween invite. "I'm sorry, but I won't be able to make it to your party."

"Of course not," Chloe chided. "I told my mother you wouldn't come; I don't know why she forced me to invite you."

Chrysta sighed. She didn't know why the most popular girl in school hated her so much, but it was getting harder to ignore her attitude. "Look, Chloe, I would go if I could," she said truthfully, "but I'm not trying to hurt your feelings by saying I can't go."

"Like you could hurt my feelings, weirdo," Chloe snapped at her, and then she shoved her way past Chrysta with her friends following close behind. Poe squawked as other students snickered. The first bell rang, and all the students filed into the building.

"It's alright, Poe," Chrysta said, reaching out to give him a brief scratch. "Go see the pretty bird in the park. I'll see you after school."

"Aw man, you mean I have to go to that bitch's party without you?" complained Mary as they walked inside. "Who else is going to dress as a sexy vampire with me?" Chrysta laughed.

.....

Chrysta's day passed without any more drama. Math, science, history, lunch, Latin, and English. Finally, she let herself into her last and favorite class of the day, orchestra. Other students were already warming up or talking. Chrysta waved to Mary as she set up her cello. Chrysta sat in the first chair while Chloe glowered from the third chair.

Their teacher, Mr. Hansen, took the podium. "Alright, everyone, settle down!" he said, and the students settled. When the room quieted, he looked over his glasses and smiled. "Now, I know it's Halloween next week, but we have to start thinking about our winter concert." He paused, letting the groans die down. "I know, the time of year when you get sick of Christmas carols before Thanksgiving." He smiled. "You're welcome," he drawled.

He started to pass out sheet music as students laughed. "I have *Dance of the Sugar Plum Fairy* for the woodwinds, *Coral of the Bells* for percussion, *Jingle Bell Rock* for horns," he paused as there were hoots from that part of the room, "and finally, *O Rest Ye Merry Gentlemen* for strings."

Chrysta helped to pass out papers and winced when she saw a solo part in her sheet music.

"As always, solo parts will have a seat saved in the front row for family members," Mr. Hansen stated. "Now, everyone, let's visit the world of Brahms today, shall we?"

Once class was over, Chrysta approached Mr. Hansen after gathering her things. "Mr. Hansen," she asked, "can I ask for a favor?"

"Yes, Miss York?" he asked, looking over his glasses and raising bushy eyebrows.

"Can someone else take my solos?"

"Miss York, I would be remiss if I didn't have my first chair violinist play the best parts," he explained while smiling. He patted her hand. "Don't worry. I have faith that you will do fine."

She nodded but didn't say anything else. She didn't know how to explain to Mr. Hansen that she wasn't nervous about playing in front of a crowd.

As she went outside to wait for her car, Mary joined her. "So," Mary asked, "how has he been lately?"

Chrysta grimaced, knowing what Mary was alluding to. "I guess he's been okay," she said.

"He said you couldn't go to Chloe's party?"

"Yes," Chrysta confessed. "I didn't want to go. I'm more upset that he took that bead Poe gave me."

"Chrysta, you know that isn't normal, right?" Mary asked as they sat down on a bench in front of the school. "I mean, parents can be strict, but your dad goes way too far."

Chrysta nodded. "I know. And I just have to keep telling myself: I will be able to move out on my own soon."

Mary sighed but nodded. "Well, if you ever need a place to stay, or he throws you out, or he ever hurts you," she placed her hand on Chrysta's, "I'm here for you."

Chrysta smiled at her friend and squeezed her hand. "Thanks," she said softly. "I appreciate it."

So they sat in the afternoon sun, talking about school, when the sound of a violin drifted towards them. They both paused and listened for a few minutes. "Is that someone we know?" Mary asked.

"I'm not sure," Chrysta replied. "Let's check it out."

They crossed the street to the park, following the sounds of the violin. There was a fountain, and in front of that, a boy stood playing what sounded like Bach. Both girls paused and sat down on a bench to listen. Mary leaned over after he finished one song and started another. "He's good," she whispered, even though the boy couldn't possibly hear them.

"Yes, he is."

"He's cute," Mary continued to whisper.

Chrysta smiled. "Yes, he is."

"Think he has a girlfriend?" Mary asked, and Chrysta could only giggle.

Calling him a boy was probably not right. He looked at least a couple of years older than the girls. But he certainly wasn't dressed like someone who could play the violin. He wore a torn black shirt that showed flashes of a grey undershirt, the sleeves rolled up to his elbows. He had several silver piercings in his ears and one on the corner of his lower lip and eyebrow. He had silver rings on almost every finger and a silver armband covering most of his left arm. The sides of his head were shaven. But the rest of his hair was long, in dreads, tied back, and had streaks of red. A chain was attached to black jeans, and the look was complete with combat boots. A folded, black leather jacket sat on the fountain beside him..

They sat enthralled, watching him play. Chrysta started digging in her backpack for her wallet. Talent like that needed to be supported. While she was looking down, she heard a shout and looked up. "What now?" Mary groaned.

Chloe was stalking up to the boy and said something. It did not sound encouraging, and the boy stopped playing. He shrugged and responded to whatever she said. Chloe folded her arms and said something with a smug expression.

Chrysta got up and started walking towards them. Whoever he was, he didn't need that kind of harassment.

He folded his arms, still holding the violin, and smirked. He said something, and Chloe's face turned red. She suddenly grabbed his jar with money inside it and ran.

"Hey!" Chrysta yelled, but Chloe was gone. The boy hadn't reacted except for giving Chloe a middle fingered salute. Chrysta stopped when she reached him. "Are you okay?"

"Yeah, I'm good," he said. "What crawled up her ass?" he asked.

"She's always like that," Mary confirmed. "She was probably mad you play Bach better than she can."

Chrysta finally found her wallet and tried handing the boy a twenty-dollar bill, the only money she had. "Here," she said. "I hope this covers what she stole."

"Nah, don't worry about it," he said, lifting a hand. "I can get the money back playing somewhere else." And he finally turned to look at them, and his eyes widened as he looked at Chrysta. "Do I know you?" he asked.

"Um, I don't think so," Chrysta said. Mary looked between the two of them and grinned. "I think I would remember someone who plays as good as you."

He gave her a smug smile. "Well, thank you, but I doubt I'm as good as someone with formal training." He gestured to Chrysta's violin case, and she felt herself blush.

Mary stuck out her hand. "Mary Jackson, lowly cello player," she joked. As shook her hand, Mary placed a hand on Chrysta's back and made her take a step forward. "Chrysta York, the best violin player in the school."

The boy's demeanor changed. He looked shocked and then angry as he looked Chrysta up and down. Chrysta hesitated to put her hand out but did so to be polite. He paused but then shook her hand, his face hard to read. "Thomas Monroe," he said in a voice that held a frosty note it hadn't had before.

"Nice to meet you," she said, not understanding his reaction.

There was a shout coming from the school. "Oh crap," Mary said. "That sounded like your driver," she told Chrysta, and the girls started to hurry back to the school. Chrysta halted and turned around. "Hope your day gets better," she yelled, actually meaning it. The boy watched her as she went, a weird look still on his face.

Chrysta crossed the street and went up to the car. "Sorry," she apologized as she climbed into the door the driver held open. She waved at Mary before the door closed, and they drove away.

Once they got home, the driver opened the car door and escorted her inside. Chrysta started making her way up the stairs but stopped when she heard her father. "Chrysta, a word," he called out. She flinched and went into his study.

Her father's study was dark, only lit with a lamp on his desk. He sat with his hands tented, elbows on the arms of the chair. The driver was next to him, face neutral.

"You were not waiting at the school this afternoon," he said. It wasn't a question but spoken more like a statement. Chrysta nodded.

"Yes, sir," she confessed. "A violin player was busking in the park across from the school. I wanted to watch him play."

Jozef York's face fell into a frown. "You are to wait at the school and come straight home, understood?"

"Yes, sir," she whispered.

"Supper is at six. You may go." He lifted a hand and waved it dismissively.

She nodded and left the room, feeling a lump in her throat. Once she got to her room, she leaned against the door and sighed. "Soon," she told herself. "You can move out, not live here anymore." She took a deep breath and let it out in a shaky exhale. "Hell, I'll play on the streets if I have to."

She studied, practiced her violin, and joined her father for a silent dinner. When done, she went back to her bedroom. At one point, Poe dropped in for a visit, and she went out to the balcony to spend time with him. Chrysta was surprised to see him holding another bead in his beak.

"Where are you getting these?" she asked the raven. But he just cocked his head and squawked. She went back inside and grabbed the other bead. She went to the bottom drawer of her chest and removed a false bottom. She mostly had items that Poe brought her and some money she kept in case of an emergency. She added the beads and replaced the false bottom. She thought for a moment and then grabbed some cash from the drawer.

After a shower, she dressed in PJs and climbed into bed. She sighed. Chrysta knew, all things considered, she had a good life. She had food, a roof over her head, an excellent school, and at least one friend's love and support. But the constant surveillance, her father's controlling behavior, and her inability to go out were chafing her, and it was becoming unbearable.

She fell asleep, strangely enough, with the music of Bach playing in her head.

. . . . .

Several hours later, in York's study, two men sat in front of his desk. They wore almost identical scowls, and each held a glass in their hand that remained untouched. York also had an entire drink in front of him. "You are sure she is not showing any ability?" asked the blonde-haired man.

"None," confirmed York, hand on his chin. "She will turn seventeen during the next spring equinox. If she doesn't show any ability in the next few months, she is not the right vessel."

"And are you sure that is not what you want, brother?" asked the other man, a red-headed man with glasses.

York's eyes narrowed. "What do you mean... brother."

"You keep her safe. No one can argue that, but maybe she needs to go out into the world a little." He gave an evil grin. "One can not expect her to perform under pressure if she never feels it."

York glared at the man. "What do you propose?" he asked.

"Call your slave," the man with glasses said.

York glared but twisted a ring on his pointer finger without comment. The men sat silently for about half an hour, not speaking again, only the sound of ice clinking in their glasses. There was the noise of a knock at the front door and someone opening it. A figure walked into the study, followed by a servant.

"Yeah?" the figure said, putting as much venom into the word as it could.

"We have a project for you," said the red-headed man. "Chrysta York. Befriend the girl. Take her places. Keep an eye on her. If she shows magical ability, report back to us."

The figure shifted from one foot to the other. It frowned at York, and he nodded.

"Alright," it responded and turned to leave.

"And slave?" the redhead said. The figure stopped and let out a low growl that wasn't quite human.

"Do not let your brethren know of her existence, clear?"

Once more, the figure looked to York for confirmation, and he nodded. The figure finally left to melt into the night.

2

The next day was almost a repeat of the last one for Chrysta, except when it was time for orchestra, she made a beeline for Chloe. She sat beside the blonde so she could talk to her in a low tone.

"That was a mean thing you did yesterday, Chloe."

The other girl blinked and then frowned. "My father says people like that shouldn't be begging for money. I asked if he had permission to perform in the park, and he became rude. He called me a bitch, so I took his ill-gotten gains." She scoffed and gave Chrysta a proud look. "What does it matter to you? Is he a friend of yours?"

"No, but I would think, as a musician, you would try to support someone trying to make a living making music," hissed Chrysta.

"Look at it this way, weirdo," Chloe said with a sneer, "if you ever find yourself living on the streets, I just got rid of some of your competition."

Chrysta felt a flash of anger at the blonde, but just got up and went to her seat. She was fuming in her chair, thinking how unfair it all was until she heard a *twang*. Chloe shouted in dismay. Her violin chin rest had snapped off, and all the strings flopped towards the floor. "Mr. Hansen!" she called.

"Oh, Miss Williams, how unfortunate," he said. "Get a loaner violin from the supply closet, will you?"

There were various murmurs and laughs as Chloe got up and grabbed a school violin. They were not cheap, but they were not the best, either. She sat down and started to warm up again. There was another *twang*, and her bow broke. She cried out again.

Mr. Hansen blinked in surprise and then leaned forward, placing his head in his hand. "Miss Williams, I'm afraid it is not your day," he said. The majority of the class laughed loudly, and Chloe turned red. "I'll give you a note to go to the library. How about you take a day off from music, hm?"

Chrysta just smiled as various students snickered. Mr. Hansen got her on her way and then returned to get them back on track.

After school, the girls made their way outside. Chloe's unfortunate accident was still a big topic among the band students.

"Did you see her face?" Mary asked. "Like she stepped in shit or something."

Chrysta smiled. "Serves her right," she agreed. She paused as they made it to the sidewalk. "Look who it is," she said, pointing.

Thomas sat on the top of a bench on the school's side of the street, his feet on the seat. He was cutting an apple with a wicked-looking knife. A guitar case was standing between his legs. He looked up at the girls as they approached and gave them a bright smile. "Hello, ladies," he said, bringing a piece of apple to his mouth. "How are you this fine afternoon?" he asked, chewing.

"We're doing good," Mary said. She pointed at the case. "How many instruments do you play?" she asked.

"Violin, guitar, and piano," he said with a smile. "And a mean ukulele if needed."

"I will remember that next time I have a luau," Mary joked. Chrysta looked between her friend and the young man on the bench, feeling slightly jealous. Mary always seemed to have such an easy time talking to new people.

There was a squawk, and Poe dropped down from a tree to land next to Thomas. He jumped and nearly dropped his apple. "What the actual fuck?!" he cried. Mary laughed, and Chrysta winced.

"Sorry, he's with me," she explained, placing a hand on the bird's back. She noticed he had another bead in his beak and held her hand out so he could drop it. Once she held it, he squawked even louder at the older boy, hopping up and down. "Poe, be nice," Chrysta scolded the bird.

Thomas blinked slowly for a few moments, just looking at the raven. "Poe?" he asked. "As in, 'suddenly there came a tapping?'"

"Yeah," she said, smiling shyly. "Poe visits me at my house, and I feed him sometimes."

Thomas gave her a bemused look and cocked his head at the bird. Poe cocked his head in return. "Ravens are smart birds," he said. "He must like you if he brings you gifts."

Poe briefly regarded the boy, then opened his mouth and said, "Chrysta." All of the humans gave him shocked looks. "He's never said that before," Chrysta said.

Poe gave a more normal-sounding squawk and flew away. The teens watched him go. "If he ever says 'Nevermore,' let me know. I'll remember to avoid women named Lenore," Thomas joked.

Both girls laughed. "By the way," Mary said once they'd stopped laughing. "You will be glad to know karma bit Chloe in the ass today."

"Chloe?" he asked, putting another piece of apple in his mouth and chewing.

"The blonde girl who stole your tips yesterday," Chrysta explained. "Her violin and bow broke today."

"Huh, sucks when that happens," Thomas said and grinned.

There was the sound of a car horn, and the group looked up. Mary's mom was waiting for her in front of the school. "Oh, that's me," Mary said. She looked between the two. "You two behave now, alright?" Mary joked, laughing and running towards the car. Chrysta waved as she went.

Left alone with the older teen, she cleared her throat and sat next to Thomas on the bench's top. She nervously made sure her skirt was covering her knees. He offered her some apple, but she shook her head. "Oh, I almost forgot," she said, reaching into her backpack.

Chrysta tried to hand him all the cash she had. "Since I couldn't convince Chloe to return your money."

He blinked in surprise. "Ya know," he said, "You keep trying to give me money. I'm not that kind of boy."

She giggled apprehensively. "I just feel bad that Chloe did that to you," she explained. "It's the least I can do."

He looked her up and down. "Why would you feel bad? You didn't steal the money."

"No, but..." she paused, attempting to find the words to voice her feelings. "If you are trying to survive by playing music, I just think you need all the support you can get."

He looked at her for several moments and then pushed the hand that held the money back. "Keep it," he said. "Like I said yesterday, I can make it all back."

She hesitated but then put the money back in her backpack. They sat on the bench for a bit in silence as Thomas sliced and ate his apple. She cleared her throat again. "So," she started, and he raised an eyebrow, "You said yesterday that you didn't have formal training. Are you self-taught?"

"Yep," he confirmed, chewing on a bite of the apple. "I hang out with as many musicians as I can, learning as much as I can, but mostly I taught myself to play."

"Favorite music?" she asked.

He looked up, thoughtfully tapping on his chin with a finger. "Jazz, rock, classical, all kinds, really," he admitted. "Except pop music. I don't like men who sound like they get kicked in the balls before they sing."

She snorted. "Favorite composer on the violin?"

He gave her a look. "Paganini."

"Piano?"

"Duke Ellington."

"Guitar?"

"Johnny Cash."

She expected him to be annoyed, but he gave her a wide smile, teeth looking very white against his dark skin. "Want to know my blood type next?" he joked. She laughed. She checked the time on her phone.

"Am I boring you?" he asked, finishing the last bite of his apple. He threw the remains of the core in some nearby bushes and wiped his hands on his pants.

"No," Chrysta said quickly. "My driver is just usually here by now."

"Oh?" he said. "Your parents don't pick you up?"

She snorted. "No, my mom passed away when I was little," she explained. "My father is..." She trailed off. Oh, how could she describe what her father was like to a stranger?

"Your father?" he prompted.

She winced. "My father is weird. He doesn't care about my grades and doesn't come to any of my concerts. He never asks how I am doing." She swallowed past a lump in her throat. "Never says he loves me."

Chrysta glanced at Thomas and was slightly astounded to see a mad look on his face.

"But at the same time, I have to stay on a tight schedule, can't go anywhere, can't wear anything he doesn't approve of." She shrugged. "It's like he doesn't care but wants to guide everything in my life at the same time."

"Sounds like an asshole," he said. Chrysta glanced at him to see if he was mocking her, but he seemed sincere. She smiled.

"Well, I guess that's why I feel so strongly about getting your money back," she explained. "Someday, I will move out, and if I have to live on the streets, playing my violin on some street corner," she sighed and shrugged, "I'll gladly do it. Just to be out of that house."

"Oh, I don't think you should do that," Thomas said. He leaned in like he was about to give her a huge secret. "Living on the street sucks balls," Thomas whispered. She laughed, and he straightened up. "Best you get the first chair in some professional orchestra. That would be better for someone like you."

She snorted. "Young and naive?"

"Beautiful and kind," he replied, and Chrysta felt herself turn red in embarrassment.

Chrysta heard her name called, and she saw her driver waiting. She leaped off the bench and started to rush over. She paused and turned around. "Thanks for keeping me company, Thomas," she said.

He held up a hand and gave her a small salute. "Anytime," he said. "And please, call me Tommy."

She smiled, waved, and hurried to the car. She didn't see Poe land next to Tommy again.

"She is certainly something, isn't she?" the young man asked the bird, watching the car drive off, and Poe just squawked in reply.

. . . . .

Chrysta found herself smiling all evening, although she couldn't put her finger on why. She wanted to talk to Mary about the strange young man they seemed to have befriended, but she knew her father sometimes read messages from her phone, so she decided to wait until morning.

Fresh from her shower, though, she sat on her bed with her laptop and looked up "Duke Ellington" on Wikipedia.

"Born 1899..." she read to herself, "Died 1974... 65-year career... wow."

She typed his name into a music streaming service and scrolled through the results. "So many songs," she said to herself. "Where do I start?"

In a Sentimental Mood caught her eye, and she clicked on it. Mellow piano and horn played through the speakers, and she got comfortable and closed her eyes. It was lovely, more delicate than most jazz she had tried to listen to in the past. After that was the song *Prelude to a Kiss*, and then *Solitude*. Chrysta put *In a Sentimental Mood* on repeat and fell asleep listening to it on her headphones.

. . . . .

The next morning, Chrysta had barely made it into her school before someone tackled her from behind. She made a squawk that would have made Poe proud and turned around to see Mary bouncing up and down in excitement. "O. M. G. Tell me everything that happened yesterday after I left."

Chrysta laughed. "Not much to report, I'm afraid. He likes all kinds of music, a self-taught musician, and prefers to be called Tommy." She thought back to the previous afternoon and blushed. "And he called me beautiful and kind."

"Awwwwww," Mary cooed. She knocked an elbow into Chrysta. "He likes you."

"I like him too," Chrysta confessed. "He's nice and smart and funny."

"And cute and a little bit dangerous," Mary continued. She sighed. "Think he has a brother?"

They stopped by Mary's locker so that she could get some textbooks. "Hey," Mary suddenly said. "If you need someone to cover for you, you know, if you want to hang out with him and don't want your dad to know, just let me know."

Chrysta sadly smiled at the other girl. "You know how strict my father is. He barely lets me see you outside of school as it is."

"Just letting you know, sis," Mary said, grinning. "You should live a little."

The day passed like most, and when the girls let themselves into orchestra class, most of the other students were already warming up. Chloe came in after them and started to set up. It looked like she had a loaner violin. They started playing the piece they had been practicing all week. About ten minutes after they started, there was a loud snap, and Chloe cried out. The neck of the violin had snapped off the instrument.

There were laughs and jeers, and Chloe got up to walk to Mr. Hansen, red-faced, trying not to cry. "So weird," Chrysta heard someone mutter, "what are the chances of that happening three times in two days?"

Chrysta also thought it was eerie. Chloe was an experienced player; she shouldn't be having such troubles. What Mary said seemed to be coming true. Karma was biting her in the butt.

.....

The rest of Chrysta's Friday afternoon was uneventful. Tommy wasn't outside the school when it let out, but Chrysta tried not to feel upset. He was under no obligation to visit her every day.

Later that night, after her shower, Chrysta was padding across her bedroom, drying her hair, when she heard a tapping on her window. She paused. It could only be Poe, but he had never done that before. She grabbed some chicken she had stolen from dinner and started to open the door to the balcony.

"Hey Poe, how are y—" She gasped and ducked back inside, closing the door. She blinked in shock, opened the door again, and leaned out, using the curtains to cover herself. "What are you doing here?" she squeaked.

Tommy stood on her balcony, leaning on a window, grinning evilly. "What's up, beautiful? Not happy to see me?"

She laughed nervously and then turned around to check that her bedroom was indeed empty. "No? I mean, it's nice to see you, but what are you doing *here?* How do you know where I live?"

He shrugged. "I have my ways," he just replied cryptically. "I scored a gig tonight and wanted to see if you would join me."

"A gig?"

"Jazz club, playing the piano. You want to see how to earn a living making music. I can help," he explained.

"I don't know," she hesitated. "What if my father finds out?"

"So? He finds out, and then, what? Grounds you?" he asked, standing up and stepping in front of her. "He doesn't let you go out anyway."

She bit her lip, thinking. Tommy had a point. "How late?"

"A few hours of music. Why? Will you turn into a pumpkin if I don't get you back before dawn?"

She laughed. Was she considering this?

He sighed loudly and crossed his arms. Chrysta thought he was angry, but he gave his next statement with a grin. "Alright, I'll throw in dinner too. Make it a proper date."

The word "date" made her blush. "Alright," she said. "I'll go. Let me just get changed."

"Aw, but I like the tank top, flannel pants combo," he whined. He leaned forward like he was trying to look past the curtains. Chrysta put a hand on his face and pushed him back. He laughed.

"Let me change," she repeated, trying to sound forceful but laughing with him.

She quickly dressed. When she let herself back out on the balcony, she wore jeans, a long, flowing black shirt with sunflowers printed on it, and a black lace buttoned-up shirt. She decided to keep her hair down and out of its usual braid or ponytail. Tommy did a chef's kiss. "Wonderful," he said.

"So how do we sneak out?" she asked. They were on the second floor, and Chrysta knew there were cameras on the house's corners. She leaned over the stone railing to look down. It did not look like a fun climb.

He also leaned over the railing. "Well, the cameras are easy," he explained. Holding up his hands, he extended his pointer fingers to show where the cameras were facing. "Once they face each other, you have 25 seconds as they rotate to look in different directions and back again. Poor design, if you think about it."

"How do you know this?" Chrysta asked.

"Let's just say I have learned the art of not getting caught on camera while doing something," Tommy moved his hand in a circle like it would help him find the right word, "questionably legal?"

Chrysta blinked and then looked down. Maybe this was a bad idea. She barely knew him. What if he was just trying to get her alone to hurt her?

"Having second thoughts?" he asked. Chrysta looked at him and blinked again. He didn't seem upset or disappointed but had a small smile on his face. She bit her lip.

"Look, if this makes you uncomfortable, you don't have to go," he said as she weighed her opinions.

"No, I want to go," she explained. "I'm just," she sighed, "nervous?"

"Understandable," he said while nodding. He held up a hand. "I, Thomas Monroe, promise to be on my best behavior and keep you safe at all times, on pain of death. Scout's honor."

"Were you ever a scout?" Chrysta asked, grinning.

"Never," he confessed. "But you have my word."

"Alright," she said. "Let's do it."

He suddenly swooped her off her feet into a bridal hold. She gasped and instinctively wrapped her arms around his neck. He grinned as he hopped onto the railing and crouched down. "Hang on," was the only warning she got as he dropped.

He held her tight with one arm around her waist as he used the other to hold on to the vines climbing up the wall to slow their descent. He paused at one point to make sure the cameras were looking in opposite directions. When it was safe, he dropped to the ground and rushed her to the bushes growing along the wall. He boosted her upon his shoulder and got her over the wall in one motion. She landed with a laugh and continued laughing as he joined her.

"You make that look so easy!" she exclaimed.

Tommy grinned and held up a hand. "But of course." He offered her an elbow. "Ready for a night on the town?"

"Yes," she said, grinning, taking his arm, and they walked into the night.

3

They walked quickly, heading downtown. Chrysta kept expecting someone to stop them and demand that Chrysta go back home, but no such thing happened. She looked around like everything was new, and in a way, it was. She just never had the pleasure of seeing it up close before.

They came to a street lined with clubs. Neon signs announced their names, and loud music oozed from their open doors. Halfway down the road, they found a club with a sign out front proclaiming it was the Jazz Nocturne, the figure of a man wearing a fedora and playing the sax underneath the letters. Tommy herded her around the corner to the back of the club. He knocked on a door. It opened up to reveal a large man.

"Tommy, yer late," he growled. He spotted Chrysta and looked her up and down. "Who dis?"

"The young woman I was bringing with me tonight," Tommy explained. Chrysta smiled and gave a small wave.

"Dammit, Tommy, where ya find her? Middle school?"

"Ha-ha," Tommy said. "Come on, Ben, that was the deal. I play, she gets to come in with me."

"You didn't say nothin' about her being underage," griped Ben. He scratched at his belly as he leaned to get a closer look at Chrysta. "Ya want me to lose my license?"

"Like you don't bribe anyone who comes in during inspections," said Tommy. He sighed, put an arm around Chrysta's shoulders, and turned her away from the door. "Well, I guess we will head out if you real—"

"Wait, you bastard!" Ben cried out. "I didn't say that!" He pointed his finger at Chrysta. "If anyone asks, you are a young-looking 21, got it?"

"Yes, sir," she said, and Ben turned around and let them inside.

Ben turned left into a small office. To the right were two doors: "Women's" and the other "Men's." There was rustling coming from the office, and then some clothes came flying out. Tommy caught them and gave them a sniff. He grimaced. "When the hell did you last wash these?"

"I haven't," Ben replied. He appeared in the doorway and leaned on the frame.

"Thanks, pal," Tommy said, looking disgusted. He went into the bathroom and closed the door.

"Yer welcome, buddy," Ben replied, chuckling. He raised his voice. "Make sure to take most of that metal out of yer face."

"Yeah, yeah," Tommy grumbled.

Ben gave Chrysta another look up and down. "So, how did ya meet this clown?"

"He was playing in the park, and I went to listen," she explained. She fought the urge to say, "sir." He leered at her.

"Oh, playing guitar, was he?"

"Um, no, violin."

Ben grunted. He raised his voice. "I wonder if he makes more money playing on the street than playing piano here. The only reason he wouldn't take my generous offer to work here full time."

"I told you, Ben," came Tommy's muffled reply. "I don't think I could handle your sunny personality all the time."

Ben smirked. "Well, my offer still stands, Tommy. The new guy is not working out." And with that, he turned back into the office and closed the door.

Chrysta waited for a few minutes, and the door to the bathroom finally opened. Tommy wore black leather shoes, black pants, a buttoned-up white shirt, a red vest, and a red tie. He had removed all his jewelry except the silver armband on his left arm. He was rolling up the sleeves, revealing toned arms.

"You look nice," Chrysta said, and she meant it.

He rolled his eyes. "Yeah, I do, but I'm gonna stink to high heaven before the night is through," he complained. He leaned towards the office door. "If only someone could be so kind as to wash these clothes."

There was only a bark of laughter in response, and Tommy steered Chrysta deeper into the club. The next room was a small kitchen where Tommy stored his clothes and boots in a locker. He opened a door for her, and they were behind the bar.

The club was dark. The decor was art deco, with dark walls and gold highlights everywhere. To their left were tables lit with candles. To the right was the stage, already set up with a piano. A man with a stand-up bass talked with a man holding a sax while a woman set up the drums.

"Well, who is this?" said a female voice. A larger woman with blue streaks in her brown hair was setting up the bar. She wore the same outfit as Tommy, minus the tie, and Chrysta could see tattoos peeking out of her shirt.

"Mandy, meet Chrysta," said Tommy as he directed Chrysta to the bar's customer side. "Chrysta, meet Mandy, the best bartender in town."

Mandy put a hand to her cheek. "Oh, you flatterer," she said sarcastically. She dropped her smile, and flatly said: "What do you want?"

"Just to keep an eye on this lovely lady for me," he replied, getting Chrysta to sit on a barstool.

"Nope, won't do it."

"I'll give you half of whatever I make in tips tonight."

"Deal," she quickly replied. "I'll get a tab started for you two. Whatcha drinking, sweetie?"

Chrysta froze. "Um, water?"

Mandy blinked and then smiled. "One Shirley Temple, coming right up." And she started making a drink.

Tommy leaned in and dropped his voice. "You good so far?"

Chrysta nodded, not trusting her voice. She was nervous, but the club was small, and as long as she stayed where she was, she could see Tommy, and he could see her. The man with the sax was snapping his fingers, and Tommy grimaced.

"Duty calls," he said. "We'll play some songs, and I will come back to check on you."

She nodded again, and he rushed to the stage. The man handed him some sheet music, and he looked it over as he sat at the piano.

Mandy placed a drink in front of Chrysta. "Thank you," she softly said and took a sip. "It's good. What is it?"

"Just ginger ale with grenadine," replied Mandy. "I have a feeling I shouldn't give you anything stronger."

Chrysta winced. "Sorry."

"No worries, sweetie," Mandy replied. "I'll make sure you stay safe." She leaned forward and winked. "So, how long have you known that rascal?"

"Just a few days," she confessed, chewing on a cherry. "How long has he worked here?"

"Oh, a little over a year," answered Mandy. "A night here, a night there, just when Ben needs him to play. But you are the first person he has ever brought with him."

"I hope to make a career playing music, so I think he wants to show me how it's done."

Mandy nodded. "Nice, you play piano too?"

"Violin," she explained, taking a sip of her drink.

"Ah," Mandy said. "Well, yell if you need anything. Feel free to use the bathroom in the back."

Chrysta nodded in thanks, and Mandy left to finish getting the bar ready.

Soon the front doors were opened, and people started pouring in, men dressed up with buttoned-up shirts and women in dresses. Chrysta began to feel a little underdressed, but no one seemed to give her a second glance. The musicians started playing slow beats and mellow tunes on stage, and sometimes couples would drift to the dance floor for a song or two. Sometimes they even dropped some money in a tip jar on the piano. Mandy stayed behind the bar, filling drink orders and taking money. Sometimes men would see Chrysta and point to her. Mandy would smile and nod and then make another Shirley Temple. "From the young man in the black shirt," she would say, or "From the man with glasses." Chrysta would just grin and nod in thanks, laughing at the men's confused expressions.

Sometimes she would catch Tommy's eye, and he would drop her a wink or grin. The songs he played didn't seem complicated, but to Chrysta's ear, they sounded lovely. Anytime he had a solo, she gave him her undivided attention and clapped the longest when the players paused between songs.

The sax player went to a microphone during one of these pauses. "Thank you, everyone," he said as the clapping died down. "We will be taking a break. Be back in fifteen."

Tommy started to get up from the piano, but two women walked up and blocked his path. He glanced between them and Chrysta, but when one woman dropped some money in the tip jar, he sat back down and started talking with them. Chrysta gave him a smile when he glanced in her direction.

"Don't worry about those two, dear," Mandy said. "They flirt with all the musicians." Chrysta nodded, wondering why she felt upset. Maybe it was the short skirts they were wearing and the tight shirts they had on. Suddenly, the sax player was standing next to her.

"So, who do we have here?" he asked, holding out his hand and smiling. Chrysta shook it to be polite.

"Chrysta."

"Jonathon," he replied. "A friend of Mandy's?"

"A friend of Tommy's," Mandy corrected as she helped some customers. Jonathon made a face, but the smile slid back on his face.

"Well, that's nice. Tommy has never brought anyone with him before."

"That's what I have been hearing," Chrysta said, glancing at Tommy. One of the women was laughing at something he said and put a hand on his arm. Tommy looked Chrysta's way and then rolled his eyes when the women weren't looking. When they looked at him again, he flashed them a bright smile. Chrysta smirked.

"So, how do you like the music so far?" asked Jonathon. "I made the song list myself."

"Oh?" Chrysta said. "I don't know much about jazz, but I think it's a lovely selection." She cocked her head a little. "A little slow, though."

"Well, I feel jazz should be mellow," he explained. "Any song you like in particular? Maybe I can fit it into tonight's rotation."

"In a Sentimental Mood," she said confidently, and Jonathon made the same face like he had just tasted some lemon. He tried to put the smile back on his face.

"Why that song?" he asked.

"I have classical music training, and that one just appeals to me the most."

"Figures you would like Duke Ellington too," Jonathon sighed and glared at Tommy. "Alright, it will make him happy if we play it." Mandy had made a tray of drinks, and Jonathon picked it up with a sigh. He stalked towards the stage, and Chrysta turned towards Mandy.

"I'm sorry. I didn't mean to upset him."

"Don't worry about it, sweetie," Mandy said with a grin. "Jonathon and Tommy are always butting heads over the playlist. He argues that no one would ever like Ellington's songs. You just proved him wrong." Jonathon got to the stage and passed out the drinks. He then got the others to lean towards him and told them something. Tommy grinned and held his glass full of amber liquid up to toast Chrysta. Jonathon got that sour look on his face again. "You just made Tommy's night," Mandy laughed.

The musicians started playing again, and Chrysta listened with her head in her hand. Part of her imagined dancing with Tommy on the dance floor. No, she guessed that he wasn't a dancer. He would want to play and have her by his side. She briefly wondered what it would be like to play with him.

After they had played about a dozen songs, Tommy started to play the first chords of *In a Sentimental Mood*. As Tommy looked her way, their eyes met, and Chrysta smiled.

The whole club fell into a trance as he played, and no one talked or got up to dance. When the song ended, the crowd gave him the biggest round of applause of the whole evening. Tommy lifted his glass in salute and continued into the next song.

Several songs later, Jonathon went back to the microphone. "Thank you, ladies and gentlemen. We had fun playing for you this evening. We hope you enjoy the rest of your night." Everyone on the stage took a bow, and Tommy joined Chrysta at the bar.

"So, what do you think?" Tommy asked her, leaning on the bar, sipping the last of his drink.

"Oh, that was wonderful," she said.

Tommy looked at her from the corner of his eye. "You don't have to lie. Jonathon's selection sucks," he said, placing the empty glass on the bar. "He always talks about playing mellow jazz but ends up putting everyone to sleep."

Chrysta smiled. "Well, I think it was wonderful."

The two women from before joined them, smiling at Tommy, ignoring Chrysta. "So, can we get that drink now?" asked one of them.

"Sorry, ladies, but I already have plans for the evening," Tommy said, placing a hand on Chrysta's back. She smiled and leaned closer to Tommy. The women frowned.

"Oh, okay," said the second woman. She held her hand out, and Tommy shook it. "Maybe we will catch you next time you're free." And the women left to go to their table.

Tommy snorted. Chrysta gave him a look, and he held up his hand. There was a piece of paper pressed into his palm. "They think they're slick."

Chrysta grabbed the paper and opened it to see the women's names and numbers. "Would you like to get to know them?" she asked, glancing at the two women as they glared at her from their table.

"Nope," he replied. Jonathon came up with some cash and handed it to Tommy. Tommy started counting it. "What do I owe you for the drinks, Mandy?"

"Nothing. Your young friend here already had your tab covered by several other interested parties tonight," Mandy said with a smile. Chrysta blushed.

"Sweet!" exclaimed Tommy. "I'll have to bring her more often." He turned to Chrysta. "Ready to head out, beautiful?"

"One second," she said. She held the paper up and made a show of tearing it up. Mandy and Tommy laughed, and Jonathon just shook his head.

"She's like you," Jonathon said to Tommy. "A smart ass."

"Best kind of ass there is," Tommy said as he handed Mandy half his tips, as promised. "Goodnight, guys."

"'Night, Tommy," Mandy said. She held her hand out to Chrysta. "Nice to meet you, sweetie. Keep this one out of trouble, will you?"

"I'll try," Chrysta chuckled. Tommy led her to the back of the club while the two women glared at them. Tommy wiggled his fingers as the door closed behind them.

Tommy grabbed his stuff, and Chrysta used the bathroom as he changed. When he came out, he was still smiling. Chrysta smiled back. "What?"

"Getting Jonathon to play Ellington, free drinks, getting those girls to leave me alone," he explained, knocking on Ben's door, "I'm starting to think you're my good luck charm."

Ben opened the door, and Tommy threw the clothes, so they hit Ben in the face. Chrysta smacked a hand to her mouth to keep a giggle from escaping while Ben's face slowly turned red. "Why, you little son of a bitch," he growled.

"Fucking wash them next time," Tommy growled back and then held his hand out. Ben's mouth moved like he was chewing on something, but he reached into his pocket and slapped some cash into Tommy's palm.

Tommy broke out into a bright grin. "A pleasure as always, Ben," he said.

Ben grumbled. "Yeah, yeah. Get out of here, you damn degenerate," he said, slamming his office door.

"See," Tommy said, offering an elbow to Chrysta and opening the door outside, "that wonderful sunny personality."

.....

Tommy guided her through the city. It was very much alive and busy, with most people waiting to get into clubs. She wondered where they were going until they came up to a restaurant. The decor was Japanese, and when he opened the front door for her, Chrysta was shocked to see a pond in the middle of the dining room with live koi. A hostess bowed and took them to a table.

"What is this?" Chrysta asked, pointing to a conveyor belt that ran along the wall.

"Well, cooks make sushi and put it on the belt, and then you grab whatever looks good to you," he explained. He grabbed some chopsticks, and when a plate came by with a roll covered in tempura flakes, he placed it in front of himself.

She hesitated to grab her own set of chopsticks. "Isn't this kind of place expensive?" she asked.

"Hey," he said, pointing a chopstick at her, "I dragged you out. Let me treat you to some good food." He expertly picked up a piece of sushi and popped it into his mouth. "Besides, I can always make more money. Having good company is harder to find," he clarified, chewing.

"If you're sure," she said, taking her own chopsticks. A simple California roll showed up on the belt, and she grabbed it.

He nodded. "Totally," he said, showing Chrysta how to hold the chopsticks.

They ate, swapping bits of sushi, as Tommy helped her choose what she wanted to try. At one point, a waitress came to their table, and Tommy asked for sake. Chrysta decided to try some Japanese soda.

"So, when do I get to hear you play?" Tommy asked her.

"I practice most nights," she said. "Anything you would like to hear?"

"*Twinkle, Twinkle, Little Star.*"

"Harder than that."

"Paganini's 24 Caprices."

"Which one?"

"Allllll of them," he hissed, and Chrysta laughed.

.....

They ate and talked about music (mostly about jazz) and laughed. Chrysta couldn't remember a better evening. He paid, and they headed out into the night. It had gotten colder, and when she shivered, Tommy took off his jacket and put it on her shoulders.

"Can we..." Chrysta started to ask. Tommy's jacket smelled like him, like the ocean and burning wood, and she blushed. "Can we play together sometime?"

"Of course," he said. "I would love to."

She squeezed his arm and smiled.

When they got to her home, Tommy helped her over the wall, and they rushed to the house. He helped her to climb up the side of the house. They got to her balcony, and she checked her room.

"Well, if my father found out I was missing, he's not waiting for me with a shotgun."

"That's good," Tommy said as he shrugged his jacket back on. "I wasn't looking to throw hands tonight."

Chrysta hugged herself against the cold and stepped up to the taller boy. "Thank you," she said. "I had a great time."

"Me too," he responded.

Chrysta shifted from foot to foot as a breeze made her shiver. He stepped closer, and Chrysta had to look up at him. She blushed. He suddenly put a finger to her chin and gently lifted her head. She closed her eyes, expecting a kiss.

She was a little bit disappointed when she felt lips brush her forehead.

She tried not to pout as she opened her eyes, and he stepped back. He smirked. "Hey, I made a promise. On my best behavior, on pain of death."

"That you did," she agreed.

She went to the door and opened it. She turned around one last time. Tommy was getting ready to leave, looking over the railing. "Thank you," she said softly, "again."

"Anytime, beautiful." And with that, he was gone.

4

Chrysta spent the whole weekend on cloud nine. She smiled and sighed and giggled. She tried to study, or play her violin, or spend time with Poe, but just felt her attention wandering back to the jazz club and sushi. She wanted to text Mary about the magical evening but couldn't risk her father finding out. She wouldn't be allowed to leave the house ever again.

Monday morning came, and she rushed to get into the car and to school. When she saw Mary walking up the steps, she almost tackled the other girl.

"What? What is it?" Mary asked, smiling at Chrysta's excitement.

"He came over!" Chrysta nearly shrieked. "He came over, and we went out!"

"What?! Who came over? Out where?!" Mary nearly shrieked back.

"Tommy! He took me out on a date Friday night!"

Mary stood on the steps, blinking for a few moments. But then she shrieked, grabbed Chrysta's hands, and jumped in delight. Other students looked at them like they were crazy, but the girls didn't care. The bell rang.

"Oh! Oh, I need more details!" Mary said.

"Okay, at lunch," Chrysta responded.

"Oh, you wanna make me wait?!" Mary cried.

"Sorry!" Chrysta laughed.

When it was time for lunch, Chrysta filled her friend in on everything that had happened. Mary looked scandalized. "I just don't believe it," she said. "Sneaking out with someone you barely know."

Chrysta laughed. "You were the one to tell me you would cover for me if I wanted to hang out with him."

"Yeah, but a jazz club? Sitting at a bar? Dinner at a sushi place?" Mary smiled. "Now, I'm jealous. Think you will go out again soon?"

"I want to," Chrysta confessed. "But only if I can make sure my father doesn't find out."

Mary nodded. "We don't want a whirlwind romance to turn into a tragic love story."

Orchestra class started, and Chrysta sat down in the first chair. She glanced over at the chair where Chloe usually sat. "Where's Chloe?" she asked Martin, the second chair violinist.

"Rumor is, every time she touches a violin, it breaks," he said. "Her parents took her out of class this week."

"Weird," murmured Chrysta.

A young blonde man opened the door. He went up to Mr. Hansen, and the teacher smiled and placed a hand on the young man's shoulder. "Everyone," he called over the sounds of students warming up. "Please welcome our newest violinist, Peter."

"Hi, Peter," most of the class called out, and he gave them all a bright smile. Mr. Hansen pointed to the string section, and Peter joined the others.

"Hi," Chrysta greeted him. "I'm Chrysta, and this is Martin. We have a third chair violinist, Chloe, but she is out today. You can have her chair."

"Oh, can I sit next to you? Just until I get settled," he asked.

"Um, sure," Chrysta said, and Martin shrugged and moved over. Peter sat down and set himself up.

"So, what are we studying today?" he said, flashing Chrysta a smile and placing a hand on her shoulder. Chrysta froze. She had a terrible feeling in her stomach.

"Music for the winter concert," she explained, fighting the urge to throw his hand off her shoulder. "Brahms's Violin Concerto."

He flashed her a smile. "Nice," he said brightly. Chrysta returned the smile nervously. Mr. Hansen stepped up to the podium, and they started playing.

After class let out, the girls were leaving when Peter caught up to them on the stairs. "Hey," he called out. "Chrysta, can I ask you a question?"

"Um, sure," she said, glancing at Mary. "Mary, this is Peter. Peter, Mary Jackson."

Peter gave Mary that same big smile, and Chrysta fought that bad feeling in her stomach. Mary held out her hand, but Peter ignored it and looked at Chrysta. "I was wondering," he said while Mary made a face, "If you can help me practice since I'm new."

"Um, sure, I may be able to help if you are having problems. Which part do you need help on?"

"Oh, I may need help on all of it. I want to make sure I'm ready for the winter concert."

The two girls glanced at each other. "It's Brahms, dude. I think you will be fine," Mary said sarcastically.

"And I think you played well today," Chrysta said.

"Well, maybe I can come to your house and practice," he asked, the smile not leaving his face.

"Um, no, if we did any extra practicing, it would have to be at lunch," Chrysta explained. She saw a familiar figure waiting on a bench near the park. "There is a friend of ours. Let's head over, Mary." Mary nodded, and the girls crossed the street to see Tommy.

Tommy held up a hand in greeting and grinned. Mary closed the last few feet of distance between them and started smacking Tommy on the shoulder. "Ow, ow, ow, hey, ow!" he protested with a smile.

"How dare you kidnap my best friend and show her a good time without me," Mary growled playfully, still hitting him.

Tommy looked between the two girls, laughing. "What? You wanted to be the third wheel?"

Mary stopped and placed her hands on her hips. "Well, I should have gone as a chaperone. I still don't think your intentions are pure regarding Chrysta."

"Chrysta, are you seeing this abuse I'm getting? Hey, stop laughing. I need your protection here, beautiful."

Both girls started laughing loudly. "So, how was class?" Tommy asked.

Mary said, "Good," while Chrysta said, "Weird." Tommy looked at her. "Chloe wasn't in class today. Every violin she touches breaks on her. Also, there is a new student, and he's kind of... creepy."

Tommy made a face as he stood up. "You mentioned that last week. Chloe was the one who stole my tips, right? And her violins started breaking on her the next day?"

"Yep," Mary confirmed, "karma biting her in the butt."

"Interesting," Tommy said. He gestured behind the girls. "And is that Mr. Creepy?"

Chrysta turned to see Peter still standing in front of the school, looking at them. She shuddered. "Yes, that's him."

Tommy gave the other boy a big smile and waved. Peter didn't move. "Yeah, he has a *Stepford Wives* vibe goin' on."

Chrysta's car pulled up. "That's me," Chrysta said. She turned back to Tommy and smiled. "Will I see you tonight?"

"Sure," he said. Mary leered at the two of them.

"I'll practice *Twinkle, Twinkle, Little Star* then," she joked and rushed to the car.

Once done with dinner, Chrysta waited on the balcony for Tommy to appear. She was nervous but couldn't put her finger on why. Poe dropped in for a visit with yet another blue bead. He dropped it on the wooden table that sat outside with a *thunk*. She picked it up. "I'm starting to think you stole someone's necklace," she scolded the bird but put the bead with the others.

As she scratched the raven's neck, Tommy pulled himself over the stone railing. He had a bag in his mouth that he plopped on the table while sitting next to her. "Good evening, beautiful," he said with a grin.

"Hello," she responded. Poe had moved his head back so Chrysta could scratch his chest. She stopped, and he did a dramatic flop onto the table, legs sticking up in the air. She laughed and continued petting him. Tommy watched them with a smile and opened his bag to bring out a burger and fries. He offered her the food, but she refused with a shake of her head.

"So I was talking to Mary," Tommy started.

"Oh yeah?" Chrysta asked. "Was she interrogating you?"

"A little. Mary's a little protective of you," he replied. "She worries about you a lot." Chrysta smiled. She was lucky to have Mary as a friend.

"What I found most interesting," Tommy continued, "was how your father reads your text messages. That sucks. I was about to ask for your number."

"Sorry about that," Chrysta said with a grimace.

"No worries, we will have to communicate the old fashion way: letters, telegrams, smoke signals," he said, grinning.

When Tommy had eaten his food, sharing a few fries with Poe, Chrysta got up and went inside for her violin and a music stand. She opened a book full of music and took a deep breath. She whipped her bow at Tommy, making it whistle in the air. Tommy scratched Poe's neck, looked at the bow currently pointing at him, and raised an eyebrow.

"I will play this music, but when I mess up—" she started.

"*If* you mess up," Tommy interrupted.

"*When* I mess up," she stated firmly but with a smile, "you have to promise not to laugh or make fun of me."

"Come on, *Twinkle, Twinkle, Little Star* is not that technically difficult."

She sighed and turned the book so he could read the cover—*Paganini's 24 Caprices for Violin*. Tommy grinned and gave an evil laugh.

"Promise me, Tommy," she tried to growl without smiling. He just laughed harder.

"You're cute when you're angry. Which one are you playing?" Tommy asked.

"Just number 1 and number 2," she replied.

He leaned back in his chair. "Ready when you are, beautiful," he said.

Chrysta took a deep breath and started playing the first piece. She had practiced Paganini in the past but had hated it. It was not the difficulty that turned her off, but his frantic melodies were not her favorite thing to play. She made mistakes but tried to soldier through.

The second piece was slower and more comfortable, and Chrysta enjoyed it more. She found herself closing her eyes and swaying to the music. Poe was hopping on the table, but Chrysta was not looking at Tommy directly.

When she finished, she was aware of just how quiet it was. She looked at Tommy and was dismayed to see him frowning. "Paganini is rolling in his grave right now," he simply said.

Chrysta's stomach dropped. "Was it really that bad?" she asked, upset.

He shook his head. "Hell no, it was perfect," he said. "I thought you would suck, and I would have to act like you weren't terrible, but," he flashed her a bright smile, "that was awesome."

She blushed and smiled back. "Thanks."

"Think you can play some more?"

"Oh no," she groaned and closed the book of music. "That's all the Paganini I can stomach in one night." And then she laughed.

She put her violin away and then went back outside to sit with Tommy. "You know," he said as she brought her feet up onto the chair to rest her chin on her knees, "you would do better to play professionally in an orchestra, not on the streets."

She smiled. "That's my plan. Try out for orchestra in a year or two. Move out on my own, maybe be roommates with Mary if I have to. Study music in college so I can be a teacher someday." She looked at him. "Have you ever tried to play in an orchestra?"

"Oh yes, they would love someone like me in the first chair," he replied sarcastically and gestured from the red streaks in his hair, down to his piercings, to his clothes and combat boots. Chrysta laughed. "The best I can hope for is to play in a club like Jazz Nocturne," he confessed.

"So why not play full-time?"

He made a face and shifted uncomfortably in his chair. "I've had to move around a lot in the past on short notice. It makes it hard to keep a job. Better I only play when they need me," he explained.

She hummed. "Playing there this week?"

"Actually, yes, tomorrow night for sure. The new pianist is flakey. His girlfriend never lets him out or something. Already asked for Halloween night off, though," he said.

"Oh?" she said with a grin.

"Yep, spending my birthday with you," he explained with a shrug. "If you want to go out, that is."

She blinked. "Halloween is your birthday?" She smiled. "Of course, we can go out. I would love to." She frowned. "But I don't have a costume."

"No worries, I'll take care of the costumes," he said with a grin.

"Oh, no," she groaned. "That sounds like a bad idea."

"You sayin' you don't trust me?" he asked, leaning forward so that his elbow was on the table and putting his head in his hand.

"Not at all," she stated, and he laughed. She smiled and looked at him from the corner of her eye. "So, how old will you be?"

"Well, let's see," he said, leaning back. "I was born 1842, so that will make me," he counted his fingers for a few seconds, "177 years old."

She blinked at him and then started giggling madly. "Funny, but really, how old are you?"

"If I'm lyin', I'm dyin'," Tommy said.

"Come on, you can be honest with me," Chrysta said. "I already know you're older. You don't have to lie."

He groaned, rolling his eyes. "I'm hurt that you don't believe me. Where is the trust? Don't I seem like a mature adult?" And he stuck out his tongue at her.

"Fine, be that way," she said and stuck her tongue out at him. They laughed, but Tommy sobered and looked at her.

"Seriously, me being older doesn't bother you?"

Chrysta shrugged. "Mary's parents have a significant age gap too. Granted, they met when her mom was 22, and her dad was 32. It caused a big scandal because she was a student and he was a teacher's aide. I guess it doesn't seem like a big deal to me?"

"Well, a decade is different than 200 years."

"True," Chrysta agreed, giving him a grin. "Maybe I shouldn't date someone who was around for the invention of the car."

"The invention of the car was nothing. I was happy when they started making toilet paper."

She grinned but suddenly felt a yawn coming on. She stretched. "Time for bed?" he asked.

"I think so," she confessed. They both stood up at the same time, suddenly standing very close to each other. Chrysta shifted and blushed. He smiled at her and then leaned down so their foreheads touched. "Thank you for playing for me," he said.

"Thank you for not making fun of me," she replied. Tommy gave her a grin and kissed her forehead. "See you Thursday?" she asked as he got ready to drop off the balcony.

"Thursday," he confirmed, and then he dropped down, and Chrysta watched him melt into the night.

5

The rest of the week was uneventful, except for Peter following Chrysta around like a lost puppy. He was cute enough that most of the other girls in their grade seemed to want to know him, but he only had eyes for Chrysta. He ate lunch with her and Mary and was still trying to get Chrysta to tutor him after school. Chrysta's feeling of unease just didn't seem to want to go away, even after several days.

"I don't know," she told Mary, "he is just giving me the creeps."

"Well, I think he is just nervous," said Mary. "But if you don't like him, don't feel like you have to hang out with him. Or, don't hang out with him alone, at least."

Thursday night, Chrysta rushed through dinner and then waited in her room for Tommy to appear. He popped over the railing as the sun dipped below the buildings around her home.

"Well," Tommy said, placing a large paper bag on the table, "I went with a couple's theme so that we could match."

Chrysta inspected the bag with a sense of trepidation. "I'm afraid of what you mean by that," she admitted. She held up a finger. "Before we head out, I have a surprise for you. Close your eyes."

Tommy made a show of closing his eyes and placing a hand over them as Chrysta disappeared back inside. She brought something out and put it on the table. "Okay, you can open them."

When Tommy dropped his hand, a giant cupcake was on the table. Somehow Chrysta had fit large candles on it that read "177" and lit them, the frosting quickly melting under the heat and weight. He looked between the cake and Chrysta for a few moments with an anxious look. The smile fell from her face. "You don't like it?" she asked.

"No... I..." he stammered. "I don't know what to say. No one has done something like this for me before."

She smiled. "Well, it's important to celebrate. I'm just sorry I couldn't get you a gift. You need to thank Mary for helping me get it for you."

He looked at the cupcake with a sad smile on his face. "Thank you," he said softly.

"You're welcome," she replied. "Make a wish before the cupcake catches fire."

Tommy smirked and leaned down. He cocked his head to the side and then blew out the candles. Tommy picked the candles off the cupcake and then broke it in half and then handed her the other piece. "So I wished—" he started. She placed a finger on his lips.

"Don't tell me!" she cried. "It won't come true if you do."

He smirked. "Alright," he said, licking some icing off his finger. "A secret it will stay. Ready for your costume now?" She nodded.

He reached into the bag and took out several items: fake white wings, a golden halo, and a white robe with gold trim. "Here," he said with a grin, "try these on."

She went back inside to her room and came back out several minutes later. It was a pretty simple angel costume, but Chrysta counted herself lucky that the robe wasn't too revealing. It went down to her knees, and the neckline wasn't too low. She put her hands up like she was praying. "How do I look?" she asked.

"Perfect," he said. Chrysta crossed her arms. "And where is yours?" she asked.

He got a package from the bag, just a red tail and red horns on a headband. He attached the tail to his pants and then put the headband on his head with a *thunk*. He grinned and held out his hands. "Do I look devilish enough?"

She laughed. "I suddenly feel overdressed."

"Well, everyone knows people only care what the woman is wearing," he said. He held an elbow out. "Ready to go?"

"Where are we going?" she asked, taking his elbow.

"Mary mentioned that your classmate, Chloe, is having a party," he stated.

"Show up to Chloe's party, fashionably late, with an older boy, for everybody to see?" She grinned. "Let's do it."

. . . . .

Chloe's house was not far from Chrysta's, so she didn't have to worry about getting cold on the way. She watched the kids running through the street in superhero and princess costumes. They held out their bags full of candy and screamed in excitement. Chrysta told each kid how awesome they looked and even cooed over the costumed babies in their parents' arms.

"You like this holiday, huh?" Tommy asked as they let some screaming kids pass them on the sidewalk.

"I do," she admitted. "It's something about being anything you want for one night that makes me love it."

When they arrived at Chloe's, they went through the opened gates up to the house. Chrysta knocked, and an older blonde woman answered the door. She wore a tight, short dress with a gauzy shirt embroidered with silver stars. A witch's hat and glitter on her face completed her outfit. She blinked at the two of them for a few moments, holding a glass of white wine, until Chrysta broke the awkward silence. "Um, good evening Mrs. Williams. It's me, Chrysta York. I know I said I couldn't make it, but I was able to come aft—"

"Oh, Chrysta! I didn't recognize you out of your uniform! You look so young!" Mrs. Williams gave a loud laugh and leaned over to pat Chrysta's shoulder, almost spilling her drink. "Of course, you can come in. The more, the merrier!" She looked Tommy up and down. "Who is your friend? I don't recognize him."

"Thomas Monroe, this is Mrs. Williams," Chrysta started. Tommy smiled and held out his hand, and Mrs. Williams grabbed it to shake but didn't let go. Tommy glanced at his trapped hand but kept the smile on his face. "A pleasure to meet you, ma'am," he said.

"Oh, the pleasure is all mine," Mrs. Williams purred. She was still holding onto his hand, rubbing her thumb on the back of it. Chrysta coughed to hide a laugh.

"And I love the costumes!" Mrs. Williams almost yelled. "Chrysta, small, innocent, pale-skinned, beautiful angel," she said, gesturing to Chrysta. "And you, tall, dark-skinned, handsome devil," she stepped closer to Tommy, "ready to sin."

"Well, that was the plan, ma'am," Tommy almost squeaked. "You know, having a *couple's* costume and all."

If Mrs. Williams got his meaning, she didn't acknowledge it, and just bit her lower lip and giggled. She suddenly blinked. "Oh, where are my manners. Come inside, you two, enjoy the party." She finally let go of Tommy's hand and stepped back so they could go inside. While she closed the door, Chrysta took a look around, and Tommy took off his jacket. A circular staircase led upstairs in front of them, a dining room full of snacks to the right, and a living room full of dancing bodies to their left. Fake bats and spiders were everywhere, with a giant spider hanging on the staircase.

Mrs. Williams suddenly appeared at Tommy's side and grabbed his arm. She held it in such a way that his elbow was between her breasts. "I have to top off my drink," she said, leaning close to Tommy and almost spilling her too-full glass on him, "would you like to join me and get a drink of your own?"

"Well, I see some punch on the table, ma'am. I'm sure that's fine," he said, trying to keep the smile on his face.

"Nonsense, let me get you something *stronger*," she sighed and pulled him through the dining room. Before they went through a far door, Tommy looked back and mouthed, "Help me" before he disappeared.

Chrysta considered going after them but decided to look for Mary first. She went to the left.

The living room had a DJ playing dance music with a small dance floor in front of him. Various teenagers from Chrysta's school were there, some dancing, some eating food, some just talking in clumps. Chrysta had to push her way to the back of the house, where french doors opened into the backyard. Someone had set up carnival-style games, and teens were wandering around shooting hoops and tossing darts at balloons. She saw Mary playing whack-a-mole, covered in a long black dress.

She approached her friend, and Mary squealed and hugged her when she recognized her. "You made it!" Mary cried, a smile showing off fake pointed teeth. "Where's Tommy? He's the one who sprung you, right?"

"He's here, he just got kidnapped by Mrs. Williams," Chrysta explained.

"Oh yeah, she's wasted," Mary agreed. "I think she flirted with most of the boys here. Should we rescue him?"

"Probably," Chrysta admitted. They made their way back to the house. Nearby, a group of teens shouted in joy when one of them rang the bell on a strength tester. "This looks fun," Chrysta said.

"Yeah, Chloe's parents like going all out for Halloween," explained Mary. "And Chloe hasn't come out of her room, so win-win!" Mary laughed.

They found the door to the kitchen and went inside. Mrs. Williams and Tommy were standing at the kitchen island, leaning on it, Mrs. Williams laughing loudly at something Tommy said. She glanced at the two girls and gestured at Tommy. "Where did you find this awesome specimen of a man, girls?"

"Playing violin in the park after school," Chrysta replied honestly. She linked arms with Tommy. "He's good."

"Oh, violin?" Mrs. Williams said. "Maybe you're better than Chloe," she growled, sipping at her drink. "She has broken five violins in the last week. *Five.* It's unbelievable."

"Oh, I'm sure I'm not," Tommy said. "And maybe Chloe is just having a spot of bad luck."

"Well, her father and I didn't pay for all those lessons for *bad luck*," Mrs. Williams continued, taking a bigger swallow of her drink and almost falling over. "Now, Chrysta here. Chrysta is a *wonderful* player with natural talent." Mrs. Williams reached out and played with Chrysta's hair, which she wore down.

"Chloe is a good player," Chrysta said honestly, "I think Tommy is right. She's just having a bit of bad luck."

"Maybe you two are right," Mrs. Williams hummed. She tried sipping more wine but realized that her glass was empty. She unsteadily toddled over to a cabinet and started messing with the bottles in it. "Oh, can't I offer you something, Thomas? White wine?"

"Wine gives me heartburn, ma'am," Tommy said, looking around the room while Mrs. Williams was occupied, like he was looking for an exit.

"Bourbon?"

"Could never use to the taste of bourbon, honestly." Tommy grabbed Chrysta's hand and tried to guide the girls to the door outside.

"Vodka?"

"A potato is better used for making fries, in my opinion." He was holding the door open and trying to wave the girls through it.

"Rum?"

Tommy paused in his frantic attempt to escape to turn towards the older woman. "Well, maybe just a little," he said.

After Tommy accepted a glass with some amber liquid, a man walked into the kitchen. His costume made him look like an extra in the Harry Potter films. A long wizard's robe embroidered with stars and constellations, a wizard's hat, a fake beard, and a large staff completed the look. "There you are, darling!" he cried. "I hope you are not torturing anyone."

"Not at all, dear," Mrs. Williams said, kissing the man on the cheek. "Just showing them around the house."

Tommy finished his drink in one big gulp and held out his hand. "Thomas Monroe, sir. Nice to meet you. You have a lovely home."

Mr. Williams looked between Tommy's open hand to the now-empty glass. "Thank you," Mr. Williams said cautiously, shaking Tommy's hand and turning to his wife. "Can you go talk to Chloe, darling? She's missing all the fun."

"Oh, all right," Mrs. Williams pouted, giving Tommy a leer. She wobbled out of the kitchen. Mr. Williams turned towards the group. "My apologies, Martha can't help but overindulge with wine during parties. Even parties where under-aged students are roaming about."

"Oh, no worries, Mr. Williams," Mary stated, "Tommy here is 177 years old." Tommy flashed the older man a broad grin and waved.

"Right," Mr. Williams said, looking confused. "Well, enjoy the party." And he backed out of the kitchen to follow his wife.

Tommy dropped the smile as soon as the man had left, and he started walking fast into the backyard, herding the girls with him. "*Don't* leave me alone with that woman," he hissed. "That woman wants to be a *cougar*, that's fine, but no one gets to yank on my tail. Oh, stop laughing, you two, it ain't funny."

. . . . .

They wandered around the games outside, the girls bouncing from one game to the next like little kids, Tommy following them with an amused look on his face. The other teenagers looked at the group with open curiosity but otherwise left them alone. The games were handing out tickets for winning, and as they passed the booth that was handing out prizes, Mary pointed out a giant teddy bear. "I'm getting that bear," she declared.

Tommy looked where she was pointing and then gave her a deep bow. "As the lady commands," he said.

Tommy proceeded to go from game to game, winning as many tickets as possible, the girls cheering him on. After about an hour, Mary had an armful of tickets that she took to the prize booth and returned to Chrysta and Tommy with the giant teddy bear. "Thank you!" she cried out.

Tommy bowed again and then linked arms with Chrysta. "Consider it a show of my appreciation for the cupcake," he said.

"No problem," Mary said. She looked Tommy up and down. "So, how old are you? Really?"

"Why is it so hard for people to believe that I'm 177 years old?"

"So that makes you a vampire?" asked Mary.

"Vampires are not the only creatures that live a long time," he stated.

"That didn't answer my question," Mary pointed out.

"No, it didn't. You're correct, I'm a vampire. That eats food. And wears silver jewelry. And can go out in daylight. And cannot turn into a bat. Why are you laughing like that, beautiful?"

Chrysta laughed for a full minute and then turned to Tommy. "Just happy to be out with my two favorite people," she said.

Tommy turned to Mary. "You hear that?" he asked. "I'm a favorite person." And then it was Mary's turn to laugh for a long time.

They roamed back inside and started getting food from the dining room. Tommy had a plate piled high with meat when they heard a shout. Chloe, dressed as a witch like her mother, stalked into the room and snatched the plate from him. "Why are you here? No one invited *you*."

Chrysta felt a flash of anger and joined Tommy by his side. "You invited me, and I brought him with me. If you have a problem with it, we will leave," she said. She placed a hand on Tommy's shoulder to push him towards the front door, but he resisted, pulled her back, and put an arm around her shoulder.

He gave Chloe a big smile. "Surprisingly, I wanted to talk to you, Chloe," he said, not looking upset. "I hear you are having problems with a curse."

Chloe snorted. "What curse?"

"The curse I put on my money jar," he explained. He grabbed a brownie straight off the table and popped it into his mouth.

"What are you talking about?" Chloe demanded as he chewed.

"Well," Tommy said thickly and then swallowed, "I put a curse on the money jar so that if anyone ever stole it, they would have a string of bad luck. If you return the jar, your problem with breaking violins will end."

Chloe saw that a crowd of teenagers had gathered around to see what the commotion was about, and she gave a hearty laugh. "I don't believe in that shit, and you are just trying to get your money back."

"Perhaps," Tommy admitted as he grabbed another brownie off the table. "But if you give me back my money and the curse isn't real, what's the worst that can happen?"

"What's going on here?" Mr. Williams asked as he and his wife walked into the dining room.

"Daddy, I didn't invite this person. He should leave," Chloe said in a whiny tone and pointed at Tommy.

Chrysta and Mary looked at each other and rolled their eyes. "It's okay, Mr. Williams," Tommy said with a grin. "I can head out if you prefer. Thank you for your hospitality, though."

"What did you say about Chloe having your money?" Mrs. Williams asked.

"Chloe stole my tip jar when I was playing in the park one day," Tommy explained, pushing the brownie into his mouth. "She said I shouldn't be begging for money, that it is stealing."

"Oh, kitten, that's horrible," gasped Mrs. Williams. "You should give the money back."

"It's okay, Mrs. Williams. When Chloe wants to play the violin again, she knows where to find me." Tommy started to head to the front door, Chrysta and Mary following him. "Just remember, if you want the curse gone, you have to give back every cent," he said with a wave.

Tommy retrieved his jacket, and he opened the door for the girls. Chrysta turned to the adults that had followed them to the door. "Thank you for inviting us, Mr. and Mrs. Williams. We had a fun time," she said, not looking in Chloe's direction.

"Thank you for coming," Mrs. Williams said. She stepped up to Tommy and held out her hand. "You make sure to get these girls home safe, you hear?"

"Of course," he replied. He took Mrs. Williams's hand and kissed it. She giggled, and the group headed out into the night.

·····

The angel, the vampire carrying a giant teddy bear, and their devil bodyguard made their way to Mary's home, passing groups of costumed children and their parents.

"So, did you curse your tip jar as you said?" asked Mary, craning her neck to look at Tommy behind them.

"Nope," he admitted. "I think Chrysta did that."

"Me?" Chrysta cried out. "I wish. If I could make people pay for their actions..." She trailed off as she thought about it and gave out a laugh. "Chloe would break out in hives."

"Or her hair would combust into flames," Mary added.

"Or her heels would always break."

"Remind me never to make you ladies mad," Tommy joked behind them, and the girls laughed. "I'm serious, though, Chrysta cursed her. I'm ninety percent certain of it."

Mary snorted. "Whatever you say."

They made it to Mary's townhouse, and she hugged Chrysta. "Goodnight, you two," she said. She started walking up to the door. "Happy birthday, Tommy!"

"Goodnight," Chrysta cried out, and they started walking to Chrysta's home.

They walked quickly, Chrysta shivering as the wind picked up. "So, if you are not a vampire, what are you exactly?" she asked.

He paused and seemed to consider her question. "The truth?" he softly said.

"Yes."

"A changeling."

"A changeling?" she asked, laughing. He nodded gravely.

"I am a part of a group of murderous creatures that can change between our true form and a human form," he explained.

"And why haven't you murdered me yet?"

"Cause I like you," he simply said. Chrysta laughed.

They made their familiar trek to sneak her back into her room. When they made it up to the balcony, Tommy paused by the railing and didn't haul himself up. He stayed low so only his eyes showed. "Chrysta?" he softly said.

"Yes?" she asked, turning around as she removed the wings.

"Thank you," he said. "I don't think you realize... how being so nice... how much that means to me."

She smiled and leaned down to kiss him on the forehead. When she stood back up, he pulled himself up so that they were on the same level and looking into each other's eyes. Chrysta leaned forward so their foreheads touched. She wanted to close the gap between them and kiss him, but she had a feeling that wasn't what he wanted.

"Do you want the costume back?" she asked, breaking the uncomfortable silence.

"Nah, you keep it. White isn't my color," he joked, and she giggled.

"Goodnight," she said but didn't move away.

"Goodnight," he said, not moving away but putting a hand on her cheek and rubbing his thumb across her skin.

They had started to move closer to each other to kiss when Poe dropped down next to them and squawked. They both jumped back quickly, Tommy almost losing his hold on the railing. "Cockblocked by a bird," Tommy muttered to himself, and Chrysta laughed nervously.

"He's protecting my honor," she joked. Tommy just glared at Poe.

Chrysta quickly kissed Tommy's forehead again and started to go inside. "'Night," she said.

"'Night," he responded, watching her go with a wistful smile on his face. Poe cawed at Tommy again. "Oh shut up, you uptight bird," Chrysta heard Tommy say as she turned away, and she smiled.

The next day at school, the only topic of discussion was Chloe's party. Only, this year, it wasn't how cool it was, but how Chloe threw Chrysta out with the mysterious stranger that no one knew. By lunchtime, Chrysta was continually explaining who Tommy was and how Chloe stole his tips. Peter seemed upset when he went to sit with Chrysta and Mary at lunch.

"I didn't know you would be at the party, Chrysta," he said, glaring at her.

Chrysta shrugged. "I was invited, but my father said I couldn't go."

"So, how did you get there?" he asked.

Mary, who was getting sick of Peter ignoring her, leaned over and said something in a loud stage whisper. "She snuck out." Peter frowned.

"And who is that boy who was with you? He's not a student at this school," he stated.

"He's a friend," Chrysta explained, getting upset.

"For how long?" Peter asked.

Mary rolled her eyes in frustration. "Dude, why are you interrogating her? You have only known us for a week. You do not have the right to ask personal questions."

Peter's frown grew, and he stalked off. "Jerk," Mary said to herself. She turned to Chrysta. "Looks like you were right about him being a creep. You okay?"

Chrysta took a deep breath and nodded. "Yeah. I guess I just realized that if I'm going to keep Tommy a secret from my father, I'm going to have to be more careful who sees us together."

Mary suddenly got a wicked grin and leaned forward over the table. "Speaking of tall, dark, and handsome, how are you two doing?"

"What do you mean?" Chrysta asked, but she was grinning.

"You know, have you two kissed yet?"

"I don't think I'm supposed to kiss and tell."

"So, you *have* kissed?" Mary asked, looking scandalized.

"No, we haven't," Chrysta admitted. She held up a finger. "But, he is a master at forehead kisses."

"Awwwww," Mary cooed. "You two are too cute." She suddenly got a serious look on her face. "I'm happy, you know, that you found someone nice."

"Thanks, Mary," Chrysta said as she placed a hand on Mary's.

.....

Later that night, after dinner, Chrysta was practicing her violin in her room when she heard the doorbell ring. She ignored it but was surprised when a servant knocked on her door about half an hour later. "Your father wishes to see you," is all he said. She followed him down to her father's study.

She was shocked to see Peter sitting in one of the chairs placed in front of her father's desk. Peter stood and smiled as she walked further into the study to sit in the other chair. "What is going on?" she asked as Peter sat back down and grinned.

"This young man and I have been conversing," her father stated. "It seems he would like to court you. I will allow it."

"You... you will allow it?" Chrysta asked, her voice rising with her anger. "What if I don't want to date him?"

"Peter is a nephew of a friend," her father continued, not acknowledging her question. "He is from a good family and plays the violin. He is now attending your school. I'm sure you two could become quite close if given a chance."

Chrysta balled up her hands in anger but didn't say anything. She knew that arguing would not change anything.

"I thought we could go out tomorrow night," Peter said, placing a hand on one of her fists. Chrysta fought the urge to pull her hand away. "Dinner and a movie?"

Chrysta felt a lump in her throat and tried to keep herself from crying. She cleared her throat. "Alright," she thickly replied.

Peter beamed at her and her father. "It's a date then," he brightly said. He got up and kissed Chrysta's hand before leaving the study. Chrysta suddenly wanted to wash her hand with the hottest water she could find.

Her father studied her for a moment, his face hard to read. He tented his fingers in front of him. "For your information," he said, "I have increased security around the house. You may notice guards patrolling the grounds. Pay them no mind, they are here for your safety."

He knows, Chrysta thought to herself. He knew about Tommy, and this was him punishing her. She felt fear bloom in her chest. Would these guards hurt Tommy if they caught him?

Chrysta tried to keep her face neutral but felt like she was swallowing a lemon when she finally responded. "Yes, sir," she simply stated.

"You are dismissed," he said, and Chrysta walked out of the study as fast as possible.

When Chrysta made it back to her bedroom, she slammed the door and started pacing back and forth. When she hadn't calmed down after several minutes of moving around her bedroom, she screamed in frustration and let herself outside on the balcony. She wanted to cry but was trying to hold onto the anger. Why? Why Peter? Why couldn't she be with someone she wanted?

She suddenly slammed a fist down on the wooden table and was shocked to see a golden light flash, a popping sound following it. Her hand felt numb, and she looked at her fingers in awe. What was that?

Poe dropped down onto the table and cawed. Chrysta put her hands up to her face and rubbed her eyes. With her rage gone, she was fighting the tears that threatened to fall. "Not now, Poe," she said.

Poe hopped but stopped to cock his head at her as she sat at the table. She lost her fight with the tears and started crying in earnest. Chrysta put her head on the table and let out loud sobs.

She wasn't sure how long she had been like that until she heard a noise come from the railing. She looked up to see Tommy climbing up. "Hey, beautiful, you know anything about the gorillas currently walking arou—" He stopped talking when he saw her at the table, eyes red from crying and trying to wipe her nose. A worried look crossed his face, and Tommy got down on one knee and took her face in his hands. "What's wrong?" he asked as he looked around the balcony as if he could find the thing that hurt her and beat it up.

"It's my father," she tried to explain. Chrysta sniffled and tried wiping her eyes and nose. "I think he found out about me sneaking out with you, and now those guards are going to be walking around. What if they catch you and hurt you?"

Tommy looked relieved and smiled. "Is that all? Beautiful, I can handle a couple of hired goons. They will never see me, I promise." He smiled at Chrysta, but the smile went away when she didn't return it. "What else is wrong?"

"Well, the reason he found out about you is that Peter came over tonight," she explained, voice rising in anger. "He wants to *court* me, and father is *allowing* him to." She got up from her seat and paced the balcony. "Like my father *owns* me, and I have no say in who I *see* or *date*. Peter probably told father about the party last night, and the mysterious man I was with."

Tommy sat on the table and nodded. "Well, it's not the end of the world. And maybe it's for the best," he said.

Chrysta stopped pacing. "What do you mean?" she asked.

"Well, I'm not saying creepy dude is the one, but maybe you should see someone else."

"What? Why?" she asked, tears threatening to come back.

"Look, I can't give you the life you deserve, beautiful," he tried to explain. He stood and placed his hands on her shoulders. "You deserve someone who can make you happy. Get that apartment, let you sleep in on weekends, and let students play horrible music when you're teaching. I don't know if I can give you all that."

"But don't I get to decide who I want to be with? Who I want a life with?" She felt tears falling down her cheeks, and she closed her eyes. "I really like being with you. I don't want to lose that."

She heard him sigh and then felt the press of his lips on her forehead as he gave her a big hug. "You will be the death of me, you know that?" he said. Before she could ask what he meant, he pushed her back and wiped the tears off her face.

"I will make you a deal," Tommy said. Chrysta opened her eyes and looked at him. "I will allow you to be the one to end things. I will let you decide when you no longer want to see me." He put a hand on his chest. "But I will always be your friend. I will be there when you call or need help. I will do everything in my power to help you because I do like you—a lot. I like you enough to realize that I may not be the right person for you. But I know you need to make that choice for yourself."

She smiled. "Thank you," she whispered.

"And speaking of being at your beck and call," he said with a smile. He reached into an inner pocket of his jacket and brought out a red object. He handed it to Chrysta, and she was amazed to see an old-style flip phone. "Feel free to text Mary too, just go easy on the minutes, okay?"

"Thank you," she said, fighting tears again. She had always considered getting a phone her father didn't know about but had never had the chance.

"Anything to see those golden eyes of yours stay dry, beautiful," he replied.

When he mentioned the color of gold, Chrysta paused and looked at her hand. She thought of the flash of gold that she saw when she hit the table in anger. She rubbed her fingers together. "What is it?" he asked.

"Nothing," she murmured. "I thought I saw something, but I think I was just upset."

"So when is your first date with Mr. Creepy?" he asked.

Chrysta felt her lip curl in disgust. "Tomorrow night. Dinner and a movie."

"Well, I got him beat with a jazz club and sushi for a first date," he said. He leaned back on the table. "But maybe what he lacks in originality, he makes up in charm."

"Still rather go out with you," she replied.

46

"You will," he said. "Just because I want you to find someone better doesn't mean I will give up without a fight. Most girls would be happy to have two people fighting over her."

"I'm not most girls," she said, with more venom than she meant.

"That you are not," he agreed.

She sighed and then rubbed her eyes. "I... I'm sorry."

"Nothing to apologize for, beautiful," he said.

She smiled. She stepped closer to Tommy, and she felt him stiffen. His eyes widened as she leaned closer. She felt his lips twitch as she kissed him on the cheek. "Doesn't seem like a fair fight," she joked.

"What's that?" He brought her back into a big hug.

"He's probably horrible at forehead kisses."

He snorted. "If he tries to do more than a forehead kiss, let me know, okay?"

"Gonna kick him?"

"After you, of course."

She giggled and returned the hug, breathing in his scent. "Thank you, Tommy. You are a wonderful person."

"Why yes, yes, I am," he stated. And Chrysta started to giggle and laugh and had to bury her face in his throat to make sure she didn't get too loud. When she had calmed down, she leaned back to look him in the eyes. "Wanna hear me play Paganini?"

"Hell yeah," he replied. "Which ones?"

"Number 4," she answered as she went inside for her violin. "I think it will help my mood," she said after she set up.

Although she made many more mistakes than she had the first time playing, Chrysta didn't care. Tonight was about playing for herself more than anyone else. It started slow and mellow but soon built into a frantic pace she poured her anger and frustration into. As the last note died and the silence returned, she opened her eyes to see Tommy looking at her with awe. He gave her a chef's kiss. "Excellent," he said. She smiled and bowed.

7

Chrysta went on her date with Peter and was surprised that it wasn't awful. She dressed in jeans and a sweater that her father approved. He showed up at 6 to pick her up and opened up the taxi's door for her. He let her choose the movie only after expressing surprise that she didn't want to see the latest romance movie. Chrysta picked a horror movie instead and was kind of happy to see he had turned green as they left the theater.

Dinner was at an expensive Italian restaurant, where Peter butchered the pronunciation of most of the plates. He tried to order a salad for her, and she had to talk over him to get the Caprese chicken instead. Peter looked shocked when she ate most of the plate. "You eat a lot for a little person," he said.

"I'm short, not a midget," she said, trying not to sound upset, and she was happy to see him blush in embarrassment.

While they waited for coffee and cannolis (Peter had not asked if she wanted any but ordered for both), Chrysta noticed someone playing guitar across the street. She smiled when she recognized Tommy, and had to focus on Peter for the rest of the dinner so he didn't see her staring out the window.

"So, who is your favorite composer on the violin?" she asked, mostly being polite.

He shrugged. "Don't have one," he said.

"You don't like one composer in particular?" she asked, surprised.

He shrugged again. "I like what we are playing now," he said.

"Okay," she said. She expected Peter to ask who she liked, but he just moved on to the next topic.

They ate dessert, Chrysta having to tactfully decline the coffee several times before Peter stopped asking if she wanted any and then went outside to wait for another taxi. She swore she saw Tommy wink in her direction.

Back at her home, Peter escorted her inside. Her father was waiting for them in the foyer, one of the guards standing by his side. Chrysta had a feeling of what Peter was going to do and tried to keep her hands folded behind her back, but he grabbed her right hand and kissed it before leaving. When her father disappeared into his study, Chrysta almost ran to her room.

Almost as soon as she turned on the lights, Tommy's phone started buzzing in her pocket. She answered. "Thank you for being there," she said.

"No worries," he said. "I wanted to make sure he didn't try anything. How was it?"

"Well, he was shocked that I didn't want to see the romance film *The Misty River* and wanted to see the horror film *Blood House 6* instead. I guess he's not a horror fan."

"Is that the one where a girl's head exploded in the trailer?"

"Yep."

"Nice. How was it?"

"Good," she confessed. "I liked *Blood House 3* better."

"And dinner?"

"He tried to order for me. A salad."

"What does he think you are, a rabbit?"

She laughed. "I ordered a chicken dish instead."

He hummed. "Good. So Peter is a bit sexist, but we figured that out when he asked your father permission to date you instead of, you know, asking you."

She smiled as she flopped on the bed. "I don't know, maybe I'm being too mean."

"Well, I'm glad I kept the title of 'Best First Date,'" he joked. "Have a nice night, beautiful."

"Goodnight," she replied and hung up. She dressed for bed and then went outside to enjoy the crisp fall air. Poe dropped down with a familiar blue bead in his beak.

"Where are you getting these, you silly bird?" she asked, scratching him on the head. He just squawked at her and said, "Chrysta," before flying away.

•••••

Come Monday morning, Chrysta went to school, hoping that Peter had moved on and gotten over his crush on her, but she was dismayed when Peter appeared and insisted on escorting her to every class. He wouldn't even let her talk to

Mary, and they had to duck into the girl's restroom to get away from him at lunch. Finally, Chrysta was able to tell Mary what had happened over the weekend.

"You know," Mary started to say after thinking in silence for several minutes, "I think your father can't stoop any lower, and then he does something like this." Mary watched Chrysta pace. Telling Mary everything had upset her all over again. "He said he would *allow* Peter to *court* you. What flipping century does your father live in?"

"I don't know," Chrysta moaned. She stopped pacing and rubbed her face. "It's all so... infantilizing."

"Well, just as long as those two don't start planning your wedding, you're fine," Mary joked, but the smile died on her face when she saw the look of horror on Chrysta's face. "Oh, sis, I was kidding."

"I would kill myself," Chrysta said softly, realizing she meant it. "I would rather die." The frustration she felt on Friday came back, and she felt the tears threaten to fall again.

"Oh, I'm sorry!" cried Mary, and she quickly gathered Chrysta in a hug. A girl entered the bathroom and gave them a look, but they paid her no mind. Chrysta calmed down and was washing her face when the girl came out of the stall.

"Congratulations," the girl said.

"For what?" Chrysta asked as she dried her face.

"Peter and you are dating now, right? He's your boyfriend?" the girl asked as she washed her hands. "He has been saying that all day."

Chrysta fought the urge to scream into the paper towel and lowered her hands, sighing. "We went on one date. He's not my boyfriend," she tried explaining in an even tone.

"That's not what he said," the girl said in a singsong voice. She glanced between Chrysta and Mary. "Are you two dating?"

"We are not," Mary said dryly. They had known each other long enough that rumors that they were sleeping together had plagued them since middle school.

The girl looked at Chrysta and smirked. "Well, you're lucky to have him."

Chrysta felt a flash of anger and balled her hands into fists. "I don't *want* him!" she yelled.

But something odd happened. Chrysta felt the fist; she imagined what it would be like to punch out with that fist into the mirror next to her, feel the glass shatter, maybe even feel the sharp pain of glass shards going into her skin, break the bones in her hand. And even though she didn't twitch a muscle, the mirror beside her broke into dozens of pieces.

All of them jumped, Mary and the girl yelping, Chrysta just staring at the mirror in shock. There were several moments of silence, and then the girl made a run for the door. Mary and Chrysta were left blinking at each other and the mirror.

"How... how did that happen?" Mary asked in a small voice.

"I-I don't know," Chrysta stammered. She took a shaky breath. "We should let someone know about this," and she left the bathroom.

Peter was waiting outside of the bathroom, but before Chrysta could turn around, he spotted her and flashed a smile. "Hey, Chrysta, wanna eat lunch together?" he asked while putting his arm around her shoulder.

Chrysta shook her head stiffly. "No, thank you," she said, walking away from him. Mary followed her.

"Oh, why not?"

"Not hungry," she admitted. The broken mirror had killed any appetite she had.

"I have to make sure my girlfriend eats," he said.

Chrysta froze in the middle of the hallway, and she could sense Mary stopping as well but then taking a step back. That made the anger evaporate in a flash, her lifetime friend being afraid of her. Chrysta took a breath and turned around to look at Peter.

"Peter, we went on one date. You are not my boyfriend, and I am not your girlfriend. Please stop telling people that," she said. She made a face. "If you want to continue to go out, we will, but you can't make decisions like that for me."

Peter smirked. "Why? Is that boy everyone saw you with your boyfriend?"

"No, he's not. He is a friend. And if I want to spend time with him, I will."

Peter's smirk turned into a pout. "Well, fine. We will see what your father has to say about this." And with that, he turned around and stalked off.

"Did I wake up in an alternate dimension?" Mary asked softly, and Chrysta let out an unladylike snort. She looked at Mary and then started giggling madly. Mary blinked at her and then started to laugh as well.

"Come on," Chrysta said, "let's go tell someone about the mirror."

.....

Chrysta, so used to being overlooked, didn't know how to handle the attention Peter brought by proclaiming they were together, but she decided to ignore everyone for the rest of the day. Orchestra class started, and she sat down with barely a glance in Peter's direction. Chloe was back, which meant Chrysta didn't have to sit with Peter anymore. Chloe had another violin to play, but 20 minutes into the class, there was a *twank*, and the violin was once again in two pieces.

There were hoots and hollers as Chloe walked up to Mr. Hansen, red in the face. Chrysta felt terrible for her. It had gotten to the point where it felt less of a lesson in humility and more sadistic. Chloe got a note and left the classroom, and Mr. Hansen spent several minutes getting the class back to work.

After school, the girls made their way outside. Mary bumped a shoulder against Chrysta, and she stopped. Mary looked worried. "Are you okay?" Mary asked.

Chrysta thought for a second. "Yes," she answered. "I'm sorry about earlier in the bathroom. I don't know what happened."

"I was talking about Peter and the rumors flying around."

Chrysta sighed. "Yeah, I'm good. I just have to learn to ignore it."

Suddenly Chloe appeared. Both girls looked at her with surprised expressions. "Chrysta, can I ask for a favor?" Chloe asked, with a very sour look on her face.

"Sure, Chloe, what's up?" asked Chrysta.

"Can you ask your friend, Tommy, to come to the school tomorrow?"

Chrysta blinked but then gave Chloe a genuine smile. "Of course. I'll get in touch with him tonight."

Chloe gave a small nod and continued down the steps. "Well," Mary said, "today's wonders won't stop."

Chrysta snorted and then laughed.

. . . . .

Chrysta texted Tommy that night, telling him Chloe had asked to see him. "Wednesday afternoon," was his reply. "Let her twist a little."

She had laid down on her bed when he texted again. "Are you okay?" and she smiled at the contraband phone.

"Peter is saying we are boyfriend and girlfriend," she responded. "I'm trying to ignore it."

"Ouch," he texted. "You weren't going to tell me you two were getting serious?"

She laughed. "Well, it was a surprise for me, too."

"Well, keep your Saturday night open, beautiful. I have plans."

"Noted," she responded. She thought about the bathroom and the broken mirror. For some reason, she felt Tommy was the only person she could tell about all the weird stuff happening, and he wouldn't think she was crazy. But she was tired and decided it wasn't worth bringing it up over text.

The next day, Chrysta went to school. If Peter made good on his threat to speak to her father, she had not heard anything about it. She waited on the steps for Chloe. "Tommy says he will be here tomorrow afternoon," she said when she saw Chloe, and Chloe only gave her a nod in return.

Chrysta still avoided Peter that day, ignoring anyone who wanted to talk about their "relationship." She was still unhappy that he had made that announcement without her, but there wasn't much she could do about it now. It helped that Tommy kept texting her throughout the day, making little jokes and comments on classical music.

Wednesday was pretty much the same, although when she and Mary were leaving school, seeing Tommy standing by a bench in the park made her feel so happy. She had to fight the urge to hug him and gave him a big smile instead.

"You okay, beautiful?" he asked, looking worried.

"She is stressed out," Mary explained.

Tommy frowned. "Stressed about what? Mr. Creepy?"

"If he throws his arm around my shoulder one more time, I'm ripping it off his body and beating him with it," Chrysta said flatly.

Tommy choked back laughter, and Mary slapped his arm. "What?" he asked while chuckling. "That's the sexiest thing I have ever heard her say."

Mary glared at Tommy. "What is wrong with you?"

"Many things, but we don't have time to cover them right now," he replied.

Chloe came out of the school and walked across the street to join them. She rummaged in her backpack and brought out Tommy's tip jar. She reached out to hand it to him, but he folded his arms and grinned at her.

"Here is your money back," Chloe said, a sour look on her face. Tommy didn't reach for it, and Chloe shifted from foot to foot. "Well? Aren't you going to take it?"

"Was hoping to hear an apology," he said with a smile, and Chloe went pale. Chrysta put a hand on his shoulder, and he turned to her.

"I think she learned her lesson," Chrysta said.

"Don't mess with people who can put a curse on you?"

"Don't be a jerk when it's not needed," Chrysta said and gave Chloe a look. Chloe, for her part, looked ashamed and nodded.

"I'm sorry I took the money," Chloe said softly. Finally, Tommy took the jar.

"Well, if Chrysta can forgive ya, so can I," he said. He put the tip jar on the bench and grabbed his violin case. "Want to test your luck now?"

Chloe paused and then opened up the offered case, taking out Tommy's violin. She held it up and played a few notes, the anxious look not leaving her face until she played a Bach piece for about two minutes. She took a deep breath and gently handed the violin back to Tommy. "Thank you," she said softly.

"No problem," Tommy said, and Chrysta smiled at him.

Chloe shifted from foot to foot nervously and then cleared her throat. "So, Chrysta, you and Peter are dating?" she asked. Chrysta groaned and put her head in her hands. She felt Tommy put an arm around her and pull her into a hug. "What, was it something I said?" Chloe asked.

"Peter asked Chrysta's dad if he could *court* Chrysta, and he said he would *allow* it," revealed Mary. "She's not happy about the arrangement and wants to forget about it."

"That's horrible," Chloe said with a frown.

"My father has always been controlling," Chrysta added, reluctantly moving away from Tommy after taking a deep breath to enjoy his scent. "I figured he wouldn't let me see anyone. I just never imagined he would force me to date a boy I didn't want to."

Chloe looked thoughtful for a moment. She then pointed at Tommy. "Would you rather date him?"

"Date a loser like me?" Tommy asked. He blew a raspberry. "As if I could be so lucky." The girls laughed as he grinned.

"We hang out, yes," Chrysta confessed. "But he's under the impression I should see other people."

"You could do better," Tommy said while nodding. Mary smacked him on the arm, and he looked between her and where she hit. "Why do you abuse me so?"

"Because you keep saying things I need to hit you for," Mary said.

There was a shout, and Chrysta turned to see her driver across the street. "Bye, everyone," she said and started walking away.

"Hey, Chrysta?" Chloe shouted behind her, and she slowed down for the other girl to catch up. Chloe looked thoughtful as they crossed the street. "I'm sorry that I have been a bitch before."

Chrysta blinked and smiled. "It's alright," she said and held out her hand. Chloe shook it, and Chrysta left, feeling much lighter than she had in days.

.....

Thursday and Friday went very well for Chrysta. Chloe and her friends started to run interference for her and would nearly tackle Peter in the hallways and keep him from bugging her between classes. It was funny to see and helped Chrysta with the anxiety that had plagued her all week. In orchestra class, Chloe, who had returned and played beautifully without a single broken violin, would answer his questions and keep him from bothering Chrysta too much. After school on Friday, Mary lightly elbowed Chrysta as they waited for their rides. "Would you like to go shopping, lovely lady?" she asked.

Chrysta suddenly winced. "Peter wants to go out," she explained.

Mary made a dismissive wave of her hand. "Nonsense," she said. "Bring him along. He can hold our bags while we shop." Mary gave Chrysta an evil grin. "Make sure you aren't alone with him."

That afternoon, Chrysta knocked on the door of her father's study. Once she entered, she asked if she could go shopping. He made a face until she mentioned that Peter was going, and he reluctantly agreed.

An hour later, Mary showed up driving her family's old car. She had already picked up Peter and had saved the front passenger seat for Chrysta.

Even though shopping was not one of Chrysta's favorite activities at the mall, she had fun looking at clothes and makeup. They were looking for new dresses for the winter concert, which gave the girls an excuse to be alone as they went into the dressing rooms without Peter.

Mary had found a beautiful red gown, but Chrysta did not see anything she liked. They were passing another store when Chrysta spotted a gorgeous dress. She gasped and ran up to the window to get a closer look. It was black, floor-length, no sleeves, with silver lace that started at the right shoulder and wrapped around the body down to the floor. "Oh, that would look great on you!" Mary cried.

"Yeah, but they won't have it in my size," Chrysta moaned.

Mary grabbed her arm. "Won't know until we try it," she said while dragging Chrysta into the store. Mary waved at Peter. "You go off and try on suits," she said.

"Why would I need a suit?" Peter asked, looking disgruntled.

"Just shoo," Mary said, making a waving gesture with one hand.

Luckily, they had a dress in Chrysta's size, although it was still a foot too long. She stepped out of the dressing room with a beaming smile and turned for Mary as she clapped. Mary took a picture with her phone while the store's seamstress started to make adjustments.

"I don't know if I can afford this," Chrysta worriedly said.

"Don't worry, I've got you, sis," Mary said, getting a large amount of money out of her purse.

"Where did you get that?!" Chrysta asked with a laugh.

"A present from Tommy," Mary explained. "He said he wanted you to have it if you ever needed it, but he knew that you would never accept money from him. So he gave it to me for safekeeping." She stepped up to Chrysta and started playing with her braided hair. "What do you think? Hair up or down."

"Up, I think," Chrysta said as Mary's phone chirped at them. Mary checked the screen. "Tommy says you are gorgeous, by the way."

Chrysta blushed. "Did you just send him a photo of me?"

"Yep," Mary giggled.

They paid for the dress and alterations and wandered towards the food court. Mary sat to Chrysta's right, forcing Peter to sit on the other side of the table, but Peter didn't seem to mind. He and Mary talked about a local sports team, and Chrysta was just happy he wasn't so focused on her. Their conversations turned to the winter concert.

"I'm just happy Chloe can play again," stated Chrysta.

"Why?" Peter asked.

"Chloe stole money from a friend, and he said he cursed her. She couldn't touch a violin without breaking it in her hands for the last two weeks," Chrysta explained while taking bites of a soft pretzel.

"You mean like on Monday?" Peter asked.

Chrysta nodded. "Once she returned the money, she was able to play again."

"According to Tommy, she was cursed by Chrysta, actually," Mary joked.

Peter gave Chrysta a shocked look. "You cursed her?"

"Not intentionally," Chrysta joked and laughed. But Peter got a serious look on his face.

They left the mall, and Mary dropped Chrysta at her home. "Thank you," Chrysta said softly. Mary smiled and nodded.

She let herself outside on the patio after she got to her room and changed into comfortable clothing. Poe was waiting for her and croaked a greeting. "What do you think, Poe," she asked, "did I curse someone?"

"Chrysta," he squawked.

"I agree. I could never," she replied, smiling.

·····

Several hours later, York waited in his study by the fire. He looked into the flames and regarded the ring on his finger when there was a knock. "Enter," he stated.

The red-headed man entered and sat down without a word. "You wish to see me, brother?" he asked cooly.

"You asked me to send the slave to watch my daughter," York stated, still looking into the fire, "and then send someone else to watch her at the same time. Tell me, Frost, do you always contradict yourself?"

"Not a contradiction, brother," Frost answered, tenting his fingers. "We need evidence of her ability. Two sets of eyes would be better than one."

York gave the other man a sour look. "I'm not blind. You wish to lead, and this is a personal insult."

Frost barked out some laughter. "Oh, York, I find your self-doubt amusing. I am here as an advisor. At worst, this is me overstepping my bounds. Call the slave here. Let us see what he has to say."

York twisted the ring on his finger, perhaps a little harder than he had to. This time it only took a few minutes before the knock at the front door came, and two security guards escorted a young man into the study. The slave glared around at his surroundings.

"Has she shown any ability?" Frost asked without a greeting. The slave crossed his arms and just glowered at York. York just continued to look into the fire and waited a few moments. Frost threw his hand up in the air in frustration, and York allowed himself to smile. "Tell him," he stated.

"She cursed a classmate," said the slave flatly.

"With a spell?" asked Frost.

The slave shifted from one foot to the other. "She did it without a spell."

"Are you sure? What proof do you have?"

"No proof."

"Then how do you know?"

"The classmate couldn't touch a violin without breaking it. Sounds like a curse to me."

Frost leaned over to York. "This is perfect, brother. If she can perform magic without spells, then she is the ideal vessel. We need more proof, though. This is not enough."

York waved his hand impatiently. "I agree," he said. He looked at his slave. "Continue watching her."

"Why do you need proof she can perform magic?" asked the slave.

"That is not any of your concern," Frost snapped, and the slave let out a growl. York held up his hand with the ring, and the slave froze.

"Leave. Now," commanded York, and the figure let out a grumble before leaving the study. The two men waited until they heard the front door close, and York got up to get himself a drink.

"You need to tell him to be quiet, brother," Frost said. He was watching the door of the study like the young man would come back unannounced.

"Why? He can't tell anyone. His brethren would kill him, so would anyone else he could go to for help. Chrysta would not believe him or shun him for lying to her," York explained while he swirled his drink in the glass. "He's trapped. He can't go anywhere." He lifted the hand with the ring so it glinted in the firelight. "He is mine to control."

After dinner on Saturday, Chrysta waited for Tommy on her balcony. She watched as guards patrolled the grounds and worried once again that they would see Tommy and catch him. But, while she watched, a shadow detached itself from the bushes, ran to the house and climbed up. Chrysta laughed as he hauled himself over the railing and crouched next to her.

"Evening, beautiful," he greeted her with a grin. He tugged on the sleeve of her red sweater. "Not wearing the dress you bought?"

"It's being altered. It was too long for me," she explained. "Besides, that is for the winter concert, not whatever we are doing tonight."

"True. As much as I want to see you in it, that dress is a little too much for where we are going tonight," he stated as he slowly stood up to look over the railing.

"How do we get out?" Chrysta asked in a loud stage whisper.

"With speed, luck, and an old movie trick," he said, holding up a stone. He waited until both guards looked towards the front of the house and then threw the rock at the house's back camera. The camera was struck so hard it was now hanging at an angle, and the guards rushed to investigate.

Tommy helped her down the wall, and they rushed to the bushes. Chrysta was amazed by how silent he could be as he grabbed something from the ground and propped her over the wall. When they both made it to the other side, Chrysta saw that it was an old quilt. "Why do we need that?" she asked.

"You will see," he said cryptically, offering her an elbow.

They walked towards the park near her home, and Chrysta let out an excited squeal when she saw a sign. It read "Edgar Allan Poe's Greatest Stories" with a line underneath, "Read Live!" A volunteer smiled at her and handed her a flyer.

"*The Tell-Tale Heart, The Cask of Amontillado, The Masque of the Red Death, The Raven,*" she read. "These are some of his best works!"

"Thought you would like this," Tommy said, grinning. She squealed again and then jumped up so she could wrap her arms around his neck. She kissed him on the cheek before jumping down. His smile grew, and they went into the park after he paid.

The theatre was open-air, and Chrysta finally understood why Tommy brought the quilt when he wrapped her up as soon as they sat down. She cuddled up to him once the stage lights came up.

The production was impressive, with beautiful costumes, detailed sets, and a live piano and violin playing music. Each tale happened in a different decade, with a narrator reading Poe's stories as actors acted out the scenes. Chrysta was enthralled and hung on every word and would excitedly clap at every intermission. Between *The Cask of Amontillado* and *The Masque of the Red Death*, she stretched to give Tommy another kiss. "What's that for?" he asked.

"A thank you for bringing me," she explained.

He kissed the top of her head. "No problem, beautiful," he said as the stage lights came back on.

The Masque of the Red Death was wonderfully done, with most of the women in beautiful ball gowns. After the final intermission, the light came on, and one actor who looked like Edgar Allan Poe himself started to perform *The Raven*. However, the play was almost ruined when the raven showed up on the stage; a horrible looking puppet that barely moved when it was time to croak out a "Nevermore." Both Tommy and Chrysta snorted in laughter at the terrible fake bird, and a lady sitting in front of them turned around and shushed them. "Sorry," Chrysta whispered.

Suddenly, after they had gotten control of themselves, Poe, the real raven, dropped down and landed on the chair next to them. People murmured and laughed at the sight of Poe jumping up and down. Tommy pointed the finger at the bird. "Don't you dare," he hissed a warning.

"He doesn't know this poem," Chrysta whispered. "He's never said that word in his life."

But of course, just as the narrator got to the famous line, Poe opened his beak, and loud enough to drown out the puppet on stage, he let out a clear "Nevermore!"

People laughed louder, and even the actor on stage noticed the creature who was upstaging him from the audience. He made a quick motion, and the puppet disappeared, and the actor got up to address Poe directly. Tommy kept a hand over his eyes, shoulders jerking as he tried not to laugh. Chrysta watched both the actor on stage and Poe, bouncing between feeling embarrassed and proud at the bird's performance.

The actor delivered his final lines with all the passion one would expect, and at the last line ("Take thy beak from out my heart, and take thy form from off my door!"), he threw himself to the floor dynamically as Poe gave a hearty "Nevermore!"

Finally, the narrator started the closing stanza:

And the Raven, never flitting, still is sitting, still is sitting
On the pallid bust of Pallas just above my chamber door;
And his eyes have all the seeming of a demon's that is dreaming,
And the lamp-light o'er him streaming throws his shadow on the floor;
And my soul from out that shadow that lies floating on the floor
Shall be lifted—

Everyone, including Tommy and Chrysta, waited with bated breath to see what Poe would do. After a minute, he ruffled his feathers and then croaked out the clearest "Nevermore!" yet. Everyone started applauding and laughing.

"Oh, how did you train him?" someone asked Tommy.

"I have never seen that bird in my life," Tommy responded.

Poe flapped his wings. "Tommy," he squawked.

Tommy glared at the raven. "Traitor."

.....

After the play, they went to a nearby food truck and got tacos. They found a tree to sit under and spread out the quilt to sit on. Poe plummeted down and hopped up and down next to them until they gave him some food. Tommy kept glaring at Chrysta until she broke down and glared back. "What?" she asked.

"You taught him to say that," he stated.

Chrysta shook her head. "Nope."

"Oh, come on, you're telling me you haven't read the story?"

"Oh, I have read it. Just never out loud." Tommy gave her a look, and she laughed. "I'm serious. I thought about teaching him some words, but he didn't start talking until recently."

"Uh-huh. And how long have you known that damned bird?" Tommy asked, taking a bite of a taco.

"Ten years. Poe showed up after my mother died," she explained, giving Poe a pet on the head. Poe croaked and leaned into her touch.

Tommy winced. "Sorry."

"Don't be. I miss my mother, but the memories I have of her are good ones."

They sat in silence for a bit and finished their food. There was a shout, and Poe saw some people trying to entice him with food. He looked at Chrysta and cocked his head. "Go ahead," she said with a laugh. "Meet your adoring fans." He took flight and started bouncing in front of a crowd of teenagers.

"So, how are things at home?" Tommy asked softly. Chrysta turned to see him with a worried look on his face.

"Better," she replied. "Chloe has been distracting Peter at school, so I don't feel like I have to dodge him all the time. Father never lets me go out, but if Peter tags along, he allows it, so that is kind of nice."

"Has your father always been that dominating?"

Chrysta nodded, playing with the sleeve of her sweater. "When mom died, he became overbearing." She shrugged. "Maybe he was always this way, and I didn't see it when I was a kid. I use to think he was just trying to protect me, but now I'm not so sure."

She sighed, bringing her knees to her chest. "I can go over to Mary's house. Rarely. Thanksgiving and Christmas, mostly. My mom and Mary's mom were friends, and she tries to keep an eye on me. She's worried father won't let me leave when I'm old enough. Nothing he does is abusive, just very controlling and creepy, so it's not like we can get anyone to intervene."

Tommy sighed. "I know I said seeing Peter might be a good thing, but the more I think about it, the less I like it." He leaned forward and placed a hand on her hand. "I can't tell you what to do, but be careful around him, okay?"

"Okay," she promised. "I'm just happy to get out of the house. I can't thank you enough for that."

He cleared his throat and leaned back on the tree. "Don't thank me. Like I said before, good friends are hard to come by."

Chrysta glanced over at Poe and smiled at the raven, who was croaking "Nevermore" repeatedly as the crowd cheered. "So what about your parents?" she asked when she looked back at Tommy.

Tommy winced. "They existed," he said after a moment.

"Oh no, I'm sorry," Chrysta replied. "I guess that was pretty inconsiderate of me to ask."

He shrugged with a sad grin on his face. "It's alright. It's something people talk about, so why not ask about them?" His smile fell away as he scowled. "My mother died when I was young, too, when I was thirteen. Dad blamed me and kicked me out."

Chrysta gasped. "Why?"

Tommy shrugged again, and his leg started bouncing. "He was right. She died protecting me. If I hadn't been born, then she would still be alive."

"But, that's what a parent should do, protect their children. Your father shouldn't blame you for that." She looked at his leg. "Are you okay?"

"Yeah, sorry," he said, looking at his leg. "It's something I do when I haven't had a drink in a while."

"You mean alcohol?"

"Yeah, I can't promise I will stay sober, though. I usually only manage a few weeks before I fall off the wagon." He frowned at her, pointing his finger at Chrysta. "Don't look at me like that."

"Like what?"

"With pity. I hate when people look at me like that."

She frowned and then gently scooted until she was in front of him. She hugged him, letting her arms wrap around him under his jacket. He kept the frown on his face, but it slowly melted when she leaned up to kiss his cheek. "It's not pity. It's me worrying about you," she explained as he started to rub her back.

"Don't worry about a loser like me," he said softly, all his anger gone.

"You're not a loser," she replied. Just then, the wind picked up, and she shivered.

"Come on," Tommy said, almost too loud. "Let's get you home. Don't want to let you freeze to death."

He picked himself off the ground and helped her up. He knocked some grass off of the quilt and wrapped it around her. There was something in his eyes she couldn't place, something she hadn't seen before. He started to walk over to Poe and the crowd watching the raven roll around in the grass. "Okay, everybody, as Mr. Poe's agent, I'm going to have to ask that be all for the evening." The teenagers groaned and walked away, Poe flapping his wings to land on Tommy's shoulder.

Chrysta walked up to him and linked her arm with his. "Are you okay?" she asked.

"Oh yeah," he said in a light tone. "I love talking about childhood trauma." He smiled at her, but it seemed strained.

"I'm sorry," she said softly.

The smile softened and seemed more genuine. "You're alright, beautiful. Being sober makes me grumpy."

They walked back to her house and paused outside. "So, here's the plan. I'll get you over the wall and then go to the other side of the house and make some noise. That should get their attention, and you run for the house."

"Are you sure?" Chrysta asked. "I don't want you to get hurt."

"To hurt me, they have to catch me," he stated with a grin.

She nodded. "Okay."

He stepped up to her, took the quilt, and folded it to hide it. He lifted her chin and frowned. "Why the worried look?"

"Maybe we shouldn't go out for a while. Wait until my father gets rid of the guards."

"Is that what you want, beautiful?" he asked. The look was back in his eyes.

"No," Chrysta confessed. "But I want you to be safe."

Tommy sighed. He leaned down and kissed her on the forehead. "Think about it. I won't come around until you tell me to."

He was suddenly boosting her over the wall. "Wait," she tried to argue. "That's not what I meant."

He shushed her and was running off before she could say anything else. She huffed and then dropped to the other side of the wall.

Chrysta crouched in the bushes, watching the guards move back and forth below her balcony. She shifted her weight and froze when a stick snapped under her heel. One of the guards heard it and started to move over to the bush to investigate. Suddenly, there was a shout from the other side of the house, and the guards ran in that direction. Chrysta waited until the cameras were pointed in the other direction as Tommy taught her and quickly climbed the wall.

She quickly slipped inside her room and changed into her night clothes. There was a knock at her door, and before she could answer it, her father entered the room with two guards. They started to search her room while Chrysta sputtered. "Why are you doing this?" she cried, trying not to sound out of breath.

"There was a suspicious person sighted on the grounds tonight," her father explained cooly. His eyes scanned the room as the guards checked in the bathroom and under her bed. "We are checking to see if you are alright."

"Well, I'm okay, so please leave," Chrysta snapped, and her father's eyes moved to glare at her.

"This is for your protection," he responded frostily. "I suggest that you adjust your attitude."

There was a croak from outside, and both guards jumped. One of them went to the window and moved the curtain. Jumping up and down on the wooden table in agitation was Poe. Jozef turned to Chrysta with a scowl.

"I told you that bird is not welcomed here," he said while making a motion with his hand. The guard let himself outside while opening a nightstick.

"Don't hurt him!" Chrysta yelled, but the guard swung at the bird anyway. Poe jumped out of the way as the nightstick hit the table with a *crack*. Poe took flight and got away.

Chrysta felt her eyes burning, but she wasn't going to cry in front of her father. However, she looked at the guard and had an awful thought: *He should know what it's like getting hit on the head*. There was a weird feeling in her chest, and something *flexed* inside her. She imagined the nightstick broken, and just like that, it shattered, even though it was several seconds after he had hit the table. The guard cried out and clutched at his hand, but her father and the other guard didn't move. Chrysta felt a surge of delight at the man's pain-filled cry.

After several moments of stunned silence, Chrysta's father gestured at the other guard and broke the stillness. "Get him to a doctor," he commanded.

"But how did tha—" the man started.

"Get him to a doctor now!"

The guard blinked and then helped the other man out of the room. Chrysta felt the anger quickly vanish, and she shivered. Her father was looking at her, but she had trouble reading his expression.

After several moments, Jozef finally broke the silence. "I will be hiring more guards to patrol the grounds. And you will have a personal guard staying with you at all times when you are not at this house."

Chrysta blinked and felt her stomach drop. "Why?"

"For your protection," he said and then turned to leave the room.

"No."

Her father stopped short and slowly turned back towards her. His face was a mask of anger she couldn't recall ever seeing before, but she didn't back down.

"This is not about my protection," she stated, anger coming back slowly. "You just want to be able to control me, and I'm sick of it. I am old enough to make my own decisions. I want to see my friends, I want to go out when I want, and I don't want some stranger following me when I do."

A muscle twitched in her father's jaw, and she saw him take a deep breath as if he was going to respond, but then he glanced at the broken pieces of nightstick on the patio and paused.

"Fine," he said. "But if there is another incident of someone trying to get into the house, I will have to take stronger precautions." And with that, he left her bedroom, and she slammed the door behind him.

She expected to feel sad and have a good cry, but the anger was back, and Chrysta had a feeling it wasn't going away. At least not that night. She grabbed her contraband phone from her discarded clothes and texted Tommy. "Are you okay? Did they get you?"

He didn't answer, and Chrysta cleaned up the pieces of nightstick still on her balcony. She sat at the wooden table and watched the night sky for Poe.

Tommy did not respond to Chrysta on Sunday, and Poe did not come back either. Every meal with her father was full of sullen silence, and she avoided him as much as possible. She noticed more guards, who would barge into her room with barely any warning like they were trying to catch someone. By Monday morning Chrysta was sick with worry and went to school with a heavy heart. It wasn't until lunchtime that she was able to talk to Mary about all that had happened: the date, Poe being attacked, and Tommy not answering her texts. Chrysta left out the part about the broken nightstick. It was too weird, and she didn't want to upset Mary again.

"Do you think he's okay?" she asked.

Mary shrugged while she looked at Peter at Chloe's table. "He probably is. I think he was right when he said he could avoid getting caught."

"So why isn't he texting me back?"

"Honestly? It sounds like he was upset that you told him not to go back to your house."

"I didn't mean it like that, though," Chrysta said, rubbing her eyes. "I just didn't want him to get hurt."

"I know, but he may not see it that way."

Chrysta sighed. "I'm going back to being the lonely weirdo no one loves."

"Don't do that. You finally got interesting."

Chloe sat down at their table and flashed them a perfect smile. She saw Chrysta's sour face and blinked. "What's up?"

"Bad date with Tommy," Mary explained.

"Oh, is that all?" Chloe asked. She finished the can of soda she had brought with her. "Just kiss someone else and post a picture on social media. That's what I do when Mark gets out of line."

Both Mary and Chrysta rolled their eyes. "Your poor boyfriend," Mary said dryly.

"Look, hate the game, not the player," Chloe said. She looked at Chrysta. "We are thinking of going to a movie on Friday. Would you like to come?"

"Yeah," Chrysta sighed. "I can get my dress and get out of the house." She glanced over at the table where Peter was laughing. "Not that I'm ungrateful, but why are you keeping Peter away from me?"

"Because I figured I had been a jerk so long, I owed you a favor," Chloe explained. "He's not a bad guy, but he is kinda obsessed with you. Always wants to be able to see you even if he's hanging out with us."

"I noticed," Chrysta said flatly, putting her sandwich down with a sigh. She had no appetite. "Can you join us?" she asked Mary.

"Sorry, going out of town to visit family this weekend," Mary said.

"Okay," Chrysta said. She gathered her stuff and got up. "I'm heading to class early. I'll see you guys in orchestra class."

Both girls nodded, Mary looking worried, and Chrysta left the table. There was the sound of birds flying, and Chrysta heard cawing, but when she looked at the sky, all she saw was a murder of crows. She sighed and pulled her shoulders up as the wind blew harder.

.....

Chrysta spent the week in a haze. She picked at her food, went to school, did her homework, and practiced her violin, but she spent the rest of her time in bed or sitting on her balcony in silence. She ignored the guards that burst into her room unannounced and didn't fuss when Peter forced her to spend time with him at school.

"I'm worried about you," Mary said Thursday night when she had called Chrysta on her contraband phone.

Chrysta tried to smile, even if the other girl couldn't see it. "I'm okay. Just feeling..." Oh, what was the best word? "...a little down."

"No word from Tommy or Poe?" Mary asked.

"No," Chrysta confessed. "I guess if they don't want to be around me, I can't force either of them."

Mary sighed. "Just hang in there, okay? Your father may be trying to isolate you, but you're not alone, okay?"

Chrysta smiled. "Thanks," she said.

When Friday came, Chloe showed up in her family SUV. She had saved the front passenger seat for Chrysta, her two friends, her boyfriend Mark, and Peter in the back seat. Chrysta was a little nervous being with a group of people that had been actively avoiding and mocking her just a few weeks ago. Still, the whole group was kind and tried to include her in their conversations, even if most of it was gossip. Mark kept Peter busy talking about sports.

They saw the latest action movie, and after eating at the food court, they went to the store that had Chrysta's dress. Mark made a wolf whistle when she stepped out of the dressing room.

"Down, boy," Chloe told him. "That looks good on you," she said to Chrysta. "I'm shocked you didn't have to shop at a children's store to get it."

"Ha-ha," Chrysta mock laughed, but she could still feel a wide grin on her face as she looked at herself in the mirror. "Thank you for letting me pick it up."

As they left the mall, Peter carrying the dress, Chloe hung back with Chrysta, isolated from the rest of the group. "Hey," she started, "that's the first time I have seen you smile all week. You okay?"

"Yeah, things are... strained at home. And I still haven't heard from Tommy."

"If you like that jerk so much, maybe you should track him down and make him talk to you."

"He's not a jerk," Chrysta quickly said.

"Okay, okay," Chloe said with her hands up in surrender. "If you like that boy so much, hunt him down and make him talk to you."

Chrysta cocked her head in thought. "Maybe you're right," she said.

Once she was home, Chrysta went to her bedroom and changed. She glared at the door and shoved a dresser in front of it. An hour later, she smiled when she heard the door bang on the furniture suddenly.

"Miss York?" a voice called.

"I'm alright," she responded. "Just making sure you guys can't barge in."

"Miss York, please let us in."

"No, I don't think I will. If you don't like it, talk to my father."

There was only silence as a response, and she smiled to herself.

Chrysta got up and grabbed her violin. She went out to the balcony with her sheet music and shivered with the cold. "You better be able to hear this," she muttered to the night sky and started playing Paganini's Caprice number 7.

.....

Nearby, on the roof of an apartment building where Tommy had unofficially moved to after meeting Chrysta, he sat in the shelter he had made with his feet up. He heard the violin and smiled. "Good," he murmured to himself, "she's playing again."

Poe dropped down and squawked at him. "Chrysta," the raven croaked, hopping up and down.

"Don't you start," Tommy told the raven darkly. "She's better off without me, you'll see."

The bird cocked its head to the side. "Nevermore," he said.

"Exactly," Tommy said, mostly to himself. "Nevermore."

10

Chrysta tried texting Tommy again to apologize and ask him to come back to her house, but when he didn't show up Sunday evening, she didn't know what else to do. She didn't know where he lived, and she had no way to track him down. She finally had a breakthrough Wednesday and went up to Peter during lunch. "Would you like to go out on Friday night?" she asked him.

Peter smiled. "Finally willing to give me a chance?" he asked.

She tried not to roll her eyes. "I guess," she said with a forced smile.

He threw an arm around her shoulder. "Where would you like to go?"

"I have a place in mind," she simply said, gently pushing Peter's arm off her shoulder. "Can you pick me up in a taxi?"

Friday night came, and Chrysta ran out to the taxi, barely acknowledging that Peter was holding the door open for her. Before he could get in the cab and tell the driver to go to the mall, she interrupted. "The Jazz Nocturne club, please," she said, ignoring Peter's questioning look.

The taxi dropped them off, and Chrysta barely waited for Peter to pay the driver before leading him to the back door. She loudly knocked while Peter started tugging on her arm as it began to rain. "I don't think we're old enough to be here."

"It's okay," she said. "I just have to check something real quick."

She knocked again, and the door finally opened to show Ben's scowling face. Peter stepped back, but Chrysta just tried to flash a bright smile. "Hello, sir." She suddenly realized she never got Ben's last name. "I haven't heard from Tommy in a while, and I'm worried about him. Is he playing here tonight?"

"He better have his ass here tonight," Ben spat out. "Jonathon and that no-good piano player both called out. If Tommy doesn't come, I will fire the whole bunch of them and start playing recorded music." He looked Chrysta up and down. "Wait, didn't you say you played something?"

"The violin, sir."

"Wanna earn some cash, honey?"

Chrysta sputtered. "I don't know any jazz," she declared.

"Tommy can sort it out when he gets here," Ben said as he ushered Chrysta inside. "You too, white bread," he said while grabbing Peter. "Fuck the age restrictions tonight."

Once the teenagers were inside, Ben closed the door and called out to the small kitchen. "Jennifer? Mandy? Can I see you, please?"

Mandy came to the back and broke out in a big grin when she saw Chrysta. "Hello, sweetie. What brings you here tonight?"

"I was looking for Tommy. I haven't seen him in a while and was getting worried. But I guess you guys need a music player tonight?"

"Can you two get her a uniform?" Ben asked as he went back into his office. "It's all hands on deck tonight."

"Well, you and I are closer in height, but I probably have 50 pounds on you," Mandy said as she looked at Chrysta. "Maybe 75 pounds," she muttered darkly, mostly to herself. "What do you think, Jennifer?"

The drummer hummed and also sized Chrysta up. "I think my clothes will fit. We will just have to hem everything. I'm at least 8 inches taller than her."

"Sorry I'm tiny," Chrysta said with a blush.

"Nonsense, sweetie," Mandy said. "We will make it work." She looked at Peter. "Come on, you, let's set you up at the bar."

"Bar?" Peter asked. "This place has a bar?"

While Peter followed Mandy to the club's front, Jennifer handed Chrysta some clothes, thankfully clean ones. After Chrysta exited the bathroom, Jennifer showed her what locker to store her stuff, then used pins to hem the pants and tighten the shirt and vest. "So, you came looking for Tommy and got roped into playing tonight, huh?" Jennifer asked.

"Yeah, I don't want you guys to lose your jobs," Chrysta said.

"Oh, Ben talks big, but if he got rid of the live music, no one would come in," Jennifer explained. She looked at Chrysta through her eyelashes. "So you like that brat?"

"Tommy?" Chrysta asked. Jennifer nodded. "Yes, I do very much." Jennifer finished the hemming and stood up, and Chrysta smiled at her shyly. "I told him I was worried my father would hurt him, and he shouldn't come back to my house, and," she sighed, "I guess he got upset. I haven't seen him in a couple of weeks."

"Ah, so that's why he has been grumpy," Jennifer said with a grin. "Well, I think you did the right thing, showing up tonight. He shouldn't be wallowing in self-pity like that."

The door to the back opened, and Tommy came in with the bass player carrying his violin case and clothes. "What the hell was Ben saying about a newbie, Jenn—" Tommy stopped short as he caught sight of Chrysta and blinked for several moments. "What are you doing here?" he asked softly.

"I got worried," she answered back. "You haven't been answering my texts."

The bass player looked between Tommy and Chrysta, cleared his throat, and held a hand out to Chrysta. "Manny. I don't think we got introduced last time you were here, darlin'."

"Chrysta," she answered, glancing at Tommy while shaking the older man's hand. She couldn't quite read the look on Tommy's face. "Ben said you needed someone else to play tonight."

"Wait. What?" Tommy asked and then blinked. He looked at Jennifer.

Jennifer nodded. "Jonathon called out too."

"Well, fuck me," Tommy said with a growl. "What we playin' then?" he asked, looking at Manny.

"Don't ask me, boss. I ain't the music expert."

"Come on, old man, throw me a bone here?"

Manny just shrugged, and Tommy made another growl while rubbing his eyes. He glared at Chrysta for a full minute and then sighed. His expression softened. "Okay, I'll bite," he said. He held up a finger and pointed at her. "But we need to talk later."

"Oh, we will," Chrysta stated, and Jennifer snorted.

"Okay, with a violin player here, it looks like we are playing *jazz manouche*," Tommy said. He went to a locker, locked up his clothes, and brought out some sheet music.

"*Jazz manouche?*" Chrysta asked as Tommy handed out papers. Manny smiled and nodded. "Gypsy jazz," the older man said as Chrysta looked over the music.

"Developed in France during the 1930s," Tommy explained. "The only thing that works with drums, bass, piano, and violin." He opened his case and handed Chrysta his violin. "Think you can handle a full-size violin, beautiful?"

She brought the violin up and tried to play a few chords. The shoulder rest was too big, but otherwise, the notes came out clear. "It will do," she confirmed.

"Alright, Jennifer, it's mostly snare and cymbal for you tonight. Manny, you have bass and third guitar. I'm piano and the second guitar, Chrysta, you are the violin and first guitar. Any questions?"

"Who is setting the speed?" Jennifer asked.

"Chrysta," Tommy confirmed.

Chrysta blinked. "Me?"

"Hey, this is all you, beautiful."

She took a deep breath and puffed out her cheeks. "Okay."

"Just remember, staccato," Tommy said. "Alright, let's crash and burn people."

As they filed out of the kitchen, Chrysta spied Peter sitting at the bar with a drink. He waved at her and leaned in close when she went to him. "I don't think we should be here. I don't think your father would approve," he said.

She nodded. "You're probably right," she agreed, but then she flashed Peter an evil grin. "But if you tell him we came here, I will say it was your idea."

Tommy overheard her and laughed as he rolled up his sleeves. "Wait, you can't do that," Peter stammered. "He won't believe you."

"Maybe you're right. My father may know it was my idea and ban me from going out. Or he will think you planned it and ban us from going out. Do you want to take that chance?"

"Looks like you are screwed, my friend," Tommy chuckled. He held out a hand. "Nice to meet you finally, Mr. Creepy. The name is Tommy."

"Mr. Creepy? What do you mean? Who are yo—" Peter saw the silver armband on Tommy's left arm, and his mouth closed with an audible snap. He didn't take Tommy's hand and just glared. The smile died on Tommy's face, and he stepped back.

"Well, aren't you a bundle of joy," Tommy muttered. He smiled, but it didn't look friendly.

Chrysta looked between them and then turned to Mandy. "I will take care of the drinks, okay, Mandy?"

"All right, sweetie," Mandy said. She was also looking between the two boys currently frowning at each other. "Your usual, Tommy?"

"Water tonight, Mandy," Tommy said. He put a hand on Chrysta's lower back and guided her to the stage. "Come on, beautiful, almost showtime."

They took the stage, and Chrysta studied the music a little more. The front doors opened, and people started filing inside. Once the club was half full, Tommy looked at Manny and clicked his tongue. Manny looked at him curiously until Tommy jerked his head to the microphone. Manny grinned and shook his head no. Tommy sighed, got up, and went to the mic.

"So we had some staffing issues tonight, ladies and gentlemen, so we are trying something new," he said with a smile. "*Jazz manouche*, also known as gypsy jazz. A little faster than what we usually play, so please forgive us if we have any hiccups."

He turned around and squeezed Chrysta's shoulder. He sat back down, and Chrysta gave a small nod to him and Jennifer before putting the violin to her chin and launching into the first song.

It wasn't Paganini, but it was light and airy and fun to play. Chrysta felt her nerves start to fade by the third song, and by the fifth song was grinning and thoroughly enjoying herself. She had played in front of an audience plenty of times, but she couldn't remember getting such a response before. People smiled, tapped her hands and feet, dropped more money in the tip jar, and danced more with these songs than they did with Jonathon's selection.

They had planned nine songs in the first set, and it made the time fly by. As the notes of the music died away, the club erupted in applause. Tommy got up and went to the mic. "Thank you, ladies and gentlemen. We will be taking a short break."

Tommy went up to Chrysta and started messing with her music. He glanced at her. "How are you doing?"

"Good," she said with a grin that almost hurt her face. "This is fun."

Tommy smiled. "Good." The smile faded. "What are you doing here, beautiful?"

"Like I said, I was worried. This club was the only place where I could think of that I might be able to find you."

He sighed and glanced at Peter, who was glowering from the bar. "It was a gamble bringing him here," Tommy said.

Chrysta shrugged. "Either he tells my father, or he doesn't. I don't care at this point."

"You should," Tommy said cryptically.

Mandy came up to the stage with a tray of drinks, and Chrysta accepted a water glass gratefully. Mandy smiled at her. "You look like you're having fun."

"I am," Chrysta confessed.

Tommy leaned on a stool towards Chrysta. "I forgot to ask, beautiful, where did you get the outfit?"

"From me," Jennifer explained, taking a drink for herself.

"Oh, didn't have to raid a children's clothing store, huh?"

"Ha-ha," Chrysta said dryly. "I'm four-foot, eleven-inches-and-a-half, thank you very much. I can fit in adult clothing with alterations."

Tommy looked at Jennifer. "Ever notice how the short ones always have to throw in that half-inch?"

"Well, how tall are you, you giant?" Chrysta asked the grinning boy.

"Six-foot, two inches." He took a sip of water. "And a half."

Jennifer laughed. "Look at you two. Why would you ever ghost someone so cute, Tommy?"

"Hey, don't comment on stuff you don't know about," he growled with very little venom.

"Well, she tracked you down, so I know you are an asshole who can't break up with a girl properly."

"Hey, screw you," Tommy said, acting hurt.

"Can't. Don't think my girlfriend would appreciate that."

Mandy shook her head. "You two are worse than my kids."

"She started it," Tommy whined.

"Nah-nuh," Jennifer whined back, and the two of them started to lightly slap each other.

"You sure you still feel bad about making him upset?" Mandy joked with Chrysta.

"Not anymore," Chrysta joked back.

They set up for the last set, playing slower and more romantic songs than the first. More couples stood up and went to the dance floor to sway slowly together. It was nice to have such a positive response from an audience.

When they played the last song, there was a round of applause, and everyone on the stage took a bow. Chrysta handed Tommy his violin and went to Peter at the bar.

"Thank you for indulging me," she told Peter, still smiling. Peter only scowled back. "I just have to talk to Tommy real quick, and we can head out."

"Not like I have a choice," he said. He glanced at Tommy, who was sitting halfway down the bar with his violin under his arms. "Why do you like him more than me? You never gave me a chance."

Chrysta blinked. "Maybe I didn't," she admitted. "But you went to my father to ask permission to date me instead of asking me personally." She felt some of the anger she had held for weeks flare up and glared at him. "And if you don't understand why I would be upset by that, I don't see us having much of a relationship."

"Well, I just don't understand why you would like *that*," he spat while pointing at Tommy.

Chrysta recoiled as if he had hit her, and even Mandy stopped wiping down the bar nearby. "Did you just say what I think you said?" Mandy asked.

Chrysta felt a presence, and Tommy leaned over her shoulder with an evil-looking grin. "Don't worry, Mandy. He's not commenting on my skin color if you are worried about that. He's just wondering why Chrysta would be interested in an asshole like me. Isn't that right, pal?"

Peter looked like he was chewing on something sour but nodded curtly. He looked at Chrysta. "I'm going to wait outside," and he marched out of the club.

"Dickhead," Mandy spat at his retreating back, and Tommy just nodded grimly.

Tommy looked at Chrysta. "You okay, beautiful?"

Chrysta just nodded numbly. She felt like she should be outraged, but she was mostly in shock. "I shouldn't have brought him here," she acknowledged.

"I didn't give you an option, did I?" Tommy asked.

Chrysta glanced at Mandy, and she seemed to get the hint and moved down the bar. "Tommy, look," she started as she sat down. "If you don't want to see me anymore, that's okay. You just have to let me know. I thought something bad had happened to you when you didn't answer."

He took a deep breath and let it out. "I'm sorry, beautiful. I'm not used to people giving a damn about me." He took a sip of his water and grimaced. "Man, I miss alcohol," he muttered. "But that jackass has a point. You can do better than..." He gestured to himself. "...*this*."

She punched him on the arm hard, and he jumped. "Stop that," she ordered.

73

"Ow! What?"

"I don't let anyone talk about you like that. I'm not going to let you do it either."

"What do you mean?" he asked.

"Well, people call you a jerk and a brat all the time," she started to explain.

"Aw, who said that," he said while looking hurt, and she laughed.

"And I keep saying that you really are not," she said. "At least not to me."

His smile faded, and he turned away. He looked anxious. "I showed up at your house, uninvited," he started.

"But you didn't force me to go out," she countered.

"I have taken you, an underaged teenager, to a bar."

"But didn't make me drink."

"I am so much older than you."

"But you have never made me nervous or pressured to do something I didn't want to do."

"I am a horrible creature," he said in a small voice, and she looked at him, noticing how miserable he looked.

She linked her arm with his and leaned in close. "You're not, though. Not to me."

He looked at her for a few minutes and opened his mouth. He winced and closed his mouth. He sighed. And then he flashed her a smile, one so beautiful and genuine it made her heart melt. He kissed her fingers that were on his arm lightly. "Alright," he said softly. "You win."

"No more disappearing acts?"

"No more disappearing acts," he confirmed.

"Good."

They just stared at each other for a minute, Chrysta not hiding the goofy grin on her face. She finally cleared her throat and stood up. "I have to get going before Peter gets more upset. We will have to find a way to meet up soon."

"You got it, beautiful," he said.

She quickly changed and brought the uniform back to Jennifer. "Sorry, I can't wash them, but thank you for letting me borrow them."

"No problem, sweetie," Jennifer said with a smile. "I'm glad you could help out."

Tommy was arguing with Ben at the other end of the bar. Tommy looked angry and leaned over the bar with a finger in Ben's face. Finally, Ben gave a loud "Alright!" and turned towards Chrysta. "Mr. Monroe has informed me," he started in a controlled growl. "That tonight's success would not be possible without you. So I'm going to pay you what I would have paid Jonathon if he was here."

Chrysta gave him a big smile. "Thank you, sir."

"About fucking time," Tommy darkly muttered while Ben handed Chrysta some cash. She didn't count it to be polite. Tommy gave her some bills as well. "Your cut of the tips," he explained.

"Thank you," she said. "What do I owe you, Mandy?"

"Not a thing, sweetie. Just promise not to bring that boy back here," Mandy said while cleaning a glass.

"Deal," Chrysta said with a laugh.

Tommy escorted Chrysta outside to a miserable and soaked Peter. Peter started to look for a taxi while Tommy turned to Chrysta. "By the way, you can call Poe back now."

"What do you mean?" she asked.

"Poe has been hounding me for two weeks. Didn't you send him?"

"No, I haven't seen him in two weeks. One of the guards tried to hit him, but he flew away. I was worried about him. I'm glad he's safe."

"Great," Tommy grumbled. "Looks like your pet is now my pet."

"He was never my pet," she said.

A taxi pulled up, and Peter called out to Chrysta. She smiled at Tommy and then kissed him on the cheek. "I missed you," she said. "But I'm glad we got to play together tonight."

"Me too, beautiful," he said.

Chrysta climbed into the cab, and Peter closed the door behind her. He gave the driver Chrysta's home address, and she watched Tommy disappear into the night.

e 11 o

Sunday afternoon, there was a knock on Chrysta's bedroom door, and she moved the dresser out of the way to let her father and a man she didn't know into her room. Something was off about him; the small smile he wore didn't make it to his eyes as he scanned the room. When his gaze stopped on her, it was cold and almost reptilian. "Miss York, we meet at last," he drawled. "Luca Guerra, at your service," he said as he held out his hand.

Chrysta shook his hand to be polite but winced as a pain burned across her throat. She snatched her hand back to rub the spot. If the man was insulted, he did not show it and kept the eerie smile on his face. Her father saw her rubbing her throat but did not comment.

"I am going to be your father's new head of security," Guerra continued as if nothing was wrong. "I wanted to discuss your new defense measures and how they can't proceed." He gestured at the dresser waiting by the door.

"I only did that to make sure nobody can barge in whenever they felt like," she explained, crossing her arms and glaring at the man. "This is my bedroom; I should have some privacy after all."

"Of course, *bella ragazza,* I would never imagine doing anything to make you uncomfortable," he said while he reached out to pull at her hair, making her nervous. She fought the urge to knock his hand away or to lean backward.

His smile got bigger, like he had made her uncomfortable on purpose. He ran a thumb across the strands of her hair. "It's just we need to be able to examine the room without notice. We will not be doing our jobs if a portion of the house remains uncovered."

"How about you guys search the room in the mornings and the evenings?" she asked, scowling.

"Ah! A worthy compromise! Only that would mean we would be on a predictable schedule, and some people would take advantage of that." He held his hands up in a "what can you do?" gesture, and his cold dark eyes flashed in amusement. Chrysta glanced at her father, but he stood silently with his hands folded in front of him, leaning on his cane.

"Who do you think would be in my room?" she asked, trying to keep her voice from rising in anger.

Guerra waved a hand dismissively. "Rascals, scoundrels, ne'er-do-wells." He also folded his hands behind his back and went back to the disturbing smile. "Someone has been trying to get on the property. We know that for sure. We just want to ensure no one hurts you, my dear."

She shifted from foot to foot. "Alright," she said. "I won't put the dresser in front of the door. But your men will have to knock."

"*Bene, bene!* So good we could agree," he cried out with false cheer, clapping his hands. "Let me know if you need anything, my dear. I am a servant of the York household, after all."

Guerra turned and left her room, her father pausing by the door. He gestured at his own throat. "You rubbed your throat. Are you... feeling alright?"

Chrysta gave her father a suspicious look. He rarely asked how she felt. "I'm fine. Just a sharp pain. Probably nothing."

He nodded and turned away, closing the door behind him. Chrysta glanced at the dresser and debated putting it back in front of the door again. But she had made a deal. And she had a feeling that Guerra's kind veneer would quickly melt if she tested him.

She grabbed her violin and sheet music and let herself outside. It was colder, but the sky was blue and clear. She started playing Bach's Violin Partita No. 1 in B Minor. When she was halfway through the song, her contraband phone chirped. She paused and checked the text message.

"That's not Paganini," Tommy had texted her.

She smiled at her phone. "You can hear me? It's just some Bach to help me relax. Met the new head of security, and he left a bad taste in my mouth."

"Someone I have to avoid?"

"Someone I would like to avoid," she texted back. "Would you like to hear anything?"

"Paganini," he answered back. She laughed.

"Why do you like him so much?"

"He is the reason I picked up a violin," Tommy confessed over a text message. "And you play him better than anyone I have heard in a long time."

She smirked at the phone and changed sheet music. "For you," she texted and then started playing.

A couple of blocks away, Tommy smiled and kicked his feet up. "Good job, beautiful," he texted Chrysta while Poe croaked next to him.

.....

Monday, Chrysta went to school feeling lighter than she had in the last few weeks. She became even happier when Peter showed no interest in following her around all day. She told Mary about finally getting in touch with Tommy but didn't give her the details. Mary smiled and gave her a hug. "See? He just needed some space," Mary said.

When it was time for orchestra class, Mr. Hansen waved to her before she could sit down.

"My apologies, Miss York, but it seems Peter has dropped out of this class," Mr. Hansen explained. "I was planning on letting the sections work on their pieces for the winter concert. Let me know if this hurts the string section, yes?"

Chrysta blinked. "Thank you, Mr. Hansen. I'll let the others know, but I think we will be fine between me, Martin, and Chloe."

When they broke off into groups, Chrysta told the others what had happened. "That's good," Chloe stated.

"Why?" Chrysta asked.

"His playing was shit, and that is coming from someone in the third chair," she explained.

Martin nodded in agreement. "His playing was robotic. Like a computer reading sheet music."

Chrysta thought about what they said and nodded. "I guess you are right."

That night, she texted Tommy about Peter's sudden departure from playing music. "Ding dong. Want to celebrate tonight, beautiful?" he texted back.

"How about sushi? At my house on Wednesday. With this new head of security, I won't be able to go out anymore."

"It's a date," he answered.

Wednesday came, and the sky was dark and grey, threatening the first snow of the season all day long. Come nightfall, Chrysta waited for Tommy on her balcony, wrapped in her heaviest blanket. She was delighted when Poe dropped down on the table in front of her. "Oh, Poe!" she cried. "I missed you!" She wanted to hug the bird but scratched his head instead. She noticed a bead in his mouth and opened her hand for him to drop it.

"Yeah, we have to break him of that habit," a voice said, and Chrysta gave Tommy a bright smile as he climbed over the railing. He was carrying a large paper bag and dropped it on the wooden table. He leaned down to kiss her on the forehead. "He gave me at least a dozen of those beads while living with me."

Chrysta looked at the blue bead with its gold flecks and hummed. "He must have found a full necklace at this point. I just hope he didn't steal it." She smiled at Tommy. "Wanna head inside? It's warmer, and the guards won't hear us."

He seemed to hesitate. "Didn't you say something about those guards bursting into your room unannounced?"

"The last visit was 30 minutes ago. They don't have a set schedule, but they wait at least 2 hours before inspecting the room. Still an invasion of privacy, but at least they knock now."

"Alright," he agreed, but he still looked worried.

Chrysta opened up the door and held it open to let Tommy in. He looked around her room, and Chrysta felt self-conscious. She wanted to tell him that the decor was her father's taste, that she would never choose the pastels and light colors he saw. He suddenly broke out in a huge grin and went to the foot of the bed. He held his arms out and let himself flop on the cover with a *flomph*. He gave a muffled groan, and she laughed.

"Oh, this is nice," he said into the cover. Chrysta sat down next to him, and he turned his head to look at her. "I can't remember the last time I slept in a bed thicker than cardboard," he explained.

"Wait, you always sleep outside?" she asked. "Isn't it too cold this time of year for that?"

"The cold never really bothered me," he said, removing his jacket. "And if the weather gets too bad, I know a couple of shelters I can go to. Just have to make sure I hide my instruments, so no one steals them."

"Well, if you need to stay here, let me know," she said. She opened up the bag and placed the containers of sushi on her bed. "Don't want you to turn into a popsicle."

He snorted. "And where would I sleep? The floor?"

"Nonsense," she said with a smile while popping a piece of sushi in her mouth. "You're a guest. You get the bed, and I get the floor."

He chuckled and wiggled his eyebrows. "Or we share the bed."

She nearly choked on the sushi and blushed. "This is not a sitcom," she growled, and Tommy laughed.

Their talk drifted to other topics, mostly music. Jonathon had returned to the club to find Tommy now in charge of the music. The look on his face when he found out was, according to Tommy, "pretty fucking funny." Chrysta told Tommy about Thanksgiving at the Jackson's and how she was hoping for a sleepover with Mary. It then went to Chrysta's upcoming winter concert. Tommy's eyebrows shot up when he saw the look on her face.

"What's wrong, beautiful? You don't look excited about the concert."

"It's the solos," she started to explain.

"You just played in front of an entire club while sightreading music you have never practiced before. I think you will do fine."

"It's not that," she said with a sigh. "Mr. Hansen saves the front row for the families of people playing solos. He always saves a seat for father, 'just in case he decides to show.'"

"And Mr. Hansen doesn't realize your father is never going to show up at one of your concerts."

"Exactly," Chrysta agreed. "I hate seeing that seat empty. It seems to be mocking me at every concert." She suddenly thought of something, and her mood immediately lightened. "Oh, I have my dress! Want to see it?" And she was hopping up to run to her wardrobe before Tommy could answer.

He chuckled behind her as she got it out. She held it out so he could see and then did a twirl with it. She held it to her body and preened in the mirror until she realized Tommy was directly behind her. She leaned back until she was resting on his chest and craned her neck to see his face. "Isn't it lovely?" she asked him.

"Not the only thing in here that is lovely," he replied, and she blushed.

He ran his fingers through her hair, then leaned down to kiss her on the forehead. She smiled and closed her eyes. He hugged her. "I should be going," he said. "Don't want us to get in trouble." She opened her eyes to see him staring at her in the mirror.

"Alright," she said, slightly disappointed. Tommy went back to the bed to grab his jacket, and she had a thought. "Hey, Tommy?"

"Hm?"

"You know how you said I cursed Chloe?"

He paused in getting his jacket on and turned to her. "Yes?"

"More... strange things. Have been happening. I'm starting to think... I don't know—"

"Don't tell me," he snapped. Chrysta almost flinched at his tone.

"Why?" she asked while putting the dress back in the wardrobe.

He winced and rubbed at his left arm. "If you talk about that stuff, you can't let certain people hear you."

"Like who?" she asked.

"Your father, Peter, and me."

Chrysta blinked and then stepped closer to him. "Why can't I tell you?"

He sighed and rubbed at his arm again. "Do you trust me?" he asked.

"Yes, of course."

"Then trust me when I say you're not crazy, but you need to keep quiet about this."

"My father was there when one of the strange things happened," she started to explain. He sighed again and ran his fingers through his dreadlocks.

"O-okay," she said. "I won't tell anyone."

He nodded. "Good."

He shifted from foot to foot and then brought her in for a hug. He placed one last kiss on her forehead and then gestured at the dress. "I can't wait to see you wearing that."

"Are you coming to the concert?" she asked.

"Wouldn't miss it for the world," he said.

She wrapped herself up in her blanket and then let Tommy out onto the balcony. She squeezed his hand before he stepped over the railing. "Thank you for coming," she said softly.

"Anytime, beautiful," he answered back, and he was gone.

·····

Thursday afternoon, while the girls were leaving the school, there was a shout, and both girls looked to see Mary's mother, Selena Jackson, walking up to them. Chrysta smiled and hugged her. "Hello, Selena, how are you?" she asked. Mary's parents had stopped being Mr. and Mrs. Jackson years ago when they insisted on being on a first-name basis with them. Because they were family, they explained.

"Doing good, little one," Selena answered back. "But I'm a little confused. I called your father to ask him about Thanksgiving, and imagine my surprise when he said I have to invite your suitor to dinner too? What is that about?"

Chrysta winced. "Sorry about that, Selena. Father is... *letting* Peter *court* me. You don't have to have him for dinner if it makes you uncomfortable."

"Well, I don't mind one more for dinner. I'm just wondering why your father sounds like he got a script from a Victorian-era movie." She paused as she thought about something. "Wait, this boy is *courting* you. What do you think about this arrangement?"

"I hate it," Chrysta said honestly.

Selena gave her daughter a look, and Mary shrugged. "I didn't want to tell you," Mary confessed. "I had a feeling your inner feminist warrior would go ballistic."

"One day, I *will* go ballistic on that man," Selena growled. "Well, if it keeps the peace, I will invite the boy." Her frown turned into a smile, and she hugged Chrysta again. "See you next week, little one." And they left, waving goodbye to Chrysta as she waved back.

12

Thanksgiving break started, and Chrysta spent the week practicing her violin and avoiding her father as much as possible. Guerra and his guards would still make their surprise inspections, Guerra sometimes examining her room personally, hands held behind his back with that false smile that made her shudder. Tommy did not visit her. Jonathon was declining to play at the club more and more, so Tommy tried to help as much as he could. At least she had Thanksgiving dinner at the Jackson household to look forward to. Her father even agreed to let her stay the night.

So Thursday morning, she rushed to the limo her father had called, barely pausing to let her father approve her outfit. Peter was waiting inside, scowling as she got seated across from him. "Um, how are you?" she asked.

He just sneered at her, so the rest of the ride was held in complete silence.

Once they got to the Jackson townhouse, Mary opened the door when Chrysta knocked, and the girls squealed and hugged each other. "Hey Peter," Mary greeted the other teen, but he just grunted in reply. Mary's father, Adam Jackson, was waiting nearby and held out a hand.

"Nice to meet you, Peter," he greeted the moody teen. "Do you like football? I have the game on TV." Peter broke out in a grin and went with the older man to the living room.

Chrysta followed Mary into the kitchen. Her mother, grandmother, and younger brother were there, the kitchen warm and smelling of garlic and cinnamon. Selena and Marigold flashed Chrysta a smile when she gave them brief hugs. "Oh, hello dear," Mrs. Jackson said, her hands covered in flour as she worked on a pie crust. "How have you been?"

"Doing good," Chrysta answered. In truth, she was just happy to be in the Jackson household. It felt more like home than her own house sometimes. Chrysta kissed Noah on the cheek, and the younger boy looked disgusted, rubbed his face, and said, "Eck." "How are you doing, Mrs. Jackson?" Chrysta asked the older woman.

"Alive for another year," Mrs. Jackson said. She paused in getting the pie crust in a pan. "I hear you are bringing a young man to dinner tonight. A new boyfriend?"

Chrysta winced. "Peter is not my boyfriend," she tried to explain without sounding upset.

"Peter? I thought the young man was named something else?"

"Grandma, hush," Mary said while washing her hands. "That's a surprise."

Chrysta looked between the two women. "Mary, what are you planning?"

Just then, there was the sound of a doorbell, and Noah hopped up. "I'll get it!" he yelled while running out of the kitchen.

"Oh look, the surprise is here," Mary joked as she started to chop some sweet potatoes.

Noah came back into the kitchen with Tommy in tow. Tommy wore a green sweater with blue jeans but still had his black combat boots on. He'd removed most of his jewelry, except one silver stud in each ear and the stud in his lip, and tied his hair up. He was also holding a bouquet of sunflowers. Tommy gave Chrysta a smile while handing her the bouquet. "Hello, beautiful."

Chrysta gave him a huge smile in return. "What are you doing here?" she asked, the grin hurting her face.

"I was invited," he explained, holding a hand up to his chest like he was offended.

Mary just threw her hands up. "Surprise!" she cried and laughed as she went back to chopping potatoes.

"Nice to meet you," Selena said while drying her hands on a towel. She held out a hand that Tommy shook. "Selena Jackson, my mother-in-law, Marigold Jackson, and I think you already met my son, Noah."

"Thank you for inviting me, Mrs. Jackson," Tommy said with a grin.

"Selena," she replied. "And thank Mary. She said you had nowhere else to go today."

"Oh, that isn't true," Tommy said. "You can find free food at a lot of places this time of year." He started rolling up his sleeves. "But at least here I am not being served by an ex-felon with face tattoos. Need help with dinner?"

Selena smiled. "Can you chop apples?"

"Of course," he replied while washing his hands.

Chrysta and Noah retreated to the small kitchen table to stay out of the way. Tommy joined Mrs. Jackson at the kitchen island. He looked at Chrysta. "Not helping out, beautiful?"

"I'm not allowed to," Chrysta explained while finding a vase for the flowers. She put her head on her hand while leaning on the table after she was done. "I'm a horrible cook."

"You can't be that bad," he said while he started to peel an apple.

"She once used salt instead of sugar in a pie filling," Mary said.

"Honest mistake," Tommy replied.

"She once burned spinach in a pan so bad it caught fire, and the house smelled of smoke for a week," Selena said.

"Burning food sometimes adds flavor to a dish," Tommy tried to explain.

"She once poured the whole pepper shaker into the mashed potatoes," Noah said. Chrysta covered her face in shame.

"Well, mistakes happen?" Tommy said uncertainly. The whole kitchen erupted in laughter.

Mrs. Jackson waved a flour-covered finger at Tommy. "I know you," she said with a smile.

"I don't think so, ma'am," he replied. "I think I would remember someone so lovely."

"Oh lord," Mary groaned. "Can you not hit on my grandmother, please? What is it with you and older women?"

"Hey, I can't help my natural charm," he said.

"More like natural sleaziness," Mary replied.

They continued cooking, Tommy even helping Selena to baste the turkey. Chrysta helped keep Noah busy by letting him perform magic tricks. "Is this your card?" he cried out while showing Chrysta a two of clubs.

"Um, no," she giggled. Noah looked at the card. "Dammit," he cursed.

"Hey now, language, we have guests," Selena said.

"Oh, the horror," Tommy mumbled, mostly to himself. "Need help learning some tricks, kiddo?" he asked the younger boy while helping Mrs. Jackson pour pie filling into the crust.

"You know some magic tricks?" asked Noah.

"I know some sleight of hand, yes," Tommy confirmed. He walked over to them, held up his empty hands, and then made a coin appear out of Noah's ear.

"Cool!" the young boy cried out. Tommy nodded while handing the coin to Noah. "The trick is to distract your audience while surprising them with something else." Tommy leaned in, while Chrysta watched Noah, to kiss her on the cheek. "Ewww," Noah cried out while Chrysta blushed.

Dinner was finally served—turkey, mashed sweet potatoes, collard greens, creamed spinach, rolls, and apple pie for dessert. Adam greeted Tommy. "Good to finally meet you, Tommy. I have heard good things about you."

"Then they were probably lies, sir," Tommy joked while he smiled at Mary. Peter came into the room and gave Tommy a scowl. Tommy just waved his fingers at Peter. "Good to see you, Peter," he cheerfully said, although Chrysta could tell it was forced. Tommy held the chair out for Chrysta, and she sat down.

"I'm surprised to see you," Peter said. "I doubt Chrysta's father would approve of you being here."

Tommy shrugged as he took the spot across the table from Chrysta. "Maybe," he admitted, "but just remember, we have dirt on you."

"Dirt?" Mary asked. "Wait, you two know each other?"

"I kidnapped Peter a few weeks ago to see Tommy at a jazz club," Chrysta explained. "I knew it was the only way my father would let me go out. I didn't tell Peter of my plans, so I'm blackmailing him so he won't tell my father." She glared at Tommy. "But I didn't tell anyone about it because I was trying to protect him." She then glared at Peter. "And Tommy is a guest here too, just like you, so be nice."

"Chrysta York, have you been sneaking out to spend time in a club of all places?" Selena gasped as she passed the rolls from her son on her left to Tommy on her right.

"Um, yes?" Chrysta hesitantly agreed.

"I approve. Carry on," Selena said, and everyone chuckled except for Peter.

"You're encouraging her?" Peter asked, almost rudely.

"We are not Jozef fans in this household," Selena explained. "Generally, I would never encourage any child to disobey their parents, but I think Chrysta has earned the right to make some decisions independently." She took a sip of wine and then turned to Tommy. "But hurt her, and I start breaking limbs."

"Noted. Your daughter pretty much said the same thing the first time we met," joked Tommy.

Mary leaned forward to look at Chrysta over Peter. "I got you, sis," Mary said, and Chrysta smiled.

"A jazz club! That is where I know you from!" Mrs. Jackson said with a cry and then put a hand on Tommy's. "You look exactly like a young man I used to see in a jazz club about an hour from here when I was younger."

"Maybe it was Tommy," Mary said.

"Oh no, dear, this was in the 50s," Mrs. Jackson explained. "It was the only club that allowed blacks inside. I was barely older than you. But it is where I met your grandfather, dancing to The Ink Spots on the dance floor."

"I don't want to set the world on fire," Tommy sang, and Mrs. Jackson joined him for the last bit. "I just want to start a flame in your heart."

"Oh, you sound *just* like him!" Mrs. Jackson cried while clapping her hands. "You must stay around and listen to some records after dinner."

"I would love to," Tommy said with a smile.

"Is that what you do for a living, Tommy?" Adam asked.

"Yes, sir. I mostly busk on the streets, but lately, I have been doing a lot of playing at the club." He looked at Chrysta. "I actually hope you can make it back to the club soon, beautiful. I could use your help in making some music."

"Wait, you *played* at the club?" Mary asked. "How was it? What did you play?"

"It was fun," Chrysta confessed. "I played something called Gypsy jazz."

"And I hope you got paid for the evening," Selena said.

Chrysta nodded. "I did. Tommy made sure of it."

Selena nodded in approval. "Do you sleep on the streets, Tommy?" she asked.

Tommy gave her a look. "Yes?"

"Well, it's going to be a cold winter. You need a place to stay, you're welcome here."

Tommy slowly blinked. "Um, thank you, ma'am, but I don't want you guys to take in a complete stranger. I can always go to a shelter."

"Do you think we would have invited you if we didn't trust you?" Selena said.

Tommy looked around the table to see all the Jacksons giving him big smiles. "No, ma'am," he said. "I guess you wouldn't." And he gave Chrysta a big smile of his own and dug into dinner.

.....

Chrysta didn't know if it was her own bias, but dinner was more delicious than anything she got at home. She had seconds, and Tommy went for thirds. Even Peter seemed to get more comfortable as the evening went on.

"Oh, I couldn't eat another bite," Tommy said, leaning back from the table. Chrysta nodded in agreement.

"No room for apple pie?" Selena asked.

"Well, maybe a little slice."

"With ice cream?"

"Of course."

Selena started taking plates to the kitchen with a smirk on her face. "Come on Peter, we cooked dinner, you clean the dishes."

Peter looked between Tommy and Chrysta. "Um, yes, ma'am."

"Oh, Chrysta, you want s'mores?" Mary asked.

"Like when we were kids? Oh, that's a great idea." Chrysta turned to Adam. "May we use the fire pit?"

"Sure, girls, just be careful starting the fire."

Mrs. Jackson linked her arm with one of Tommy's. "Can you help me with the record player, young man?"

"I would love to," he said, following her to her room.

The girls went outside, taking a heavy blanket and the ingredients for s'mores with them. Mary got wood into the pit and tried to light it while Chrysta watched from a bench. "Fother mucker," Mary cursed to herself, and Chrysta laughed. "Sorry," Mary apologized. "Mom is trying to get me to stop cursing in front of Noah." She frowned at the lighter. "Stupid thing isn't working."

"Let me try," Chrysta said. She crouched down next to Mary and reached out with the lighter. She tried to use the lighter, but every turn of the wheel just clicked. As she felt a stab of annoyance, a crackling sound started, and sparks appeared in front of her fingers and lit the wood. Both girls yelped and leaned back.

"Do you... how did... what!?" Mary cried. "Was that from the lighter?"

Chrysta looked from the lighter in her right hand to her left hand, where the sparks had come out. "No," Chrysta admitted. "I think that was me."

Just then, Tommy came out with Mrs. Jackson and Noah, carrying a large case. He saw the looks on the girls' faces and paused. "What's up, you two. You look like you saw a ghost."

"Yeah, Chrysta just ha—" Mary started but abruptly stopped when Chrysta grabbed her arm.

"It's nothing," Chrysta said. "Nevermore," she said. She prayed Tommy understood what she was trying to say.

Tommy looked at them with narrow eyes, but then his eyebrows shot up. "Ah, got you," he said while nodding. He put the case on a towel Mrs. Jackson had put down and started to open it. Mary gave Chrysta a weird look, but she just shook her head. "Later," she murmured.

Mrs. Jackson was going through her record collection while Tommy plugged the record player in. "What do you think?" she asked Tommy. "Dean Martin or Frank Sinatra?"

"Can't go wrong with Ol' Blue Eyes," Tommy responded, crouching beside the fire. He warmed his hands and looked at the girls. "You two want your s'mores?"

"Yeah," Chrysta said, and she accepted a marshmallow and stick from Tommy and handed them to Mary. Mary numbly took them. Chrysta took her own set, and they speared the marshmallows and started toasting them.

The first cords of *Fly Me to the Moon* started, and Mrs. Jackson danced over to Tommy. "Come on, young man. You have the first spot on my dance card."

"Yes, ma'am," Tommy said with a grin. He got up, and the two started swaying.

Mary groaned. "Stop flirting with my grandma," she said with a smirk. She took her marshmallow out of the fire and started making her first s'more.

"I can't help it. I'm a weak man who loves attractive women," he said with a grin. Mrs. Jackson chuckled, but with the smile on her face, she indeed looked stunning.

Noah made a face. "Eck," he grimaced.

"Give it a few years, kiddo, you'll understand," Tommy replied as *All I Need Is the Girl* started playing.

Tommy and Mrs. Jackson danced for a few more songs, the girls continuing to roast marshmallows and make s'mores, Noah stealing any that he could. Finally, Mrs. Jackson laughed as Tommy carefully dipped her. "Oh, I haven't danced like that in years," she gasped, turning to her grandson. "Come on, dear, it's your turn."

Noah groaned but obeyed his grandmother, and they danced to *That's Life*. Selena came out with three plates of apple pie and handed one to Tommy. She grinned at the sight of her mother-in-law and son dancing.

"Where's Peter?" Chrysta asked.

"Inside, watching sports," Selena explained. "Doesn't want to leave until Tommy does."

"Worried about me being here with Chrysta?" Tommy asked.

Selena made a face. "Yep."

"I'll head out soon then," Tommy said. "Get Mr. Creepy out of your hair," he said as he took a bite of apple pie.

"Oh, don't rush out on his account," Mrs. Jackson said. The Frank Sinatra record had ended, and she was going through her collection. "You owe Chrysta one dance."

"Oh no," Chrysta said with a laugh. "I have never danced. We shouldn't. I'll be terrible at it."

"Never?" Tommy asked.

"No one has ever asked me to," Chrysta confessed. "I mean, Mary and I have gone to a couple of school dances together, but that's it."

"A crime we are going to correct right now," Tommy announced, and he placed his plate of half-eaten pie on the patio table and tugged Chrysta out of the blanket and onto her feet. Selena smiled and took her place, snuggling next to her daughter and wrapping herself up in the blanket.

Mrs. Jackson had put another record on the record player, and a song started playing. Tommy put a hand on her left hip and grabbed her right hand, and they were swayed to the music.

Tommy kept her at a respectful distance, but she could still feel the heat coming off his body. She heard him humming to the song and realized it was the same one he and Mrs. Jackson had sung at dinner. Chrysta accidentally stepped on Tommy's foot and blushed. "Sorry!" she cried.

"No worries, beautiful, you're too light to hurt me," he joked.

"Ha-ha," she deadpanned. But when he pulled her closer, she let him.

"Hey, I need to see some space between you two," Selena told them, and Tommy rolled his eyes but backed off.

"Let me guess, school dance chaperone?" Tommy asked her with a grin.

"Exactly," she replied.

The song ended, and Chrysta reluctantly moved away. Noah came over and made a large bow. "May I have this dance?" he asked in a deeper voice, and Chrysta laughed. They danced to the next song as Tommy grabbed his pie and squatted beside Mary.

Noah was silly and dancing wildly, and Chrysta tried to follow him while giggling. She noticed that Mary was leaning towards Tommy, gesturing towards the fire. Tommy was just nodding with a sour look on his face, pie forgotten.

Finally, the song ended, and the adults clapped. Tommy's scowl was replaced by a bright smile. "See, beautiful? You're a natural."

Tommy stood up. "Well, ladies and gentleman, I must depart." He went over to Selena and held out a hand. "Thank you again for the invite." And then he walked over to Mrs. Jackson and held out a hand. "And thank you for the music."

"Oh no, dear, you get a hug," Mrs. Jackson said, and she stood to give Tommy an embrace. She pulled him down and then whispered something in his ear. He just grinned.

"Walk me out, beautiful?" he asked. Chrysta started walking with him to the front door. "'Night, Mary!" he cried out in a singsong voice. .

"'Night, jackass!" Mary responded.

"Language!" Selena cried at her daughter while Noah laughed.

At the front door, Adam was on the phone. He smiled when he saw Chrysta and Tommy. "I just called a cab for Peter. Do you need one as well?"

"No, thank you, sir, I can walk," Tommy explained as he got his jacket. The sweater looked good on him, but Chrysta had to admit that it was good to see him in his old jacket. "Thank you for having me."

"It sounds like you showed my mother a wonderful time. I haven't seen her use that record player in years." Adam held out a hand with a grin. "You let us know if you need a warm place to sleep this winter, alright?"

"I will," Tommy replied with a smile; Chrysta could tell it was genuine. Adam went back to the living room.

"Hope you had fun tonight," Chrysta said.

Tommy nodded. "Dinner was delicious, music was great, dance partners were wonderful," he said. "Couldn't ask for a better night. Hope you have fun with your sleepover, beautiful."

He turned away but stopped when she put a hand on his arm. "Hey, Tommy," she started.

He stopped and raised an eyebrow, but then she remembered what he had said. "Nevermind," she said.

"Don't you mean Nevermore?" he asked, teasing. She smiled with a blush.

He chuckled and then pulled her close to place a kiss on her forehead. "'Night, beautiful," he said before melting into the night.

13

Later, the girls stayed up, a movie playing on the TV, but they were too engrossed in conversation to notice. Chrysta had told Mary everything that had happened so far; not only the mirror and the fire but also the broken nightstick. Mary sat on her bed, thinking, while Chrysta watched her from the air mattress on the floor.

"So, what?" Mary said after several minutes. "You have telekinesis?"

Chrysta sighed. "I don't know. Maybe?"

"Let's not forget, Tommy said you cursed Chloe. That's not a psychic ability."

"But if I was unconsciously breaking the violin Chloe was holding, it could still be telekinesis."

"But what about the violins she broke at home? You weren't there to see her holding a violin."

"True," Chrysta admitted. "And what about the fire?"

"That's pyrokinesis," Mary said. "I don't watch horror movies, and even I know that."

Chrysta groaned. "One strange thing happening is uncanny, but all of them together? It's a pattern."

"A weird, freaky pattern."

"And why is Tommy saying I can't tell Peter or my father? Or him? I mean, my father, I kind of understand. But why not Tommy?"

"And you said Peter and Tommy acted like they knew each other when they met?"

"Peter did, for sure. And they instantly seemed to hate each other." Chrysta sighed again and flopped onto her back. "It's just so... frustrating. Like something is going on, and I just only see the tip of it."

Mary joined her on the floor and got Chrysta to put her head on Mary's lap. The girls sat in silence for a few minutes until Mary snorted to herself. Chrysta looked at her friend while the other girl started giggling.

"Just look at this way," Mary said with a chuckle, "if playing violin doesn't work out, you can go into magic."

Chrysta laughed and sat up, lifting her arms in the air. "Presenting, for your entertainment, Chrysta the Great!" She made a show of bowing to an invisible crowd. Mary clapped and made a wolf whistle. The girls laughed louder, and Chrysta collapsed back into her friend's lap.

They sat in silence for a few minutes, both girls giggling to themselves. "Mary?" Chrysta said after they had calmed down.

"Hm?"

"Thanks for inviting Tommy tonight. I appreciate it."

"Weeeelllll..." Mary started to say. "That was mostly mom's idea. After she found out about Peter, she started to ask me questions. I slipped up and said, 'Well, she likes Tommy more than she likes Peter,' and *that* was a fun conversation because then I had to explain how Tommy is older, but he's really fantastic and respectful, not like Peter, who is our age, but a jackass." Mary took an exaggeratedly long breath, and Chrysta giggled again. "And well, mom said she wanted to invite both of them to see who was really the jackass but don't worry because I think Tommy got the Jackson seal of approval."

"So glad he does," Chrysta said with a smile.

There was a knock at the door, and Adam stuck his head in. "Alright, ladies, it's almost one in the morning. Lights out."

The girls groaned, but the TV was promptly turned off, and Mary climbed back into her bed.

"'Night," Chrysta said.

"'Night," Mary responded.

Soon Mary's breathing was deep and even, but Chrysta was still awake. She grabbed her phone and opened up a music streaming app and brought up The Ink Spots. She started playing *I Don't Want to Set the World on Fire* and finally drifted off to sleep with a smile on her face.

.....

The slave was pulled out of deep sleep by the pull of the summons. He grumbled as he rubbed his eyes in the early morning's grey light. The call felt like an electrical shock, running from his middle finger up his left arm to his shoulder blade, pins and needles that wouldn't stop until he was in the presence of his master. If he didn't respond quickly enough, his whole arm would go numb. He had been stubborn in the past and let that very thing happen, trying to rebel by being difficult, but now he moved quickly to respond. He had a feeling he would need his arm in perfect working order.

He walked the few blocks to the York mansion, knocking on the door, and was let in by a servant. He expected to be ushered into the study but was led upstairs without a word instead. He tried to keep his face neutral as he was guided into Chrysta's room.

Jozef York was standing in front of the wardrobe, Chrysta's black dress hanging in front of him. He was staring at it with a scowl. A second man in the room looked at a framed picture of young Chrysta with her mother. The slave felt his skin crawl when he recognized him.

"Ah, the slave! At last!" Guerra cried out in false cheer as he put the picture back. The smile plastered on his face did not reach his eyes. "It has been a long time, no?"

The slave frowned at the other man. "Not long enough, Guerra," he flatly responded.

"Oh, don't be like that, Mr. Monroe," Guerra said with that false smile.

Tommy just scowled at both men.

"Tell me, has she shown any ability?" York asked.

"No," Tommy lied, and the band on his arm burned dully. Technically, Tommy had not seen anything, and Mary telling him about the fire last night was hearsay. As long as he didn't see anything himself and kept Chrysta from telling him directly, he wasn't lying. Guerra looked at him with that broad unnerving grin like he knew Tommy was fudging the truth.

"Nothing?" asked York.

"Nothing," Tommy said, the band on his arm still burning. He tried to keep his face blank.

"If I may," Guerra started, folding his hands behind him, "you said she destroyed something? When she was upset?"

York nodded, still looking at the dress.

"Then a little pressure may be needed," and Guerra's smile grew into something obscene, something predatory and dark. Suddenly a part of Tommy wanted to kill him to ensure that this man never even looked at Chrysta again.

Tommy blinked and shifted. He was getting too protective of Chrysta and had to be careful. These bastards had something planned for her; he couldn't let his feelings for her cloud his judgment. If the Butcher was here, it meant bad news for Chrysta.

"Perhaps," York mused. He lifted the dress from the wardrobe to get a better look. "I am still not convinced that the proof we need is required right now."

"The winter solstice is in several weeks," Guerra said. "How much more time do you think you have, sir?"

York was carefully folding the dress over one arm. He started walking out of the room. "If we make her have a reaction now, we run the risk of her being too strong for the ritual."

Tommy's stomach dropped at the word ritual. He *knew* it. Whatever was going on, it was not in Chrysta's best interest. Guerra and Tommy followed him into the hallway, where York handed the dress to a waiting servant. "Put this upstairs and lock the door," he ordered.

"Why are you taking it away?" Tommy asked before he could stop himself.

York turned to him with a scowl, like he had just remembered that Tommy was there. "None of your concern," he snapped. He held a finger up in Tommy's face, the finger with the ring on it, and Tommy had to bite back a growl. "Continue watching her, and report back with anything you see."

The band on Tommy's arm constricted, and he winced. But he bit his tongue and nodded. Better play along for now. If they didn't think Chrysta was useful, maybe they would leave her alone.

He glanced at the cold smile of Guerra. Or maybe if they didn't think she was useful, they would get rid of her.

York waved his hand impatiently. "You are dismissed."

Tommy nodded again and started making his way down the steps. He suddenly understood why Chrysta was so uncomfortable around her father. Except for her room, the house felt vast and empty. Well-kept and expensive for sure, but it had no personality or warmth. The men were murmuring to themselves as he let himself outside.

He paused when he got on the sidewalk to get a deep breath of cold air before turning around. Tommy glowered at the building. He knew more than before, thanks to those bastards treating him like a piece of furniture. But what he heard, he didn't like. There was a ritual happening on the winter solstice, and York was going to use his daughter as a part of it.

Tommy was glad he had followed his instincts and stopped drinking. He needed to keep his head clear and make a plan. He turned away from the building and started making his way back to his roof.

He needed to get her out of there.

. . . . .

Chrysta woke up the next morning to the smell of blueberry muffins and pancakes. She joined the Jackson family for breakfast and felt her face hurt from smiling after a few minutes. This is what a family was supposed to do at meals. Sit and laugh and talk about their days. Not eat in complete silence. She put her head on Mary's shoulder. Mary leaned her head on Chrysta's.

"Thank you," she whispered. "For letting me be part of the family."

"Of course, sis," Mary responded. They hugged, and Noah gave a loud "Ewwwww!" from across the table.

Generally, on days when her father allowed her to spend the night, he would let her stay until supper. Selena got out the Christmas decorations, and they started to decorate the house. Chrysta's home was always bare during the holidays, so it was her only chance to enjoy putting up anything festive. But she was surprised that after a lunch of leftovers, her father called and told her to be ready for the car he was sending.

"What?" Mary growled. "It's too soon."

Chrysta shrugged. "Well, there is always Christmas day," she tried to say with a smile.

She hugged everyone and said her goodbyes. The car appeared, and she climbed in. Once home, she was surprised that her father was not waiting for her at the front door. She went upstairs to her bedroom.

Opening the door, she noticed her father was there, with a man she didn't know. "What is going on?" she asked.

"I noticed you had gotten a dress for the concert," he explained. "I didn't think it was appropriate, so I got you something else."

He gestured to the bathroom, and Chrysta went in to see a pale pink dress hanging there. It was floor-length, with sleeves and big puffy flowers made of gauze. It was hideous and something Chrysta would never pick for herself. She turned to her father. "What happened to my dress?"

"It's gone," he simply said. "As I said, it wasn't appropriate."

"I don't care," she said, voice rising in anger. "It was my dress. I want it back."

"No," he said cooly. He gestured again at the pink dress. "Try it on. It needs to be altered."

She looked at the dress with tears in her eyes. She looked at her father. "I hate you," she said and meant it.

He blinked. "I know," he said.

She went into the bathroom and slammed the door, ripping the dress from its hanger. She put it on and stomped out to let the seamster do his alterations. Her father was not in the room while the man worked. The man left and took the dress with him.

Chrysta fell on the bed and cried.

$\backsim$ 14 $\backsim$

Chrysta's rage did not die over the weekend, and when she went back to school on Monday, it only got worse. She was sullen in class, snapped at people in the hallways, glared at Peter when he tried to get near her. She was moody and felt justified in her anger. She didn't even tell Mary what was going on, wanting to wallow in her hurt.

After orchestra class, she gave her sheet music to Chloe. "You may want to learn the solo parts," she simply said. "I don't know if I will be at the concert."

Chloe blinked but took the music. "Are you sure?"

Chrysta nodded. "I have a feeling I'm coming down with something," she said.

She refused to eat with her father, and so wasn't allowed to eat. She even ignored Tommy's texts for a few days. Maybe she was overreacting, but having the dress taken from her felt like her life's biggest betrayal.

Wednesday night, her father dropped off the new dress, and she could barely wait until he was out of the room before she was crying.

Thursday night, Chrysta was trying to concentrate on homework when there was a tapping on the door to her balcony. She got up and wasn't surprised to see Tommy.

"Hey, beautiful," he said as she let him in. "You have been really quiet lately. Everything okay?"

She sighed and rubbed her eyes. "Yeah, it's just been a rough week."

Tommy frowned. "Something your father did?" he asked with a growl.

She didn't answer but went to the wardrobe and brought out her father's dress. She hung it on the outside and turned around. Tommy was looking at the ugly thing in horror and started searching the many pockets of his jacket.

"What are you doing?" she asked.

"I think I got a lighter somewhere," he explained. "We are burning that fucking thing to ashes."

She snorted, and just like that, the storm cloud that had been over her head for days broke, and she was laughing. She laughed so hard she started to cry, and Tommy brought her into a fierce hug. Once she calmed down, she began to murmur into his chest. "I'm not going to the concert. Not in that. I loved that dress, dammit."

"I know, beautiful," he said softly, shrugging out of his jacket and getting her back into his arms. She turned around so she could look at the dress.

Chrysta sighed and leaned back into Tommy's warmth, feeling calmer in the hug. She ran her hands up his arms as he placed a kiss on her head. Abruptly her hands stopped on his left arm. She had always assumed that the band on his arm was fabric, even though it appeared metallic. She had thought that he was covering up something shameful, but she figured that it was rude to ask, and he would tell her about it when he was ready. But it was smooth, cold metal under her palm, which made no sense because she didn't see a seam. She didn't see how it could be taken on or off. It was so tight on his skin that she couldn't even feel a way to get her fingers under the edges. Something like that couldn't be comfortable.

"Tommy, I have never asked—" she started.

"Chrysta, don't worry about it," he said softly.

"No, I'm serious. I have never asked, but this band on your arm, what is it?"

"Beautiful, it's fine," he said again.

"But it is metal, isn't it?" she asked, turning around to face him, tugging his arm so that it was between them. She looked up to see him grimacing. "Isn't it too tight? How did it get on your arm? Doesn't it hurt?"

"Only every damn day," he responded softly, and she saw something sad and hurt in his eyes.

"How do we get it off?" she asked. "Does it need to be cut off? Do we need to take you to the hospital? Do you need money? Tell me how to hel—" But before she could continue her barrage of questions, Tommy kissed her.

It was not a gentle kiss. Chrysta knew Tommy was only using it to stop her from talking, but the part of her that should feel outraged at being silenced was currently being drowned by the thought that *he was kissing her*. She moaned, and the kiss got softer. He had cupped her face with both hands, but one moved to her back to pull her closer. She was now very aware of Tommy's body and where it touched hers.

He started to pull away, but her hands shot up to his neck and pulled him back down. Tommy chuckled, lips still on hers. He sat down on the bed and brought her into his lap. One hand stayed on her cheek, but the other tugged her hair out of its ponytail. She sighed. A part of her was screaming, *he's only doing this to distract you*, but she wanted to ignore it. They could talk about his arm after he was done kissing her.

He ran his fingers through her hair, and Chrysta suddenly hoped *after* would be a long time from *now*.

There was a knock at the door. The couple froze. Chrysta's heart had been pounding already from the kiss, but now it was going even faster, probably so loud Tommy could hear it. She leaned back to look at him, eyes wide in terror. Tommy looked like he was trying not to laugh. Of course, he would find this hilarious.

"Just one minute, please," she called out, surprised her voice was so even. She scrambled out of Tommy's lap and hissed at him. "You need to hide."

She started her way to the door, trying to smooth her hair and praying her cheeks were not too red from blushing. She turned to see where Tommy was and was shocked to see he had vanished. Out the door? Maybe. But she hadn't heard the latch.

She counted to ten and then opened the door. Guerra himself was on the other side with two men. She let them in, trying her best not to search her own room with her eyes. Guerra stepped inside but stopped with his hands folded behind him. "I trust you are having a fine evening, Miss York?"

"I am," she said, trying to not follow the two men with her eyes. Focusing on Guerra's strange smile was not easy, either. "Just debating if I want to go to school tomorrow or not."

She didn't know why she said that to him. Guerra certainly didn't care about her feelings, but she was surprised to see him look at the pale pink dress and grimace. "Ah, yes, the dress. I don't quite understand why your father took the other one. It was certainly a lovely thing." He shrugged. "But your father is in charge, is he not?"

"Yes, he is," she said bitterly.

One man was looking in the wardrobe while the other was inspecting the balcony. One of them was about to look under the bed, but Guerra called out to him. "Let us leave Miss York alone this evening. She looks flushed. Maybe she is unwell. She must sleep."

Chrysta tried to keep herself from blushing more while they filed out of the room. Guerra paused and turned around. "Until the morning, my dear," he said with that creepy smile and a deep bow. Chrysta just nodded and closed the door.

"Tommy?" she loudly whispered after counting to thirty. Maybe he was able to make it outside? She didn't think so. He had no time. She looked around the room, trying to find a clue to where he was hiding.

"Under here," came a muffled reply from underneath her bed. She grinned and crouched down to peer into the small space.

"How are you doing under there?" she asked.

"Well, I have met the dust bunnies. They are a kind and benevolent race. Easier to conquer. I am now their king."

She laughed and then got up to give him space to come out. He emerged with his jacket, looking slightly embarrassed. He tossed his jacket on top of the bed and leaned on it. "Was that the famous head of security?"

"Yes," she confirmed while nodding. "Such a lovely man, isn't he?"

"Oh, just peachy," he agreed. He cocked his head to the side. "Would you like me to head out, beautiful? Let you get some sleep?"

She blinked and then smiled at him. "Can you stay?"

His eyebrows went up, and he grinned. "The night?"

"Until I go to sleep?" she shyly asked.

"I don't know..." he started, taking a deep breath.

She looked at him through her eyelashes. "Please?"

He let the breath out in an explosive sigh. "Alright, you win."

She smiled, gave him a quick kiss on the cheek, and rushed to the bathroom to change. When done, she came out to see that he had turned down one corner of the cover. His shoes were at the foot of the bed with his jacket. He had one foot up and was removing a knife holder from his calf.

"Why do you carry that?" she asked.

He took the knife out of its holder, letting the blade move across his knuckles before grabbing the handle and holding the knife out. "Living on the streets, have to protect yourself," he stated before putting it back in the holder. It joined his boots at the foot of the bed.

She climbed into bed, and he covered her up and tucked her in. Tommy stayed on the top cover, stretching out and crossing his legs. She put her head on his shoulder, and he wrapped his arms around her, running his fingers through her hair. She burrowed as close to him as the cover would allow.

Chrysta wasn't sure for how long they stayed like that. Chrysta felt warm and protected. She could hear the thump of his heart, slow and steady. "Tommy?" she asked.

"Sshhhh, you should be asleep," he told her.

"What are you doing?" she asked.

"Just trying to commit as much of this to memory as I can."

"Why?"

He didn't answer; he just kept running his fingers through her hair. "I still want to talk about the band on your arm," she said, and his fingers stopped moving. She lifted her head to look at his face. "Let me know if I can help you get it off."

He gave her a sad half-smile and then kissed her on the lips. He put his forehead on hers and ran a finger across her lips. "Don't worry about it, beautiful."

"I'm serious. If it hurts you, I want to help you get it off."

"I know," he whispered, pulling her back into a hug. He said the next bit into the crown of her head. "That is why I love you so much."

She froze. The admission Tommy just made hung in the air. Would he expect her to say it back? He chuckled. "Don't worry, beautiful, you don't have to say it."

She huffed. "You don't think I lo—" Tommy was clamping a hand on her mouth before she could finish. She growled, and he chuckled again.

"No, I don't doubt you care for me," he explained. "But you say that word, you are never getting rid of me." She smiled, and he dropped his hand. "Besides, you will get to know me better, and then you will regret it later."

"I doubt it," she said. They fell quiet, and Chrysta was almost certain Tommy had fallen asleep when his breathing slowed after several minutes. She lifted her head again to look at his face. "I love you too."

Tommy curled a lip and groaned. "Why did you have to say that, beautiful? Now I can never leave." And she was laughing as he kissed her again.

·····

Chrysta was dreaming.

It was her room, it was her bed, it looked the same and smelled the same, and everything was where she expected it to be. Tommy wasn't in bed with her. He must have left after she fell asleep like he said he would. There was only one thing there that shouldn't be, and that was her mother sitting at the foot of the bed.

Cassia York didn't look like a rotting zombie. She didn't look misty or see-through. Didn't look like the monsters in any of the horror films Chrysta had watched before. She looked healthy and human and so lovely.

"I never liked putting you in pink things," her mom simply said, looking at the offensive dress hanging on the wardrobe. "Even as a baby, I never dressed you in pink. It didn't suit you." Her voice was weird, distant but clear.

Chrysta slowly sat up, moved slowly down the bed, and then hugged her mother from behind. Cassia felt warm and firm. Her hair was down, and she was wearing a black dress. "I've missed you," Chrysta told her mother.

"Oh, I have missed you too, little one," her mother responded. She placed her hands on Chrysta's arm and squeezed. "Although I was never far away, I'm sorry I couldn't talk with you before."

Chrysta wondered why she was not crying, but all she felt was calm. She scowled at the pink dress. "I wish you could have seen the other one," she said.

Her mother pulled away, turned around, and gave her daughter a mischievous grin, the same smile she would use before giving Chrysta ice cream before dinner when she was little. "Maybe I still can," Cassia said and pulled her daughter from the bed.

They stood in front of the wardrobe. Cassia held up a finger. "First, we find it. Poe can help you with that." Now, Chrysta was confident it was a dream because Poe was there with a pop, hopping on the bed even though the balcony door was still shut. "Cassia! Cassia! Cassia!" he cried with each hop.

Both women laughed, and Cassia turned back to Chrysta. "Visualize the dress. Think about it."

Chrysta closed her eyes and thought about the dress—

black dress, beautiful dress, silver lace dress that she chose, altered, Tommy helped her pay for it, wanted to wear it for him

—and then she could see it, upstairs in the third-floor bedroom.

"Oh, it is upstairs!" Chrysta cried, looking up. "But we can't go in there. Father will know I was in there. He always does."

"That's because your father has wards in that room. They let him know when someone has been inside." And Chrysta just wanted to ask, *how do you know all this?* But it was a dream, wasn't it? And a dream didn't have to make sense. In a dream, her dead mother would totally know all this, and she would be able to see a lost dress, and Poe could materialize in her bedroom with no warning.

"Now send Poe to the dress," her mother said.

"How?"

"People don't know this, but there is space between atoms," Cassia explained. "What you think is a solid object is really not. You can move the atoms in the ceiling and in Poe and make them move past each other."

"But how?" Chrysta asked with a laugh. "What you are describing, it sounds like..."

"Magic?" her mother asked. Chrysta looked up at the woman who was giving her a grin. Black hair like hers, but with olive skin and blue-grey eyes. Chrysta couldn't help but smile back. "Try it," Cassia said, and Chrysta shut her eyes. And then she did understand because she could *feel* it, the space between atoms could feel how easy it would be to shift Poe's to one side and the ceiling's to the other.

She held her hand out, and Poe started to glow gold. She pointed to the ceiling, and space glowed up there as well. Poe flapped his wings and vanished into the ceiling, only a few feathers falling down where he disappeared. Chrysta could only give a laugh of disbelief.

"Now that he is with the dress, bring him and it back here," her mother said.

She was about to ask how she would do that when Chrysta could feel something flex inside her chest, and suddenly, she felt herself pulling Poe and the dress downstairs. The dress and Poe landed on the bed, and he gave a loud squawk. How was it so simple? It had to be her imagination.

She grabbed the dress off the bed and twirled with it, laughing. Poe hopped up and down with her. She hugged her mother, and both women laughed, her mother quickly shushing her. Chrysta finally understood what she missed most about her mother: her laugh. All the silent dinners, the empty chair at her concerts, the distance her father held Chrysta at, her mother would not act like that. She filled the emptiness with light and laughter.

Chrysta glared at the pale pink dress. "You know," her mother said, "Tommy did mention burning it."

Chrysta matched her mother's wild grin and fixed her gaze on the offending dress. This she had already done. She reached out and snapped her fingers. The dress immediately caught fire, flames licking up from the bottom hem, all the way up the front, fake gauze flowers turning to ash. The fire did not touch the wardrobe or the clothes hanging inside it, and when the last flame died out, nothing was left of the pink dress.

Chrysta put the black dress up where the pink dress had been hanging and stepped back to smile. Her mother hugged her from behind, just like Tommy did before, and mother and daughter looked at it with matching smiles on their faces.

"You will look beautiful," Cassia sighed, her voice starting to sound weak and distant. Chrysta felt some of her joy fade. This was a dream, after all. Soon it would end, and her mother would be gone again. Her mother squeezed her then. "Don't worry, little one, I'm not going to be far away," she said like she had read Chrysta's thoughts.

Chrysta tried to swallow past the lump in her throat. "I want to ask you to stay."

"Oh, I would if I could," Cassia confessed. She held Chrysta's hand up. "One last thing before I go."

Chrysta felt a warmth go up her arm, and she watched as the silver lace on the dress slowly turned gold. "So you can wear those golden hairpins I like," Cassia whispered in Chrysta's ear, and Chrysta felt herself grinning. Once the last bit of lace had turned colors, the dress started to shift and change. "Just a glamour," Cassia said as the black dress began to look like the pink one. "Make sure your father can't see what we did."

The two women stayed like that for several minutes, just looking at their work and hugging each other. Chrysta looked down and realized that her mother's arms were starting to fade. She turned around to look at her mother's face, panicking when she saw Cassia slowly disappearing from sight. Her mother was still smiling, but her eyes looked sad.

"Listen, little one," Cassia started to say, "I don't have much time. Trust in Tommy. He will protect you."

"Protect me? From what?"

"Your father."

Chrysta blinked. Her father was controlling, but she never felt like he would hurt her. Did she really need protection from him?

Cassia grabbed her hand and started to lead Chrysta to bed, tucking her in. "I am proud of you. Of who you are now and what you will be in the future." Chrysta could barely see her mother now but felt the weight of her sitting on the bed.

"What is going on?" Chrysta asked her mother, feeling her eyelids getting heavy.

"Don't you know, little one?" her mother said with a smile. "It's a dream." And just like that, Chrysta was asleep.

❧ 15 ❧

The next morning, Chrysta's alarm went off. She had replaced *Morning Mood* with *In a Sentimental Mood*. She spent a few seconds stretching and rubbing her eyes when she remembered Tommy coming over. Oh. They had kissed. She was still worried about the band on his arm, but she felt her cheeks burn with a blush as she remembered how it had felt kissing him. She burrowed into the covers and giggled.

Suddenly, she frowned. There had been something else that had happened last night. What was it?

"You will look beautiful."

Chrysta shot up in bed. Her mother, her dead mother, had been in the room with her. She looked around her bedroom. There was nothing out of place, no sign of Poe. She hopped out of bed and opened the wardrobe, expecting to see the black dress.

The pink dress was there instead.

Chrysta's stomach dropped, and her eyes started to burn with tears. The dream felt so real that she was shocked that her black dress was not there. She reached out and touched the pink dress and sighed. It wasn't real. None of it was real.

The phone she got from Tommy chirped, and she glanced at the screen. "Good morning. Still going to the concert, beautiful?" he asked.

She glared at the pink dress. But she sighed. "Yes," she replied. "I hate this dress, but I have to go to the concert and play. It's the right thing to do. Just promise not to laugh tonight."

"Wouldn't dream of it," he replied. "I'll see you there."

She sighed again and got ready for school. It was a disappointment, knowing that her dress was lost to her, but really, what did she expect.

It had been a dream.

.....

When Chrysta got to school, she found Chloe and went up to her during lunch. "I'll be at the concert tonight," she said. "You don't have to do the solos."

"Oh, thank God," Chloe said. "I wasn't looking forward to trying to play your parts tonight."

"Wait, what do you mean?" asked Mary.

"I... wasn't going to the concert tonight. But I changed my mind. I should go. It's only right," Chrysta explained. "Just, please don't laugh when you see me. Or take pictures."

Mary and Chloe shared a look. "I don't understand," Mary said. "Why would we laugh?"

"You'll see," Chrysta said with a sigh.

Once she got home, Chrysta ate dinner with her father and made sure he had called for a car to pick her up for the concert. She went up the stairs to her bedroom, a feeling of dread settling in her bones. The dress was hideous, but she had to go and play her parts.

She was astounded when the black dress was waiting for her in the wardrobe.

She laughed in disbelief and looked in the wardrobe for the pink dress. It was nowhere to be found. Did her father have a change of heart? She wasn't sure.

Was it Tommy? Sure, she could imagine him breaking into the house and finding the dress for her. But that didn't explain the gold lace. She reached out tentatively with one hand and ran it down the side. It was real. And if it was real, then the dream... did that really happen?

She decided that she would worry about the dream later. Right now, she had a concert to get to.

She put on the dress and found a black fur stole to keep herself warm. She wore her hair up in a large bun, finding some gold hairpins in the shape of leaves and flowers to decorate her hair. She didn't have much makeup but could put on some lipstick and dark eyeshadow. She checked herself in the mirror, smiled, and grabbed her violin case to get to the concert.

As she descended the stairs, her father was waiting for her at the door. He wasn't looking at her, but when he heard her approach, he turned to her. Judging by how his eyes widen, he did not expect to see her in the black dress, and he scowled as she neared.

"What are you doing in that dress?" he asked. "I thought I told you it wasn't appropriate."

She shrugged. "I found it in my wardrobe. I thought I was allowed to wear it."

"No, I forbid it. Go change to the other one."

"I can't," Chrysta said with a smug smile. "The pink dress is gone."

His eyes narrowed. "What do you mean, gone? What did you do to it?"

"Nothing," Chrysta said. Which was true. She didn't do anything to the pink dress. Burning it had been part of a dream. She smiled at her father. "Mom said she liked this dress better."

Jozef York's mouth opened in shock, and Chrysta used it as an opportunity to move past him to the car waiting outside. As she settled in the car, and it left the curb, she glanced at her father to see him scowling from the door as they moved away.

.....

Chrysta was running late, and ran to the band room without looking for Tommy. She stored her stole and then went to warm her instrument up. Mary and Chloe saw her and crowded around her. "You're late!" Mary cried. "Have you seen Tommy?"

"No, I haven't. Why?" Chrysta asked.

Mary and Chloe exchanged a look and flashed evil grins at Chrysta. "Oh, you'll see," Chloe giggled. Chrysta was surprised. She didn't know Chloe could laugh like that.

"What? What is it?" she asked with a smile.

"You'll see," Mary just echoed.

Chrysta warmed up with the others. Several minutes before the curtain call, the orchestra traveled as a group to the auditorium. The first piece was the first movement of Brahms' Violin Concerto. Chrysta's solo was three minutes after it started, so Mr. Hansen wanted her to wait off stage and walk on when it was her time to play. "Add to the drama," he had explained to her with a wink. She tried to find Tommy in the seats she could see, but couldn't spot him. She bit her lower lip. Had he left?

Mr. Hansen walked onto the stage, and the audience clapped as he bowed. He held his hands up and started the first movement. Chrysta was aware of someone sneaking into an empty seat in the front row, but couldn't make out who it was with the house lights so low. She took a breath to calm her nerves and started walking on stage when Mr. Hansen gestured to her.

Halfway to her spot, she finally made out the latecomer in the front row. Tommy wore a black suit with a black tie and vest, a red shirt underneath, and black cowboy boots on his feet. He had a bouquet of roses in his lap and was grinning from ear to ear. While she stared at him in shock, he kissed his fingertips and offered his hand.

She snapped out of her surprise when Mr. Hansen started to wildly wave his hand at her. She was about to miss her intro. Chrysta felt tears in her eyes but blinked them away and walked to her place on stage. She quickly recovered, put the violin to her chin, and started to play.

So weird that she would have this reaction, playing in front of Tommy. She had played for him a dozen times now, but knowing he was sitting in that front-row seat made her deliriously happy. She had to keep herself from staring at Tommy's infectious grin and force herself to watch Mr. Hansen instead.

The first movement moved onto the second one, and finally, the third, the 40-minute concerto flying by in a blur. As the last note died, the audience broke into a round of applause, giving the orchestra a standing ovation. Chrysta gave a small bow, but before she could sit down, Mr. Hansen pulled her to the front of the stage to accept Tommy's roses.

"Thank you," she said with a small smile as Tommy gave her a kiss on the hand.

The orchestra played the rest of their music, Christmas songs for each section. There was another round of applause when the Christmas carols ended, and the curtain was drawn. Mary ran up to Chrysta while laughing. "I have never seen you play like that!" she cried.

"Never had anyone to play like that for," confessed Chrysta, smiling so hard her face hurt.

The girls went back to the band room for their cases and jackets. Someone had set up dessert in the courtyard, where they usually ate lunch, and the girls went outside with the rest of the orchestra to mingle with the audience. Chrysta said a quick hello to the Jacksons but then went looking for Tommy, getting stopped ever so often by members of the audience congratulating her on an excellent performance. She finally found Tommy at the other end of the courtyard with Mr. Hansen. They seemed to be having a heated debate.

"I'm sorry, Cage's *4'33"* is not music," Tommy was saying. "It's just lazy."

"Oh, but it's not lazy, Mr. Monroe, it's art," Mr. Hansen said with a grin.

"It's the auditory equivalent of putting a blank canvas on the wall and saying the viewer makes their own art by viewing it. You don't even need to have any performers, they just sit on their hands the entire time," Tommy complained.

"Sounds fun," Chrysta joked as she linked arms with Tommy. He glanced at her with a grin. "Have you two been introduced?" she asked.

"Yes, Miss Jackson acquainted us," Mr. Hansen said. "She was the one who thought you should get your flowers during the concert. That was a marvelous performance, Miss York. You should be very proud of yourself." Mr. Hansen gestured at Tommy. "Your friend here was saying something about you playing Paganini for him? We may have to set up a solo concert for you in the spring."

Chrysta groaned. "Sorry, Mr. Hansen, I'm horrible at playing his music." She glanced at Tommy. "Maybe I can convince Tommy to play instead."

"Me? Oh no, no, no, no, beautiful, I'll leave Paganini to the professionals," Tommy said with a smile.

Mr. Hansen chuckled at the couple and then saw someone waving to him. "Pardon me," he said and melted into the crowd. The wind picked up, and Chrysta shivered. Tommy brought her closer to him. "Thank you for coming," Chrysta told him again. "It really means a lot to me."

"The pleasure was all mine, beautiful," he said softly. He looked at some of Chrysta's classmates. "I think that dress is going to earn you a few admirers tonight."

Chrysta didn't even glance where he was looking. "Well, their loss. I'm already seeing someone."

"Oh, really? Who?" Tommy joked.

"Oh, a very handsome man, tall, dreadlocks, plays piano, violin, and guitar, sometimes the ukulele," Chrysta joked. She slowly gave him a hug under his jacket with the one arm not holding her roses. "Currently dressed in a very handsome suit."

"Sounds like a real catch," he joked while giving her a kiss on the forehead.

"Hey, let me see some space between you two," Mary said as she came up with Chloe and Mark. "You clean up nice, Monroe," she joked, and he gave a small bow.

Mark gave Tommy a scowl and gestured at the flowers. "Why did you have to bring those, man? Now Chloe won't shut up about them."

"Oh, just making sure the star of the show gets some of the attention she deserves," Tommy admitted. Chrysta tipped the bouquet towards him, and he tugged two roses out, handing one to Mary and one to Chloe. "Doesn't mean we can't share, though."

Chloe giggled while Mark frowned some more. Mary sighed and shook her head. "Horrible flirt," she called Tommy, although she was grinning when she said it.

The group talked for a few minutes, occasionally interrupted by someone praising Chrysta on her solos. Chloe kept frowning at her until she snapped her fingers. "Now I see what is wrong. You changed the lace on the dress. Wasn't it silver?"

"Oh yeah," Mary agreed. "You're right. How did you change it?" she asked Chrysta.

Chrysta froze. If it was just her and Mary, she would talk about the dream and not worry about her friend thinking she was crazy. But with Tommy and the others here, she wasn't free to talk about her dead mother's visit. She bit her lip. "Um, it's a long story," she said. "But someone said they liked the gold better, and I agreed with her."

"Who?" Mary asked innocently.

Chrysta felt some panic. She didn't want to lie. Tommy squeezed her arm, and she glanced at him. "Nevermore?" he asked.

"Nevermore," she said, and he nodded.

"So, Mary, when are you and I playing Brahms' Cello Sonata together?" Tommy asked in an almost too loud voice. Mary glared at him while Chloe looked confused.

"Nevermore?" asked Chloe.

"I don't know. It's some code word they use when trying to be secretive," Mary explained.

"Hm, weirdos in their natural habitat," Chloe joked. "Are you two coming to the orchestra after party? My house, no end time."

"No thanks, I still have nightmares from Halloween because of your mother," Tommy said.

Chloe tried to look offended. "Mom says that she is just looking for husband number two. You should be honored."

"Oh, I'm thrilled," Tommy replied dryly, making Chrysta laugh.

"I would love to come, but father says I have to get home," Chrysta explained. She sighed as she saw the car driver coming towards her. "Actually, that is my cue to leave."

Chrysta hooked one hand in Tommy's tie and tugged him down, standing on her toes to close the distance. He chuckled as she gave him a kiss on the lips but returned it with no comment. After several moments, she broke off the kiss, noticing Mary's shock and Chloe's smirk. She blushed. "Goodnight, everyone," she said, quickly walking away to get to the waiting car. She glanced back and waved, Tommy lifting his hand to his lips to give her one last kiss goodbye.

. . . . .

Jozef York was in his study, nursing a drink. Chrysta had returned several hours earlier and gone to her bedroom, carrying roses and a smile that made her look so beautiful. She was looking more like her mother every day. Bright and elegant and able to command a room with that smile. The driver had confirmed that she was with someone after the concert, someone who fit the description of one Thomas Monroe.

"You were supposed to watch her, not become infatuated, you idiot," York said to himself, taking a sip of bourbon. But maybe he shouldn't be surprised.

"Mom said she liked this dress better."

Why did that statement haunt York so much? Because it implied Chrysta had been talking to her mother. Cassia would have chosen that black dress for their daughter. He was sure of it. Cassia York, with her own bright smile, love of dark clothes, and infectious laugh. Jozef was amazed that Chrysta had taken after her mother, even after Cassia's death a decade earlier.

York had searched the third-floor bedroom as soon as Chrysta left, confirming that his daughter's black dress was not a double. Somehow she had gotten into the room without tripping any of the wards. A single black feather was his only clue. Somehow that blasted bird got into a locked room and transported the dress. He wanted to feel annoyed but felt an odd sense of pride instead.

What abilities did his daughter have now? What would it be like to help her develop them? How many more would show themselves over time? Maybe he could convince the others to leave her alone. Perhaps she could help them control their enemies.

No, if he knew his daughter (and of course he knew her well), she did not have the heart to rule over others. Especially by force.

Her fate had been decided already, long before she was born. Long before he had been born, even. There was no changing course now.

There was a knock on the door, and a servant brought in Jacobs, Frost, and Guerra. York tried not to smile at the other two men who gave Guerra a wide berth. York found it such a source of amusement that he was the only one not afraid of the Butcher.

"We are going to test Chrysta tomorrow night," York stated as he swirled his drink. "But, I think I have better bait that can be used."

"Why now?" asked Frost. Always the contrarian. York tried to not show any annoyance.

"She is showing signs of clairvoyance," York explained.

Guerra chuckled with his dead smile. "We can't have her speaking to the spirits around here."

"No, we can't," York agreed. "Unfortunately, I believe the slave can no longer be trusted. I will send him away."

"No need to worry," Frost said with an evil smile. "I have just the person to help." Frost glanced at York. "For her alone," he said.

"For her alone," York replied, almost without thinking. Yes, all of this was for her, their Lady. A plan put into motion centuries ago. One that Chrysta held such an essential role in.

Too bad, it meant she would die.

16

Chrysta spent Saturday by herself, mostly practicing music outside and doing homework. She would find herself staring at the roses in her room dreamily and remembering the concert from the night before with a goofy grin on her face. If her father disapproved of the flowers, he did not make a comment at lunch or dinner. He had not mentioned the black dress, which now lived inside the wardrobe. Chrysta considered it a small victory.

Once night fell, the first snow of the season started to fall. Chrysta wrapped herself up in a blanket and went out to her balcony to enjoy the weather. She loved how quiet the city got as it snowed and loved watching it slowly build until everything was white and puffy.

Suddenly Poe dropped down on the table and started to hop around, croaking loudly. "Hey, Poe, what's wrong?" she asked. Chrysta tried to pet the bird to calm him down, but he would jump out of her reach, squawking loudly. She got a horrible feeling in her stomach. Was Tommy okay?

She headed inside to get her contraband phone out of its hiding spot when someone pounded on her door. She hesitated. If it was the guards, she couldn't let them see the phone. She went to the door instead, the pounding still happening. She was shocked when she recognized Peter when she opened the door.

"Quick," he nearly shouted. "Tommy is in the park. He's hurt. I think someone jumped him."

"What?"

"He's in the park near here. He was barely awake. I think someone mugged him for money."

Chrysta sprang into action, grabbing some boots and getting them on as Peter waited. Poe was still outside, hopping on the table, and croaking loudly, but she ignored him and closed the door. She joined Peter, and they ran downstairs. Chrysta didn't even pause to get a jacket to cover her light sweater. She was surprised that her father and the guards did not see them leave and stop them.

They ran several blocks, not meeting anyone on the streets. When they made it to the park, Peter tugged on her hand and led her deep into the trees.

After several minutes, Chrysta tried to tug her hand back. Something wasn't right. If Tommy was busking in the park, he wouldn't be this far into the trees. There was no foot traffic this late for him to make money. "Wait!" she said, digging her heels into the ground. "Where is Tommy?"

"He's this way!" Peter said, tugging on her hand. She pulled back and broke off Peter's hold on her.

"No, where is he?"

Peter bounced up and down excitedly, looking at Chrysta and then glancing deeper into the park. "Come on!" he cried, walking several feet and gesturing to her. "He's this way!"

Chrysta paused, bad feeling returning. She slowly shook her head. "No, I don't think so."

Peter's look of distress slowly melted, and he laughed. "Sorry," he said with a chuckle. "Was my acting that bad?" He started to walk back towards her.

Chrysta folded her arms. Now that her panic was fading, she became acutely aware of the cold and shivered. Anger flared up, however. "Why would you lie like that?"

Peter casually shrugged. "I figured it was the only way to get you out of the house. Since you like that thing."

Chrysta blinked, then felt her face flush in anger. "Don't call Tommy a thing."

Peter barked a laugh. "You don't even know what it is, but you like it anyway."

Chrysta glowered at Peter and then turned around to walk back home. Suddenly Peter ran in front of her and shoved her. She almost lost her balance in shock and shouted as she stumbled.

"What are you doing?" she asked but pulled back as Peter got in her face. He was no longer smiling.

"Chloe told me you two were kissing last night," Peter said with a growl. Chrysta tried to move back, and he followed her further into the park. "It was all she would talk about today. How *cute* it was. I still don't know what you see in that thing."

"At least he was at the concert," Chrysta said, trying to keep her voice even. If she kept him talking, maybe she could run. "You didn't even show up."

"I learned how to play the violin for you, and you don't even notice," Peter continued, not acknowledging what she said. "You never gave me a chance." He shrugged. "Well, not like we could actually have a future together. But maybe we can have some fun tonight."

Oh no. Chrysta's stomach dropped. How could she have been so stupid and let him get her alone like this? She never thought she would miss her home with its multitude of guards.

She stopped trying to back up and waited until Peter was leaning into her face. She grabbed his shirt, pulled, tried to knee him in the groin, and then ran when he tripped. He shouted something, but she didn't look back.

Chrysta ran for a few minutes, the sounds of Peter close behind her. She tried to not look behind her, but he caught up to her and grabbed her. She yelped, and he clamped a hand over her mouth as he lifted her up, legs kicking the air uselessly.

"Now, here is something I want to ask you," Peter growled in her ear as she struggled. He put her down but then forced her to turn around. "Was that your first kiss? From that *thing*? Maybe you should get a kiss from a real man."

He kissed her roughly. She tried to slap him to stop, but he wouldn't. She got his lower lip in her mouth and bit down. He shouted and pushed her away. "Shit!" he cursed, slapping her on the face.

Chrysta stumbled, tears stinging her eyes. She panted for a few moments, trying to clear her head. Run, she needed to run, but before she could get to her feet, Peter pulled her up with a fistful of her hair in his hand. She hissed in pain, but the murderous look on his face told her he didn't care.

"Now, that is some horrible technique," Peter snarled. He had some blood on his chin, and he glanced at his thumb when he wiped it away. "Definitely have to break you of that habit."

Peter slapped her again, hard enough to make her ears ring. He was trying to pull her into the trees, and Chrysta dug in her heels. He cursed again and raised his hand.

"Enough!" she growled. "Don't touch me!" And then his raised hand was glowing gold. He looked like he was trying to move his arm, but it was being held in place. He grunted with the effort of trying to move.

"Let me go!" she shouted. But Peter didn't, so Chrysta *flexed*, and there was the sound of a muted snap. Peter yelped and grabbed the arm with his other hand, letting her go.

She walked backward from him, not letting him out of her sight while she rubbed the sore spot on her scalp. He was cradling his arm close to his chest. "You broke my arm!" he cried. He started to stalk towards her.

"Stop!" she shouted, and the flexing feeling happened again, and there was a flash of golden light that hurt her eyes and sent Peter flying backward at least a dozen feet.

For a few seconds, Chrysta stood panting, actually worried that she may have hurt him. But he started to moan and curse on the ground, so she turned around and ran.

She went deeper into the park, the opposite direction of her home, but instinct told her she had to hide. She found the outdoor theatre and ran through the seats up to the stage. The stage was bare except for a fake tree. She quickly ducked behind it and tried to control her breathing.

Stupid, stupid, stupid, she chanted in her mind as her heart slowed. So dumb letting Peter get her out here alone. She needed help and didn't even have her phone with her.

Chrysta thought about the dream with her mother and how she was able to move the dress. Could she do that now? Get herself back home without Peter knowing? She tried to think of her room—

warm, safe, behind glass and stone and guards, oh, she will never complain about the guards again, never again

—but she couldn't get that flexing feeling to happen again. Didn't find herself home, no matter what she tried to imagine.

Poe. If she couldn't move herself, maybe she could move the raven. She closed her eyes, took a deep breath, and thought about the bird instead. There was a soft *pop,* and suddenly he was in front of her, squawking.

She gently shushed him and rubbed his head. "Shhhh, Poe, I'm sorry." He quieted down and cocked his head at her. "Were you trying to warn me about Peter? I'm sorry I didn't listen. Can you go get Tommy?"

The bird moved his head in the other direction. He croaked a soft "Tommy!" and then took flight, disappearing into the dark sky. Chrysta brought her knees up to her chest and waited.

.....

Tommy felt the summons and made his way to the York mansion. There were more guards around, some sneering at him as he was led into the study. York waited by the fire, drink in one hand and cane in the other.

"You are not to contact Chrysta anymore," York said without preamble. "You are not to see her, call her, leave notes, or try to communicate in any way. Am I clear?"

"Clear," Tommy growled back. It didn't surprise him, really. The winter solstice was in two weeks. York would want Chrysta to stay home to keep an eye on her for whatever they had planned. What York didn't know about was the phone Tommy had given Chrysta. He just needed to use someone like Mary to get a message to her.

They could make all the rules they wanted; Tommy had enough practice in bending them.

York dismissed him, and Tommy headed outside. He thought about trying to sneak into Chrysta's room anyway, say goodbye in person, and tell her something, anything, so she didn't wonder if he had disappeared again. *I'm not abandoning you, I'm here, I will keep you safe.*

He had a plan. It was a stupid plan. It would result in a lot of pain, suffering, and possibly death on his part. But if it worked, she would be safe from her father. If it took Tommy dying to make sure she was protected, well, that would not be anyone's loss but his own.

Tommy was making his way down the street, debating whether he wanted to get a drink or not, when Poe suddenly appeared in front of him, squawking frantically, flapping so he was at eye level. Tommy hopped back, throwing an arm up to protect his face. "What the fuck, Poe?!" he shouted, but he suddenly realized that what he thought was random squawking was actually words.

"Chrysta! Park! Hurt! Come! Come help!" Poe croaked desperately. "Chrysta! Help!"

Tommy lowered his arm. "Show me," he commanded, and Poe flew away, Tommy running behind him.

·····

Chrysta stayed behind the tree, shivering, from the cold or fear, she couldn't tell. She was trying to keep quiet, listening for Peter. He was still looking for her and not being calm about it, and she could occasionally hear his panting and cursing. Every time he went away, she would start counting from one and start over if she heard him again.

...374, 375, 376...

Had Poe understood her and found Tommy? What if Tommy was at the club? How long would it take Tommy to get here if Poe did find him? She couldn't count on him saving her.

...498, 499, 500, 501...

Slow, even breaths. Count slowly. Keep still, keep your head. If Peter can't find you, maybe he will give up. It is just a few blocks to get home. Get to the street, and he shouldn't be able to hurt you.

...752, 753, 754...

She had a thought and started giggling, trying to stifle her hysterical laugh into her hand. Everyone always asked her why she loved horror movies so much, but maybe they would help save her tonight.

...997, 998, 999, 1,000.

She slowly stood up, climbing off the stage and walking through the seats towards the exit, steps deafening to her ears. The snow was really falling now, and Chrysta folded her arms over her chest. She tried to keep her breathing even, ears strained for any noise. Nothing. She picked up the pace.

Chrysta saw the exit, and she rushed to get to the street. Before she made it there, Peter stepped out from some brushes by the gate, right arm cradled close to his body. His face was twisted in rage, and Chrysta stopped while she was still about a dozen feet from him. "Stay away," she said, trying to sound stern, but her voice trembled in fear.

"You know, I was supposed to only scare you, but now, I can't let you go back until I get some revenge."

"Peter, I'm sorry, really I am," she stammered as he started to walk towards her. She began to back up in retreat. "I don't know what is going on, but I can't really control it."

"Oh, we know that," he growled.

She stopped moving back. "Wait, what do you mean 'we?'"

Suddenly he lunged toward her and grabbed her arm. She yelped and tried to get away, but he dug his fingers into her arm until she winced. She attempted to raise her hand to blind him, hurt him, anything, but only useless sparks appeared. He smirked.

"Out of juice already?" he said in a mocking tone. He pulled Chrysta close, twisting his fingers into her arm until she cried again. "Come on, hit me. I dare you."

Suddenly, an arm wrapped around Peter's neck, lifting him off his feet. He let go of Chrysta as his right arm was twisted behind him. Peter screamed but clamped his mouth shut when the arm at his throat shifted, and a hand pressed a knife to his throat. Chrysta saw Tommy's face over Peter's shoulder, set in rage as Peter squirmed in his arms. Poe landed on Chrysta's shoulder, croaking loudly at the two fighting figures.

"You okay?" Tommy asked Chrysta as Peter whimpered, voice low in steely rage. Chrysta nodded numbly.

"His arm, it's broken," she mumbled.

"Oh, is it?" Tommy asked as he raised his eyebrows. He pulled Peter's arm higher, and Peter gave a shout. "Would suck if someone used it to hurt him."

"No! Tommy, please," Chrysta pleaded. "Please let him go."

Tommy's look of cold rage softened, and he glared at Peter's back. He planted a foot on Peter's backside and kicked hard, sending the blonde flying. Tommy spat on the ground and walked over to Chrysta. He ran his fingers across her face, and she shivered. He shrugged out of his jacket and wrapped her up in it. "I'm sorry," Chrysta said, tears starting to run down her face.

"Why the fuck are you apologizing, Chrysta?" he said softly.

"He said you were hurt, and I followed him out here alone. I was so stupid. I'm sorry," Chrysta said again, tears in her eyes.

Tommy wiped at her eyes. "Only one who needs to apologize is that asshole. You're in shock. Let's get you home."

There was a shout, and Tommy looked behind them before pulling Chrysta in front of him and shielding her. He grunted, and when Chrysta looked behind them, she saw that Peter had stabbed Tommy in the right shoulder. Tommy slashed out with his left hand, a flash of light following a wide arc. Peter fell back with a shout, and Chrysta realized Tommy had cut him with his knife.

"Tommy!" Chrysta yelled as he pulled Peter's knife out. Tommy looked at the blood-stained weapon and then glared at the boy on the ground. "We need to get you to the hospital," she cried.

"I'm fine," Tommy snapped, throwing Peter's knife into the trees. "Just let me take care of this asshole."

"No!" she cried. She glanced at Peter to see him rolling on the ground, hand on his face. Chrysta wanted to hate him, but she felt numb. "Just... take me home. Please."

Tommy scowled, but he just nodded, took her arm, and started to guide her home.

They walked down the street, no one in sight. And what a sight the couple would make. Chrysta, bloodied and bruised, clutching at a too-big jacket; Tommy in just a light shirt with a growing bloodstain, scowling, Poe perched on his left shoulder. She regularly glanced at Tommy, trying to read his expression, but his face was hard to read. Once they were a block from her home, a guard saw them coming and shouted. By the time they got to the front gate, Guerra was waiting for them. Poe took off.

"Miss York, aren't you a spectacle!" Guerra said with that false smile Chrysta hated. She wondered if he ever sounded genuinely happy, or was false cheer all he could manage. "How about you go to your bedroom and clean up?"

Chrysta removed Tommy's jacket and handed it to him. She started to make her way inside when her stomach dropped. "Tommy wasn't the one who hurt me. It was Peter," she explained. She didn't want them to blame Tommy. "I don't want Peter inside the house anymore."

"Noted, Miss York. Now, please, head inside," Guerra said. The smile was fading from his face, and Chrysta glanced at Tommy nervously.

"It's okay, beautiful, go inside," Tommy told her.

"Are you going to the hospital?" she asked. "Are you going to be okay?"

He gave her a small smile. "I'll be fine, beautiful. Go."

Chrysta nodded and finally entered the house, climbing the stairs to her bedroom.

.....

As soon as Tommy was sure Chrysta was out of hearing range, he rounded on Guerra, shoving a finger in the man's face. "What the fuck, Guerra?" he growled. "All this security, and you can't make sure she's safe?"

Guerra blinked. "Don't worry, Mr. Monroe. She was never in any real danger."

"Bullshit."

Guerra gestured to Tommy, ignoring his outburst, and they went inside. They went into the study, York, Frost, and Jacobs waiting for them.

"What happened?" asked York, using his cane to get up and stalk up to Tommy.

"Mr. Monroe just escorted Miss York home," Guerra explained.

York glared. "You were under orders not to contact her."

"I don't fucking care, that asshole was going to hur—" Tommy started, his complaint cut off when York backhanded him, using the hand that had the ring on it.

Tommy reeled for a second but recovered and let out a deep-throated growl. He let the knife drop from his left sleeve into his hand and swung at York. The blade stopped inches from York's throat, and Tommy grunted from the effort to close the distance.

Both Jacobs and Frost stepped back, but neither York nor Guerra moved. Guerra kept that false smile on his face, chuckling while York just raised one eyebrow. York held up the hand with the ring on it. "Know your place," he said in a low voice, and Tommy stopped trying to stab him and dropped his hand.

Two guards entered the study, supporting Peter between them, cradling his arm and blood streaming down his face. He balked when he saw Tommy and tried to backpedal out of the room. "Keep that thing away from me!" he shouted.

Jacobs went up to his nephew as the guards left the room. "What happened?" he asked.

"I did what you told me to do!" Peter stammered. "I got Chrysta out of the house, threatened her, slapped her, and she broke my arm! And then this *thing* came up and slashed my face!"

"How did she break your arm?" York asked as Tommy felt his chest constrict in rage. He knew Peter was involved with these bastards, but hearing him say it was another thing.

"She used magic," Peter continued, flinching when he heard Tommy growl. "You didn't say she was that strong. I wasn't expecting it."

"And what color was it?" York asked.

"Gold."

In the ensuing silence, Tommy didn't think any of them dared breathe, including himself. York shook his head slightly. "Are you sure?"

"Very sure," the young man replied.

Frost and Jacobs rushed over to York, and they started to fiercely whisper. Peter looked at Guerra. "Well, are you going to punish him?" he demanded, gesturing to Tommy.

"For?" Guerra asked. "He protected Miss York."

"By attacking me!"

"Looks like he was returning the favor," Guerra grumbled as the smile died on his face, and he gestured to the bloodstain growing on Tommy's shirt.

"Oh, you will be sacrificing her in two weeks but want to protect her now?" Peter asked sarcastically. Tommy felt his stomach drop as he looked at Peter in shock.

"Peter!" York shouted, and the young man flinched. "Hold your tongue!" York pointed at Tommy. "You have your orders. Do not contact my daughter, and do not come back here. Understood? Now, get out!"

Tommy nodded and headed out, glaring at Peter as he went. As soon as he got outside, he circled around the mansion to check on Chrysta. Her room was dark.

Poe dropped down onto his good shoulder and croaked. "Chrysta?" the bird seemed to ask.

"Yeah, we need to get her out of there," Tommy confirmed, rubbing the wound on his other shoulder. "Before those bastards really hurt her." And he turned reluctantly from the mansion.

ᴄ 17 ᴐ

Chrysta felt like she was in a fog, walking up to her bedroom. She sat on her bed, getting her boots off. She meant to get up, and maybe take a shower, but suddenly all her strength left her. She lifted the covers and laid down, fully clothed. Just a few minutes to lie down. Then she would feel better, more like herself. She thought she heard raised voices but made the mistake of closing her eyes, and sleep took her.

She woke up slowly, feeling like something was wrong but not quite remembering what. It was only when she realized that the sun was shining in her window that she got up. It was afternoon. She had slept most of the day. Then the memories of the night before came back. Peter, the park, him attacking her, him stabbing Tommy.

Tommy.

Chrysta carefully got out of bed, wincing at the dirt- and blood-stained sheets; she took them off and left them at the door. Into the bathroom, she grimaced in the mirror at the crusted blood on her chin and the bruises on her arm. The sweater was a loss, too much blood dried black and too many holes to repair. The jeans went into the laundry. "Are you alright?" she texted Tommy before stepping into the shower. She felt a hundred times better after getting clean. She dressed and got her contraband phone. Tommy had not responded, so Chrysta switched over to her messages with Mary.

"Why weren't you at school?"

"Are you okay?"

"Hey, seriously, give me a call when you can."

Chrysta stared at the messages in confusion until she glanced at the date. Monday? That couldn't be right; that meant she had been asleep for almost two days. Her feeling of dread started to grow. She dialed Mary's number.

"Oh, thank the lord, sis, you had me worried," Mary answered. "I was about to call the police to check on you."

Despite her anxiety, Chrysta smiled. "Sorry to worry you. I have been asleep for forty hours, apparently," she explained.

"Forty hours?! What happened?"

Chrysta sighed as she let herself out on the balcony. "Peter came over Saturday night. He said Tommy was hurt and lured me out of the house. He attacked me. Evidently, he wasn't happy that I kissed Tommy."

"Oh, that asshole, when I find him I'm killing him."

"He wasn't at school?"

"No, but I was more worried about you," Mary said. "What happened?"

"Well, remember the fire I started on Thanksgiving?"

"Yeah?"

"I broke his arm with a thought."

There was stunned silence on the other end of the line. "Well, as far as parlor tricks go, that is an impressive one," Mary said after a few minutes. "Then what?"

"Well, I asked Poe to find Tommy," she said, not mentioning how she summoned Poe out of thin air, "and before I could leave the park, Peter found me and wouldn't let me leave. Tommy knocked him down before Peter could hurt me more, but then Peter stabbed him."

"Holy shit!" Mary cried. Chrysta heard Selena talking in the background. "No, mom, you have to hear this." And Mary put Chrysta on speaker. "Say what happened again."

"Peter came over on Saturday and lured me out of the house. He attacked me and then stabbed Tommy when Tommy tried to stop him."

"Holy shit," Selena said. "Are you okay?"

"Yeah, Tommy got me home. I guess I had a concussion? Because I went to sleep and just now woke up."

Selena started to curse in Spanish. "And your father didn't take you to the hospital?"

"No," Chrysta confirmed.

"Okay, we will talk more about this tomorrow. We need to speak to Tommy too, maybe bring charges against Peter."

"Alright," Chrysta said. "I'll call Tommy, make sure he's okay."

"Take care, little one," Selena said, and they ended the call.

Chrysta tried calling Tommy, but the call went straight to voicemail. It was strange, he always answered, unless he was at the club.

Chrysta let herself out of her room and went downstairs to her father's study. Her father and Guerra were there in front of the fire, speaking, an amber drink in her father's hand. "Ah, Miss York!" Guerra said. "You are finally awake."

"What happened Saturday night?" she asked. Mostly looking at her father.

"Well, Mr. Jacobs is no longer welcomed here," Mr. Guerra answered. "I apologize for the lack of security that allowed him to slip in."

"And Tommy? Did he go to the hospital?"

"Alas, your friend had some powerful words about what happened Saturday night. He blamed you. I don't think you will be seeing him anymore."

Chrysta felt her stomach lurch. She knew that couldn't be true. If Tommy wasn't returning, it was because of her father, not what happened on Saturday. She swallowed past the lump in her throat. "I think we need to talk to the police. I want to make sure Peter doesn't bother me at school."

"There will be no more school," her father stated, and Chrysta's heart stopped.

"You can't do that," Chrysta almost growled when she recovered.

"I can and will."

Chrysta balled her hands into fists and felt the flex happening in her chest. The glass in her father's hand started to shake, and a ringing sound reverberated in the room. Jozef glared at his daughter as she glowered back, not moving his hand from the drink. Mr. Guerra smiled, looking between the two of them.

"So was that your plan along? Have Peter attack me and then use it as an excuse to lock me away?"

Her father's jaw clenched before his face went neutral again. "My apologies Chrysta, I truly felt Peter was a fitting suitor." He took a sip from the now-silent glass. "But that is neither here nor there. You will stay home, safe. No more going out, no more dates, no more time at the Jacksons."

Chrysta relaxed her fists and crossed her arms. "Fine."

"Are you hungry?" her father asked.

"Yes," Chrysta confessed.

"You can eat in your room." And with that, Chrysta turned around and stalked to her room.

Once the door was closed, Chrysta started to prepare a backpack with her things. Violin, clothes, all the money she had, her only photo of her mother. She only paused when someone knocked on her door, throwing the backpack under her bed. The servant dropped off some chicken alfredo, and she sat down to eat. She would text Mary after eating and run away. Maybe Tommy could help her hide from her father. She just knew she wasn't staying in that house another night.

As she chewed, Chrysta found herself getting tired. By the time her meal was half-way eaten, she was yawning and rubbing her eyes. Alright, maybe a small nap, and then she would head out.

Chrysta barely had the energy to hide her phone and put fresh sheets on her bed before lying down with heavy eyes. Before she knew it, she was asleep.

.....

Chrysta woke up to sunlight that told her it was morning. She groaned. She would now have to wait until nightfall to try to leave. She grabbed her phone to check her messages, shocked to see about a dozen texts and several missed calls from Mary. Tommy still had not gotten in touch with her.

She called Mary.

"Chrysta! Where have you been?" Mary answered the phone.

"My house. I ate some food after we talked and went back to sleep. Why are you worried?" Chrysta asked.

"Chrysta, it's Thursday. The last time I talked with you was Monday night."

"What?!" Chrysta cried, and she checked her phone. "But, I don't understand, how—" And then it hit her. "The food, my father must have drugged me."

"That's not the only thing," Mary continued. "My mom and I were worried, so we went to your house last night. We asked your father to see you, and this... Chrysta, this girl came out, and she sounded like you and looked like you, but it wasn't you."

Chrysta felt her skin crawl. "I don't remember that," she said.

"Well, I realized it wasn't you when I said something about us both being vampires for Halloween, and she didn't correct me. But Chrysta, this girl, she looked so much like you. It was disturbing."

"Alright, tonight, I'm running away," Chrysta said.

"Good. Will you come to my house?" Mary asked.

"I... don't know. I don't want you guys to get in trouble," Chrysta explained. "I would go to Tommy, but he's not answering any of my texts or calls." Her stomach dropped. "Guerra said he didn't want to talk to me anymore. Maybe he wasn't lying."

"Well, leave and get to my house if you need to. You shouldn't spend another night in that house." There was the sound of a school bell. "I have to go, be safe."

Chrysta paced her room for several minutes and then dialed Tommy's number. It rang several times, each ring making her heart hurt more until he finally picked up. "Oh, Tommy," she sighed, letting go of a breath she was barely aware of holding. "You're okay. I was worried."

"Hey, beautiful," he said, voice strained. "How are you doing?"

"Terrible," she admitted. "I went to sleep Saturday night and woke up on Monday. My father said he was taking me out of school, so I was going to run away, but then I ate some food and just woke up today." She started to pace her room again. "I think my father drugged my food."

"Fuck," he cursed. "Okay, beautiful, I got a plan. But I don't have much time. Listen carefully."

She let herself outside and glanced over the railing of her balcony. She was shocked to see three guards standing right where she and Tommy used to climb down. She felt panic build in her chest. There was no way she could run away now.

"Pack some stuff you need," Tommy continued. "Clothes, violin, anything you would miss if you left it behind."

"Already did," she whispered, sinking to the floor.

"Good. I'm going out of town. Talk to some people who can help you. I'll let you know when I'm back and when I'm coming to get you, alright?" His voice was sounding more forced as he talked.

"Are you hurting? Did you go to the hospital?" she asked.

"I'm good, beautiful," he replied, but she didn't believe him.

"Tommy?"

"Yeah?"

"I'm scared."

Tommy sighed. "I know, Chrysta. Just try to stay strong. Act like you are listening to your father. Make him have a false sense of security, okay?" He sighed again, this time with more pain. "Just remember, I'm not ditching you, okay?"

She felt tears running down her cheeks. "Okay."

"Beautiful?"

"Yeah?" she said, wiping at her face.

"Think of this as a way to force yourself to practice Paganini," he said, and Chrysta laughed, a laugh that almost sounded like a sob.

.....

Tommy sighed as he ended the call. He looked at his left arm and the band that was so hot that it was glowing. Sticking his arm into a pile of snow, Tommy hissed as it sizzled. As he tried to get the band to cool, he removed the bandage on his right shoulder.

The stab wound was a puckered red welt that would be gone in a week. Peter had gotten lucky and hit the muscle that moved Tommy's arm, and he had wasted almost a week waiting for it to heal. Now he needed to get his ass in gear.

He stood, getting on a black sweater and his jacket, rolling his shoulder to make sure it had the range of motion he wanted. Poe dropped down on the rooftop and started to hop around, squawking.

"I'm heading out of town," Tommy started to tell the bird. "You stay here and keep an eye on her. If I'm right, you are her familiar. She needs a friend right now, plus you can help her out of there if I don't come back."

The raven cocked his head to the side and squawked. "Chrysta. Friend," Poe croaked.

"Exactly," Tommy replied.

"Tommy. Friend," Poe croaked again.

Tommy paused. "Well, I would prefer a friend without feathers, but I will take what I can get right now." He scratched the bird's head. "Wish me luck." And he left the rooftop.

18

Mandy let herself into Jazz Nocturne's back door but froze when she heard a banging noise. She cursed to herself. It wouldn't be the first time Mandy got to the club early and bumped into someone robbing it. She just prayed that they didn't have a weapon. She got her taser out and went to investigate.

She found Tommy, head buried in his locker, cursing to himself. She let out a breath. "For crying out loud, Tommy, you scared the shit out of me," she said.

He glanced over his shoulder and went back to banging in the locker. "Sorry, Mandy. I'll be out of your hair in a minute," came his muffled reply.

"What are you doing here? Ben has been trying to get a hold of you."

"Well, I got stabbed in the shoulder, so I've been letting it heal," Tommy said. Mandy blinked at the young man's back. Tending bar, you met many characters, both customers and musicians alike, and Tommy was no exception. But sometimes, the things Tommy said didn't make sense, like how he talked about music from the turn of the century like he had been personally there for a performance. Or telling Ben he played in a club in the 50s. And now, something about being stabbed when he was whaling on the locker with no pain?

There was a final bang, and something shifted in the locker. Tommy gave a bark of triumph as he started throwing items on a nearby table. It took Mandy a minute to realize that it was rolls of money. Lots of it. "Where did all that come from now?" she asked.

"Just because I live on the streets doesn't mean I'm poor," he said with a smirk. "Hiding it here was the safest place I could think of. No one would steal it if they found it." He paused in counting the money. "Well, maybe Ben would steal it. I don't know."

Mandy snorted. "He's not as bad as you think," she chided Tommy and then started to help him count the money. "Why do you need this much cash now? Running away?" she joked.

He winced and started to rub his left arm. "Remember Chrysta? Her father has locked her up for the last week. He's not even letting her go to school. I think he's going to hurt her. I'm helping her get out, hopefully, next week."

"Aw shit," Mandy cursed. She liked the young girl Tommy had found and how Tommy had changed since he met her. He was more content, less surly, and Mandy was happy he found someone so kind. "Well, now I feel like an asshole. So, this may be the last time I see you for a while, huh?"

"Probably," he admitted with a sad smile, and they continued counting.

They made a pile of money for every thousand dollars he had, and when they were done, there were thirteen completed rolls and one roll of about two hundred dollars in ones. The ones went into his pocket, and the rest were going into a compartment in a backpack he had. He paused while putting the money away, grabbed three bundles, and handed them to Mandy. "For you, Jennifer, and Manny," he said.

She sputtered as she held the money. "Tommy, I couldn't," she started to say.

"Yeah, you can. Didn't you mention your kids needed braces?" he asked with a smile, and he started to make his way out the back door.

"Wait!" Mandy cried out, and she ran to him and gave him a hug. His face darkened in a blush, and he hugged her back. "You take care of that girl, alright?" she said. Mandy gave him a kiss on the cheek. "You're a good man, Tommy."

Tommy huffed. "I keep telling you guys, I'm not a nice guy."

"Yes, you are," Mandy argued as she stepped back from him. "I'll tell everyone you said goodbye."

"And tell Jonathon he's a bastard," Tommy joked, and Mandy laughed as he left through the back door.

. . . . .

The next morning, Tommy bought a bus ticket to go north. He sat down in the waiting area, leg bouncing, eager to get moving. The other riders avoided him, and that suited Tommy just fine. The main reason he dressed the way he did, really.

When the bus driver announced it was time to board, Tommy was one of the first people to get on, and he was happy to see that everyone avoided sitting in front, back, and next to him. His guitar and violin went into the compartment above him, his backpack at his feet. He put headphones on and got ready to spend the next few hours pretending no one else existed.

So imagine his surprise when he felt a tug on his jacket thirty minutes into the trip. He cracked an eye open to see a young girl, maybe 6 years old, standing next to him, holding out a cookie. He took the headphones off and smiled at the girl. "What's up, kiddo?"

"Wanna cookie? My grandma made them."

Tommy looked over to the girl's mother to see she was asleep. An older gentleman watched Tommy and the young girl, probably worried about what Tommy would do to her. Tommy grinned and leaned in. "I don't think your mother would like it if you ate a cookie before lunchtime," he said in a loud stage whisper.

"But if you eat one, I can eat one," the girl explained, also in a loud whisper.

Tommy put a hand to his chest like he was offended. "Making me an accomplice to your crimes?"

"What is an a-comp-lance?" she asked.

"Means you are making me do something naughty," Tommy explained.

The girl's eyes got wide. "But you look so sad. A cookie will make you feel better," she explained.

Tommy's smile softened. "Alright, I'll make you a deal. I will eat one, but only after we stop for lunch, and if your mommy says it's okay."

"Aw, okay," she said with a pout. And without another word, she climbed into the seat next to Tommy, putting the cookie back into a baggie.

He raised an eyebrow at the little person sitting to him and sighed. So much for a quiet ride. He held out a hand. "Thomas Monroe. Friends call me Tommy."

"Olivia Jones. Daddy calls me Olive," she said seriously while shaking his hand. "Whatcha listening to?"

Tommy took the headphones jack out of his phone, and Brahms' Violin Concerto started to play. It was one of Chrysta's solos, and Olivia's eyes widen. "Wow, that is so pretty," she said with a grin. Tommy noticed that the older man had a smile on his face and turned away. Tommy assumed the man realized the girl was in good hands.

"Yep. This is from a friend's concert last week," he explained. "Wanna see a picture of her?"

The girl nodded, and Tommy brought up a picture of Chrysta when she first got her dress. Chrysta was looking down and not at the camera, but you could still see her beautiful smile, one hand tucking a strand of long hair behind her ear. Olivia let out a gasp. "She's so pretty!"

Tommy nodded and started rubbing his left arm without thinking. "Yes, she is," he agreed.

"Is she your girlfriend?"

Tommy chuckled. "No, but I do love her a lot." Funny, telling Chrysta directly how he felt was hard, but revealing his feelings to this wholesome little girl was easy.

Olivia rolled her eyes. "Just don't pull her hair if you like her. Boys at school pull my hair, and grandma says they like me. Mommy says that they are just jerks."

"Noted," Tommy said with a grin.

About 45 minutes later, Mrs. Jones woke up. She looked around in a panic when she realized her daughter was not next to her, but spotted Olivia several rows behind her and relaxed. The young girl had broken out her makeup kit and was in the process of painting Tommy's nails bright pink. Tommy already had on red lipstick, and one eye was covered in baby blue eyeshadow, while the other was purple.

Mrs. Jones moved down the aisle to sit across from her daughter and the young man. She felt a pang of regret for thinking the young man was unfriendly based on his clothing and piercings. Obviously, he couldn't be so bad if he let her daughter have free range of his face. "Sorry if she was bothering you," she said with a giggle.

"No bother," he said, inspecting his free hand while Olivia worked on the other. "She just keeps insisting on putting me in spring colors when I told her I'm obviously an autumn." He sighed, putting his head in his hand. "But, I will let the artist do her work." Olivia giggled madly.

When the bus stopped for a break, Mrs. Jones requested that Tommy join them for lunch in the local diner after washing his face, and she did let her daughter share a cookie. Mrs. Jones noticed that he was rubbing his arm and wincing. "You okay?" she asked.

"Oh yeah," he responded. "Just got cursed by an evil wizard."

They climbed back on the bus, and Olivia curled up next to Tommy, covered in his jacket as she slept. "You will make a good dad someday," Mrs. Jones told him.

Tommy balked at her statement. "Me? No, nope, not in a million years," he said, shaking his head. "They say you learn how to parent from your parents, and my father was the worst."

Mrs. Jones smiled as she leaned over to get some hair out of Olivia's face. "But the fact that you think you will do a terrible job shows that you care enough to be better than your father."

Tommy looked at her in shock for a minute and then smiled. "Maybe," he admitted. And he closed his eyes and listened to music for the rest of their ride.

.....

Their next stop was a small village called New Bendigo. Olivia and her mother were continuing north, but Tommy was getting off. Olivia gave him a hug as he got his guitar and violin down.

"Have a good trip, kiddo," he said in goodbye.

New Bendigo was a small town, just a few blocks making up its downtown area, surrounded by modest homes and bungalows. People looked at him, but no one stopped him or seemed upset by his presence. Hopefully, they would think he was a musician just passing through. There was magic there, he could smell it, but there weren't any wards that he could see. The town was mostly normies as far as he could tell.

He ran into his first sorcerer while walking east.

It was a man, tweed suit and bowler hat, a greyhound walking by his side without a leash. Tommy could smell the tang of magic, even half a block away. The man was engrossed in a book and didn't notice Tommy as they passed each other, but the dog sniffed the air and whined. Tommy glanced behind him and ducked into a store, but he could hear the dog barking to alert her owner.

It was a small department store decorated for Christmas, and a single loss prevention guard took notice of Tommy as he made his way to the makeup counter. He grabbed a perfume bottle like he was reading the label while the dog ran in behind him. "Hey, you can't have that dog in here!" the guard yelled as her owner ran inside behind her.

"I'm sorry, I don't know what's got into her!" the man with a hat cried.

Tommy clenched on the bottle in his hand, and it shattered, dousing him in perfume. The smell overwhelmed his sensitive nose, but that was what he was counting on. The dog, who had been ignoring her owner and the guard, stopped and starting sniffing the air. She looked at Tommy but seemed uncertain of what to do next.

"Oh, are you okay?" the girl behind the counter cried. She grabbed some paper towels and started to clean up the stinking mess.

"Yeah, I'm good. I can pay for that if you need me to," Tommy said, accepting some of the frantic girl's towels.

"No, you're fine. I just never have seen them shatter like that," she said.

After a few minutes, Tommy strolled out of the store, the man with the bowler hat still trying to convince his dog to leave.

Tommy continued his way east, passing businesses and houses. He crossed some train tracks and was in the forest, trying to keep a steady pace. He realized that black clothing wasn't the best thing to wear in the snow-covered woods, but he didn't have much choice.

He came upon the wards after about two miles of hiking. Black pieces of wood with white runes, set on trees about 20 feet in the air. Whoever made them was lazy. It would have been better to carve them directly into the trees, but these were just attached with twine. Easier to mess with.

He tied his knife to some rope and threw it as hard as he could. It hit with a *thunk*, and green sparks appeared. Tommy smirked to himself, pulled on the line, dislodged the ward, and got his knife back, leaving the ward where it fell. He started his trek again, ears straining in the silence.

He heard a group crashing in the forest several minutes later and crouched down to let them pass. Four sorcerers with one giant Maine Coon cat familiar draped across her owner's shoulders. They rushed back towards the destroyed ward, the cat scenting the air, but she didn't sense that Tommy was there. He resumed going east when they were out of sight.

He found a stream, and one bank was falling into the water, exposing a large tree's root system. Tommy stuck his instruments and backpack as far into the roots as he could, hoping they would stay dry. If he could come back for them, he would, but right now, he wasn't hopeful of that outcome.

Hope for the best, plan for the worse.

He paused to dip his left arm in the ice-cold stream, sweater rolled up. The band hurt more the longer he was out of his master's reach, and he could only hope to finish his task here quickly.

He continued east, and after three more miles of the dense forest, he finally found it.

The Academy.

It was Neo-Gothic architecture, four stories tall, about the length of two football fields, with towers in each corner of a square structure. It was impressive, although the air was full of magic, thick even in the trees around the building, making Tommy's nose burn and eyes water. The walls could probably talk with how much magic bled through them. Tommy wondered briefly how many of his kind had been brought here. Probably not alive.

He patrolled the grounds as close to the building as he dared. The entrance was facing north, the south end opened onto manicured gardens, the east side faced a river. With the cold and snow, not many people were outside, but with the holidays, he could only assume that the people left lived here full time. There was only one person he needed to find. He prayed to any god listening that he would find them.

Chrysta's life depended on it.

.....

It took four days to find the healer. Four days of stalking in the trees, making sure he wasn't seen, fishing in the river when he was hungry, and keeping the band on his arm from burning too badly. Really, for the most prominent organization for magic in the New World, Tommy was appalled at their security measures. Only one circle of wards? No walls? They had sorcerers walking the grounds, but they and their familiars never spotted him. One came close, but he suspected it was because she was a hunter, her black sword a dead giveaway of her profession. He climbed a tree and waited for them to pass, one hand resting on his knife. The familiar, a caracal, wound his way through the trees, sniffing on the remains of Tommy's lunch. The hunter looked up, but Tommy moved out of her line of sight. They knew he was there; they just couldn't find him.

He saw several adults come and go, staff that didn't live on the grounds and probably lived in New Bendigo. He noted their appearance and cars.

He finally got lucky on Tuesday, when he had almost given up hope, and the band on his arm was becoming agony.

A teacher brought a gaggle of students out to the gardens, and they started working on fire magic. Tommy watched them with interest. It was rare to watch fireballs being tossed around without one of them being aimed at his head.

One of the students slipped up, and a fireball got the arm of her jacket. The teacher was able to put it out almost instantly, but the girl held her arm like it was hurt. Another student was sent running inside, and when he came back, it was with a woman. Glasses, brown hair, slightly overweight, but she had a big smile and kind voice. She held her hands over the student's arm, and with a flash of blue, the girl was better. Although the jacket was probably a lost cause.

Bingo.

The woman with glasses drove a late-model Volkswagen Beetle. Tommy waited until it was time for her to leave before slinking up to her car parked in front. A late-model vehicle meant no car alarm or electronic locks, and he was able to unlock and slip into the trunk, hoping she didn't have to use it. After a few minutes, he heard her walking over the gravel to get into the car and turn it on.

The ride was blessedly short, considering Tommy was folded almost in half. Every bump and turn was torture, on top of the burning on his arm. When the car stopped, it sounded like it was in an enclosed space, and Tommy waited until he heard a door close.

He opened the trunk. He was in a small garage, with enough room for only one car, although the little Bug barely took up half the space. He went to the door—a small laundry room with coats and boots. He went to the second door and cracked it open.

It was a tidy little bungalow, with an open kitchen, a living room, and stairs to the second story on the far wall. Windows showed a tiny backyard that barely had room for a tree and patio set. The healer was on the phone, pacing her living room.

"Yes, Mom, I'll be there for dinner," she was saying. "No, just dinner. Because I need to be at the Academy if anything happens. Yes, one of the other teachers could help out if needed, but the kids need me, Mom."

She paced into her kitchen and grabbed a kettle. She took it to the sink, which was across from Tommy. He eased the door open and waited for her to get off the phone.

"Yeah, well, that is what I do, Mom. Sit around and wait for bad things to happen," she said. "I have gotten very good at crocheting."

There was a noise over the phone; it sounded like laughter. The healer filled the kettle with water. "Yeah, love you too, Mom."

The phone beeped as she hung up, and before she could grab the kettle and turn around, Tommy closed the distance and grabbed her, one hand on her mouth and one arm around her waist.

He winced when the kettle fell to the floor. The healer kicked his shin and bit his hand. He tried shushing her as she struggled, but he didn't let go as she tried to scream. After a few minutes, she stopped, heart pounding so hard Tommy could feel it on his chest. "All done?" he asked, and she nodded after a moment, still breathing hard.

"I'm sorry I'm here. I'm sorry I had to break in," Tommy explained, keeping his voice even. "I don't want to hurt you, but I need to talk to you. I just need a few minutes of you staying calm, okay? I know it's a lot for me to ask, a stranger in your house. But it's important, I swear."

She was calmer but still scared. But after another minute, she nodded. Tommy slowly took his hand off her mouth and backed up.

She whirled around, eyes wide, and he held up his hands to show they were empty. She looked him up and down. "W-who are you?" she panted.

"Someone who doesn't want to hurt you," he said. "I'm going to take off my jacket, okay?"

She didn't say anything, so he slowly took his jacket off, folding it on the counter. When he rolled the left sleeve up, her eyes got even wider. "Is that... Is that a slave band?" she asked.

"Yes," he said.

"They're illegal. No one is even supposed to know how to make bands like that anymore," the healer said.

"Yeah, well, I found the one person who did. Mind if I use the sink?"

She thought about it but nodded. Tommy went to the sink, letting the healer circle behind him. He turned on the cold water and let it run over the band, groaning as the metal cooled.

"Who is your master? They can get in a lot of trouble for using a slave band," she said.

He snorted. "Oh, believe me, he has a lot on his record without adding my slavery to the list." He turned off the water and dried his arm with a towel. "Besides, I'm not here for me."

She looked confused. "You don't want me to help you get that off your arm? I don't know how, but I can find out."

Tommy sighed and leaned on the counter, folding his arms. "I'm here to help my friend, not free myself."

The healer frowned. "Okay. Okay. Who is your friend?"

"Chrysta York," Tommy said. "Jozef York's daughter."

She gave out a bark of laughter. "You want me to help the daughter of Jozef York? I rather help you. You're the victim here, not her."

Tommy sighed. "Look, she is nothing like her father, trust me. For some strange reason, he has kept her in the dark about the magical world. She only started showing magical ability a few months ago, and now York is talking about using her in some ritual during the winter solstice. That's this Saturday. One of their members said they will sacrifice her. I don't know if that is true, but I doubt he plans to take her to see Santa."

The healer gave him a look. "I know the acolytes have a reputation for human sacrifices, but that hasn't been in years, and I doubt York would harm his own daughter." She started to move forward, focusing on his left arm.

"You don't know them like I do," he started.

"Well, let me free you first, and then we can talk about helping her."

Tommy sighed again and screwed his eyes shut. He didn't want to do this, but it looked like he had no choice. Tommy changed, feeling that prickling sensation in every part of his body. He heard a scrambling noise, and when he opened his eyes, the healer had retreated to the other side of the kitchen. She had spilled the contents of her purse, grabbing some pepper spray. She was aiming it at him, breathing hard.

"Still think I'm the victim here?" he joked in a rumble, crouching down. Humans felt better when he wasn't towering over them.

"You... you are... you're a changeling!" she cried.

"Yep," he agreed. He was fighting the urge to grin. He didn't need to scare his new friend with all those sharp teeth. He really did need her help; he shouldn't frighten her that badly.

"Wha... How..." she stammered.

"Deep breathes," he told her.

"There were rumors, speculation, that the acolytes had a changeling working with them," she said, mostly to herself. "You're saying that this entire time, you were their slave?"

He nodded. "The slavering was passed down from one leader to the next. They don't have much of a lifespan once they get in power."

"So Jozef York is your master now," she said. She lowered the pepper spray. "Why are you reaching out now?"

"If you asked me a hundred years ago if I would like my freedom, I would have taken it," he said with a shrug. "But now? I'm tired. I don't care if I live or die. Even if I got free, where would I go? There isn't anywhere I could go where I wouldn't have to keep looking over my shoulder." He winced and rubbed at his left arm. "If I'm going to die, I can at least make sure Chrysta is safe before I kick the bucket."

She stared at him for a full minute. Then she put the pepper spray on the counter and grabbed a towel. She went to the freezer and filled it with ice cubes. She reached out to hand it to him, snatching her hands back a little faster than necessary. He tried to not notice as he mumbled a quiet "Thank you."

She retreated back to the other side of the kitchen. "Why her?" she asked.

He sighed. "Chrysta... she lights up a room. She's kind, even to people who have wronged her. She's so used to people abandoning her that she pays it back tenfold if you show her an ounce of loyalty. I don't know how she is the way she is, given her father is a horrible bastard, but she deserves to get out of there." He paused. "She deserves to be happy."

"You love her," the healer said in a whisper.

Tommy looked at her, not admitting she was right. "Let me die, turn me into dust. I don't care. But she doesn't deserve it. Even if her father wouldn't kill her, he might end up hurting her."

"Why me?"

"You're a healer. You want to help people. And you may get the others to listen when they would kill me before I could get them to hear me out."

She nodded slowly. "I understand." She blinked. "I know someone who can help."

"Good," he said, and he changed back into his human form, and she visibly relaxed. He suddenly felt so tired and rubbed his eyes.

"Abigail Normandy," he heard her say, and when he looked up, she held a hand out. He smiled and shook her hand. "Thomas Monroe," he replied.

She sighed as he stood up. "So, what is the plan?"

He handed her his phone. "Program your cell phone number on my phone. Saturday night, when I have her, I will text you. There is a park at the north end of the city. Morningside. You get there to wait for us with, I don't know, some transportation spell, however you sorcerers do it. I will bring her to you, you bring her here."

"If you can't bring her to the park?" she asked, handing him his phone.

"She has a family she knows, they may be able to protect her. I will tell her to get in touch with you if she needs to." He paused and rubbed his eyes again. "I have a backpack full of all my money. It's in the forest near the Academy if you need it."

She nodded. "Okay."

"Thank you," he said. "I don't know how I can repay you for this."

"Don't die," she replied.

He snorted. "I don't make promises I can't keep, Miss Normandy."

"Seriously," she said. "You need to live long enough for me to get that slave band off your arm."

He shrugged. "Wouldn't do any good." He grabbed his jacket. "Let me get out of here."

"Wait, where are you going?"

"Bus depot. I will catch a bus back to the city in the morning."

"Stay here," she said. "You can get a meal, get some sleep."

He held up his left arm. "This won't let me get any sleep. Trust me."

"I insist," Abigail said, and before he could argue, she was gone. When she returned, she had sheets and a pillow to place on the couch, but Tommy had disappeared, the back door left open to the cold night.

19

Chrysta spent the next few days waiting for Tommy's return feeling like an animal trapped in a cage. The balcony was no longer a means to escape, and when she tried her door, she found it locked. She suddenly felt sympathy for every animal she ever saw in a zoo as she was reduced to pacing back and forth with no chance at freedom.

Thursday night, Chrysta was out on the balcony, scowling at the guards below her, when Guerra himself delivered a meal to her bedroom. She glared at him as he set the plate on the wooden table outside. "I'm not eating that," she said.

"And why not, Miss York?" he asked innocently. "The salmon smells superb this evening."

"The last meal I ate made me sleep for three days," she said. "You and father must have drugged my food."

"We would never, Miss York," he said, holding a hand to his chest like he was insulted. "Would you feel better if I was your food taster?" And he made a show of cutting a piece of fish, slowly chewing it, and swallowing.

Chrysta continued to frown at the man, but when her stomach grumbled, she sat down and started to eat. "Mr. Guerra?" she asked the smiling man who stood in front of her with his hands folded behind him, "I have a question."

"What's that, Miss York?"

"Peter said something I didn't understand last Saturday. At one point, I hurt him. I broke his arm with a thought. And when I told him I couldn't control it, he said, 'we know.' And I have been thinking, since father doesn't want to involve the police, maybe he sent Peter to hurt me."

"That is not a question, Miss York," Guerra said, a fake smile stretching wide on his face.

"What is going on?" she asked. "Father won't tell me, but I feel you know more than you are letting on."

"Me? Oh, Miss York, you flatter me. I am but a servant of the house of York. A hired hand." He held a hand up and made a circle with it. "All this talk of breaking Peter's arm and magic. I think, in my humble opinion, you were just stressed from the attack and imagined it. But your father feels it is better to forgive and forget and move on. And keep you here for your own safety."

Chrysta stopped chewing and stared at him. Magic? She hadn't said anything about magic. There was the sound of cawing in the distance, and while Guerra looked away, Chrysta hid the dinner knife. She didn't know if she needed it, but better to be safe than sorry.

When she was done with her meal, Guerra took her plate and turned away. He paused and then turned back. "The knife, Miss York," he said with a smile, and Chrysta reluctantly gave it up.

"You are a smart woman, Miss York, but please, don't get any ideas that may get you hurt," he said, leaving the room. Chrysta was not surprised to find the door locked when she tried it.

She leaned her forehead on the door and sighed. "Please, Tommy," she said to the empty room. "Please hurry up."

．．．．．

The wait to hear from Tommy was slow torture. Chrysta was just happy that she had the contraband phone to help pass the time after realizing the phone her father gave her had disappeared. Mary was not pleased to hear that Chrysta was virtually a prisoner in her own home, but there was not much she and her mother could do.

"We have asked social services to drop by and talk to you," she told Chrysta. "But if your father is doing homeschooling and you're are being fed and not physically abused, they won't do anything to get you out of there."

"Well, I'm not being homeschooled," she said. "Maybe that will mean I can go back to school."

Chrysta tried to read to pass the time but found herself pacing her room more and more as the weekend dragged on. Guerra always delivered her meals, made a show of trying a bite, and declaring how good it was with his false cheer. She felt like he was mocking her.

Monday evening, Mary called. "Did you talk to social services?" she asked.

"No."

Mary cursed under her breath. "They said they dropped by and talked to you, and apparently you told them you were being homeschooled, allowed to go out whenever you wanted, was not attacked by Peter, and quite happy with everything. I had a feeling they would use that weird double."

Chrysta groaned and rubbed her eyes. "Why? Why is my father doing all this? Just to keep me locked up?"

"I don't know," Mary said. "What do we do?"

"Tommy said he was going out of town to talk to some people that could help," she sighed. "I guess I have to wait to hear from him."

"Do you trust him?" Mary asked. "You did say Peter acted like he knew him. Maybe he is in on all this too."

"Trust in Tommy. He will protect you."

"Yes," Chrysta replied with no hesitation. "I believe him, Mary. I don't think he would leave me here."

"Alright, sis, just let me know if you need my help," she said. "I hate feeling like I can't do anything to get you out of there."

Chrysta smiled. "I know. Don't worry. Tommy will find a way to get me out of here. He has to."

A few minutes after she had hung up with Mary, Guerra came in with her dinner. He placed it on her vanity and then sat on her bed. He patted the cover next to him, a fake smile stretching wider than she could remember ever seeing. Chrysta felt like she had no choice and sat down.

"Tell me, Miss York, how would anyone outside this household know what happened with Peter?" he asked.

"I don't know, Mr. Guerra," she said, trying to sound innocent and training her eyes on his disturbing smile and not glancing at her hiding spot.

"Oh, come now," he said. "You are smart, Miss York. But so am I. You have a way of talking to someone. Maybe your friend, Mary Jackson?"

"I don't know what you mean. Father took away my phone."

He tsked and then placed his hand on hers. Chrysta winced when she felt a pain in her temple. But after a moment, it disappeared, and Guerra's smile faltered for a second.

"Well, that is unexpected," he said. "Maybe I need to make a visit to Miss Jackson?"

Chrysta didn't know what he meant by something unexpected, but she knew his comment about Mary was a threat. She tried to make the flexing feeling happen in her chest, and the knife on her plate started to move and shake until it was pointed at Guerra.

"Don't mess with my friend," she growled.

"Noted," he said, smile back with full force. He took back his hand and stood. "Looks like I'm stressed and imagining things. Goodnight, Miss York." And then he left.

Guerra let himself into the study and quickly bowed to the three men there. "I know why she is not sleeping," he said, addressing Frost. "She's becoming resistant to magical influence."

"How do you know?" York asked.

"I just tried causing her pain so intense she should have been left on the floor writhing in agony. She barely felt it."

"Dammit," Frost cursed. "She's too strong."

"Hence why I wanted to wait," York said. "Increase the guards watching her balcony. We can't have her sneaking out."

Guerra bowed and left the study, leaving the three men alone. Frost took a sip of his drink, scowling. "What do we do?"

"Nothing," York said. "We get the ritual ready and make sure she doesn't leave."

"And how do we get her to the third floor?"

York smiled, looking at Jacobs. "I think Thomas Monroe can help with that."

. . . . .

Chrysta noticed that the house became busy with noise and activity on Tuesday and Wednesday, with the doorbell almost continually ringing and people moving around the third floor. Chrysta didn't know why the biggest bedroom in the house was off-limits to her. Or why anyone would be up there now. It was just an empty ample space from what she remembered when she wandered in there as a child, her father yelling at her to get out almost immediately. But knowing that there were people in there now gave Chrysta a weird sense of unease.

She almost cried in relief when Tommy called her Wednesday night. "Oh, I'm so glad you're back," she told him when she picked up.

"Hello, beautiful," he responded.

Chrysta bit her lower lip. "You sound so tired. Are you okay?"

"Yeah, just haven't slept the last few days. How are you?"

She sighed. "Well, something is happening upstairs, and it has me worried. Guerra threatened to visit Mary a few days ago because she asked social services to check on me."

"Remind me to give him a present in the form of a knife in the back next time I see him," he said. "Him and Peter both."

Chrysta paused. "You know them personally, don't you?" She started to pace her bedroom, voice rising in anger. "You knew what was going on. About the strange things, about *magic* being real, don't you? Why didn't you warn me?"

He went quiet so long that Chrysta was afraid he had hung up. But he sighed, and it sounded so defeated Chrysta felt guilty for her outburst. "You don't have to be with me when this is over, beautiful. I don't expect you to. But I'm begging you, please trust me for a little longer. Then I will tell you everything, and you will never see me again."

Chrysta swallowed past the lump in her throat. "You promised no more disappearing acts."

He laughed a bitter sound. "And *I* warned *you*, you will get to know me, the *real* me, you will hate me, and you will never want to see me again."

Chrysta let herself outside, looking around like she could find Tommy standing on the lawn. "How could I hate someone who gives the best forehead kisses in the world?"

He chuckled, a warmer sound than his previous laugh. "Whatever you say, beautiful." He went quiet again and then made a small sound, something that seemed like a whimper. "I shouldn't ask this, it's the worse time, but could you... nevermind."

"What?"

"Could you play for me? Please?"

She smiled sadly. "It won't be Paganini."

"Oh gods, no," he said and laughed, sounding more like his old self. "Bach's Violin Partita No. 2 in D minor."

"That is what you were playing when we first met," she said.

"Yeah, it was my mom's favorite," he explained. "She played it all the time."

"Your mom played the violin?" she asked. She felt tears on her cheeks. "My mom played the violin too."

"Wonderful women, both of them."

Chrysta laughed and then sniffed. "Okay. For Cassia York."

"For Jemila Monroe," Tommy responded.

"For Cassia York and Jemila Monroe," she agreed. She ended the call and got her violin. When she let herself back outside, Poe dropped down on the table next to her. She smiled at the raven and started to play.

.....

Several blocks over, Tommy sat on his rooftop, left arm in the snow up to his elbow. Tears were streaming down his face, and when Chrysta's playing reached him, he let out a sob.

"Forgive me, Chrysta," he said as he rubbed the tears off his face. "Please forgive me."

.....

Thursday and Friday, the bustle of activity continued in Chrysta's house, even in the early morning hours. Guerra proceeded to deliver her meals, but he didn't make a show of trying her food. She thought about trying to sneak out over the balcony, even with the guards standing there. Maybe if she ran, she could make it to the wall.

"Don't do it," Tommy texted her when she asked for his opinion of her chances. "I'll come to get you Saturday. Just wait until I text you."

Friday evening, Guerra did not come into her room with a meal. She tried to open the door to find it locked. Chrysta pounded on the door calling for anyone to tell her what was going on, but no one responded. She barely slept that night.

Saturday, the house was quiet. After almost a week of activity, the silence was ominous and foreboding. She could barely stay still, walking her room regularly. Guerra did not show up with any meals at all, and Chrysta felt her stomach rumble as time passed.

In the late afternoon, there was a soft knock on her door. She paused in her pacing. Guerra rarely knocked before letting himself in the room, and when he didn't open up the door, she tried the handle. The door opened, and Tommy was on the other side. She stood blinking at him for a few seconds before she tackled him in a hug. She took a deep breath as he returned the hug. He smelled like sandalwood. She could barely believe it had only been two weeks since she last saw him; it felt like forever.

"Oh, I'm so glad to see you," Chrysta whispered. "I thought you said you were going to text before you came?"

"Sorry, I saw an opportunity to get into the house and took it," Tommy explained. "Come on, I know a way out." He started to pull her out of the room.

"Wait, what about my stuff?"

"Leave it," he hissed. "We have no time."

He pulled her to the staircase, but instead of going down, he tugged her upstairs, and she started to resist. "Wait, we can't go up there. Father will know."

"It's fine," he said. "I found a way out." She stopped resisting and followed him upstairs.

He opened the door to the bedroom and drew her inside. The room was still empty, except now there was a table at the far end. It was huge, not as long as the dining room table, but taller and wider. One end of the table had an incline carved into it, stained with something dark. How it got in there, she couldn't tell; it was larger than the door behind her. She paused as Tommy tried to draw her deeper into the room.

"Tommy, I don't like this," she whispered. Except for the stains, the table looked ordinary, but something about it felt off. It seemed like an infected wound, pulsing with energy. It hurt her eyes to look at it directly. "How will we get to the ground from here?"

"Trust me," he said with a grin, and in the late afternoon sun coming through the windows, she noticed something was... off about him. Then she realized that his piercings were on the wrong side of his face. She pulled her hand out of his.

"You're not Tommy," she said, her stomach clenching in fear.

"What do you mean, Chrysta?" he asked, confusion on his face.

She scowled. "You are not Tommy," she repeated.

"Of course I am," he said, smile turning from gentle to nasty. "Who else could I be?"

She didn't answer but turned around and tried to run. Unfortunately, she ran into someone who immediately grabbed her upper arm. A man with glasses she didn't recognize grinned at her and held up a hand. "Sleep," he simply said, and Chrysta instantly felt her eyes get heavy.

The man who was not Tommy was walking towards them, but his features were melting like warm wax. Even his clothes were shifting. By the time he stood in front of Chrysta, he looked the complete opposite of Tommy. White skin, blonde hair, wearing a suit. Chrysta was fighting her sudden urge to sleep while the man holding her arm frowned. "I told you, you didn't look right," he said.

The blonde man shrugged. "It worked, didn't it?" He blinked and looked at Chrysta. "Shouldn't she be asleep by now?" he asked.

"She's fighting me," the man with glasses growled. He held up a hand again, and orange sparks flew up from his hands. Chrysta felt herself begin to pass out, blackness starting to deepen at the edges of her vision.

Fight! something screamed in her head, and Chrysta focused on her feeling of terror to stay awake. Her hand started to glow gold, and Chrysta tried to lift it. The blonde man took a step back. "Frost," he said, voice rising in fear.

Frost glared at her. "Don't you dar—" he started to say, but before he could finish his warning, Chrysta got her hand up to his face and blasted him with the brightest flash of light she could. He flew back with a shout, and the moment his hand left her arm, Chrysta felt wide awake.

Chrysta glared at the blonde man, and he started to raise his hands up in surrender. "You tricked me," she snarled.

"Now, Miss York, stay calm," he said, trying to smile but only producing a grimace.

Chrysta wanted to hit him with a blast of light but thought it would be better to leave that room with the strange table. Before she could turn to flee, an arm grabbed her across her shoulders, and a hand holding a rag clamped on her mouth. She started to struggle while Guerra made shushing noises in her ear.

"Sh, sh, shhhhh, Miss York," he cooed. "It will be all over soon." She saw her father come out of the corner while Frost tried to pick himself off the floor. She pawed at Guerra's arm, trying to get him to let go, while a metallic smell filled her nostrils. Her vision was darkening again, but this time Chrysta suspected it was not magic that caused her to feel heavy. She raised her hand again, a gold glow already forming at her fingertips, but her father lifted his hand and said a word under his breath, and the light she was holding winked out.

"I told you she was too strong," her father said coldly, glaring at Frost, who was inspecting his broken glasses.

Frost just glared back. "It was worth trying," he pouted.

Chrysta was still struggling as they spoke, limbs getting heavier by the second. She tried raising her hand again, the light returning. Her father grimaced. "*Interclusit*," he said with more force, and the glow died at her fingers for the second time.

"Is she fighting you too?" Frost asked in awe.

Her father nodded. "Yes," he confirmed. He leered at Frost. "Still wonder if she is the right vessel?"

And before Chrysta finally lost consciousness, Tommy's face appeared in front of her. "*Please help me,*" she tried to say, but only darkness came to her call.

·····

Tommy was across the street, watching the York mansion. He was waiting for nightfall when he heard a voice right behind him. "Please help me." He whirled around, eyes wide and heart racing, searching the alleyway for the sound's source. No one was there, but Tommy could have sworn that was Chrysta's voice.

When his heartbeat had slowed down, he turned back to the mansion and glared. Something was wrong, he could tell. A light turned on in the third story bedroom, and almost as if that was a cue, cars started to line up to drop off their riders at the front door.

"Fuck," Tommy cursed under his breath. It had been a few decades since the acolytes had made a human sacrifice, but they were always large affairs. If others were showing up, they were getting ready to start. He thought he had more time, thought he had until midnight before they began their ritual.

Lucky for Tommy, he had made a backup plan. He grabbed a smooth grey ball made of rock from his jacket with a small pin of red crystal. He put each piece in separate pockets so they wouldn't touch and then waited. Once it looked like they were starting, he would slip in and grab her. And he had a surprise waiting for the bastards.

20

Chrysta was slowly being pulled back to the waking world with a headache throbbing at her temples. There was the feeling of lying on a hard surface, arms above her. She tried to bring her hands down to rub at her eyes but felt resistance. The inability to move her arms finally snapped her out of her stupor. Her eyes flew open.

She was on the table, arms tied above her head, something tied around her mouth to gag her. To her left stood her father, Guerra, Frost, and the blonde man. They were leaning over a bowl, adding herbs and stirring, murmuring to themselves. To her right stood three dozen figures in robes, chanting and holding their hands up. Most of them were glowing, reds, blues, greens, oranges, and a few purples. Ever so often, some light would break off from them and travel to the bowl, disappearing in the liquid. It would have been beautiful if Chrysta wasn't terrified.

Chrysta tested the bonds above her head and even attempted to move her legs to find them tied up. She tried to scream, "What are you doing?" at the men at her left, but it just came out as an indignant muffled shout.

They finished whatever they were mixing, and Frost turned to her with the bowl. Guerra ungagged her, and she screamed, praying that someone, anyone other than the maniacs currently chanting around her, would hear her. Guerra clamped a hand over her mouth.

"Hush now, *bella ragazza*," he said like she was a screaming toddler and not tied up on a table. She glowered at him.

Frost tried to place the bowl to her lips, but she locked her jaw and refused to open her mouth again. Guerra moved his hands so one was on her forehead and the other held her nose shut. She tried to move her head away, but they waited until her lungs were burning, and she had to take a breath. The liquid burned down her throat, sour and thick, and she started to cough as she accidentally breathed some of it in. Guerra replaced the gag, and Chrysta struggled to catch her breath, tears burning her eyes.

The blonde man handed a bundle to her father, and he moved the cloth to reveal a wicked-looking stone knife. He held it up, and the light caught several red crystals that ran down the blade. The last one at the tip was gold. Chrysta felt fear claw at her throat.

"Brothers," he boomed, and the room fell silent, the robed figures losing their otherworldly glows. "Seven hundred and eighty-two years ago, the Lady was taken from this plane. We, her loyal followers, have kept the faith and have made her return our only mission." He lifted his hands, the knife pointed down at Chrysta's chest, and Chrysta felt her stomach drop. "May this offering tonight bring her to us. For her alone!"

"For her alone," the other robed figures echoed, and once their murmurs died, her father fixed his eyes on her.

Chrysta began to fight the ropes holding her down, twisting as hard as she could, screaming against the gag. The robed figures were utterly silent, and all Chrysta could hear was the pounding of her heart in her ears. She felt the flexing in her chest, and the ropes started to glow. Frost grabbed her legs while Guerra held her arms down. "Quickly, York!" Frost hissed. "She's going to get free!"

Her father looked Chrysta in the eyes, placing a hand lightly, almost lovingly, on her forehead. He lifted the knife, pointed at her chest, and Cyrysta felt herself tense, waiting for the blow.

Suddenly there was a thunk and a shout from Chrysta's right, and the robed figures started to murmur. A ball had been thrown into the middle of the crowd, hitting one in the head. The murmur began to build into panicked shouts. "Bomb!" someone yelled, and the figures started to pull away from the round object.

"Quickly!" Jozef York yelled. "Get it out of here!" But even as he shouted, a red dot started to flash on the ball, and the world exploded.

Chrysta was yelling, but she couldn't hear herself. She was blinking, but the white flash did not fade. Other than a horrible ringing in her ears, she didn't feel any pain. So it was not a bomb but some kind of flash grenade. She continued to twist at her ropes, hoping that the ball left everyone else in the room just as disoriented as she was.

Something reached out, and when it found her hair, it tangled itself painfully into a fist. Chrysta winced at the burning sensation on her scalp, but suddenly the hand was ripped away. She felt someone tugging on the ropes on her legs, and when her feet were freed, she brought her knee up sharply and felt it connect with something. Whatever it was didn't stop, however, and started to unhook her hands. When they were able to move, she began to punch out wildly. Suddenly someone grabbed her hand. She was able to feel lips pressed into her palm and caught the scent of the ocean and burnt wood.

Tommy! She reached out until she felt his jacket and grabbed it like she was drowning. She pulled him closer, and he picked her up in a bridal hold. She wrapped her hands around his neck and buried her face into his throat.

He turned and started to run, dodging and twisting with her in his arms. She still couldn't see or hear, so she thought he was trying to get her out of the room without any of the men instinctively grabbing them. He suddenly came to a stop and jumped back, twisted, and ran in another direction. She sighed in relief when she felt him running down the stairs, finally free of the room.

He lifted a leg and kicked out, Chrysta feeling the impact of his foot hitting something. He ran again and paused. They were blasted with cold air, and Chrysta realized they must be on her balcony. He twisted around, and suddenly they were falling, Chrysta instinctively grabbing onto his neck so hard she had to be hurting him. Tommy landed on his feet, dropping to one knee and giving out what felt like a grunt. He was back up and running without a pause.

They were in the bushes, branches pulling at her face and sweater. Tommy shifted her, so she hung behind him, and he was scrambling up the wall faster than she thought possible.

They dropped to the other side, and Tommy picked her back up. He ran for what felt like several minutes and then crouched down, his heart thundering against her cheek. He gently removed the gag, and Chrysta nearly sobbed in relief.

They waited. Chrysta felt the tension leaving her body as she panted. When she was able to hear Tommy's heartbeat as well as feel it, she tentatively opened her eyes. They were squatted next to a dumpster, Tommy leaning forward slightly to watch the street. Poe was on the corner of the dumpster, softly cawing to himself. Tommy was scowling, lip split and bleeding. "T-Tommy?" she asked, starting to shiver.

"Hey, beautiful," he said, glancing at her from the corner of his eye. He flashed her a smile, and Chrysta couldn't help but smile back. "Hope I didn't break up your father's party. It seemed like a real rager."

She giggled a high twitter that sounded a little unhinged. "You were f-fashionably late, but got th-there just in time. Any longer and my f-father would have... would have—" She faltered, shuddering. Tommy suddenly crushed her to him, and she let out a sob.

"Hey now, beautiful, hey," he whispered. "You're alright. You're good."

"He had a knife. He had a *knife*. There was s-someone that looked like you, and he took me upstairs, but then he didn't look like you. One of them tr-tried to get me to go asleep by touching me, and then Guerra drugged me, and when I w-woke up, father had a *knife*, and I think he was going to st-stab me."

"Shhhh, sh, sh, you're okay, beautiful," Tommy cooed. He kissed her forehead, and when he leaned back, he cupped her face in his hands. "I know it's a lot, but hang on a little longer, okay? I promise you can have your mental breakdown later."

She nodded numbly and then reached up to touch his lip. "Who hit you?" she asked.

"You did," he admitted, wiping at his lip with a thumb and looking at the blood. "Very nice shot."

"S-sorry."

He waved her apology away with one hand. "Don't worry about it." He shrugged out of his jacket and wrapped her up. "Listen up, beautiful, if you have recovered, so have those assholes, so we don't have much time. I'm taking you to someone who will hopefully take you somewhere safe."

"What about Mary's house?" she asked, putting her arms into the jacket's sleeves. He grabbed his phone out of a pocket.

"After everything you have seen tonight, do you really want to drag them into this?" he asked. Chrysta bit her lower lip. He was right, this was dangerous, and she didn't want to bring the whole mess down on the Jackson household. He was texting someone. "If the people helping us don't show up, we will get on a bus and leave the city. Only go to the Jacksons if something happens to me."

"Do you trust them?" she asked as he stood up and tugged her to her feet, putting the cellphone in one of his pants pocket.

"Honestly, I barely know them," he admitted. "But right now, I trust them more than your father." He paused when he saw the look on her face. "Please, Chrysta, believe me. I just want to make sure you're safe." And he held out a hand. She looked at it and nodded, placing her hand in his. She didn't have much choice, really.

They ran deeper into the alleyway to a wooden fence that cut the alley into two parts. Tommy got her to hop on his back again, then vaulted it with minimal effort. When they got to the mouth of the alleyway, he paused and looked around the deserted street. He glanced back at her and looked her up and down. "How you doing?"

"C-cold," she confessed. She was just wearing jeans, a light sweater, and socks, and as the adrenaline started to wear off, she was beginning to become aware of how cold it was. Tommy's jacket helped to keep her warm, but it wasn't the best solution.

"Here," he said, crouching down to remove his boots and socks. Chrysta protested as he stuffed the socks in the toes, but he shook his head. "You need them more than me," was all he said. He helped her get them on, and Chrysta almost giggled. With the oversized shoes and coat, she looked like a small kid who raided her older sibling's closet

They started to make their way down the street when men in robes appeared at the next intersection. Tommy cursed under his breath and started to tug her in the other direction, the men shouting when they saw the couple. They broke out into a run, but another group of men appeared in front of them at the other intersection.

"Shit, shit, shit," Tommy started to chant. He pushed Chrysta back into the alley, and he tried to climb the fence, Poe landing on it and croaking loudly. Before Tommy could grab her and pull her up, a ball of light sailed by his head, and he fell off the fence with a loud "Fuck!" Poe flew away, squawking.

He grabbed her and pulled her back to the street. The two groups were closing in, and as Chrysta looked back, two more men cleared over the fence. One of them brought up his hands, and balls of fire danced at his fingertips. Chrysta jumped and whimpered, and Tommy tucked her behind him, turning to keep an eye on all of the approaching men. Poe landed on his shoulder and cawed at the advancing men.

"Mr. Monroe," a voice rang out, and Chrysta recognized Frost. The redhead was grinning as he held out his hands at his sides. "I should have known. What did you hope to accomplish tonight, hm?"

"Oh, you know," Tommy said, glaring at the other man. "Save the damsel in distress, fuck up your plans, the usual."

"This will only end in death for you," Frost said.

"Probably," Tommy said, nodding.

Chrysta felt fear claw at her throat. "Tommy, no," she whispered.

Tommy glanced at her but looked back at Frost. "But as long as I keep her from you assholes, I win, don't I?"

Frost scowled. "Bring her here, and you live to see the sunrise."

"Not how that works, Frost, you know that," Tommy said, and while he was distracted, the man with the fire swung at him. The fireball was aimed at his chest, but before it reached him, Chrysta reached out and somehow stopped the ball in mid-air. It shook and fluttered and then exploded, leaving flames on the ground. All the other men other than Frost ducked and backed away from Chrysta as her arms glowed gold.

"Calm down, you idiots," Frost yelled at the retreating men. "She can't control it." The men glanced at each other and started to close in again.

Chrysta tried to do something, anything to stop them, but the gold was dying. "No, no, no, no," she begged. While she was looking down at her hands, one of the men lunged for her. When he grasped her upper arm, she shouted, but Tommy landed a punch on his jaw, and he let go. Poe took flight and tried to fly at one of their attackers, but he was thrown to the side. Another fireball was flung at Tommy, and Chrysta barely got him to duck in time. They hunched down, Tommy trying to cover her with as much of his body as possible.

The men continued forward, and suddenly Tommy let out a sound that reminded Chrysta of a large predator, a deep rumble that came from his chest and vibrated against her back. It was so low and primal that it was impossible to believe a human was making that sound. All the men paused and moved back again. Even Frost took a step back, fear blooming on his face.

"You wouldn't dare," Frost whispered, and Chrysta gulped when Tommy repeated the noise. He was definitely the one making it; there was no way it was coming from anywhere but his chest.

"You kinda backed me into a corner, asshole," Tommy growled back, his voice deeper and rougher than Chrysta had ever remembered hearing.

Tommy hugged Chrysta close to him with one arm, leaning close to her ear. "Listen, beautiful," he whispered, and she shivered as his breath tickled her ear. "Just remember, it's still me in here, okay?"

"What do you mean?" she asked, but he didn't answer.

Chrysta suddenly felt him shift behind her, and even though she was trying to watch the men closing in on them, she saw the arm around her get larger, his sweater straining against new muscle. The hand on her arm grew, the skin turning a dark grey, nails changing into black talons. She swore his legs got longer and could feel him looming over her. The men around them jumped, fear on their faces. When a growling noise started behind her, Chrysta finally glimpsed back.

Chrysta wasn't sure what she was seeing, but it wasn't human. Tommy had grown, shoulders wider and straining the material of his sweater. The skin she could see was grey and hairless, spots dotting his face and neck. His head had a feline shape, ears flattened to his head, lips on his snout curled up in a snarl, golden eyes trained on Frost in front of him. With the growl coming from his chest and his teeth bared, he was the purest form of hatred and hostility. "Tommy?" she asked in a small voice, and he glanced at her but quickly looked back at the men around them.

"Now, be reasonable, Mr. Monroe," Frost said, holding his hands out in a calming motion. Tommy started to stand, impossibly tall, snarling and making everyone, including Chrysta, jump.

"What's the matter, Frost?" Tommy growled, voice deeper. He actually had a tail that was lashing back and forth in agitation. "Not so high and mighty when someone shows up that can rip your throat out?"

For several agonizing moments, no one moved, holding their breath. "Well," Tommy said with a rumble. "Anyone want to get this party started?"

Suddenly, the man who could make fireballs threw one at Tommy. He ducked as the fire hit his shoulder, but it died, burning Tommy's sweater but nothing else. He broke out in an evil grin. "Looks like we have a volunteer," he said, and he was running to attack the man.

Chrysta looked on in horror as Tommy knocked the man to the ground and slashed at his face. Blood arced in the air, and everyone scattered. She may have run with them; only someone grabbed her arm and made her get up. Frost started to pull her away, face set into a frown. The man on the ground screamed for help as Tommy leaned down. Chrysta could only see Tommy's back, but she could imagine he was putting his sharp teeth to good use. She fought Frost, but he held onto her arm, and when she tried to blast him, nothing but sparks appeared at her fingertips. "You lack the malice needed to control that spell," Frost said to her, leering at her.

"Lucky for us, I have enough malice for the both of us," a voice sounded behind her, and Frost's smile died. Tommy's hand shot out and grabbed Frost by the face, and he let go of Chrysta, yelling. Tommy lifted the man off the ground, nails cutting deep into his scalp.

Chrysta backed up, watching as Frost struggled to get Tommy to let go, feet kicking about a foot off the ground. His glasses broke, and blood was running down his face. When Tommy reached up with his other hand to grab Frost's throat and squeeze, Chrysta realized Tommy would kill him. "Stop!" she screamed, and Tommy paused. "Don't hurt him!" she yelled.

"Why? They were going to kill you," Tommy said. Frost only grunted as the nails at his throat broke the skin, and blood began to flow.

"Doesn't mean you have to stoop to their level," she said.

Tommy seemed to think over her words, and with a snarl, he threw Frost over to the injured man. Someone was helping the wounded man up, and when Frost was thrown at their feet, Tommy let out a roar. The message was clearly received as the two men grabbed Frost and ran, barely letting their leader regain his feet. Chrysta watched them go while biting her lip.

Tommy's hand appeared next to Chrysta's head, long fingers and claws covered in blood, and she gasped, ducked, and turned around to look at him with wide eyes. He snatched his hand back, his own eyes going wide and ears going back and tail wrapping around his legs. They stood looking at each other for a few moments, Chrysta panting and a strange look of sadness slipping onto Tommy's face. He shook his head and mumbled a small "Sorry" before turning away and going back into the alley.

She watched him go, feeling her heart slowing down as the shock wore off. She tentatively walked to the alleyway's mouth and looked at him, Poe landing on her shoulder. He had squatted down and grabbed some snow, wiping the blood off his hands and snout, making it turn pink. He glanced at her but quickly looked away, face looking blank.

"Go north. There is a park called Morningside. We were going to meet the people there," he explained in a rumble. He was not looking at her but at the ground. "One of them is a woman. Her name is Normandy. She's nice, she will help you."

"What are you going to do?" she asked, voice low.

"Stay here," he said. "They will come back here. Try to pick up our trail." He took a deep breath and let it out with a growl. "I'll try to slow them down."

"They'll kill you," she realized.

"Doesn't matter," he said, closing his eyes and letting his head hang back, hands dangling between his legs. "I'm going to take as many of those bastards with me as I can."

She watched him, trying to read his face but couldn't decipher it. Did he really think she would leave him here, alone, to die?

After a few minutes, she made a decision and walked up to him. He flinched when she took one of his hands but otherwise didn't do anything as she tried to tug him back into standing. He let her get a few tugs in before he cocked his head to the side. "What are you doing?" he asked.

"You are coming with me," she said, trying to sound as forceful as possible as she strained to pull him up.

"Chrysta, you should—"

"No!" she yelled. She dropped Tommy's hand to point a finger in his face. He blinked and leaned as far back as he could, yellow eyes wide and ears straight up. Crouched down as he was, they were eye to eye, and she used that to her advantage to show him how mad she was. "I'm not leaving you here, with some bullshit excuse, to commit suicide. You said no more disappearing acts, and that includes letting some jerks kill you just to protect me."

He blinked at her, mouth moving, ears lying flat on his head. For a second, she was worried she had angered him and he was about to bite her finger off. But suddenly, he threw his head back and started laughing, a deep warm sound that thundered. It took a few moments, but he recovered, chuckling to himself as he rubbed his snout. "You use the word 'bullshit,' but call those assholes 'jerks,'" he snickered.

"You know what I mean," she said, breaking out in a grin. It fell off her face. "Come on, you can't give up like this. I won't let you."

He sobered up and let out a grumble. "You need to go."

"Not without you," she said softly, and to prove her point, she crouched next to him, trying to keep herself from shivering.

He looked down at her, ears perked up, face back to being hard to read. He sighed and held out his hand, and she took it, marveling how huge it was compared to her own. He gently wrapped his fingers around hers and stood up, helping her to her feet.

"Come on," he rumbled. "Let's go before those jerks get back."

21

The York mansion was currently in chaos. Those hit by the flash grenade had fumbled and cursed for several minutes until they recovered their sight and hearing. Most of the men immediately ran out of the house, trying to find Chrysta and whoever took her. Some stayed behind, including York and Guerra, to figure out exactly who had interrupted their ritual.

The half-dozen men left to guard the door had been attacked, and some of them would have to spend time with a healer before they would wake up, but the two still conscious gave the same story while clutching knife wounds: Thomas Monroe, known to most of the acolytes as the slave, had appeared and fought them. Both men seemed amazed that Monroe could even harm them.

York went down to his daughter's room and saw the opened door to the balcony and cursed. He twisted the ring on his finger but seriously doubted that it would work to bring Monroe back. There was no way to tell which direction they had gone. So York was forced to dowse in his study with a map of the city and a crystal on a chain. Guerra joined him, but he was no closer to locating them after about twenty minutes of fruitless work.

"You have known him the longest," York said to Guerra, still frowning at the map. "Has he ever done anything like this before?"

"The slave has been obstinate in the past, but he has never done anything like this," Guerra confirmed, looking very solemn as he watched York work. "This is not just refusing to follow orders. This is..." Guerra paused like he was trying to find the right word.

"Suicide," York finished for him.

Guerra nodded. "Precisely. Looks like we were both wrong about the strength of his feelings for her."

They spent the next few minutes in silence, York cursing under his breath as the crystal swung but did not land on the map. After another ten minutes of work, he slammed a fist on the table and stood there, breathing heavily.

"Who are you searching for?" asked Guerra.

"Both of them," York said. "I'm not surprised it's failing with him, but I was hoping to locate her. She must be immune."

The door of his study opened without a knock, and Jacobs ran inside. "I wasn't able to find her," he said breathlessly. He glanced at the map. "Any luck here?"

"None," York started to explain when a shout came from the front door. Suddenly two figures stumbled into the study. Frost was dumped in the nearest chair, face and throat dripping blood. "Get a healer," York ordered. The other man nodded and left the study. York's annoyance at the blood staining his rug was almost as intense as his glee at seeing Frost hurt. "What happened?" Guerra asked as Frost moaned in pain.

"It's Monroe," Frost panted, one hand covering the right side of his face. Broken glass had been pressed into his skin, and he was trying to get the blood to stop. "He's the one who took her. We found them south of here. He transformed and attacked me."

York brought the map to the injured man. "Where?"

Frost grimaced as he squinted at the paper. He jabbed a finger at it and then fell back into the chair with a hiss. "He transformed?" Guerra asked as York scowled at the map. "In front of Miss York? How did she react?"

"I'm sorry, I was not in a position to assess her mental state as the slave dangled me a foot off the ground," Frost replied sarcastically.

"So he may have taken her by force if she was frightened," York murmured, mostly to himself. "But the question remains, where?"

"Isn't there a nest of changelings south of here?" Jacobs asked.

"Two hours south," Guerra confirmed. "But I doubt he would take her there. They would kill her. And him."

"Unless he has made some kind of deal," Frost said.

"Her life in exchange for his freedom?" York mused. "It's possible. It makes more sense." He looked at the map. "If only we could confirm it."

"That bird you think is her familiar was with them," Frost said.

York scowled deeper and then went to his desk. He brought out one of the raven's feathers. He wrapped the chain around it and swung it over the map again.

This time the crystal began to tug until the chain was pulled at an angle. Only, the crystal was straining north, not south.

"Guerra, head south," York barked out. "If he's transformed, he's probably staying in that form. Which means no public transportation." Guerra bowed slightly and left. "Jacobs, you're with me."

"Where are we going?"

"North," York said as he grabbed his cane. "We can't risk them escaping."

.....

They stuck to back alleyways and dark streets, pausing to let cars pass and doubling back. It made Chrysta dizzy, and she lost her way, although Tommy told her they were still heading north.

"I have to make sure you are safe," was all he kept saying.

At one point, he pulled her beneath an overpass, crouching down and leaning on a pillar. He was breathing heavily and was wincing. "I need a break," is all he said, and she was glad to take it.

The band on his arm was glowing. It seemed impossible, but with everything else that had happened that night, she started to think she needed to believe in the impossible. She was about to touch it when he growled. "Don't touch it," he rumbled. "I don't want it burning you."

"If it could burn me," she reasoned, "then it must be burning you." He didn't deny it, so she went out into the road. He called out to her, but she ignored him.

She found a dirty shirt and started to place the cleanest snow she could find on it. When she had several handfuls, she brought it over to Tommy and put it on the band. There was the sound of sizzling and an awful smell, but he rumbled, and the glow went down.

"Thank you," Tommy said, and she glanced at his face. His ears were twitching, following distant sounds she could barely hear. Strange golden eyes looked back at her. His jewelry was missing, but she could see the cut on his lip she gave him. She reached out to touch his snout but hesitated. He closed the gap to her hand, and she felt a tickle as he took a deep breath, nose twitching in her palm.

"What are you?" she whispered.

"I told you, beautiful," he said. "A changeling."

"No, *what* are you?" she asked. "You look like a cat, but you have no fur."

He cocked his head. "My mom was a leopard," he explained. "My father was a tiger shark. I inherited his skin."

"But how can that be?" she asked. "They are two totally different species. How could they have offspring?"

He chuckled, a deep warm sound in his chest. "Out of everything that has happened tonight, *that* is what you are focusing on, beautiful?"

She laughed too. "Sorry, you will have to forgive me; this is my first time meeting a magical creature. I don't know the social rules to follow."

"Oh, we are simple creatures," he said. "Just don't piss us off, or we eat you."

She smiled but felt it melt off her face. "Are you going to look like this forever now?"

"Nah, I can change back whenever I want. I just want to make sure you are safe before I do. Miss my ugly mug?"

She snorted. "No, just making sure you didn't give up your humanity for me." He cocked his head at that and raised an eye ridge. It was something she could imagine him doing. *It really is him.* She gestured to the band on his arm, which was starting to glow again. "And what about that? Is it hurting you?"

He glanced at his arm. "No more than usual," he rumbled.

"I'm serious," she said. "Is it hurting you? I don't want you to be in pain because of me."

He looked at her and cocked his head in the other direction. "If I'm lyin', I'm dyin'," he said.

She blinked and started to giggle. It dissolved into hysterical laughter, and she pressed herself into Tommy's chest to help keep herself quiet. He chuckled with her and loosely put his arm, the one without the band, around her.

A car passed nearby, and Tommy pulled her closer to him, letting the lights pass them. "Come on," he said. "We better get moving." And with that, they moved on, holding hands.

·····

They continued north, but as time went on, Tommy started to slow down and falter, but he didn't stop, only pausing to scoop up snow and press it to the band on his arm. He tripped while they were crossing the street, and Chrysta tried to help him up. "I'm alright," he rumbled as he got to his feet.

"No, you're not," Chrysta told him, glad that the late hour and weather kept the streets deserted. "Lean on me. Is it the band on your arm?"

"Yeah," he admitted as he put an arm on her shoulder.

"What is it?"

"A slave band."

"What's that?" she asked as they walked down an alleyway.

He started to growl, and Chrysta was worried that he was upset with her for prying, but she realized he was thinking. "A thing that is supposed to make me listen to my master, whoever owns the ring attached to it. He's been trying to call me back."

"And who is your master?" she asked as he suddenly lurched to the side and leaned against the wall, talons marking the brick.

He let out a rumble. "Don't worry about it."

"Well, maybe we can get him to stop hurting you."

"Only way that will happen is if I take you back to your father," Tommy said, leaning his forehead on the brick. "And no way in hell I'm doing that."

She waited as he took a break, taking deep breaths. Finally, he turned to her. "Let's get going."

They approached the park, a small space with dead grass surrounded by apartment buildings. It was deserted as far as Chrysta could see as they hid in an alleyway. "Where are the people who can help us?" she asked.

"Don't know," he said. "They may have left. They may not have even come to help us."

"What do we do now?"

He was growling, probably trying to think of an answer, when a car pulled up in front of them. They ducked as her father and a blonde man got out of the vehicle. "Shit," Tommy hissed, pulling Chrysta back into the alley's shadows, crouching with her in front of him.

"That's the one who looked like you!" Chrysta fiercely whispered when she recognized the second man.

"Jacobs," Tommy explained. "He can mimic the way people look."

"He didn't do a very good job. He put your piercings on the wrong side of your face."

Tommy snorted. "Lazy," was all he said.

"How did they find us?" Chrysta asked.

"Not sure," he whispered. Chrysta's father held up something, and Chrysta saw it catch the light. Tommy's ears perked up, and his tail lashed. "Dowsing. But what is the bastard tracking?" Poe clicked his beak from the fire escape above them, and Tommy glanced at him and growled. "I think it's Poe."

"What do we do?"

"I'll take Poe and lead them away. Get into the park, wait for me there. If Normandy shows up before I do, you get out of here."

She shook her head. "I don't want to leave without you."

"Looks like we don't have a choice, beautiful."

Chrysta looked up at him, lip curled in a snarl, ears flattened on his head, yellow eyes fixed on the two men in front of them, and suddenly felt her heart breaking. She ran a hand up one of his cheeks and leaned up to gently kiss the other. "Be careful," she whispered. "I love you too much to lose you."

He leaned back in shock, eyes going wide and ears standing straight up. He looked at Chrysta for a minute, barely moving, but abruptly his face softened. He pressed her to him in a firm hug, burying his face into her shoulder and squeezing so hard she could barely breathe.

"Love you too, beautiful," he thickly whispered. He suddenly got up and turned away, walking back down the alleyway. "Come on, Poe," he said, voice back to a rumble, and Chrysta watched them go until they disappeared.

22

Chrysta waited, watching the two men standing between her and the park. Suddenly the object her father was holding flashed and moved so it pointed east. The men quickly climbed into the car and drove off. Chrysta waited and counted to herself for five minutes, and she crossed the street when they didn't return.

It was a tiny park with a jungle gym for kids to play on, a few trees, benches, and a small patch of dead grass. She found a spot between a tree and bench, mostly in shadow, and hunched down to wait. She didn't even know what she wanted more; Tommy to come back safe so they could leave together or for the woman named Normandy to find her so she could get away from this nightmare.

Would she even be safe with these mysterious people Tommy found? What did they look like? Did they know her father? Could they fight her father?

She shivered and trembled as thoughts ran through her head. She tried to take a deep breath to calm her nerves. Tommy said she could have her mental breakdown later, but being alone was making her panic worse.

She saw someone walking down the street, slinking from one parked car to the other. The figure moved in the shadows, crept into the park, and stood up, and she saw its outline. Inhumanly tall, just like Tommy. But was it him? Were there others like him, large and alien-looking? Were they friendly?

The figure was walking towards her, the sound of sniffing getting louder as it got closer. It finally stood next to the tree Chrysta was hiding next to. "Chrysta?" a deep voice rumbled.

"Tommy?" she whispered back, and the figure turned towards her voice. He crouched down, and she finally saw his face, yellow eyes bright in the dark. She sagged in relief. "Oh, thank goodness you're okay."

He reached out a hand. "Of course," he joked. "I don't think anyone would mess with me looking like this."

She giggled as she took his hand. "The people you said would help us are not here. What should we do?"

"Leave the city," he said. "Come on, we'll head south."

"South? Back towards my house?"

"Only for a little bit." And with that, he was tugging her up.

They stepped into the light of a streetlight, and Chrysta glanced up at Tommy's face. She noticed that his lip was completely healed. She started to slow down, and he looked at her. "What's wrong?"

She looked down, biting her lip. "Just... it's been such a crazy night. W-with my father and finding out you're a changeling." She sighed. "Wondering if we can ever go on a normal date again. Like when we saw Shakespeare in the park."

"Don't worry, Chrysta, we will get out of this," he said, and he turned to continue walking, but she pulled her hand away from his and started to back away from him. "Chrysta, we have to get going. I can't be seen like this."

She shook her head. "I'm not going anywhere with you, Mr. Jacobs."

His ears went back. "Well, aren't you a clever little thing," he hissed.

"You really need to get better at copying people," she said, hoping that Tommy was on his way back and all she had to do was stall this man.

"It's not as easy as people think," he stated. He brought up a hand and studied the long fingers and black claws. "Considering I have only seen Monroe in this form once, I think I did a good job capturing his likeness."

"Please, just leave me alone," she said, trying to sound forceful and not like she was begging.

"I'm sorry, but we can't do that, Miss York. We need to complete the ritual by morning." He turned back to her and started to lean toward her. "Now, will you come with me willingly, or will I have to start taking off pieces of your body?" He clicked his claws together, so she knew exactly what he meant.

"I... I will go with you," she said.

"Good," he growled, and Jacobs grabbed her upper arm and pulled her towards the street. Chrysta winced but did not complain. His features started to flow, and by the time they were standing by the road, he looked like himself. He rolled his shoulders and sighed. "So good to be in one's skin," he purred, pulling a phone from his pocket.

He dialed a number and said, "I have her," when the person on the other end picked up. He hung up, and they waited. Snow started to fall, and Chrysta tried to keep herself from shivering.

"So, where were you two going, hm?" Jacobs asked.

"Not sure. Tommy wouldn't tell me," she lied. If she got away, she didn't want them to know that the park was a meeting point.

"Well, you should be happy we found you, Miss York. If Tommy was taking you to other changelings, they would kill you."

"Why?" *Keep him talking, stall him until Tommy gets back.*

Jacobs shrugged. "Not really sure. Mr. Monroe seems to have gained the ire of his brethren before he came to be employed by us. They tend to attack him on sight."

Chrysta glared. "Employed? Don't you mean enslaved?"

Jacobs chuckled. "Semantics, my dear."

A car pulled up and parked, and Chrysta's father climbed out. He walked over to them. "Well, this was an interesting exercise," he grumbled. "Where were they going?"

"Not sure," Jacobs said.

Her father scowled and twisted the ring that he always wore. "Time we get Mr. Monroe to answer for his actions."

Chrysta looked at the ring and felt her stomach drop. "You're the one Tommy was talking about. The master that the slave band is connected to." She tried to remove her arm from Jacobs' grasp, but he held on. She looked her father in the eye and scowled back. "You're the one hurting him."

"Only one hurting him is himself for not listening to orders," her father said.

They waited in silence as the snow gathered on the ground, their breath turning into fog in the air. A figure started walking towards them from the street, and Chrysta recognized Tommy's inhuman outline. As he got closer, she could see he was letting his left arm hang down, out from his body, his right hand clutching his elbow. The band was white, so bright it actually hurt to look at. She could see his snout wrinkled in a permanent snarl, and when he stopped in front of them, he was breathing heavily. Jacobs pulled Chrysta in front of him, grabbing her shoulders in a vice-like grip. Poe landed in a nearby tree and started to hop up and down in agitation.

"Let her go, York," Tommy said. He paused to take several deep breaths. "Killing your own daughter. This is low, even for you."

"Hold your tongue," her father replied coldly, slapping Tommy across the face, using the hand with the ring on it. Tommy staggered and went down on one knee, holding his face.

"Leave him alone!" Chrysta cried out, straining to run forward and help Tommy, but Jacobs held on. "Stop! Stop hurting him! I'll do whatever you want," she said. "I won't fight anymore. Just please *stop!*"

Her father ignored her and hit Tommy again, this time with his cane. Tommy reeled from the hit, but he recovered and glared.

Chrysta started to fight, trying her best to wrench herself free, but Jacobs held on no matter how much she twisted. Chrysta began to feel the flexing in her chest, and she closed her eyes and tried to focus on one thought—

go away, leave us alone, go away, go back home, go away, go away, GO AWAY

—and she heard Jacobs gasp behind her. She opened her eyes and realized she was glowing gold, not just her hands but everywhere. It was coming off her in waves. Jacobs finally let go and started to back away from her, hands held out in surrender.

"Chrysta," her father said, voice low and tight. "Whatever you are doing, stop it."

She balled up her hands at her side and glared at her father. "I'm just sending you away so you can't hurt us," she growled.

Her father reached out. "Wai—!" he yelled. But before he could finish his command, both he and Jacobs disappeared with a loud *POP*. Chrysta and Tommy stared in shock where the two men had just been standing a second before.

"Good job, beautiful, I'm pr— I'm proud of you... r-really working tha— that magic muscle..." Tommy trailed off, and suddenly his eyes rolled into his head, and he fell forward, chin making a loud cracking sound when it hit the pavement.

"Tommy!" she yelled, running to him, glow quickly fading away.

.....

Back at the York mansion, York and Jacobs popped back into existence outside of Chrysta's bedroom. York was about six inches above the balcony and fell painfully to his knees with a shout. Jacobs was not so lucky, appearing several feet from the balcony and falling all the way to the lawn below. He screamed in pain as he broke one of his legs.

York got to his feet, using his cane as his hip screamed in protest. He looked over the railing with a little bit of morbid curiosity at the wailing man below. She did it. With no spell or training, she transported two grown men across the city, completely intact. Somehow he wondered if hurting Jacobs was intentional or a rookie mistake.

He glanced at his watch. Almost midnight. If they didn't get the ritual finished by daylight, it would be too late. And he doubted they would be able to try it again; Chrysta was getting too strong.

He limped down the stairs and to his study, grimacing at the bloodstains in the hallway. Call Guerra. Send him to the park. York poured himself a drink. Maybe she would still be there. Monroe was not looking well; he couldn't go on much longer. She wouldn't leave Monore behind if he collapsed. He took a gulp of his drink. Get a healer for Jacobs. The man would be busy tonight.

York finished his drink in one long swallow. He had to set this right. Because if Chrysta got away, York would not be in charge much longer.

He winced. That wasn't quite right. If Chrysta got away, York might not be *alive* for much longer.

23

Chrysta struggled to get Tommy turned over. He had landed on his stomach, his arms underneath him. The band was burning him; she could hear an awful sizzling noise. He was bulky and heavy, and it took her several tries, but she got him flipped on his back, left arm flopping on the ground. It brushed Chrysta's hand by accident, and she yelped. Poe landed next to her and cawed. "I'm alright," she tried to explain.

She frantically gathered snow, piling it on his arm, ignoring her own burns. When the band stopped melting the snow, she crouched by his head. She started to rub his cheeks, taking no mind of the rough sandpaper-like texture of his skin.

"Tommy? Tommy, can you hear me? Can you open your eyes? Please?" He didn't respond. She sniffed but fought back the tears. She needed to stay calm if she was going to help him.

But how could she help him? Calling the police wouldn't help. Not when Tommy looked like this. They would lock him up, maybe try to take her back to her father. Who could help them then? The Jacksons? No, that had to be Chrysta's last resort. Her father may hurt them for helping her.

She had a thought and reached into Tommy's pocket. She found his phone and tried to unlock it. It needed a seven-letter password to open. She bit her lip and tried, "Chrysta." It went to the home screen, and she sighed in relief.

She opened the texting program and found a conversation with a contact listed as "Normandy." She typed out a message. "Please, Miss Normandy, we need your help. Please hurry."

She waited, kneeling on the cold ground, checking that Tommy was still breathing every few minutes. Poe stayed by her side, pecking at the now-cool band on Tommy's arm. How long should she wait? An hour? Two? Would her father send someone to the park? She looked at her hands. Would she be able to send anyone who threatened them away?

There was a flash of blue in the patch of grass, and when Chrysta's eyes recovered from the light, she saw two figures standing there. Her stomach dropped, and she shifted so she was shielding as much of Tommy's body as she could. Were they friends of her father's? The people started to walk towards her, and when they stepped into the light, they both stopped.

It was a man, dark hair and skin and slightly overweight, and a woman, brown hair and glasses, and they seemed to be in as much shock as Chrysta was. They stared at her and Tommy while she stared back. "Chrysta York?" the woman asked, and Chrysta slowly nodded. The woman put a hand on her chest. "I'm Abigail Normandy. What happened?"

Chrysta's shoulders sagged in relief. "Tommy fainted. Please, Miss Normandy, can you help him?"

Miss Normandy rushed to kneel next to Tommy, not caring about his appearance, and gently shooing Poe away. The man reached out as if to stop her but paused. She ran her hands over the burnt sweater, checking the wounds on Tommy's chest and stomach. "What caused this?"

"The band, it was glowing. It was so hot it burnt Tommy when he fell," Chrysta explained while showing Miss Normandy her hand.

Miss Normandy gently took her hand and covered it with her own. There was some blue light, and when Miss Normandy took her hands back, the burns were gone. Chrysta looked at her hand in wonder. "How?"

"I'm a healer. It's my ability," Miss Normandy said with a smile.

"Ability?" Chrysta asked as Miss Normandy went back to check on Tommy.

"Her power," the man said in a British accent like that would explain everything. She gave the man a confused look. "You don't know what that is?"

"No," Chrysta said while shaking her head. "I didn't even know magic was real until recently."

"Seriously?" the man asked, giving her a suspicious look. He gestured at Tommy. "And did you think this was a costume?"

"He transformed earlier when he was saving me from my father," she said in Tommy's defense.

"Akrur, can you interrogate her later?" Miss Normandy murmured.

The man looked guilty for a moment and then reached his hand out to Chrysta. "Akrur Cross. I don't know if it is a pleasure to meet you, Miss York. I'm saving that assessment for later." Mr. Cross studied Tommy's prone body as they shook hands. "Bloody hell, Abby, what have you gotten us into?"

"I didn't get you into anything," she responded, checking Tommy's chest and stomach. "I was perfectly able to come here by myself, but you insisted on coming with me."

"Couldn't let you get in trouble all by yourself," he said. He looked at Chrysta. "What happened?"

"My father was going to kill me," Chrysta started. "Tommy stopped him and got me out of the house. We came here to meet Miss Normandy. My father showed up, and I sent him away. And then Tommy passed out."

"Wait, you sent your father away? What do you mean?"

"I didn't want him here anymore because he was hurting Tommy, so he disappeared. I think I sent him to the house? I'm not sure."

Mr. Cross blinked at her but didn't comment. He looked at Miss Normandy. "So, what is the plan, Doc?"

"Don't call me that," Miss Normandy responded in a singsong voice, not looking up from Tommy's chest burns. "We need to get him to the infirmary," she said more seriously. "I can try to help him wake up there."

"Is that a good idea?" Mr. Cross asked.

"Probably not," Miss Normandy said with a sigh. "But we can't stay here. Chrysta's father may come back."

Mr. Cross looked from Tommy on the ground to where they'd appeared. "No way we can carry him," he murmured. "Well, if you can't bring the changeling to the transportation circle, you bring the transportation circle to the changeling." And with that statement, he was jogging over to the grass.

"The band has stopped glowing," Chrysta explained. "Is that a good thing? Can you wake him up now?"

Miss Normandy looked worried. "Honestly, I'm not sure if I can." She reached over to squeeze Chrysta's hand when she saw the worried look on Chrysta's face. "I will help him, I promise."

Mr. Cross came jogging back with several blue crystals in his arms. He set up what looked like a compass near Tommy's head, and it opened up like a flower, and small beams of light came out of it. Mr. Cross made some adjustments, and the lights moved in six different directions. He started placing crystals where the lights shone, making a circle.

The circle he made was small, so they had to roll Tommy onto his side and bring his knees up. "Take a breath, hold it," Miss Normandy explained. She gestured at Poe. "Is he with you?"

"Yes," Chrysta said.

"Then you may want to hold onto him. Animals don't do well with transportation spells."

Chrysta nodded and gently picked up Poe, shushing him as he started to caw loudly. Mr. Cross double-checked the crystals, and then he held out his hands. The crystals began to glow as he muttered to himself. *"Vritta bana prakaash aur patthar,"* he said. *"Hamen ghar le aao."*

The crystals got brighter, and a slight hum filled the air. Chrysta felt the hairs on her skin stand up on end, and she took a breath and held it. Chrysta felt the air moving around them, pressing down on them, and even the hair on her head started to lift up.

There was a blinding light, and suddenly, they were gone.

.....

Chrysta felt a lot of pressure. Her ears popped, and she gasped in surprise. Poe started to squawk and flap his wings, and she let him go as soon as the light died around them. She looked around them, and somehow they were now in a forest clearing, surrounded by trees and snow, blue crystals now joined by green ones, twelve in total. Chrysta looked up and saw clear skies and thousands of stars on display. She had never been outside the city, and any other time would have been delighted to study the night sky. But she tore her eyes from the sky when Tommy started coughing.

He was hacking hard, body curling in on itself. Chrysta started to rub his back while Miss Normandy held his hands. He calmed down, and Chrysta peered over to see one eye cracked open, the yellow eye looking blank.

"Tommy?" she asked softly, and the eye seemed to focus on her. "Hey, we did it. We're out of the city. You got me out safe, just like you promised."

The eye unfocused, and it rolled up into his head again. He took a deep, shuddering breath and let it out in an explosive sigh, and he was still, breathing soft and steady. Chrysta tried placing a hand on his shoulder and shaking it, but he didn't stir.

"Miss Normandy? Why is he not waking up?"

"I'm not sure," the older woman responded. She put one fist in the middle of Tommy's chest and rubbed with her knuckles. When Tommy didn't answer, she frowned. "Thomas? You in there?" she asked loudly.

"Shouldn't he have recovered by now?" Mr. Cross asked, arms folded, trying to stay warm. Chrysta suddenly realized how cold it was and shivered.

Miss Normandy studied the slave band, twisting Tommy's arm to check all sides. "If he wasn't wearing this, I think he would be fine." She looked at Chrysta, who was frantically rubbing her bare hands. "Come on, let's get both of them inside."

Suddenly, something was crashing towards them through the woods, voices shouting as they got closer. Mr. Cross looked in that direction. "Oh, sod it all," he muttered to himself. "We must have tripped one of the wards."

"Akrur," Miss Normandy said in a low voice.

"I know, I know, they can't see him," Mr. Cross answered, voice low.

"Is it my father?" Chrysta asked, fear clawing at her throat. *How?* How did they find them again so fast?

"Oh no, dear," Mr. Cross said, leaning down to squeeze her shoulder in reassurance. "You're safe. You have my word." He nodded at Tommy. "He is not."

Mr. Cross stood up and squared his shoulders. "Alright, ladies, I'll try to keep them from finding you."

Chrysta watched as Mr. Cross disappeared into the woods. She tried to keep her voice from shaking as she whispered. "Who is out there? Why is Tommy in danger?"

"Hunters," Miss Normandy said. "They are trained to find and kill changelings."

"They would hurt him? Even though he's not dangerous?"

"Generally, all changelings are dangerous," she explained. She laid a hand on Tommy's chest and then looked at her watch. "Tommy may just be the exception to the rule, but he's not exactly in a position to defend himself."

Chrysta waited, straining to hear anything in the silence. She almost thought she could hear voices in the distance but wasn't sure. There was movement from where Mr. Cross disappeared into the trees, and a large cat emerged from the darkness. Solid brown, larger than a house cat, pointed ears with black tuffs at the ends; it paused when it saw the two women and the changeling on the ground, Chrysta, and Miss Normandy staring back at it. It hissed, and Chrysta was shocked when she heard it say, "Monster!" before it turned around and ran back into the woods.

"Did that cat just talk?" she asked.

Miss Normandy blinked at her. "You mean you heard it speak?"

Before Chrysta could tell her yes, she most certainly heard that cat talk, the crashing in the forest started rapidly coming towards them again. Four figures broke into the clearing, and they all stopped at the sight of Chrysta, Tommy, and Miss Normandy. Three were dressed in black, but the man in front wore a tan suit and pea-jacket. Older, with a white beard, he was a tall and imposing figure with a large dog by his side. His face went from shock to anger as Mr. Cross caught up to them, slightly out of breath. "Miss Normandy," he said in a low voice. "What is the meaning of this?"

"He asked for my help," Miss Normandy said. "I wasn't going to ignore him." She gestured at Chrysta. "She was in danger."

"Chrysta York, daughter of Jozef York, was in peril. According to the changeling that broke into your home," the man said, voice getting louder in anger. He extended his hand, and a ball of light rose from his palm to float in the air, bathing the clearing in an eerie glow. A young woman, the cat standing next to her, started when she saw Tommy in the light, and she leaned over to whisper in the older man's ear.

"Are you sure?" he murmured back, and she nodded. His face turned grim. "Normandy, get away from him," he said in a louder voice.

"Headmaster Burke, please. I promised I would help him."

The woman stepped up and took a sword out of a scabbard. It was black and shone in the white light.

"It's too risky, Normandy," Burke said as the young woman started towards Tommy. "There are too many lives at stake."

Chrysta started shaking her head. "Please, sir, you don't know Tommy. Please, don't hurt him."

"Move out of the way," the young woman said coldly. Miss Normandy stood up, put her hands out, and opened her mouth, probably to say something in Tommy's defense, but the young woman grabbed her and shoved her to the ground. Mr. Cross ran to her to help her up. Chrysta scrambled so that she was covering as much of Tommy's torso with hers as she could.

"Please, don't hurt him!" Chrysta yelled, but the woman lifted her sword anyway.

"Move!" the woman commanded.

"No!" Chrysta shouted back. The woman's face contorted in anger, and she lifted the sword higher, aiming at Tommy's head.

Mr. Cross gave a shout, but before the sword came down, Chrysta felt the flex in her chest, and the young woman went flying backward. Once she landed with a shout, the cat positioned itself between her and Chrysta and hissed loudly.

Everyone else in the clearing was frozen in shock as Chrysta's hand glowed gold. She glared at all the adults around her. "No one *touches* him," she growled.

Mr. Cross was looking between Chrysta and the older man. "Is she... is she glowing gold?" he asked in a hushed whisper.

"It seems she is," the older man said. Just then, the young woman got up with a snarl and started stalking towards Tommy again, rage etched on her face. She raised her sword again, and Chrysta raised her other hand, getting ready to send her away if needed. "Nyla, that's enough!" the man shouted.

"No! It should die!" she screamed back.

"Nyla!" he shouted, and the woman finally stopped, looking at Chrysta's glowing hands with the same air of confusion as the others.

"Nyla, go back to the Academy," the older man said. His voice was calmer as he stepped closer to Tommy and Chrysta. Chrysta kept her attention on the young woman, not breaking eye contact.

"Burke, you can't be serious," she said. She lowered the sword but kept it ready like she still wanted to swipe at Tommy.

"Go, Nyla," he responded. "We will talk later. Smith and Ellis, go with her."

The woman waited, her scowl getting deeper. Finally, she turned, and the two men went with her back into the forest. The cat hissed again but left with them. Once she couldn't see the woman anymore, Chrysta relaxed and then shivered.

The older man paused, then took off his coat and wrapped it around Chrysta's shoulders. He backed up and then sat down on the ground out of Tommy's reach, the dog cautiously walking up to Tommy to sniff him. "Thank you," Chrysta murmured, and he nodded.

"My apologies, my dear," he said. "I was letting emotions run wild, including my own." Miss Normandy tentatively came back to crouch next to Tommy and put a hand on his chest, but now she was staring at Chrysta in awe. Mr. Cross also came forward and sat next to the older man. "Neil Burke," the man said to Chrysta, holding a hand to his chest. "You are Chrysta York, is that correct?"

Chrysta nodded. "Yes, sir."

"Tell me what happened tonight, in your own words."

Chrysta took a deep, shivering breath and then let it out shakily. She wasn't really sure where to start. "Two weeks ago, someone attacked me. Tommy saved me, but my father used it as an excuse to lock me up. He wouldn't even let me go to school. So Tommy left the city. He said he was going to find someone who could help." She paused and rubbed her face, feeling tired. She brought her hands down, and Miss Normandy squeezed one of them. She smiled at the older woman. "When Tommy came back, he said he found someone to help."

"How long have you known the change—How long have you known Tommy?" Mr. Burke asked. Chrysta took it as a good sign that he was using Tommy's name.

"Two months."

"And he didn't tell you he was a changeling?" asked Mr. Cross.

"No, he told me." Both men looked at each other in shock, and Chrysta continued. "He told me Halloween night. It was his birthday, and he said he was over 175 years old. So I asked how he could be so old, and he said he was a changeling. I thought he was joking."

Both men looked at her in confusion, and Miss Normandy spoke up. "Tommy said her father kept the magical world a secret from her."

"Why?" Mr. Cross asked.

"You would have to ask my father," Chrysta said, and he looked thoughtful at that. "Earlier tonight," Chrysta continued, but she faltered and hesitated. Was it really earlier that night? It felt like days. "Earlier tonight, someone who looked like Tommy showed up and took me to my house's third story. But it was a trap. It was a man named Jacobs who could look like Tommy. A man named Frost tried to make me go to sleep. It didn't work, but then Mr. Guerra drugged me."

Mr. Burke's eyebrows went up while Mr. Cross shifted next to him. "Guerra?" Mr. Burke asked.

Chrysta nodded. "Yes. Do you know him?"

"Not personally," Mr. Burke said dryly. "Please, continue."

"When I woke up, I was tied to a table, they made me drink something, and my father... my father had a knife, and he was going to stab me," Chrysta said the last part in a rush, feeling ashamed. "Tommy showed up, and we ran. He turned into this when Frost found us," she gestured at Tommy's prone body, "and scared him and a group of men away. Then we ran again. Father found us, and I sent him away because he was hurting Tommy. I guess... I guess my father is the one who controls the slave band."

Mr. Burke glanced at the slave band on Tommy's forearm. "And then Miss Normandy and Mr. Cross showed up."

Chrysta nodded. Mr. Burke turned to Mr. Cross. "Cross, a word?"

Chrysta watched both men stand up and move away to murmur to themselves. She turned to Miss Normandy. "Miss Normandy?" she asked in a tentative voice. "Why does everyone seem so scared when I'm glowing?"

"It's... it's a long story, dear," Miss Normandy simply stated.

They both watched Mr. Cross and Mr. Burke talking for several minutes, Mr. Burke standing with one hand to his mouth in thought, Mr. Cross waving his hands around. At one point, Chrysta saw Mr. Cross reach into his coat, but he saw Miss Normandy glaring at him and stopped. Snow started to fall, and Chrysta shivered, even with Tommy's and Mr. Burke's jackets wrapped around her. "Gentlemen," Miss Normandy called out, "I have to get these two out of the cold."

The two men returned, Mr. Cross crouching to pick up his crystals. Mr. Burke looked at Tommy. "I assume," he drawled, "you need some transportation, Miss Normandy?"

"That would be lovely," she replied. She turned to Chrysta. "Hold your breath again."

Chrysta did as she was told, and Mr. Burke moved his hands in small circles over the ground. His hands began to glow white, and the light worked down his arms. Chrysta felt the same sensation as before, her hair standing on end and tremendous pressure. The light in Mr. Burke's hand got brighter to the point it hurt to look at. They winked out of existence.

Poe came back several minutes later and dropped down where Tommy and Chrysta had been. He hopped around and squawked. He then cocked his head to the side and flew into the air, going deeper into the woods.

ॐ 24 ॐ

When the light disappeared this time, they were in a large room. There was a desk with a fireplace and a bookcase behind it. Opposite the desk was a wall with large windows with an examination table sitting there under them. A young man was snoring at the desk, but their arrival did not wake him, and he didn't even move when Tommy started coughing again, and Mr. Burke's dog had a sneezing fit. Miss Normandy glared at the young man but didn't say anything. "Come on, let's get him in one of the private rooms," she said.

She got up and opened a door leading to a short hallway lined with more doors. Miss Normandy unlocked one of them. It was a white room with a bed and private bathroom, old looking but clean. Miss Normandy went back to Tommy and grabbed one of his shoulders. "Come on, Akrur, heave-ho."

"Shouldn't we get that wanker up?" Mr. Cross asked, gesturing to the snoring young man.

"Him? We wake him up, and every student will know there is a changeling on the grounds before the sun rises. Come on, Akrur, lift with your knees, not your back."

Mr. Cross grumbled, but he grabbed Tommy's other shoulder. Chrysta got between them and supported Tommy's head, and they dragged him down the hall, Mr. Burke just looking on in amusement.

They got Tommy in the bed, but his legs were so long his feet dangled off the edge. He didn't stir or move throughout the process, but he was still breathing, slow and steady. Miss Normandy was rechecking his chest while watching her watch, Mr. Cross breathing heavily from the strain.

"Is he okay?" Chrysta asked softly, covering Tommy with a blanket.

"Well, his heart rate is steady—forty beats per minute. But I have no idea if that is normal or too low."

Chrysta inspected the slave band, making sure it was still cold to the touch. Tommy suddenly twitched, making all three of them jump in surprise, but he settled down with a sigh and didn't stir again. Miss Normandy cut off his ruined sweater while Chrysta found another blanket to cover Tommy's legs. Chrysta was surprised when Miss Normandy got up and started pushing her out of the room.

"But... we aren't leaving him alone, are we?"

"Don't worry, I'm coming back. But first, we are getting you to bed."

"But, what if he wakes up? I should be here."

"You need to eat, shower, and get to bed. That's an order."

"Doctor's orders?" Mr. Cross joked, and Miss Normandy glared at him.

Chrysta gave Mr. Burke his jacket back while Miss Normandy locked the door to Tommy's room. Miss Normandy then sighed and grabbed a book from the bookcase. She lifted it and dropped it next to the young man's head. He started awake with a yell.

"Edwin, thank you so much for covering while I was gone," Miss Normandy said in a too-loud voice. The young man rubbed his eyes and blinked at everyone looking at him. "Looks like we will have to work on making you a night owl next."

"Sorry, Miss Normandy," he replied thickly.

"No worries, Edwin. Sleep deprivation is sometimes part of the job. Go to bed." She waited as the young man got up and left. When she was confident that he was gone entirely, she turned to Mr. Burke. "You are the only other person with a key to that room, yes?"

Mr. Burke nodded. "And I will make sure Nyla does not get it." He turned to Chrysta. "Miss York, I will see you tomorrow after you have gotten some rest. There is still more for us to discuss."

"Thank you, Mr. Burke. For letting me and Tommy stay."

"It's against my better judgment. But I feel that I need to give you a chance to explain yourself, my dear. Just know that you will have to answer to me if you hurt anyone in this school."

"Yes, sir."

All four left the office, Mr. Burke and his dog turning right as the other two adults guided Chrysta to the left. They were in an older building, with wide hallways with tall ceilings, their footsteps echoing on the tile as they walked. They came to a wooden door, and Mr. Cross opened it for the two ladies.

They exited the building into a garden, bushes without any greenery but covered in snow so perfect they looked like fluffy clouds. There was a fountain, but the water was solid ice. Chrysta took the opportunity to look up and started the fruitless task of counting the stars. Miss Normandy was smiling at her when she looked back down a few minutes later.

"I have never been out of the city before," she explained, a small smile on her face. "I could never imagine the night sky could look like this."

They kept walking until they were leaving the gardens. Chrysta thought they were going back into the forest until she noticed that they seemed to be going towards a massive oak tree. It was bare, but the branches were covered in white icicles that twinkled in the dark. Chrysta saw several white objects as big as her forearm that hung from the limbs. She thought they were massive icicles, but she saw they were crystals, softly glowing, as they got closer. Little lights floated in the dark around the tree. Chrysta wondered if they were fireflies, only it was too cold, and they were purple in color. She held a hand out as one drifted towards her, and it moved through her hand, making it feel warm.

"Who set up the lights?" Miss Normandy asked.

"Ichiro," Mr. Cross explained with some pride. "He's getting good with them."

Mr. Cross was slightly in front of them, and Chrysta almost laughed when he started to sink into the ground. As she and Miss Normandy caught up, she saw that he was going down a flight of stairs curving around a stone wall. It was a room set into the ground, with corners full of snow. There was a door at the far wall, and someone had hung a wreath of holly and golden bells. The roots of the tree stretched over the space, creating a natural ceiling.

Mr. Cross went to the wooden door at the far wall, and he opened it with a flourish, bowing slightly.

"Welcome, Miss York," he said to Chrysta with a smile, "to the Disaster Club."

.....

They entered a large round room, seven doors running along the wall at regular intervals. There was a large wood stove in the middle of the room, throwing off light and warmth, exhaust pipe running along with the ceiling to the outer wall. The large room was full of furniture, couches and chairs mostly, all different styles, old-looking but clean, and several mismatched rugs were strewn about.

One couch was facing the wall, a TV set in front of it. And as the door opened with a jingle, a group of teens turned to look at them from the couch: two girls, close to Chrysta's age, three boys, one who was Chrysta's age, slightly heavyset with glasses, one who looked like he was 12, and one who looked older. They all looked at Chrysta and the adults with open curiosity.

"What the... you all should be in bed by now. It's almost two in the morning," Mr. Cross said as he offered to take Miss Normandy's coat. Chrysta reluctantly took Tommy's jacket off and put it on a coat rack by the door, already full of other jackets.

"We were concerned," one of the girls said. She had on PJs and a headscarf and gave Chrysta a small smile. "You left so suddenly we were worried about you."

"Well, you should be in bed," Mr. Cross said sternly as he took off his coat and hat, keeping his gloves on. He turned to Chrysta as she got Tommy's shoes off. "I know you are tired, Miss York, but we need to do a reading before you get to bed."

"Really, Akrur, you have to do it now?" Miss Normandy asked.

"Yes, I do. Because I have to make sure Chrysta's claims are true if she is staying the night." He shrugged. "I have to protect everyone here like Burke said."

"It's okay," Chrysta said. She didn't know what reading was, but she was okay with it if it put Mr. Cross at ease.

"Wait," the other girl said. "Did you just say York? Like Jozef York?"

"Yes, Rosa, Chrysta is Jozef York's daughter," Mr. Cross explained. The girl and the older teen glanced at each other. "But first, we are doing a reading before I make a judgment call of Chrysta staying here." The other girl made a face like she was eating something sour.

Mr. Cross stepped in front of the couch and took a seat. He waved at one of the teens who was gathering. "Grab a chair, won't you." The older teen nodded and went to grab one. He returned with what looked like a dining room chair, with one leg shorter than the others.

"Thank you," Chrysta said, and the teen just smiled and nodded, and then he moved, so he was behind her. Miss Normandy stood on her other side and put a hand on her shoulder. Chrysta gave her a small smile.

Mr. Cross was removing his gloves, and when he was done, he blew on his fingers. Blue sparks flew into the air like he just blew into a fire. Chrysta flinched as they floated in front of her, but they disappeared before they hit her. He held his hands out over the water-stained coffee table. "Your hands, please."

Chrysta looked to Miss Normandy for reassurance, and the healer smiled at her and nodded. She slipped her hands into his, her heart pounding. He ran his thumbs along the back of her fingers, making more of the blue sparks. She tried to lean back and snatch her hands back, but Mr. Cross clamped down so she couldn't have them. Chrysta felt fear claw at her throat.

His eyebrows instantly furrowed, and Mr. Cross made a small sound. "Sshhh, my dear, this is not going to hurt," he tried giving her a small smile and her hands a squeeze. "You're terrified. You don't have to be. It's not going to sting." He shifted on the couch slightly and leaned towards her. "Let's take a deep breath, shall we?"

She nodded and copied him when he took a deep breath and let it out slowly. The sparks came back, but Chrysta didn't flinch this time. Mr. Cross smiled bigger. "See, no big deal." He took a deep breath. "Now, Miss York. I'm gonna ask you some questions, and you try to concentrate on them. Okay?"

Chrysta nodded, not trusting her voice.

"Alright. Your father is Jozef York, correct?"

her father, looking stern at the dinner table, never greeted her with a smile, always seemed angry, always seemed distant, never went to one of her concerts, the empty chair, mocking her, upsetting her, the way he acted when she and Tommy were running away, was he even worried about her now?

"Do you know what your father had planned for you?"

Chrysta looked down, trying to gather her thoughts. This was bringing back some memories for her that were still fresh and frightening. "He and Guerra put me to sleep," she said. She took a breath and continued. "When I woke up, I was tied to a table, and my father had a knife. He was going to stab me. I don't know why. Then Tommy showed up and saved me."

"Tommy?" the boy with glasses asked.

"The changeling," Miss Normandy offered. Mr. Cross glared at her but then turned his attention back to Chrysta. "Can you tell me about Tommy, dear?"

Tommy, the first time they met, Tommy, when she saw him again, more open and friendly, when she brought him the birthday cupcake, Tommy treated it like the most precious thing in the world, when they played in the jazz club together, Tommy followed her lead with no complaint or comment, watching him play the piano, cuddling with him and hearing his heartbeat, "I have to make sure you are safe," he says, looking like a monster, but still the man she knew and trusted with all her heart

"Whoa there, dear, slow down," Mr. Cross said. When she brought her attention back to him, she saw that he looked like he was in pain. The blue sparks were traveling down his arms, and Chrysta noticed gold light coming from her skin and leading into his. "What are you doing to me?" she asked in awe.

"Psychometry," he said, "the ability to read emotions with touch." He took a deep breath and let it out in a shaky exhale. The gathered teens looked on in wonder, jaws dropped and mouths open. Chrysta glanced back at Miss Normandy and saw her lips were thin in worry. "I usually can spot a liar a mile away. It's hard to fake true emotion. Only, you are kinda stronger than I expected." Chrysta felt bad. She was scared, but she wasn't trying to hurt him.

"Can I do something to stop it?" she asked.

"Try to think of one memory," he said. "It will help with the emotions." The gold was already starting to retreat to her, and Mr. Cross looked a little more comfortable. Chrysta tried to focus on one memory.

her latest concert, and Chrysta knows that the chair in the front row will be empty, it always is, she is backstage, feeling anxiety, but it is not because of the people, it's not playing in front of them, no, it is the knowledge she will stand on that stage, and no one will be there to cheer her on

and she steps out, takes a deep breath, and tries not to feel the disappointment as she walks across the stage, but the chair is not empty, Tommy is sitting there, he is sitting in the chair, holding what must be a dozen roses, and he kisses his fingertips and offers them to her

Tommy, in a suit, for her

and she is standing on the stage, trying not to cry, for so long she almost misses her cue, but it's okay, because Tommy is there, and he is paying attention and when she finally puts the violin to her chin, and the bow to the strings, she plays

she plays because he is listening

Mr. Cross gasped and, finally, let go. Chrysta wiped at her eyes and noticed Mr. Cross do the same. The teens were glancing between them, sharing looks of fear. Chrysta swallowed past the lump in her throat, fighting the tears that threatened to fall down her cheeks. She felt a hand on her shoulder, but it's the teen and not Miss Normandy this time. Miss Normandy had rushed to Mr. Cross's side and put a hand on his arm.

"Are you okay?" she asked. Mr. Cross nodded and almost touched hers, but pulled back when blue sparks crackled between them. He quickly put his gloves back on and smiled. "I'm fine," he said, but his voice sounded strained.

He looked around for a minute, almost like he was getting his bearings. He took a deep breath. "Alright, everyone, she's staying here," he announced.

Everyone seemed happy by his announcement, except for one girl who cried out, "What?!" She rushed to Mr. Cross and started to whisper to him while the other girl hugged Chrysta. The boy with glasses raced up to Chrysta and began to dance from foot to foot in excitement. "Awesome! You can tell us all about the changeling!" he said.

Mr. Cross groaned as he stood up. "Easy, easy, everybody. Miss York has had a long night. We'll talk more in the morning, alright?" He looked around as he put his gloves back on. "Kevin, can you get her some dinner? Rimsha, you look like you guys are the same size... almost. How about you get her a change of clothes?"

The girl who had hugged Chrysta hopped up with a shout of glee and ran to a door. The boy also ran off to another door. The other girl who was standing by Mr. Cross glared at him. "Are you seriously letting her stay here?" she nearly yelled at him.

"We'll talk more in the morning, Rosa," Mr. Cross replied.

"Mr. Cross!" This time she did yell, and then she glared at Chrysta with hate in her eyes. Chrysta took a step back. The boy standing behind her stepped up and frowned back at Rosa. Rosa saw his look and scoffed. She stomped towards the door Rimsha had disappeared into and slammed it shut.

Mr. Cross blew some air out of his nose. "Teenagers will be the bloody death of me," he muttered under his breath, and then he clapped his hands together. "Right, then," he said, trying to sound cheerful, "Guys, get Miss York into the kitchen. Miss Normandy and I have to chat before she leaves."

Chrysta hurried over to Miss Normandy. "Will you keep an eye on Tommy tonight? Please?" she asked, a little frightened.

Miss Normandy smiled at her and took one of her hands to squeeze it. "Don't worry. I'll keep an eye on him tonight. And you are in good hands with Mr. Cross," she said. "I wouldn't have brought you here if I didn't believe that."

"Aw, how touching, you like me," Mr. Cross joked. Miss Normandy gave him a look and snorted.

"Can I see Tommy tomorrow?" Chrysta asked.

"Of course," Miss Normandy said, and then they shared a brief hug.

Rimsha came back to the common room with a scared look on her face. "Mr. Cross, Rosa is punching a pillow," she said with wide eyes.

Mr. Cross winced and sighed. "Yeah, I thought that would be her reaction. Give her a minute, Rimsha." He reached for Miss Normandy's arm. "Come on, Abby."

Miss Normandy gave Chrysta another smile, and the two adults moved to the exit. Mr. Cross held the door for her, and then they were gone.

The young boy went up to Chrysta and held out a hand. "Ichiro Takahashi," he said as they shook hands. He pointed to the taller, older boy. "Julien LeBlanc." The older boy smiled and waved. "He's deaf but can read lips if you need to talk to him," Ichiro explained. He pointed to the girl bouncing up and down excitedly next to Chrysta. "Rimsha Khalil."

"Oh, it's so good to have another girl here finally," she said, handing some clothes to Chrysta. Chrysta accepted them with a smile.

"Let's get you something to eat," Ichiro said, and they moved to the door that the other boy had disappeared behind.

Inside was a small but well-equipped kitchen. There was a dining room table in front of them with eight chairs, but none of them matched. The boy stood at a stove, moving a pan back and forth. He glanced over his shoulder at the group and called out. "Sorry, I forgot to ask. You don't have any food allergies, do you?"

"No," Chrysta called back. Julien had pulled a chair out from the table, and she sat down. Ichiro chose to sit next to her while Julien and Rimsha took the other side of the table. There were several minutes of uncomfortable silence while everyone looked at her. Chrysta had nothing to do but look back as food sizzled from the kitchen.

When Chrysta felt like she couldn't take the staring any longer and was about to ask if she could leave, the boy came and placed a pan full of bacon and eggs in the middle of the table. He went back to the kitchen to get plates and went back a third time for the toast and some jars from the ancient-looking fridge. Chrysta felt her stomach clench in hunger, and she piled food on her plate when it was in front of her.

The others also got some food, although Rimsha stuck with the toast the boy gave her. He finally sat down across from Chrysta but was startled when Ichiro kicked him under the table. Ichiro nodded at Chrysta, but the other boy just looked confused. "Introduce yourself, dumbass," Ichiro hissed.

"Hey!" Rimsha shouted at the smaller boy and pointed a knife covered in peanut butter at him. "Language."

Ichiro stuck out his tongue, but the boy wiped his hands on his shirt and held one out over the table. "Kevin Butler, at your service," he said as they shook hands. "Ha! Butler, at your service," he said with a laugh. "That joke never gets old."

Chrysta went back to shoveling more food into her mouth. The others didn't seem to mind her bad manners. "So," Kevin started to say, "you're the daughter of Jozef York?"

Now it was Rimsha's turn to kick Kevin underneath the table. He yelped and glared at her. "Did you just say that?!" she hissed at Kevin.

Chrysta dropped her eyes to her lap. "Yes, I am," she softly replied. "Everyone seems to know who he is. Why is that?"

"He has done some horrible things," Rimsha explained. "You don't know about what he has done?"

"No, I don't," Chrysta softly replied, and the table got uncomfortably quiet.

Just then, the door to the kitchen opened, and Mr. Cross came through. He sighed and rubbed his eyes as he sat at the table's head next to Julien and Chrysta. "You okay, Mr. Cross?" asked Rimsha. He shook his head.

"No, I am not," he replied. "That reading took a lot out of me." He sighed again and finally dropped his hand and looked at the table. "Dear Lord, I said feed Miss York, Kevin, not a damn army."

Kevin just shrugged. "You know I can't make food for one person." He then shoveled a large portion of eggs and bacon into his own mouth.

Rimsha was still looking at Mr. Cross with a worried expression. "Do you need anything, Mr. Cross?"

"Yeah, grab my bottle of pain pills, will you?" he asked the teen, and she got up to leave the kitchen. He looked Chrysta up and down. "So, how you doing, Lady York?"

"Better, thank you," she replied, actually meaning it. Her plate was empty, and she was thinking about going for seconds.

"Well, eat up, then you can shower and go to bed," he said. Rimsha came back and put a bottle on the table. He picked it up and started to open it. "I'm not going to pepper you with a bunch of questions right now. I got the cliff notes from the Doc, so I'm not going to demand your life story. But I do have to ask about the changeling."

"What about Tommy?" she asked.

"Just tell me about him," he said. "I know how you feel about him, but tell me what he is like."

Chrysta looked around the table and saw that she had everyone's attention. She cleared her throat. "Well, I met him about two months ago. He was playing violin in a park, and I..." she paused momentarily. "He was a good player. He *is* a good player. I play the violin too and wanted to listen."

Mr. Cross had poured several pills into his palm and swallowed them dry. "So, he didn't approach you?"

She shook her head. "No, I wanted to meet him," she explained. "I know that is strange, but I don't know. I saw him playing and just wanted to get to know him."

Rimsha sighed, and everyone looked at her. "You two play the same instrument. It's so romantic."

Mr. Cross and Kevin rolled their eyes, Ichiro stuck his tongue out in disgust, and Julien smirked.

Mr. Cross nodded at Chrysta. "So you two started seeing each other?" he asked, putting the cap back on the bottle.

Kevin held his hands up close to his face and said in a soft, mocking singsong voice, "It's so romantic." Rimsha kicked him again.

"Yes," said Chrysta, ignoring the small fight across the table. "It's just since my mom died, my father wouldn't let me go out. So I would sneak out to be with Tommy. He's my friend."

Mr. Cross nodded. "And the memory you showed me?"

"My music teacher would insist on saving my father a seat in the front row for my concerts, even though he would never be there. The empty seat would be there, mocking me during a performance," Chrysta explained. She dropped her eyes down to her lap, where her hands were wrapped together. The others stopped fighting and looked at her. She took a breath. "I was telling Tommy about how upset it made me and how I didn't want to do the concert. And that night, when I got on stage, he was sitting there instead. With roses." She laughed at the memory, and the emotions it brought with it made a lump form in her throat. She swiped at her eyes.

Ichiro put a hand on her shoulder, and she smiled at him. "He didn't have to be there, but he was. To support me," she continued. "That was a few weeks ago."

Mr. Cross was looking at her with a thoughtful expression. "So, he encouraged you when he didn't need to?"

Chrysta nodded. "Mr. Cross, can you tell me what a changeling is?"

Mr. Cross mulled over her question. "It's a long story, not something I want to get into tonight," he said. He reached over to the pan and swiped a piece of bacon to chew. "But, let me just say that changelings are cunning, evil creatures, and I have never heard of one doing anything that didn't benefit it."

"Mr. Cross, if that is true, why is Headmaster Burke letting him stay here?" Rimsha asked.

"Not sure about that myself," Mr. Cross confessed. "The only thing that the Doc and I can think of is that he is not a threat since he is unconscious."

"Mr. Cross, I'm sorry, but *what* is a changeling?" Chrysta asked. "I mean, Tommy didn't always look like he does now. He looked like a human."

"That is what a changeling is, Miss York. They can change between their true self and their human form. That is why they are feared and hated. They were able to become our friends and wreak havoc. They could be anyone."

"But how, Mr. Cross? And who made them that way?" Chrysta asked as the flood of questions started to fly out of her, but Mr. Cross held up his hand.

"Again, Miss York, it's not something I want to get into today," he said. "I know you have questions, but I think we should save them for the morning."

Chrysta nodded, although she wanted to press the adult for answers.

Mr. Cross loudly cleared his throat, and the rest of the table jumped. "Lady and gentlemen, I will ask you to refrain from overwhelming Miss York with questions. We will all have a house meeting tomorrow where everyone can get their queries out in one go, okay?" He popped the last bit of bacon into his mouth and chewed. "And if Rosa gives her grief, you let me know, understood?"

"Rosa?" Chrysta asked. The rest of the teens looked uncomfortable as Mr. Cross nodded.

"The furious young woman you met earlier, the one who has probably set fire to half her room by now," he explained. He then sighed and leaned over the table. "Her family was killed several years back, so she is a ward of the Academy."

"Who killed her family?" asked Chrysta, who had a feeling she already knew.

"Rumor is, your father did," answered Mr. Cross.

The whole table went still, and no one dared breathe. Chrysta felt the burning in the back of her throat come back. "I don't know my father at all, do I?" she whispered.

Mr. Cross reached out and put his gloved hand in front of her. She brought one of her hands from her lap and put it in his, glad for the small comfort.

"You are not your father, Miss York. We believe here at the Disaster Club is that your family's past does not define you," Mr. Cross explained.

"The Disaster Club?" Chrysta asked.

"Tomorrow, Miss York," Mr. Cross said again. He took his hand back. "Kevin, thanks for the food. Ichiro, Julien, you clean up. Rimsha, can you show Miss York around? She will be staying in your room."

Rimsha nodded, and as the boys got up and started to clean and gripe about cleaning, she led Chrysta out of the kitchen. Mr. Cross stayed at the table and started chewing on his second piece of bacon thoughtfully.

They went back into the common room. Rimsha pointed to the door to the outside. "Outside, obviously," she said with a grin. She pointed to the door next to it. It was covered in faded stickers. "Girls' room." Next door. "Bathroom." The next door, covered in silver stars. "Boys' room."

She pointed to the door behind them. "Kitchen. Kevin cooks mostly, so let him know if you want anything. Lunch is usually leftovers from the night before."

The next door had a red and gold family crest hung on it. "Mr. Cross's room." The one after that. "A guest room. It's hardly ever used."

The last door. "The greenhouse."

"Greenhouse? Underground?" Chrysta asked.

Rimsha nodded. "It's nice too. Feel free to use it whenever you want. Just please be careful of the plants. They like company but just don't touch."

Rimsha guided Chrysta to the bathroom. It had six stalls, three of them for toilets and three for showers, and three sinks. There were a washer, dryer, and cabinets on the far wall, old-looking like everything else in the Disaster Club, but the bathroom was spotless. Light moonlight streamed through a skylight in the ceiling, but Rimsha turned on the lights. Rimsha grabbed towels and soap for Chrysta from one of the cabinets, and she went into a shower stall.

The hot water felt wonderful, and Chrysta sighed as her muscles relaxed under the water. "Thank you," she said.

"For what?"

"For helping me," Chrysta explained.

"It's no problem," Rimsha said. "We try to welcome everyone here, especially for those who need it." She paused. "Mr. Cross says to be nice to everyone you meet. You don't know what kind of battle they may be fighting."

When Chrysta came out of the shower dressed in the borrowed clothes, Rimsha winced at the bruises on her arms. "You okay?"

"Yeah," Chrysta said, looking at her arms. "They don't hurt, but I had a lot of people grabbing me tonight."

Rimsha showed her where to hang up the wet towel, and they snuck into the girls' room, Chrysta carrying her ruined clothes and Tommy's shoes. There were four beds, Rosa at one end of the room, on her side facing the wall. Chrysta wasn't sure if she was awake or not but didn't want to find out. Rimsha gave her the bed at the other end of the room.

"'Night," Rimsha softly said with a yawn.

"'Night," Chrysta responded. Rimsha smiled and went to her bed.

Tired as she was, Chrysta lay under the covers, looking up through the skylight for what felt like an hour. The purple lights blotted out some of the stars, but she could still see them through the branches. She didn't know how she should feel; Chrysta was in a strange new place, with people she didn't know, who knew more about magic than she did. She was glowing gold, and everyone acted like she was a bomb, ready to go off at the drop of a hat. Tommy was hurt, and she didn't know how to fix it, and everyone was treating him like a wild animal. She was worried about Mary and knew she would be worried sick about Chrysta.

But she was free. Free of that house. Free from her father. The future was uncertain, but it was finally hers to control. She turned onto her side and eventually fell asleep.

ᓚ 25 ᓂ

Chrysta was walking through the gardens. It was snowy, and she only wore the borrowed PJs but kept walking despite the cold. Her mother was standing by the fountain, looking like she did a few weeks back, hair down and wearing a red dress this time.

"Mom?" Chrysta said softly. Her mother turned to her and smiled. Chrysta reached out, and her mother pulled her into a hug. The skin on her mother's arms felt like ice.

"Why?" Chrysta almost sobbed. "Why did my father do it?"

"Oh, little one," her mother crooned. "I'm so glad you are alive." Her mother was gently petting Chrysta's hair, but suddenly she grabbed a fistful of it and pulled Chrysta's head back. Chrysta gasped as her mother grinned at her evilly. "Now, I get to kill you myself."

Chrysta cried out and pushed her mother away, stumbling when her mother slapped her. She fell to the cold ground and gaped as her mother produced a knife, the same one her father had tried to use. The stones glittered in the moonlight, and Chrysta scrambled back as her mother advanced on her.

"Looks like the thing can't help you now," her mother said in an abnormally high voice, almost a screech. Chrysta kept backing up until her back hit the fountain.

"It didn't save you. It just delayed the inevitable." Cassia lifted the knife above her head. "Maybe I will visit it after I'm done with you!"

Chrysta screamed "No!" as her mother took aim, a mad grin on her face, and when she brought the knife down, Chrysta felt it pierce her throat.

.....

Chrysta sat up straight in bed, gasping for air, clawing at her throat. She didn't recognize her surroundings for a few moments and was worried that her mother had followed her to this room. But when her mother didn't materialize out of one of the room's dark corners, she relaxed. A dream. A nightmare. Her mother would have never hurt her, not in a million years.

She climbed out of bed and looked at the skylight to see blue skies beyond the tree's branches. It was midday if she had to guess. This time yesterday, she was locked in her room, worried about Tommy and her father's plans for her. So weird that so much had happened in a day.

She padded out to the main room, bare feet slapping on the cold floor. No one was in sight. She went to the bathroom, and when she came out, she tried the kitchen, which was also empty. She tried knocking on the boys' and Mr. Cross's rooms but got no answer. Finally, she pushed the door that led to the greenhouse.

She gasped. It was warm and bright and full of plants, every available inch of space colored in a shade of green. An easel was set up in the middle of the room, currently holding a canvas and paints. Chrysta went over to look closer at the painting in progress when she noticed Rimsha on the floor nearby, kneeling on a prayer mat. The other girl had her eyes closed and murmured to herself, although she stopped when Chrysta got close.

"Oh, I'm so sorry," Chrysta said softly, feeling a blush on her face.

Rimsha just smiled. "No problem. I was just finishing up." She got up and rolled up the mat, putting it in a corner when she was done. "I'm glad you're up. Mr. Cross was worried you would sleep the entire day away."

"Sorry, I guess I was exhausted," Chrysta said. "Where is everyone?"

"The boys went to New Bendigo for food." Rimsha saw the confused look on Chrysta's face. "That is the nearest town. Mr. Cross went for a walk with Rosa." Rimsha twisted her hands nervously. "I'm sorry if she is mean to you. She is not happy that Mr. Cross invited you to stay."

Chrysta nodded. "I kind of understand where she is coming from. I lost my mother when I was younger. If someone had hurt her, I wouldn't want them or their family to be around me either." Chrysta let them fall into silence as she looked around, trying to find a way to change subjects. Her eyes fell on the painting. It was a study of several of the flowers in the greenhouse. "That is very good."

"Thank you," Rimsha replied with a beaming smile. "I love painting flowers. They are my best subjects. No complaining, no moving." She stretched out a hand,

and it glowed green. One of the trees nearby shivered and grew about an inch. "Unless I want them to move, that is."

Chrysta gasped. "What was that?"

"My ability," Rimsha said, looking bashful. "I can make plants thrive and grow."

"Wow," Chrysta said as the tree started to flower.

Rimsha looked down and then looked dismayed. "Oh, let's get you some clothes and shoes; the floor is too cold to go barefoot."

They returned to the girls' room, and Rimsha gave Chrysta a change of clothes. She turned away to provide Chrysta with some privacy. "So, what is everyone's ability?" Chrysta asked as she got dressed.

"Well, I can make plants grow. Like really fast. I have made a tree grow from an acorn in under two minutes. I don't like doing it, though. It can harm the plant, and they die quickly. Kevin can talk to animals. He's hoping to be a vet someday, a regular Dr. Dolittle, he says. Rosa can control fire, like setting something on fire from ten feet away. She has trouble controlling it sometimes, though. Julien has several mental abilities. He can see into the past, into the future, and walk dreams."

"Walk dreams?" Chrysta asked.

"He tried to explain it to me once. Apparently, dreams are a gateway to people's innermost thoughts, and you can get a lot of information from someone when they are dreaming. It's really dangerous, though. He said walking in someone's dream means you can get hurt if you are not careful."

Chrysta started to roll up the sleeves of her borrowed shirt and the legs of her borrowed pants. "And Ichiro?"

"Ichiro glows purple. It means he is like Mr. Burke and will have several abilities. I have seen him move things with his mind and control fire and water. Mr. Cross says he will get stronger as he gets older."

Chrysta folded her borrowed PJs and put them on the bed. She checked that her clothes were still folded with Tommy's boots underneath the bed. She would clean them when she had the chance.

"I saw you glow gold last night," Rimsha said softly. "Do you know what that means?"

"Not really," Chrysta admitted. "But everyone gets very scared when they see me glow." She sat down next to the other girl. "Can you tell me why?"

"My father told me a story once," Rimsha started. "About a mighty sorcerer who glowed gold and could do *anything* she wanted. Go anywhere in the world, read people's minds, transform anything into whatever she wanted. But she went mad with power and started to force people to worship her. I always thought it was a fairy tale, a story about being careful with your powers. But maybe it's not."

Chrysta looked at her hand and tried to start a fire like she saw the man doing last night. But golden sparks flew uselessly from her fingertips. She signed in frustration. "I don't feel like an all-powerful sorcerer. I can't really control it."

"Well, that is why people come to the Academy," Rimsha explained. "To get better control of their abilities." She got up from the bed. "Come on, let's get you something to eat. We can wait for Mr. Cross."

As they made sandwiches in the kitchen, Chrysta looked through the skylight to watch the sky above. "What is this place?" she asked Rimsha.

"It was an old tower that fell down," Rimsha said. "Only the basement remained. So they cleaned it up and made it into a place people could stay. It's cold in the winter but comfortable once you get used to it."

After half an hour, just as Chrysta finished her lunch, Mr. Cross entered the kitchen with Rosa. Rosa seemed calmer than the last time Chrysta saw her, but she waited to see what the other teen would do. Rosa came up to her with a scowl on her face. She suddenly stuck out a hand. "Rosa Torres," she said softly. Chrysta took her hand and shook it. "Mr. Cross says your father tried to hurt you too, so... I'm sorry for the way I acted."

"It's okay," Chrysta said. "You don't have to apologize. I understand why you are upset."

"Well..." Rosa paused as she rubbed her neck. "I promise I won't treat you like shit unless you turn out to be like your father."

"Language," Rimsha chided the other girl, but she was smiling.

"Alright, ladies," Mr. Cross said. "We are heading out. Miss York and I have some talking to do."

"Good luck," Rimsha said as Chrysta and Mr. Cross left the kitchen.

They went to the coat rack, Chrysta wearing Tommy's jacket again. She paused to breathe in Tommy's scent. It may have been her imagination, but it seemed to be fading. They went outside and slowly climbed the steps. Mr. Cross motioned for Chrysta to follow him, and they started toward the gardens.

Now that it was daylight, Chrysta got a better look at the large building they had walked through the night before. Four stories tall, square in shape, with towers at the corners. It was an enormous and foreboding structure.

They walked through the gardens, Chrysta shuddering when she saw the fountain but trying to tell herself that she was safe in the daylight. Mr. Cross paused by a stone bench so they could sit down. He reached into his jacket and brought out a case of cigarettes. "Horrible habit, my dear," he growled as one cigarette hung from his lips, and he checked the pockets of his jacket. "Don't ever, ever smoke."

He couldn't find what he was looking for, so he sighed and raised his hand. "*Aag*," he said curtly, and a small flame started at the tip of one finger. Chrysta watched in fascination as he lit the cigarette and started puffing.

"So magic is real," she said.

"Oh, it is extremely real," he agreed. He puffed and seemed to be gathering his thoughts. "As long as there have been humans, there have been sorcerers, people able to call on and command magic."

"And wizards?" Chrysta asked with a smile.

"I know what you are thinking about," he said with a smile. "And I wouldn't mention those books or movies while you are here. They are considered very juvenile and poorly made." He snorted. "Yes, there were wizards at one point. You just don't see them much anymore. Wizards are people who learned to perform magic with wands, staffs, and spells. Sorcerers are born with natural abilities. Sometimes, we need spells, but that is for when we perform magic that does not come naturally to us." He reached into one pocket and brought something out with a smile. "And sometimes, it's easier to use a lighter than try to make a fire spell work, which is why you don't see wizards anymore," he said while wiggling the lighter playfully.

"So everyone has one ability?" she asked.

He hummed as he considered her question. "Yes and no. You see, everyone has one ability, but as they get older, their ability can grow and evolve. For example, in my family, we mostly have psychometry as our ability. We can touch people and objects and read emotions and memories. As we have gotten older, my brother has also become clairvoyant. He has visions of not only the past but the future as well. I'm starting to become clairaudient, meaning I hear things, sometimes it is spirits, sometimes of conversations people have had or going to have."

He paused to take a drag of his cigarette. "What abilities have you shown?"

"Me?" she asked, and he nodded. "Well... I broke a mirror and a nightstick with a thought. I made a fire." She paused, suddenly feeling embarrassed. "Tommy says I cursed someone."

"A curse?" he asked in surprise. "How so?"

"When I first met Tommy, someone stole his tip jar. When she wouldn't return it, her violins started breaking. She broke five of them in one week. Tommy told her he cursed his tip jar, and if she gave it back, she wouldn't be cursed anymore. But then he told me he thinks I did it." She blinked. "Maybe he was the one who did it after all."

"I doubt it," he said. "Changelings can't perform magic. And magic doesn't work on them."

"What are changelings?" she asked, but he started to shake his head.

"In due time, Miss York," Mr. Cross said. "Continue."

"Well, the next thing that happened is..." she paused. "It seems kind of silly."

"Chrysta, I don't care if you saw a talking moose. Trust me, I have heard of stranger things."

She laughed. "For my concert, I got a dress. My father didn't like it, so he took it away and replaced it with... this pink monstrosity." She shifted. "I was so upset because it was *my* dress. And I knew everyone would laugh at me if I wore what my father gave me. And so, the night before the concert, I dreamt that my dead mother came to me, and she helped me get the dress back."

"How so?" he asked softly.

"Well, she told me to send Poe, the raven who traveled with me last night, to the dress. And I *felt* it. I felt how to make him move through the wall."

"Phasing," Mr. Cross said.

"And then I brought the dress back with him."

"Transporation spell."

"It had silver lace, but my mother showed me how to make it gold."

"Transformation spell."

"And then my mother said to hide it. So after I burnt my father's dress, I made my dress look like his."

"A glamour spell," Mr. Cross said. Chrysta glanced at his face and saw him wearing an expression of wonder. "Anything else, my dear?"

"Um... a few days ago, Mr. Guerra put his hand on mine, and I felt a pain in my head. But he seemed upset? Like he was expecting something else?"

"Guerra's ability is the opposite of a healer's," Mr. Cross revealed. "Where a healer can mend the body, Guerra can injure it. He probably tried to hurt you, and you were resistant."

"That makes sense," she said. "Last night, Frost tried to get me to sleep, and he said something about me fighting him?"

"You're becoming too strong," Mr. Cross murmured. "I have a feeling if I tried to reread you, you would be able to shut me out. Totally blank me if you wanted."

He fell silent, holding his cigarette in his hand, lost in thought. It burned down to his fingers, and he cursed and flailed his hand to knock it away. Chrysta waited as he got another cigarette and lit it, using the lighter this time.

"Is that why everyone is afraid of me?" she asked.

He paused, taking a deep breath and releasing it in an explosive sigh. "You see, Miss York, generally, when we use our abilities, we glow. Blues, reds, greens, oranges. Those are the common colors." He looked at her. "Purples and whites are rare. People who glow those colors have several abilities at once. Ichiro glows purple. He started showing his abilities when he was nine. Headmaster Burke, he glows white. I have seen him perform magic that others could only dream of." Mr. Cross looked at her from the corner of his eye. "I hear your father glows white too."

"He... he made me stop glowing."

Mr. Cross nodded. "He can stop others from performing magic. When your ability is, say, throwing a fireball to protect yourself, you become defenseless when you lose the ability to make that fireball. Your father is known for being dangerous, not for what he can do, but for what he can take away."

Chrysta shifted. "And what about glowing gold? What does that mean, Mr. Cross?"

He looked at her. "You see... Those that glow gold, Miss York, are possibly the most powerful magic users to ever exist."

"Possibly?" she asked.

He hummed. "Well, there have only been two people who have glowed gold that we know of." He pointed at her. "And you, my dear, are one of them."

183

She gulped. "And the other one?" she asked.

"The Golden One."

.....

Mr. Cross had jumped up after uttering that name, pacing in front of Chrysta. He was scowling and seemed aggravated, the cigarette leaving puffs of smoke like a train behind him. She waited for a few minutes, not wanting to disturb his thoughts.

"We know very little about her," he started. "She was born in the seventh century, not to nobility, but a commoner, somewhere in Europe. Most of us start showing our ability when we are 10 to 12 years old. Like yourself, she didn't show any power until she was older. One legend says she was married off to some older gentleman, and when it was their wedding night, he beat her because she wouldn't go to bed with him. So she turned him into a toad, her first spell."

"That doesn't seem bad," Chrysta started to say.

"It gets worse."

He paused in his pacing, moving his hands, making the end of the cigarette glow. "Whatever the Golden One did, she was able to get the attention of one of the most potent sorcerers of the time. Even though magic was accepted back then, sorcerers still had to be careful with their abilities. Anger the wrong people, and you could find yourself tied to a stake at the first natural disaster. So he took her under his wing. Tried to teach her restraint."

He started pacing again. "His account is one of the few to survive history. He described the Golden One as powerful, to the degree that even he was scared of her. She performed spells that could kill a lesser sorcerer. She had no moral compass. She took whatever she wanted simply because no one could stop her. She would kill whoever angered her with no regret. She would perform taboo magic only because she could."

"So, she was evil?" Chrysta asked,

Mr. Cross's lip twitched at the corner. "Some would say you are evil, my dear. Curses are illegal, after all."

"What?!" Chrysta sputtered. "I di-didn't know. I'm sorry, will I have to go to jail?"

Mr. Cross laughed but gave her a reassuring pat on the shoulder. "You're alright, my dear. I was merely playing. New sorcerers are given a pass as their powers grow. Just don't do it again now that you know better."

A frown came back to his face, and he started walking back and forth. "People who studied the legend of the Golden One, and there have been many, have labeled her a sociopath. No impulse control, antisocial behavior, slightly sadistic, all of it made worse because she was able to bend magic to her will. No one could stop her, and she knew it.

"The sorcerer who attempted to be her mentor realized after several years that he was not going to change her. So he wrote down all he knew about her and had an assistant hide the journal. The sorcerer wrote that he would try and stop her, kill her if he could, bind her if he couldn't.

"That night, his lab was burnt to the ground. His smoking corpse was found tied to a chair with a sword through the heart. She was nowhere to be found."

Chrysta winced, and Mr. Cross paused and got his cigarette case out. He took out a third cigarette but then stopped and put it back. The case went back into his jacket.

"If they wanted fame or fortune, most sorcerers of the time would find a nobleman or king to be their patron and perform magic spells as needed, sometimes helping out in battles and wars. Those that wanted to live simple lives would find a village where they could live their days being healers and helping the crops. Others would hide their abilities and just live as peacefully as they could. The Golden One was different. She traveled the world and revealed her powers to everyone. She wanted to be worshipped and made normies, people who couldn't perform magic, think she was a god."

"Why do you keep calling her the Golden One?" Chrysta asked.

"We don't even know her name," he explained. "She had statues made of her, whole temples constructed for her, but she didn't let people write anything down about her. It was all oral history, stories and legends, fact and fiction bleeding together."

Chrysta sighed and rubbed her face. "So what does this have to do with my father? And if I'm going to be as powerful as you say I will be, why would my father try to kill me? Is he afraid of me too?"

Mr. Cross started to pace again. "As the Golden One traveled the globe, she started to gather followers, a cult. They are called the acolytes, and they were fanatic followers. Because the Golden One demanded total loyalty, their hierarchy was based on the things they sacrificed for her. If she wanted their land. It was hers. Their money? Hers. Their children." He waved a hand. "Hers. They came up with a saying. 'For her alone.' It meant that anything they had was hers to take, and the more you gave, the more standing you had.

"Your father is the current leader of the acolytes. He became the leader shortly after you were born. As for why they were trying to hurt you last night, I have a theory, but I have to backtrack a little bit.

"First, I have to tell you about the changelings."

26

Suddenly, there was an enthusiastic caw, and Poe dropped down to land next to Chrysta on the bench. She laughed as he hopped up and down, flapping his wings, each hop punctuated with "Chrysta! Chrysta! Chrysta!"

"Oh, Poe! You're alright!" Chrysta reached out and scratched his neck, and the bird cocked his head to one side.

"Tommy?" Poe croaked out.

"He's okay. He's in the infirmary. I'll be going to see him soon."

"How long has he been your familiar?" Mr. Cross asked.

"My what?" Chrysta asked.

"Familiar. An animal that becomes attached to a sorcerer and helps them perform spells. Over time, the legend has changed so that people say they are demons in animal form who listen to witches, but they are simply animals who become a companion to magic users. You did say he helped you when your mother visited you?"

Chrysta nodded. "He showed up shortly after my mother died. Father hated him. But he has been a friend for a long time."

Mr. Cross smiled. He then frowned and shook his head. "Where was I?" he murmured to himself.

"Changelings?" Chrysta started.

"Ah, yes," Mr. Cross muttered, almost to himself. "Couldn't forget them, could we?"

"Sometime in the eleventh century, the Golden One became obsessed with having an army of her own."

"Wait, the eleventh century?" Chrysta interrupted.

"That's right," Mr. Cross said with a nod. "She was over 400 years old at that point." He suddenly smiled. "How old would you say I am?"

"Um..." Chrysta hummed, not knowing how this question tied in with their conversation. "33?"

"Damn," he said with a pout. "I was hoping I still passed as 28. I will actually be turning 42 next year. Your own father is in his 60s. And Burke is 93 years young.

"You see, sorcerers have longer lifespans than people who don't perform magic. The average for most is 150 years. People who glow white, like Burke and your father, are known to live around 250 years.

"The Golden One lived for centuries, and by all accounts, she never aged. Although that could have been a glamour spell. But yes, by the time she created changelings, she had traveled around the world for years and gathered followers the whole time. But they were just human, just mortals. She wanted an army of creatures that lived longer, healed faster, but loyal to her alone."

Poe had settled on Chrysta's lap, so Mr. Cross sat down again.

"At the time, only a few magical creatures were running around that could fit that bill. Orcs, ogres, and trolls, for example. All of them lived longer than a human, were more formidable than a human. The only problem was getting their loyalty. Orcs and ogres are much more animalistic than what modern fantasy films would have you believe. They are about as smart as gorillas and stubborn as hell. You can't train them to listen, even if you are an all-powerful sorcerer with god-like powers. If she tried to threaten them with violence, they would just attack her or her followers at the first opportunity.

"Trolls are bigger and dumber. They saw humans as a food source and weren't impressed by her either. No, if she wanted an army of creatures who only listened to her, she was going to have to make one." Mr. Cross shrugged his shoulders. "And so she did."

Mr. Cross paused, putting a hand to his mouth. "She started to create animal hybrids made with magic. Manticores, griffins, chimeras, Sharabhas, you name it, she tried it. She could travel the world, remember, so her ability to create was only limited by her imagination. Fearsome creatures, loyal to her, their creator, with fangs and wings and claws."

Mr. Cross got up again, and the pacing resumed, his agitation back in full force. "But at the end of the day, they were only animals. Smart, yes, loyal, most certainly, but she wasn't happy with them. She wanted more."

He hesitated. "No one knows why, but the legend says one night she was frustrated. A creature had angered her, broken something, or gotten an order wrong.

She killed it. Even her own creations were not immune to her rages. But she decided she wanted her monsters to have human intelligence. They couldn't just be fierce or loyal anymore. They had to be able to think too. So when she heard a human baby wailing in the distance, she ordered that it be brought to her."

Chrysta's eyes went wide when she understood his meaning. "She didn't."

"She did. She never shared the process with anyone, so she went into a chamber with a human baby and an animal by herself that night. And when she came out, she had a creature that was a mixture of the two."

They were silent for several minutes, Chrysta feeling slightly sick to her stomach. After clearing his throat, Mr. Cross continued.

"Some say it was a lion, others say it was a wolf, but it was a success either way. It took about 20 years for it to mature, just like any human child, but the creature she made was healthy and intelligent, and most of all, it was loyal. She could teach it things, and it could think for itself. And either by design or by accident, it could change into a totally human form. It couldn't perform magic, but it was immune to magic. It was a perfect design and only took the abduction of one human child."

"But she didn't stop with one human child, did she?" Chrysta asked in a small voice.

"No, she did not."

· · · · ·

Chrysta shuddered, and Mr. Cross blinked at her. "Oh, my dear, I apologize. Here I am, rambling, and you're in the cold. Let's get you inside." Chrysta didn't have the heart to tell him it wasn't the cold that made her shake.

He helped her off the bench, and they headed to the building. Poe settled on Chrysta's shoulder, and she expected Mr. Cross to make him leave before they stepped inside. But he barely hesitated as he opened the door for Chrysta and ushered her inside.

"The changelings would prove to be her downfall," he continued as they walked. "Up to that point, sorcerers and normies alike were too scared of her to do anything about her. As long as she wasn't hurting them directly, they let her do whatever she liked. No one was strong enough to stop her, you see. But when she made changelings, she had to use children. The nearest human settlement would be raided for babies, and heaven help anyone who tried to stop her. Her irrational behavior had to stop."

They came to the infirmary door, and Chrysta reached out to open it, but Mr. Cross stopped her, shaking his head. "We have to see Burke first," he said.

They resumed walking. "With children being stolen, sorcerers and normies united to fight her. They were led by the strongest sorcerer of the time, Marlamin Strifelaughter."

Chrysta looked at him from the corner of her eye to see if he was joking. "Strifelaughter?" she asked.

"Laugh at his name if you want, but as strange as he was, he was powerful. Some say he was the one who inspired the legend of Merlin. And after several decades of amassing an army, they went to war.

"It was not a quick battle. The Golden One had settled in a castle in the mountains of what is now modern-day Scandinavia. First, they had to drive her and her forces back. Then they found a way to keep her from transporting herself and her forces away. It took almost a year, but they started to tighten the noose on her. There were substantial losses on both sides, but at one point, Marlamin thought it was time for a final battle. He gathered several of the strongest sorcerers at the time, and they went to defeat the Golden One."

They had reached the bottom of one of the towers, and there was a twisting staircase running up the side. But Mr. Cross guided Chrysta to an elevator that took up the middle of the building, made of wrought iron. He closed the door and pressed a button, and they started to ascend.

"No one knows what his plan was, but the Golden One must have realized something was up," Mr. Cross said as he leaned on one side of the elevator. "She sent most of her acolytes and changelings away. Witnesses say the sky lit up, and explosions were heard miles away, but then there was a final flash that could be seen hundreds of miles away, and the Golden One and her castle vanished."

"Marlamin destroyed her?" Chrysta asked.

"Maybe," Mr. Cross said. "Or he bound her." Mr. Cross noticed her look of confusion. "It means to make a prison that she couldn't leave. Either way, she was gone, and the magical community could breathe again.

"Unfortunately, that was not the end of her legacy. Even though the acolytes and the changelings serve the same master, they have always been jealous of each other and have become mortal enemies. The changelings maintain that the Golden One is alive. The acolytes say she is dead but can be brought back."

Mr. Cross pointed at Chrysta. "And that is what I think your father was trying to do last night. Sacrifice you to bring her back. They have attempted the ritual in the past, but maybe they thought using the soul of someone so strong would finally accomplish what they wanted."

Chrysta didn't respond, lost in her own thoughts. The elevator finally stopped, and Mr. Cross opened the door for her, ushering her out.

They climbed up a final flight of stairs, and Chrysta gasped when she saw the tower's top. It was an office with a large desk in the middle and bookcases on the walls. But the ceiling was painted in silver and blue, dozens of silver stars shining down on them. A metal staircase led up to a catwalk that circled the tower. Clear windows let sunlight stream in, revealing dust floating in the air. Mr. Burke was on the catwalk, speaking to Nyla. Mr. Burke had taken off his jacket, sleeves rolled up and tie tucked into his shirt. His dog and her cat were on the first floor with Chrysta and Mr. Cross. Mr. Burke's dog approached Chrysta and licked her hand when she held it out. Nyla's cat just hissed at her.

"I just don't trust it," Nyla was saying. She glanced down and saw Chrysta and Mr. Cross. She raised her voice. "How do we know it's not pretending to be hurt? To get our guard down so it can kill us?"

Chrysta glared at her; she knew Nyla was referring to Tommy. Mr. Burke rubbed his eyes and also raised his voice so that two people on the first floor could hear him. "That is what I am trying to figure out before we make any rash decisions." He put his hand down and looked at Mr. Cross. He looked exhausted. "Did you do a reading, Cross?"

"Yes, sir, I did. Last night," Mr. Cross responded, guiding Chrysta to sit in a chair in front of the desk.

"Then let's hear your story, Miss York," Mr. Burke said as he descended the stairs and sat behind his desk. Mr. Cross sat beside Chrysta, but Nyla stayed standing.

So, once again, Chrysta detailed everything that had happened. From the night Peter lured her out of the mansion to the night before. She also went over all the magical things she had done. Mr. Burke did not interrupt her, but Nyla would sometimes give a scoff or huff as if she didn't believe Chrysta. Chrysta tried to ignore her.

"Your mother, she never showed any ability?" Mr. Burke asked when Chrysta was done.

"None that I remember," Chrysta replied.

"And you never saw your father use his ability until last night? You didn't know anything about magic or your own magical background?"

"No, sir."

"And Tommy, he told you he was a changeling?"

"Yes, sir."

"You thought he was joking?"

"What else was I supposed to think? That he was actually a magical creature?" she asked, slightly upset.

"What did Peter mean when he said he learned violin for you?" Mr. Burke asked without answering her question.

"I... I don't know, sir. He played it well. It just seemed..." She hesitated. "Robotic?"

"A mimic?" Mr. Cross asked.

"Possible," Mr. Burke murmured. He stared at Chrysta for several minutes, making her squirm under his piercing blue stare. Finally, he looked at Mr. Cross. "What do you think?"

"Her feelings are real," Mr. Cross said without hesitation. "There is a lot of fear and confusion from last night. Her father scares her, and she holds some hate for him. Tommy has always supported her, and she cares for him deeply." Nyla snorted, and Mr. Cross gave her his own glare. "I believe she is telling the truth. I would not let her stay with the other kids if I thought she was here to harm us."

Mr. Burke did not respond. He went back to staring at Chrysta for another long minute. And he finally reached for a piece of paper on his desk and handed it to her.

"There is a possibility," he explained as Chrysta looked it over, "that your father may try to get you back if he finds out you are here. Legally, he is your father, and he can say he wants you to leave and go home. Of course, he is a wanted man, and if he tries to take it to the courts, it will leave him exposed to arrest. That being said, you should know that it may happen."

Chrysta felt her stomach drop as he talked. So she had escaped only to have to go back?

"However," he continued, and Chrysta looked at him. "That piece of paper, if you sign it, states that you want to be a ward of the Academy. You will have to stay here, but you will be protected and cared for. Mr. Cross will be your guardian. I will do everything in my power to make sure you do not go back to your father. Even if you had been helping your father, I would never send anyone back to that kind of fate. When do you turn 17?"

"In March, sir," she said, trying to speak around the lump in her throat.

"Your father can try to contest this decision. But again, if he does, he will have to take it to the courts, where he would be detained on the spot. When you turn 17, you will be considered a legal adult in our society. He will have no control over you anymore." Mr. Burke paused for a second as if to let her think it over. "Do you wish to get legal counsel, or would you like to sign the paper now?"

"Now, please," she said, her voice barely over a whisper. Mr. Burke handed her a fountain pen, and she signed it. Mr. Cross took it from her and signed the space below her name. He gave it to Mr. Burke, and he signed it on the bottom line. All three signatures glowed white briefly, and Mr. Burke rolled up the paper.

"Your name is infamous, my dear. I can't promise that all the teachers and students will treat you fairly. But I think I have a plan to accelerate your training, make it so that you can choose to stay or go when you are old enough." Nyla glanced at him and glowered but didn't say anything.

"Thank you," Chrysta said. She then looked at Mr. Cross. "Thank you. I don't know if I'm going to be as powerful as you think I will be. But I do want to control it."

"Now, about the changeling," Mr. Burke started.

"What about it?" Nyla interrupted. Chrysta shot her a frown, but she continued. "It needs to die. It's that simple. Even if she is telling the truth, and it did save her, it deserves to die for its crimes."

"Tommy is not a thing. Stop calling him 'it,'" Chrysta growled at her. "What crimes has he committed?"

Nyla leaned forward, putting both hands on the desk. "Do you want to know what it has done? When I was younger than you, my sister and I were snatched from our beds one night. We were thrown into a closet with our grandmother. Locked in. We heard our father come home, and there was yelling. When the door opened,

Guerra grabbed me. He brought me to my father and said if my father didn't help them, Guerra would kill me in front of him. Do you know who was holding my father so he couldn't fight? Your friend, the changeling."

Chrysta flinched but didn't look away from the furious woman in front of her. Nyla smiled, but it was a grimace of anger and not of joy. "Your father was there too, and when my father went with them to give them whatever they had broken into our home for, there was a shout, and I was let go. I ran to my father, but he was dead, his throat cut, the monster towering over him in that horrible form."

"The slave band..." Chrysta started to explain, but Nyla hit the desk, making her jump. Mr. Burke grabbed Nyla's hand to either give comfort or stop her; Chrysta wasn't sure. She knocked his hand away and glowered at Chrysta.

"Ordered to kill my father or not, it doesn't matter, it still murdered him. And I swore that I would become a hunter, like my father, and avenge his death."

"He deserves to defend himself," Chrysta said, and Nyla blinked. "If you want justice for your father, don't hurt him while he is asleep, and let Tommy defend himself when he wakes up."

"He may not wake up," Mr. Burke said in a low voice and Chrysta turned to him.

"Wha... What do you mean?" she asked.

Mr. Burke got up from the desk and went to a bookcase. He grabbed a book and placed it on his desk. "I have been reading up on slave bands. What is happening to your friend is the final stage of defying direct orders from his master. The band would first cause immense pain, and if the slave kept resisting, it would make the slave fall into a coma. And then die."

Chrysta felt her stomach drop. Nyla gave her another of her cold smiles. "You see, it would be a mercy killing."

Chrysta saw red, and she felt the flexing in her chest. Every glass object in the room started to vibrate. Poe cawed, and Chrysta heard Mr. Burke's dog whine and Nyla's cat hiss. Nyla's smile died on her face, and she actually took a step back. Mr. Cross placed a gloved hand on Chrysta's. "Surely, there must be a way to help him," he said calmly.

"There is," Mr. Burke said, also trying to be calm. "There are three ways to wake him up. First, you can return him to your father, and he will make a recovery."

"Not going to happen," Chrysta said. Yes, Tommy would be alive, but she wasn't about to force Tommy back into slavery while she was free.

"You can get the ring," Mr. Burke continued. "Either your father can give the ring to you willingly, or you can kill him and take it."

Chrysta blinked. No way her father would give her the ring. Did she hate her father enough to kill him? Maybe. If it meant Tommy would be alive and well. "But if I have the ring, he's still a slave. He's not free to do what he wants."

"What does it matter?!" Nyla suddenly shouted, and everyone else jumped. "Just let me kill it," she yelled at Mr. Burke, and Chrysta tried to keep herself calm. "It deserves to die. Surely, you see that."

"Nyla, let us discuss thi—"

"No! No more talk. Just let me go down to the infirmary," Nyla said. Mr. Burke frowned at her, and she snorted. "Come on, I know that is where it is."

"Nyla, come with me," Mr. Burke said, and he led her to one of the windows. He opened it up, and they went outside onto a balcony.

"Mr. Cross," Chrysta whispered as she watched the two figures arguing. "Do you think Mr. Burke will really let her kill Tommy?"

"Burke is a former hunter, so killing changelings used to be his profession. But I doubt he would kill Tommy in cold blood," Mr. Cross gave her hand a squeeze. "It's Hafeez I am worried about. She is out for blood." He looked at the desk, and his eyebrows went up. "But maybe he has given us the chance to save Tommy ourselves."

Chrysta followed his gaze and noticed the book about slave bands was still on Mr. Burke's desk. "Do you think he wants us to take it?"

"Probably. Burke did say there was a third way to save Tommy." Mr. Cross stood up, keeping an eye on the other two adults. He started to whistle *My Country Tis of Thee* as he waited for the two figures outside to turn their backs, and when they did, he grabbed the book and Chrysta's hand. "Come on, my dear," he said as he pulled her downstairs to the elevator. "Let's get to the infirmary as quickly as possible." Poe cawed and landed on Chrysta's shoulder just as the door to the elevator closed.

. . . . .

They took the elevator, Chrysta straining to hear any noise from above that would tell her Nyla was coming after them. "How do we get him out of here?" she asked.

Mr. Cross reached into his coat and took out a bag. He opened the drawstring and revealed crystals. "Transportation spell," he said with a grin. "We will steal him away to the Disaster Club."

They almost ran down the hall, entering the infirmary. Mr. Cross went to the door to Tommy's room and knocked. Miss Normandy, looking extremely tired, opened the door. "Sorry, Abby," Mr. Cross was saying before she even had the door all the way open and pushed past her. He handed her the book, and she gaped at it. "We have to have a change of scenery."

"Wha-What?!" Miss Normandy asked. She looked at Chrysta while Mr. Cross started to set up his crystals on the floor.

"Nyla is coming to hurt Tommy," Chrysta explained. She went over to Tommy to check on him. She gently lifted his hand. He didn't react.

"What?" Miss Normandy asked again. "What did Mr. Burke say?"

"He is talking to her now, but I don't want to rely on his negotiation skills," Mr. Cross said. "Come on, let's get him on the floor."

"I don't think this is a good idea. Tommy's heart rate is slowing down. He may stop breathing if we use a transportation spell."

"We have to chance it," Mr. Cross replied, trying to lift Tommy's legs at the knees. "We certainly can't get him to the Disaster Club by carrying him unless you have a dozen friends you can call for help in the next five minutes."

Miss Normandy looked worried, but she helped Chrysta to lift Tommy by his shoulders. They got him in the circle. "I'll get back to the club and set up the return circle," Mr. Cross said. "Do you know the incantation?"

"'Circle made of light and stone, bring us home?'" Miss Normandy asked.

"Exactly. I'll text you when it's ready."

"Poe," Chrysta said. Poe clicked his beak in response. "Go with Mr. Cross." Poe squawked but obeyed, landing on Mr. Cross's shoulder.

"Give me fifteen minutes, ladies." And with that, Mr. Cross was jogging out of the room.

Miss Normandy locked the door behind him, then joined Chrysta in the circle, opening the book. Chrysta gently rubbed Tommy's cheek and then touched his chest, feeling his heartbeat on her palm. "Has he opened his eyes at all?" she asked in a whisper.

"I'm afraid not," Miss Normandy answered, her voice just as low. "But this..." She turned a page in the book and read it. "This will help," she said with a smile.

Twelve minutes later, Miss Normandy's phone chirped. She checked the screen and then sighed. "Deep breath," she reminded Chrysta, then she put her hands out, parallel to the floor. "Circle of light and stone," she murmured as the crystals started to glow, "bring us home." And after a moment of humming and bright light, they disappeared from the room.

⚬ 27 ⚬

When Chrysta was aware of her surroundings again, she heard gasps. They were in the large main room, the members of the Disaster Club peering around Mr. Cross. "He's huge!" Chrysta heard Kevin say as Rimsha stood next to him, hand over her mouth.

Miss Normandy suddenly dropped down and checked Tommy's chest. "He's not breathing," she loudly said, handing the book to Chrysta. While she pushed Tommy onto his back, Mr. Cross came forward.

"What can we do?" he asked.

Miss Normandy shook her head as she thought. "CPR?" She pried Tommy's mouth open while Mr. Cross started chest compressions.

"I hope you aren't planning on giving him mouth-to-mouth," Mr. Cross said.

"I have to make sure his airway is clear," Miss Normandy growled.

"Miss Normandy?" Chrysta said as they continued. "Please say he will be okay." Miss Normandy didn't say anything.

They worked on Tommy for several minutes, Chrysta feeling sick to her stomach. When tears started falling down her cheeks, she felt a hand on her shoulder. Rimsha squeezed, and she looked at the other girl in despair. Abruptly, Tommy lurched and coughed, and Miss Normandy pulled back quickly before Tommy bit her. Tommy didn't open his eyes, but he settled down and sighed. Chrysta let out a breath she wasn't aware she was holding and smiled.

"Oh, thank you," she said, wiping the tears off her face.

Miss Normandy sighed. "We are *not* doing that again," she grumbled at Mr. Cross. "If you have to move him, we're carrying him."

"I don't think we can do that," he said. "We can't move him fast enough. Hafeez will not stop until she has his head on a platter, and she will be here soon."

"Then we have to hide him," Miss Normandy said.

"Hide him? Are you serious? Do you see how big he is?" Rosa asked, Kevin and Julien nodding in agreement.

"Maybe we don't have to hide him," Ichiro said while looking at Chrysta.

.....

Burke followed Nyla through the gardens, the young woman stomping furiously to the Disaster Tree. Her cat struggled to stay by her side, and Burke and his dog were barely keeping up. When done with their argument, they had gone inside the tower to notice Cross and Chrysta were gone. Nyla had turned purple. She dragged Burke to the infirmary, insisting he open all the locked doors. The room he had seen Normandy take the changeling into was empty. If they weren't there, there was only one other place they could be, and Nyla could not be stopped.

Burke was glad that the young hunter was too infuriated to notice that the book he left on his desk was gone. It would have been so hard for him to act upset.

They had reached the tree with its solar crystals, and Nyla flew down the stairs. Burke quickly followed as she burst through the door, bells ringing.

The main room was warm and bright. Mr. Cross was on one side of the room with Kevin, Julien, and Rosa. Miss Normandy was on the other side, Chrysta sitting in front of her, Ichiro and Rimsha by Chrysta's side on a couch. Cross jumped up when the door blew open. "What is all this then?" he said, accent getting thicker in his anger.

"Where is it?" Nyla demanded, and Cross gave her a confused look.

"Where is what?"

"Oh, don't start with me. The changeling. Where is it?"

"Hafeez, now is not the time," Cross started.

"You're telling me that you were talking about helping it, and then you disappear, and now the changeling just happens to be missing from the infirmary?" Nyla said as she stepped up to Cross and stuck a finger in his face. "Do you think I'm stupid?!"

"Nyla, calm down," Burke said. He looked over to Chrysta, noticing her shoulders shaking, her bird familiar on her lap, clicking his beak. "What happened?" he asked Normandy.

"Tommy... passed away. The slave band made his heart stop. I texted Akrur to tell him, which is why he and Chrysta left your meeting," she said softly. But there was something in the way her eyes shifted to Nyla and then back to him that made Burke not believe her.

"Where's the body?" Nyla commanded, and Chrysta let out a sob.

"He's gone, okay?" Chrysta said, giving the woman a red-eyed glare. "You got what you wanted, so just go."

"Not until I see the body," Nyla said, and she went to one of the doors and opened it.

The teens, silent up to this point, started shouting at her.

"Hey, get out of my room!"

"There isn't a body, you psycho."

"Just leave Chrysta alone. She just lost her friend!"

Julien just glared and made an obscene hand gesture.

Burke had to keep himself from smiling.

Nyla stalked from room to room, ignoring the teens and their jeering. She checked everywhere, in closets, under beds, but there was no sign of the body she was looking for. Kevin started following her. "Cold, cold, colder," he said in a low monotone voice. "Cold, colder, *ice-cold*. Really, do you know how to play this game?"

Burke went up to Cross, who was glaring at the young woman turning the Club upside down. "Cross?" he said in a low voice.

"Yes?"

"You do remember the rules of borrowing a personal book of mine?"

"Return the book in the condition I got it."

"And?"

"I'm responsible for my own safety."

"Hm," Burke hummed. He noticed Siad and Willow curiously sniffing at the couch Chrysta was sitting on. Well, Cross was undoubtedly a fast thinker. And Chrysta was stronger than Burke thought. He whistled at the animals to get their attention before they alerted Nyla. "Nyla," he called out. "Let's go."

"I need to see the body," she responded.

"Why?" Normandy asked, a scowl on her face. "Going to sell the parts on the black market?" Nyla frowned and started to open her mouth to counter.

"Nyla," Burke said softly. The young hunter finally looked at him. "Let's go."

Nyla's frown faded, and a look of disappointment settled on her features. She looked around at the mess she had made and stomped out the door to climb the stairs. Burke looked around, gave everyone a slight bow, and turned to follow her.

·····

Chrysta took several deep breaths after Mr. Burke and Miss Hafeez left, rubbing at her eyes. Mr. Cross stood by the open door, looking up. After several minutes Mr. Cross turned around. "They're gone," he said.

Everyone sighed and visually relaxed. Chrysta screwed her eyes shut, and the couch underneath her, Rimsha, and Ichiro started to shift and change. It was no longer a large couch when it stopped. It was Tommy, lying on his side. Rimsha and Ichiro quickly stood up, but Chrysta slowly sank to the floor.

Miss Normandy quickly crouched down next to her side. "Are you okay?"

"Yeah," Chrysta said, sniffling. She leaned over, hair covering her face. "Yeah, that was just really difficult. Like tensing a muscle and not being able to let it go." She slowly sat up and brushed at her eyes again.

"Well done, my dear," Mr. Cross told her, a grin on his face. "I give you an A-plus."

"A-minus," Ichiro joked, "that was the lumpiest couch I have ever sat on."

Mr. Cross grinned and then looked around. "Alright, ladies and gentlemen, we have some official business to address." He turned to the other teenagers in the room. "I'm calling a meeting of the Disaster Club."

All the teens gave him their undivided attention. Mr. Cross paused and then raised a hand. "All in favor of making one Chrysta York part of the Disaster Club, raise your hands." All hands went up, including Miss Normandy's. Chrysta noticed Rosa hesitate.

"It's okay," she said. The other girl shifted from foot to foot. "I understand."

Rosa looked around. "Looks like I don't have much choice."

"Six in favor, one abstain," Mr. Cross said, a soft smile on his face. "Motion granted. So, what happens when a member of the Disaster Club needs help?"

"The Disaster Club answers the call," Kevin said.

"Bloody right," Mr. Cross said with a smile. "So, everyone, let's save a changeling."

28

Since Tommy was so large, they couldn't fit him on any bed or couch, so they grabbed pillows and blankets and rolled Tommy onto them in the middle of the main room, near the woodstove. Kevin seemed fascinated by the changeling and spent several minutes writing down details in a small notebook. "Oh, if only dad was here, he would have a fit," he said, mostly to himself.

"Why is that?" Chrysta asked as she covered Tommy up.

"Dad has studied changelings all his life; he would give his right arm to examine a specimen like this." Kevin went over to a bookcase and brought several books to Chrysta. The author listed for all of them was Paul Butler. He looked excited until he noticed Chrysta glaring at him. "Sorry. Too much?"

"Too much," Chrysta agreed.

"Um, ah, sorry," he stammered. "Um, let me go get dinner ready." And he retreated to the kitchen.

Chrysta noticed that Tommy's shoulder was almost completely healed in the spot where he got stabbed. She checked his chest and was shocked that the wounds looked better. "He really is healing faster than a human," she said in wonder.

Miss Normandy sat down with the book on slave bands in an armchair, and Chrysta sat down with the books about changelings while leaning on Tommy's chest.

Chrysta tried to concentrate on her book, but she found herself looking at Miss Normandy, trying to guess what she was reading by her facial expressions.

"Miss Normandy," Ichiro asked as he watched Poe poking at the slave band on Tommy's arm. "What is a slave band?"

"They were popular a long time ago," Miss Normandy started to tell the teen. "But they are inhumane, so in the 1500s, they were banned and made illegal. I'm actually shocked that anyone knew how to make them." She lifted a page of the book. "This is the only book in existence that I know of that details how to create them."

"I thought that slave bands made the person like a zombie," Rosa asked.

"There are actually two kinds," Miss Normandy said. "The first does take the slave's free will away. But they lose all ability to think for themselves. They won't eat, sleep, or do anything without being told. So it's not good for long-term enslavement." She raised an eyebrow. "I don't think the first kind would work on a changeling. They are immune to magic, after all."

"And the second?" Rimsha asked. She slowly approached Chrysta and just as slowly sat down next to her, watching Tommy like an animal that could bite her. Well, maybe he was, Chrysta considered.

"The second type of slave band lets the slave keep their free will, but uses pain to make them obedient." She turned the book so the teens could see an illustration. It was a drawing of someone's arm, marked with cuts and scars. Even though it was drawn, it was realistic enough to look very painful. "This was someone who had worn a slave band for a *month*. I can't imagine what it would look like for someone who had to wear it for years.

"And Mr. Burke was right. There are three ways to wake him up. Take him back to the person with the slave ring, take the slave ring away from the person who has it, or perform a spell to remove the slave band."

"That's it," Chrysta said hopefully. "That is what we need to do. We need to make sure he wakes up and recovers, but he should be free." She looked at his face, strangely serene, even though it was so inhuman.

"I agree," Miss Normandy said. "Changeling or not, I promised him I would help him, and I plan to keep my promise."

The wonderful smell of food wafted from the kitchen, and Mr. Cross came out with a chicken and pasta plate for Miss Normandy. "Generally, I don't allow food in the common room," he told Chrysta, "but tonight, I'm making an exception."

All the teens joined them, sitting in various chairs and eating chicken stuffed with cheese. Rimsha had a plate of stuffed mushrooms. After everyone had eaten most of their meal, Mr. Cross turned to Miss Normandy. "So, what is the plan?"

Miss Normandy sighed, consulting a page of the book. "The spell is simple enough. I can make it in under an hour with common components. There is just one ingredient that will be hard to get."

"What's that?" Mr. Cross asked.

"The blood of Tommy's master," Miss Normandy said with a grimace.

"Bloody hell, is that all?" Mr. Cross said sarcastically. "How hard can it be to get a blood sample from one bloody Jozef York? 'Excuse me, sir, I just have to have you bleed into this basin. There is a fine chap, thank you for your donation.'" The teens snickered at Mr. Cross's exasperated tone as he rubbed his eyes.

"So, I have to get blood from my father?" Chrysta asked.

Mr. Cross stopped rubbing his eyes and frowned at her. "No, my dear, *I* will have to get blood from your father. I am not letting you walk back into the lion's den."

"It has to be me, Mr. Cross," Chrysta started to explain. "I'm immune to their magic. They can't hurt me like they could hurt you."

"They could try to sacrifice you again," Rosa said.

"Actually, they missed their chance," Mr. Cross said. "They only had the winter solstice to perform the ritual. The next time they can perform the ritual is in the summertime."

"But then they would just imprison her until it's the right time again," Miss Normandy said.

Suddenly, Julien turned to Mr. Cross and started to move his hands rapidly in the air. Chrysta realized he was using sign language. Whatever he was saying, Mr. Cross disagreed with him because he started shaking his head no. Mr. Cross then held up his right hand, holding his thumb out with the pointer and middle fingers together, making a pinching motion over and over. "No, no, no, no, we are not doing that," Mr. Cross said.

Julien huffed, put his hands down, and then started talking. "Yes, Mr. Cross, it has to be me that helps you two," he said, a little louder than needed. "Rimsha would just throw flower petals at them."

"True," Rimsha said.

"Kevin would trip over his own two feet," Julien continued.

"Hey, man," Kevin said, looking slightly hurt. "It's true, but still, hey, man."

"Rosa would set you on fire," Julien resumed.

"Screw you, LeBlanc," Rosa growled.

"And Ichiro has to stay here," Julien concluded.

"Wait, why?" Ichiro asked.

"Hafeez may come back," Miss Normandy said. "And if she does, I need help protecting Tommy. Besides Chrysta, you are the strongest magic user here."

"Looks like I'm practicing glamour spells," Ichiro muttered.

"If, and this is a very big *if*, I let you two come with me," Mr. Cross said, still rubbing his eyes, "we need a plan, a foolproof one. Because I am not putting you two in danger."

"I'm 17, Mr. Cross," Julien said. "I am an adult, and I want to help."

Chrysta leaned over to Rimsha. "How do I say thank you in sign language?"

Rimsha smiled, put her open hand up to her chin, palm facing her chest, and then moved it forward. Chrysta copied the motion at Julien, and he gave her a small bow.

"Whatever plan you come up with, it has to be soon—tomorrow night," Miss Normandy interrupted. "Tommy's heart can stop completely if we wait longer than that."

"Then remind me to update my will tomorrow," Mr. Cross quipped.

"You don't have to do it, Mr. Cross," Chrysta said. She looked at Julien to make sure he could read her lips. "Neither of you has to do it. Tommy is my friend. I have to help him. I should be the only one to put myself in danger."

"Nonsense, my dear, you are part of the Disaster Club now," Mr. Cross said. "We help our own."

"So, what is the foolproof plan you want to make?" Miss Normandy asked Mr. Cross.

"Have any experience with sleep spells?" Mr. Cross asked back.

"Of course."

"Then, that is a start." Mr. Cross paused while Miss Normandy suddenly yawned and stretched. "But the rest will have to wait until morning. I'll take first watch."

"Are you sure, Akrur?" she asked.

"Oh yes, how hard could it be?" he countered.

Suddenly, Tommy let out a deep rumble in his sleep, muzzle curling in a snarl. Rimsha yelped and ran across the room, hiding behind Mr. Cross. Mr. Cross made an audible gulping noise.

"Well, first watch with Chrysta," he amended.

.....

It was Rosa and Rimsha's turn to do the dishes, so the boys went to the TV and put on a movie. Chrysta stayed with Tommy, still looking through the books. Miss Normandy and Mr. Cross went to the other side of the room, Miss Normandy taking off her shoes and putting her feet in his lap. They were talking low, but Chrysta could still hear them. It seemed like they were talking about other teachers who worked at the Academy. At one point, Miss Normandy stretched and yawned again, looking drained.

"I hope that the guest room is clean, Akrur," she said through a yawn. "A warm, fresh bed sounds divine."

"Of course, it's clean," he responded. "That's where my girlfriends stay the night."

"Girlfriends?" she asked, laughing. "With an 's?'" He hummed in reply, looking smug. "What are these girlfriends' names?"

"Well, there's Sara," he started. "She comes over on Mondays."

"Oh."

"Tammy, her night is Wednesday."

"Ah."

"And Monique, she stays on Thursdays."

"Oh," Miss Normandy said while giggling. "Why not Friday nights?"

"Oh, Friday nights, she's dancing at the strip club," Mr. Cross explained, and Miss Normandy threw her head back and laughed, Mr. Cross joining her. Chrysta smiled at the two adults.

After another hour of talking, Miss Normandy finally got up and made her way to the guest bedroom. She paused by Chrysta to check on Tommy. "Miss Normandy?" Chrysta said.

"Yes, dear?"

"Whatever happens... thank you for all your help. For giving Tommy a chance."

"You're welcome, dear," Miss Normandy said with a smile. She then yawned. "Let me get to bed before I fall asleep where I stand." She got up and gave everyone a small wave. "'Night, everyone."

There was a chorus of "Goodnight!" that followed her to the room. The movie ended, and Kevin came over. "Hey, I'm sorry about earlier. The whole 'specimen' stuff. I get excited about changelings and kinda put my foot in my mouth."

"It's okay," Chrysta said. "People keep calling Tommy a thing and 'it,' and it's frustrating because he's not a thing to me. He's Tommy." She looked at Tommy's sleeping face as Mr. Cross came over to sit with her and Kevin. "He looks different, but he's still Tommy."

Kevin gestured to the books. "Learning anything new?"

"Honestly, it's a little hard to follow," she admitted.

"Oh, those are mostly about the types of changelings and their sizes. Try this book. I think it actually has a chapter about Tommy," Kevin said, grabbing one book and handing it to her.

"A whole chapter?" She leafed through the book and was shocked when she came across a black-and-white picture of Tommy. He was dressed like a Prohibition-era gangster, with dark striped pants and buttoned-up white shirt, suspenders, and two-toned shoes, hat tipped forward over his eyes. His sleeves were rolled up, and he was holding a gun and wearing a crazy grin on his face, staring at something off-camera.

"Yup, this book is about the famous changelings, the ones we know the most about. Tommy is known as the Heretic because he was never seen with other changelings and just seen with the acolytes."

"We knew a changeling was helping the acolytes," Mr. Cross explained as Chrysta examined the photo. "But the people who studied changelings didn't know why he would serve the acolytes. It was always assumed he believed in their cause."

"Well, they didn't really study hard enough," Chrysta said, and she turned the book so he could see the slave band on Tommy's arm on display in the photo.

"Again, like Miss Normandy said, no one had seen a slave band in centuries. And enslaving a changeling can't be an easy task." Mr. Cross glanced at Tommy. "I would be interested in hearing that story if Tommy ever wants to share it."

It got late, and the teens started to file out of the room, waving goodnight to both Chrysta and Mr. Cross. Chrysta stayed where she was, only pausing in reading the book to pull Tommy's hand into her lap. At one point, she felt a vibration and realized Tommy was purring. Mr. Cross, who was still sitting nearby reading his own book, looked over with his eyebrows raised. "Well, he has to be aware of his surroundings to some degree if he's doing that."

Chrysta looked over and smiled at the adult, then cleared her throat. "So, are you and Miss Normandy together?"

"Together? As in dating? Oh no, my dear. I was head of the Disaster Club when she joined. She was already an adult, but I still think of her as one of the kids."

"So adults can learn at the Academy just like kids?"

"Not exactly. Remember when I said most of us start showing our ability when we become teenagers? Miss Normandy comes from a healer family, but her ability didn't show until she was 22. She had actually gone to school to become a doctor when her ability finally showed itself in her last semester. So she dropped out of pre-med and came here."

"So, is that why you call her Doc?"

He shrugged. "Abby went through all that schooling, so in my mind, she has earned the title. She's a fantastic healer too. She could have gone off and made a lot of money, but decided to stay here at the Academy for the last five years."

"So, what are the requirements to be part of the Disaster Club?" Chrysta asked with a smile.

"Oh, there are many," Mr. Cross started, closing his book with a snap. "You see, my dear, in the sorcerer society, it is not the color of your skin, what religion you follow, what gender you are, if you love someone who is the same sex as you, but it's all about your abilities and lineage. And if people think those two things are off, you can get shunned.

"Julien is one of the strongest readers I know. Unfortunately, he had a great uncle who became a necromancer, so his whole family is now avoided by others. Rimsha and Kevin both have normie mothers. It's slowly becoming more acceptable, but it used to be a massive deal in the old days, sorcerers taking on normie spouses.

"Ichiro has no magical ancestors that we can find, which is very rare but can happen. Throw in the fact that he is young and powerful, people become leery of being around him. Rosa is a powerful fire user, but she can't control it. Fires tend to spread when she uses it.

"Abby was a late bloomer." He held up a gloved hand. "And I can't completely control my ability. Unfortunately, every time I touch an object or person, I do a reading. Makes going through life very hard when you can't touch someone without worrying if you are going to learn their deepest, darkest secret."

"And I am Chrysta York, daughter of Jozef York, leader of a cult. With a normie mother, I just started showing magical ability. I'm glowing gold, which means I may possess the powers of a god. People will associate me with an evil sorcerer that lived over 700 years ago and made an army of murderous magical creatures," Chrysta added, suddenly laughing in disbelief.

"See, you're the perfect candidate. You check all of the boxes, Lady York," Mr. Cross joked and joined her in laughing.

Their laughter died down, and Chrysta spent a few moments gathering her thoughts. She glanced at Tommy, whose eyes were moving under his eyelids. "I don't know, Mr. Cross. I don't know how I'm going to help him."

"With friends, Miss York," he replied softly. "That is the Disaster Club, my dear. It was made to help the ones that our society would rather forget. We will come up with a plan. And we will help him. Together."

∾ 29 ∾

Peter stamped his feet and rubbed his hands in an attempt to stave off the cold. The sun had barely gone down, and he was already freezing. He tried to keep himself from scratching the healing scar of the knife wound the slave gave him. The healer said it would disappear completely only if Peter left it alone. He realized that he was scratching it without thinking. He forced his hand down. It was going to be a long, chilly night.

He didn't know why they insisted he be the one to watch the Jackson household. All the other acolytes agreed either Chrysta was killed by the slave or its deadly brethren. The fact that she had been missing for two days proved that she was gone and wasn't coming back.

Peter shivered and blew warm air into his hands but tried to stay in the shadows of the alleyway. Actually, he knew why he was here. He had opened his big mouth and let the slave know about the ritual. His uncle's intervention was the only reason York hadn't killed him already. So here he was, outside in the bitter cold, watching for Chrysta York as a form of punishment. How long would York insist he stay out in the cold? Probably until York was killed himself.

Peter smiled. The rumors were already flying. Soon York would be disposed of for letting his daughter escape. And Frost would take his place, and then Peter's uncle would be second in command. Maybe his uncle could help Peter get some of his clout back.

Suddenly, Peter saw a figure coming down the sidewalk on the other side of the street. It wasn't strange to see someone, it had only gotten dark after all, but the figure was short and limping. It kept looking behind it but was walking fast. The person finally walked under a streetlamp, and Peter was shocked to recognize Chrysta. Well, this was unexpected. Maybe Peter would be able to gain some notoriety among the acolytes by himself.

He quickly and quietly crossed the street, thankful that it was deserted. If he had to grab Chrysta and run, he didn't want any witnesses. He trailed behind her at about two dozen feet, trying to keep his footsteps light. She turned around, however, and Peter froze underneath the shadow of a tree.

"W-who's there?!" she cried, and Peter instinctively stepped closer so he could try to stop her from screaming. When he stepped out of the shadows into the light, she looked relieved and ran to him. "Oh, thank goodness, I thought it was the things!" She was wearing the slave's jacket and boots, just like Peter's uncle had described, but she had a black eye, a bleeding wound on her forehead, and cuts on her hands. She was covered in mud and dirt. Most of all, she was scared, more scared than the night Peter lured her out of the mansion.

"The things?" Peter asked. He was a little troubled that Chrysta seemed happy to see him, considering what happened the last time he saw her. But she looked behind him like she was more worried about some unseen foe than she was concerned about him.

"You were right," she whispered, still looking down the deserted sidewalk and not at Peter. "Tommy was a *thing*, a monster, and when he took me, he... he took me to others like him. They looked like humans, but they weren't human." Her words were spilling out in a rush, her voice getting higher. She took a deep breath and let it out shakingly. "Please, just let me get to the Jacksons. They can keep me safe."

Peter felt his mind race. He couldn't let her go to that bitch Mary's house. Then the acolytes would really have a hard time getting her back. "You can't do that," he said, trying to make his voice calm and even. "What if they follow you? Then Mary would be in trouble, too."

Chrysta bit her lip. "They... they did follow me—two of them. I got away, but two of them have been following me. I could see them. I have been hitchhiking for hours, but they just kept finding me." She looked at him with frightened eyes. "But Peter, you don't understand. My father tried to kill me, I can't go back home."

"Look, your father has told everyone looking for you to not hurt you. You will be safe." That was mostly true. Chrysta York was to be taken alive, but if she would stay that way remained to be seen.

She looked at him for a long moment, still biting her lip. She finally nodded. "Alright," she agreed. "Alright, please, let's go." She crossed her arms in front of her and started walking towards the mansion. "Come on," she said, looking back at Peter. "Hurry up. I think they were just behind me."

Peter glanced behind him, her paranoia making him nervous, but he didn't hesitate for long. As they walked away, two figures came around the corner and started to follow them.

. . . . .

"We need to come up with an explanation of where you were for the last two days," Mr. Cross said. In the middle of the night, Julien and Rosa had come out to relieve Chrysta and Mr. Cross of their vigil over Tommy. Now, at the kitchen table, they ate eggs with biscuits and gravy while Miss Normandy kept an eye on Tommy.

"Is there anywhere else that Tommy could have taken you to?" Mr. Cross asked. "We need to make sure your father doesn't realize you have been here for the last few days. Then he will realize you will know about the acolytes and their plan for you."

"Not that I know of," Chrysta said. She took a bite of food and thought about it. "Tommy just said he was taking me to someone who could help us."

"Well, they wouldn't think he was bringing you here," Mr. Cross said. "It would be suicide for a changeling to get close to the Academy."

"What about other changelings?" Rimsha asked.

"Tommy was attacked several times by other changelings. It wouldn't be much safer for him to go to his own kind," Kevin said.

"Mr. Jacobs said something about changelings at one point," Chrysta said. "He said I should be happy he found me and not the changelings. He said they would kill me."

"He said that?" Mr. Cross asked. Chrysta nodded. "Then, that is the narrative they came up with without knowing that Tommy was really bringing you here." He smiled. "If that is the story they thought of, that is the story they will believe without you having to go into much detail. That is the story we will feed them."

. . . . .

Jozef York was in the third-story bedroom, hands crossed on his cane, studying the sacrificial table. It was a simple thing, notable only for its size. But, it had been the Golden One's table, and therefore passed down from generation to generation of her followers like some morbid heirloom. He had never seen it used before, but he felt the negative energy coming off it, a psychic stain that would fade, but only after decades after its last use.

Frost and Jacobs had announced they were coming back that evening. They didn't say, but York suspected they would bring other high-ranking acolytes with them. They would demand he step down, and it would be his choice to do so or fight for his position.

Let Frost lead. The money and power were not worth the constant need to look over his shoulder and make sure an acolyte was not about to put a knife in it. But if he stepped down without a fight, they may kill him just on principle alone. He tapped the useless slave ring on his cane. Damn that changeling. York didn't care what they said. No one could have predicted he would play the hero two nights ago.

Suddenly, someone opened the door and rushed into the room. Jozef felt a stab of annoyance. "I said I was not to be dis—" he started, already deciding whoever it was would die later for their insolence.

"Your daughter has returned," the guard said, not letting him finish.

"What?!"

"Your daughter, she's back."

York paused. She was alive. And she came back? Maybe it was a ploy to get him downstairs. Well, only one way to find out.

He limped down the stairs as fast as his hip allowed, entering the study. There, in front of the fire, was Peter Jacobs and his daughter. She looked ragged and worn, with wounds on her face and hands that she didn't have before, but very much alive. He felt a rush of relief and tried to tell himself he was only glad she was living because it meant he would survive. Chrysta looked at him with wide eyes as he stalked up to her and inspected the wound on her forehead.

"What happened?" he said.

"She was going to the Jackson household," the idiot boy started, looking smug. Chrysta glanced at him and then looked down, biting her lip. York glared at Peter, and the boy's smile died, and he cleared his throat.

"What happened?" York asked his daughter.

She crossed her arms in front of her like she was trying to form a shield. She shifted from foot to foot. "Tommy took me to some people," Chrysta softly explained, "but they weren't people. They changed like he did. They h-hurt him and imprisoned me." She glanced at York but then looked down. "I escaped. I was t-trying to get to Mary's house, but I don't want the things to hurt her." She looked up at her father. "Can you help me?"

York was trying to think of an answer when the door opened without a knock, and Guerra burst in. He stopped in shock at the sight of Chrysta. "Miss York," he said brightly but without that fake smile on his face. "We were worried about you."

"You didn't seem that concerned for my safety last time I saw you," Chrysta said sarcastically.

Guerra chuckled. "No, I suppose not. Please, Miss York, what happened?"

.....

Chrysta came out of the girls' bedroom, wearing her clothes from two nights ago. "Good thing I didn't wash them," she told Mr. Cross. "I doubt my father would believe the changelings would have let me clean my clothes while they were holding me."

"That's not the only thing we need to do," Kevin said. He was with Rimsha on the floor near Tommy. Rimsha was drawing Tommy on Kevin's insistence. It was a good drawing, with many little details like the spots on Tommy's back and shoulders, the hair running down his spine, and

his long fingers and talons. "*When someone is captured by changelings, they usually get pretty roughed up.*"

"*So, who do you want to punch you?*" *Ichiro joked.*

"*I don't mind taking a shot,*" *Rosa said dryly, reading the book on slave bands. Miss Normandy smacked her on the arm.*

Chrysta thought about it for a minute and then looked at Mr. Cross. "*Guerra can hurt people, right?*" *she asked.*

"*Yes?*" *Mr. Cross replied.*

"*Then, I should have that ability too.*" *Chrysta paused and placed her hand on the other one. She tried to think of an injury, a cut she once got. She hissed as pain flared across the back of her hand, and when she lifted the other one, there was a fresh wound, weeping blood.*

"*Whoa,*" *Kevin said. Miss Normandy rushed to Chrysta while the others gasped.*

"*Easy,*" *Miss Normandy said.* "*You don't want to cause too much damage.*"

"*What do you think?*" *Chrysta asked.* "*Maybe a black eye?*" *Miss Normandy looked uncomfortable while Chrysta put a hand up to her eye. After thinking for a moment, she hissed again, and when she lowered her hand, a purplish spot had formed around her left eye.*

"*Very impressive, Miss York,*" *Mr. Cross said. Chrysta smiled at him.* "*Very disturbing, but very impressive.*"

.....

"I... I don't really know," Chrysta said. "After I sent my father home, we ran. South? I think? We finally came across a man and a woman. They seemed friendly at first, but then they transformed and attacked Tommy." She took a deep, shaky breath, and York gently placed a hand on her back and guided her to a chair in front of his desk. Surprisingly, she let him lead her without protest.

"He was already in pain, and they hurt him. Bad. T-there was so much blood. But he was alive. They put us in a van, and then we traveled for what felt like hours. They put me in a room in a warehouse. They wouldn't tell me what they did with Tommy. They didn't talk to me. They didn't feed me. Well, they gave me food, but it was raw meat." She started shivering and paused, rubbing her arms.

York looked at Guerra. They shared a look of disbelief. "A changeling nest. It would make sense that Tommy would take you there," Guerra said. Actually, it made no sense at all. Monroe was always attacked by the others when they saw him. "Tell me, did you see their leader? She would look like a spider."

.....

Kevin picked up a book and started to leaf through it. "*There is a changeling nest two hours south of the city. If they think Tommy would take you to other changelings, it would have to be there.*"

"*Not too much detail,*" *Mr. Cross warned.* "*Think of things Chrysta would notice as a prisoner but nothing that she would learn from a book.*"

"Um," the young teen hummed as he thought. "There are all kinds of changelings that live there. But the leader, he's a bat changeling." Kevin paused as he turned the pages of the book and handed it to Chrysta. One whole page was an illustration of a bat creature attacking some men. If the drawing was accurate, the bat was at least five feet tall. "His name is Camazotz. He's one of the oldest changelings and rules in the Americas."

"What about details that Chrysta shouldn't know?" Rosa asked.

"What do you mean?" Kevin asked.

"Like, are there any questions York could ask that would show him Chrysta is lying?"

"Ummmmm... Oh! There are no bug changelings. Just mammals, birds, reptiles, and fish. The Golden One never made insect ones."

"Why?" Mr. Cross asked.

Kevin shrugged. "No one knows. Either she didn't like them or couldn't make one."

"Well, that is a start. Anything else?" Chrysta asked.

.....

Chrysta paused and bit her lip. "No, there were no spider creatures. The leader, the one that they listened to... He changed into a bat at one point, to s-scare me." Chrysta shivered and sighed. "Um, there was a wolf, one that attacked Tommy. And I think a cat one? Like a lynx? Most of them stayed in human form."

York glanced at Guerra, who was standing behind Chrysta, and he gave a slight nod, frowning. Camazotz, the bat changeling, leader of all the Americas. That was a detail that only a person who went into the nest or studied it for a few years would know.

"Did they say why they kept you alive?" York asked his daughter.

"No, they didn't say anything. The people watching me wouldn't tell me anything, like if Tommy was still alive or not."

"And your escape?" Guerra asked.

"They always had two of them watching me, but at one point early this morning, one of them fell asleep. The other one came into the room and hit me." Chrysta gestured to the wound on her forehead. "So I blasted him with light and ran. I... I made it to a highway and started to hitchhike here. I didn't really have a plan. I was just trying to g-get away."

York regarded his daughter for a moment. He then looked at the other men in the room. "Leave us," he said. Guerra looked startled but complied with a slight bow. Chrysta glanced at him but quickly looked away.

Once he was sure they were alone, York went over to the drink table. He poured a glass of water and then brought it back to her. She glared at it for a long moment but took it. "Thank you," she whispered, taking a small sip. He sat down, using his cane.

"I have to say," he said slowly, choosing his words carefully. "I am most impressed with your performance the other night. You fought off several grown sorcerers, teleported me across town, and now you say you were able to get away from the most dangerous changelings that we know of."

She glanced at his face but looked down again. "I wasn't trying to be impressive. I was just trying to survive."

"And no one can fault you for that," he said. He tapped the head of his cane with a finger, the one with the slavering on it. "I can make sure the others don't hurt you. You know that, right?"

She gulped and then took another sip of the water. "They weren't the ones holding the knife."

"True," he said. He let them lapse into silence. After several minutes he cleared his throat. "I apologize, Chrysta. I see the error of my ways."

She looked at him, not a glance this time, but she held his gaze for a long moment. "You do?" she asked.

He nodded. "You are strong, Chrysta. Given time, you will become the strongest sorcerer ever. Stronger than me, than anyone else on the planet right now." He leaned forward. "I shouldn't have tried to use you for the ritual. I should have tried to help you to grow your powers."

She bit her lip and looked at him.

．．．．．

"Chrysta," Mr. Cross said. She looked up from her empty lunch plate, and he made a motion with his hand. "Can we talk?"

She nodded, and they left the kitchen. They passed Tommy and Miss Normandy in the main room and went outside. Poe cawed and landed on Chrysta's shoulder, taking flight as soon as they got outdoors. Mr. Cross sat down on a bench at the foot of the tree, and Chrysta followed.

"When you go back," he said, "try to appeal to your father's ego. Don't act upset. Just act scared. Keep your emotions in check. We want to lure your father into a false sense of security."

Chrysta nodded. "I understand."

"But mostly..." Mr. Cross hesitated and moved his hand in a circle like it would help him think of the right words. Poe made lazy circles above them, croaking to himself. "Remember, your father and the other acolytes crave power. I don't know if he loves you. I can't speak to that. But I think he will try to get you to listen to him. So he can use your powers for his own gain. Don't let him give you false hope."

Chrysta swallowed past the lump in her throat. "Okay, Mr. Cross. I won't."

．．．．．

Chrysta took a sip of the water. Her edgy look was starting to be replaced with anger. "So you're sorry you tried to kill me, not because it was wrong, but because I could be useful to you now?"

York tried to not show any irritation. She had a right to be angry, he recognized that, but she had to trust him if he was to control her. "Don't you see, Chrysta, this could benefit us both. If these men fear you, they will listen to you. And you can get rid of anyone that stands in your way."

"And you will tell me who I should get rid of," she replied flatly. She shifted in her chair and leaned forward to put the glass of water on York's desk. "What about Tommy?" she asked unexpectedly.

.....

Miss Normandy checked on Tommy while Kevin went over some details about changelings he felt Chrysta should know. She was leafing through the book on famous changelings when she came across a photo, old and grainy, with several men around a lion changeling. The creature was dead, torn apart, its tongue lolling out of its head. The men were posing with the corpse, dwarfed by the changeling, but it was still smaller than Tommy. The caption listed the men's names, but what caught Chrysta's eye was "One of the Heretic's victims."

"What happened here?" she asked Kevin. He studied the photo.

"A changeling attacked Tommy, and Tommy had to kill him," Kevin explained. "It happened... yeah, it happened in 1890 in Australia. Witnesses say the lion changeling went after Tommy, they transformed and fought."

"So his own kind attack him?" Chrysta asked.

"Yep, every time. No one knows why."

Chrysta looked over at Tommy. "So the acolytes enslaved him. His own kind attack him whenever they see him. And he's lived like this his whole life?"

"Yeah, seems kinda messed up, doesn't it?" Kevin asked.

"Something he said has stuck with me since he came to see me," Miss Normandy said. She leaned her head to the side for a second in thought. "'If you asked me a century ago if I wanted my freedom, I would have taken it, but now I'm just tired.'" She finished checking his heart rate. Chrysta realized that he hadn't stirred for hours, and his chest barely moved as he breathed. "I think he has been all alone this entire time and lost all hope of being freed. But Tommy wanted to save Chrysta, so he did what he had to, even if it meant he would die in the process."

Chrysta swallowed and gently picked up one of his hands. "Well then, I'm going to do everything I can to save him. I owe him that much."

.....

York felt his face betray his annoyance, and it took longer for him to wipe his expression blank. "What about him?"

"He may be alive," Chrysta continued. "Will you help me free him?"

York paused. As much as having the slave had helped the acolytes over the years, it was clear Monroe would not obey anymore. A slave who did not listen was useful to no one. And what would the wretched creature whisper in Chrysta's ear if he came back? "I can't do that, Chrysta. I'm sorry, but going to war with some of the most bloodthirsty monsters alive is suicide. I won't do it."

He got up from the desk and walked around her, trying to make sure she couldn't see his face. "Why does it have to be Monroe? You can make more of them if you want another changeling. You will be that powerful. They would serve you and only you."

"It's not about service," she said softly, her face hidden by her hair. "Tommy's my friend. I want to help him."

"He took you to the others, Chrysta. He put you in danger. The man he attacked in the street? He lost an eye. Monroe is dangerous. Surely you see that."

"He saved me from *you*," she replied. She looked at York with anger. "I want to save him now. If you want me to trust you, help me save him."

.....

It was an hour before sundown, and Tommy stopped breathing again. Miss Normandy came running out of the kitchen, where she and Rimsha worked a potion for most of the afternoon. She performed CPR on Tommy herself, doing chest compressions for several minutes. Chrysta stood nearby, biting her lip and trying not to cry, Poe on her shoulder, clicking his beak. Mr. Cross was by her side with a hand on her other shoulder. The others were behind them, trying to give Miss Normandy some space. Tommy finally took a breath on his own, and everyone in the room relaxed.

"Akrur," Miss Normandy said, slightly out of breath. Chrysta waited for her to finish her thought, but Mr. Cross finished it for her.

"He doesn't have much time left," he said. He took a deep breath and looked at Chrysta and Julien. "And you two still want to help me?"

"Yes," Chrysta said while Julien held up a fist and made a knocking motion.

"Alright, we leave in half an hour."

.....

York glared at his daughter. He was losing her trust, and he needed to get back in control. "You're tired and in shock." He stalked to the door and opened it. "Come take Chrysta to her room," he ordered the two men who entered. "One of you stay on the balcony, the other at her door."

He turned back to his daughter as she stood up. "Shower, get some rest. I will have someone bring you food in an hour. We will talk more in the morning."

She scowled at him but allowed the two men to escort her out. Once she was gone, Guerra let himself into the study. "What are you doing, brother?"

"What do you mean?" York asked. But he knew what the man meant.

"We serve our Lady. Don't believe that you could place yourself above her. That's blasphemy."

"I would never do that, Luca," York lied. "If Chrysta is as powerful as we think she will become, she can be an asset. A tool that can help us with our goals."

"And if she doesn't fall in line?"

"Then we will perform the ritual again," York said. "And she will be the vessel our Lady needs."

Guerra stood there, hands folded behind him, just staring at York. York looked back, keeping his face blank. Guerra was a faithful zealot. York knew he would only listen as long as he thought York was one as well.

"Very well," Guerra finally said. He turned to leave. "I am glad she is back. I missed her playing. And Frost shouldn't be in charge. He is not a true believer." And with that, he left the study.

· · · · ·

"I still don't see why I can't go with you," Rosa told Mr. Cross.

Mr. Cross paused in setting up the transportation circle. "This is a job that needs to be quick and quiet, Miss Torres. Chrysta gets into the mansion, she helps us get in. We use the sleeping potion, we get York's blood, and we get out. I'm sorry, my dear, but you are too emotionally invested."

Rosa looked down, crossing her arms. "You could bring someone with you, have him arrested."

"Yes, but then they may not let us take his blood," Mr. Cross explained. "The only reason we would take it is if we were doing a spell. They may not let us do it if they know it's to help a changeling. This is, after all, a plan to save Tommy."

Rosa sighed. "Fine. But promise to give him a kick in the ribs when he's out for me, okay?"

Mr. Cross just smiled. He turned to Chrysta, who had just made a fresh wound on her forehead after getting some mud on Tommy's jacket and boots. "Where are we going, Miss York?"

She looked at the map of the city he had brought out. "There," she said, pointing to an area near Mary's home. "If I got away from something dangerous and didn't want to go back home, I would go to Mary's house. They should be watching it."

Mr. Cross nodded. "Transportation circle, the sleeping potion, Miss York is wearing her clothes from that night. Are we missing anything?"

"Yeah," Miss Normandy said. "Don't die."

"Ah, yes, sound advice." He looked at Chrysta and Julien. "If anyone wants to back out, now is the time."

Both teenagers shook their heads.

"Then let's head out," Mr. Cross said. He stood up in the circle, pulling Chrysta and Julien in with him. Poe landed on Chrysta's shoulder and croaked a quiet "Tommy." Mr. Cross looked at the others. "Miss Normandy, you have the helm. Take care of everyone?"

Miss Normandy nodded, looking worried. "Just be careful," she said softly.

"Yeah, Mr. Cross," Kevin added. "We need you to come back."

"Promise, Chrysta," Rosa suddenly barked. "Promise to keep them safe."

"I promise," Chrysta said. And Mr. Cross held out his hands and chanted to himself, and with a bright flash and a lot of pressure, they were gone.

30

Chrysta went upstairs with the two men while Guerra pushed past her to enter her father's study. Hopefully, they wouldn't talk about Chrysta's story and how many holes it had in it. She needed to be convincing enough to keep them out of her bedroom for a few minutes. Peter stood in the foyer and leered at her. She ignored him.

When they got to her bedroom, Chrysta waited until the door was closed before she made a run for the balcony. One of the men shouted, but both followed as she threw open the door and ran out into the cold. Instead of hopping over the railing, she turned, however, and waited for the men to grab her. She made sure she was touching their skin, and she started chanting in her head—

sleep, sleep, go to sleep, sleep, sleep, sleepsleepsleep

—and both men froze and dropped like stones. Chrysta panted for a moment, making sure they were indeed passed out before she turned to the railing and leaned over. She lifted one of her hands and let gold sparks float in the air.

Two figures materialized out of the bushes, and they ran to the mansion and started climbing. Julien made it up first, and he and Chrysta helped Mr. Cross up the last few feet. He got over the railing and paused, hands on his knees and out of breath. "Bloody hell," he said while Poe dropped to the table and squawked at the two prone men. "I didn't know this would be a blasted physical exam."

As he recovered, Mr. Cross checked on the two men. "Are they alright?" Chrysta asked, trying not to feel guilty. They were acolytes, after all.

"They're breathing," he said. "They should be up soon unless you hit them a little too hard with the sleep spell. Then they may be out for a few weeks." Mr. Cross saw the look of guilt on her face. "No worries, my dear. They will wake up refreshed, like the best nap of their lives."

They went into Chrysta's bedroom, and Chrysta took the opportunity to grab her backpack. She checked that everything was in it and started adding as many of her clothes as possible. Mr. Cross had taken some items out of his own backpack and set up a cauldron with two large glass jars next to it. He handed a flat round stone to both Chrysta and Julien.

"This is a magic stone," he explained to the teens, holding up his own stone. "Keep it in your mouth, and the potion won't affect you." He pointed to the jars. "Once I mix these two liquids, it will turn into a gas. It's colorless, it's tasteless, it's odorless. It will fill the entire house from this story down. We wait five minutes, and everyone should be asleep. Then we have thirty minutes to get York's blood and get out."

Both teens nodded. Mr. Cross placed the stone in his mouth, the teens following his lead, and then he poured out the two jars into the cauldron. The liquids swirled together, and it started glowing blue and bubbling. Tendrils of mist began to lift above the rim of the cauldron and then float back to the floor, the gas disappearing after it reached a few feet. Mr. Cross glanced at his watch, smiled, and gave the teens a big thumbs up.

. . . . .

Guerra left the study and was immediately grabbed by Peter Jacobs. Guerra looked at the teen clutching his arm and raised an eyebrow. Most of the others knew not to get too close. "So what happens to me now?" the young man asked. "Am I still in trouble? I can't be in trouble anymore. I brought her in."

"You found her, yes," Guerra agreed. "But I would argue that it was more luck than skill."

The teen grimaced. "I just need to get my standing back with the acolytes. Can you put in a good word?" Suddenly, Peter yawned, jaw actually popping as his mouth stretched wide.

Guerra flashed the teen his widest smile, and Peter took a step back. Guerra hated the acolytes' politics sometimes, with his brothers' obsession with their power and standing with the others. If they just listened to the leader and did what they needed to free the Lady, then that should be reward enough.

"The Lady sees all," he said to the teen. "Know that she is pleased with you, and be content." And with that, he got the teen to let go of him, and he started up the stairs, wanting to check in with Miss York.

Halfway up to the second story, Guerra felt light-headed and actually had to put a hand out to lean on the wall. He blinked and shook his head. His eyes felt heavy, and Guerra had to keep himself from yawning. He heard a thump and looked behind him to see Peter passed out on the floor.

Guerra cursed under his breath and clamped a hand over his mouth and nose, trying to take shallow breaths. A sleep potion, and a potent one, too, if it was working so fast. He knew Miss York coming back to them was too good to be true. He rushed up the stairs.

No one was outside Chrysta's bedroom door, and he burst in. The room was completely empty except for a bubbling cauldron in the middle of the room which was emitting a gas. Guerra hurried to it, to pick it up and throw it outside before it filled the entire house, not checking the bathroom as he passed.

Before he could get a hand on the cauldron, a figure tackled him from behind, and an already weakened Guerra was knocked to the floor. He fought the figure, trying to turn over or at least get his hands on some exposed skin to get them incapacitated with pain. He was shocked when he saw a young man with black hair fighting him, not one of the acolytes. Chrysta and an older man came out of the bathroom. "Grab his hands!" the man cried, voice muffled. "So he can't hurt him!"

Chrysta slammed his arm into the floor, using all her weight to pin him, avoiding his bare hand. The older man grabbed his other arm, but he couldn't get it pinned in time, and Guerra was able to reach his face. The man's eyes widened even though Guerra hadn't used his ability yet.

"No!" Chrysta cried, and she put her hand in his, and Guerra felt the overwhelming need to sleep overcome him again. His hand felt so heavy, and he let it drop. He tried to shake his head to wake up, but another wave of darkness came over him, and he swore he heard a voice—

sleep, sleep, sleep, sleepsleepsleep,

—that seemed to be saying something he really wanted to do. And so he finally gave up fighting and let sleep claim him.

. . . . .

As Guerra went limp, Mr. Cross lurched so that he was standing and ran to the bathroom. Chrysta made sure Julien was looking at her. "You okay?" she asked, trying to move her lips without losing the stone in her mouth.

Julien nodded and jerked his head towards the bathroom door. "Check on him," he said as he examined the cauldron.

Chrysta hurried to the bathroom to find Mr. Cross leaning over the toilet, heaving. She saw that he had taken out the stone and was holding it in his hand. She went over to him and placed a hand on his back. "Mr. Cross? Are you okay? Did he hurt you?"

Mr. Cross panted for a few minutes and then spit. He flushed the toilet, placed the stone back in his mouth, and turned to her.

"No, my dear, he didn't hurt me physically," he said in a rasp. He wiped his mouth with the back of one hand. "But he triggered a reading when he touched me. I think I saw every murder and torture session that man has ever done."

"Oh, Mr. Cross, I'm so sorry," she whispered. She helped him up.

He patted her hand, still looking pale, smiling weakly. "No worries, my dear. I needed some nightmares to haunt me for the next few months."

They exited the bathroom. Julien gave Guerra a kick to the ribs. Mr. Cross touched Julien's shoulder, and the teen turned. "What are you doing?" Mr. Cross asked. Julien made some motions with his hands. Mr. Cross nodded. "Yes, yes, I'm fine. But why are you kicking him?" Julien made another set of motions. "No, she said to kick Jozef York. You just tackled and fought Luca Guerra, the Butcher," Mr. Cross explained, and Julien jumped back like Guerra was a snake who would bite him.

"Come on," Chrysta said. "The potion should be working now. Let's find my father."

·····

They made their way downstairs, and Chrysta pointed to the door to the right: her father's study. They passed Peter on the floor, who was lightly snoring. "Ass!" Poe croaked at him from Chrysta's shoulder, and she hushed the bird.

Chrysta tried the study's door to find it unlocked, and she eased the door open. There was no one in the room.

Chrysta quickly checked behind the desk to make sure her father hadn't passed out behind it, but he was nowhere in sight. Mr. Cross frowned and turned to her.

"Anywhere else he could have gone?" he asked, trying to talk around the stone. Chrysta thought about it and nodded. She led the others out of the study.

They went to the french doors across the hall, and Chrysta opened them to the dining room. Several guards were passed out at the table, some on the floor. They crept past the sleeping men, and Chrysta opened the door to the kitchen at the back of the room. Two cooks were sleeping on the floor, a pan on fire on one of the stoves. Mr. Cross rushed to put the flaming pan in the sink as Chrysta made sure all the burners were off.

"Where else?" Mr. Cross growled as smoke billowed out of the sink.

Chrysta thought for a second and gestured for the others to follow her. The servants' quarters turned into a security room when her father installed the cameras, which was on the first floor. If her father wasn't in there, then the only other place he could be in was his bedroom on the second story.

Or he could be in the third-story bedroom. But Chrysta didn't want to think about that.

They crept into the hallway behind the staircase, Mr. Cross tapping Chrysta's shoulder and getting in front of her. He was making so much noise trying to open the locked door, none of them noticed the entrance to the basement gently clicking open behind them.

Chrysta was watching Mr. Cross struggle with the door when Poe squawked at something behind her. Before she could turn around, Poe was knocked off her shoulder and went tumbling to the floor. Someone wrapped an arm around Chrysta's shoulders and yanked her back. She bit back a cry when a knife was pressed to her throat. "Who did you bring into my house?" her father hissed in her ear.

Mr. Cross whirled around, making Julien turn around in curiosity. Julien's face settled into a scowl, and he almost stepped forward, but Mr. Cross held him back. Mr. Cross put his hands up, showing Chrysta's father that they were empty. "Easy now," he said, voice muffled but calm. "Don't do anything rash."

"Stones out of your mouths, please," her father said, and Mr. Cross complied, gesturing at Julien to do the same. Chrysta felt a tap on her cheek, and she spat her stone out as well. Poe had gotten up on his feet, feathers ruffled, croaking to himself. Chrysta's father swayed a little and shook his head.

"And who are you, hm?" he asked. "Not changelings, they couldn't make a sleep potion, and even if they could, they wouldn't use one. Too subtle." His knife started to lower, then jerked back up, nicking Chrysta's throat. "Not hunters, he is too young, and you are too fat."

"Now you are just being mean," Mr. Cross joked.

Chrysta's father chuckled, a sound with no warmth in it. "So not changelings or hunters. The sleep potion was a nice touch, but keep in mind that some acolytes practice mithridatism. You will not get a chance to try something stronger, I'm afraid."

"Mr. York, let us be reasonable," Mr. Cross started to say as Chrysta's father tightened his hold on her shoulder.

"Trying to assassinate me?" he continued. "My brothers want to kill me, and now my daughter does as well?"

"I just want to help Tommy," Chrysta said, trying to turn so her father could see her face while avoiding the knife. "I meant what I said earlier. I need your help to save him."

"So Monroe is still breathing?" he asked. "But he won't wake up, will he? So you want the ring to bring him back. Did your new-found friends tell you how to get it, hm?" He leaned down to whisper in Chrysta's ear. "Either I give it to you, or you kill me. And I don't like either of those options."

"Well, we found a third option," Mr. Cross said.

"And what's that?"

"We free him," Chrysta said. She caught Mr. Cross's eye. He nodded his head slightly. "All we need is your blood."

Her father gave a bark of laughter. "Not going to happen. The beast can rot for all I care."

"I was hoping you would say that," Chrysta said, and she placed her hands on her father's hand. She started to focus on one word—

sleep, you are so tired, sleep, you need to lie down, sleep, close your eyes, sleepsleepsleep,

— just like Ichiro had taught her, and her father stumbled.

"Wha... what are you doing?" Jozef York asked in a small voice.

"Making sure we can get what we want without you hurting us," Chrysta explained. "Just like I promised."

Chrysta closed her eyes, and she continued the chant in her head—

sleep, so tired, sleep, lie down, sleep, close your eyes, sleepsleepsleep,

—until her father's hold on her loosened, and the knife started to move away from her throat. She kept her hold on his hand for a few moments longer, and finally, he dropped to the ground. Julien rushed to kick the knife away as Mr. Cross rushed to grab Chrysta. "Are you alright?" he asked, looking Chrysta over.

Chrysta nodded. "I think so."

Mr. Cross looked at her father on the floor. "Good job, my dear."

"Now what?" she asked.

"We get what we came for."

They knelt down, each of them putting their stones back into their mouths. Mr. Cross brought an empty vial out of the backpack. He grabbed York's knife and made a cut in the man's palm. None of them said anything as the vial slowly filled. Chrysta gently brought Poe into her lap and scratched at his neck as the bird croaked to himself. When Mr. Cross was done, he stopped up the vial. "Right, let's head out before there are any more surprises." He and Julien started to walk back to the staircase but paused when they realized Chrysta was not following them.

Mr. Cross looked at the young woman on the floor with raised eyebrows but just nodded to himself when he recognized why she was still kneeling by her father. He tapped Julien's shoulder. "Go back upstairs," he signed. "Throw out any of the sleep potion that is left, and set up the transportation circle." Julien nodded and accepted the backpack. Mr. Cross went back to Chrysta and knelt back down next to her.

"Are you alright?" he asked around the blasted stone.

Chrysta nodded, watching her father sleep. "What did he mean that his brothers wanted to assassinate him?"

"The other acolytes, I would assume," Mr. Cross explained. He grimaced and then spit the stone out of his mouth. He took a deep breath, and when he didn't get light-headed, he continued. "Losing you, not once but twice, will be a death sentence for sure."

Chrysta bit her lip. "Why?" she asked. Mr. Cross cocked his head, and she resumed after removing her own stone. "Why do I care if they hurt him? He was going to kill me. He was going to let Tommy die. Why should I care if the others in their cult will hurt him?"

"He is your father, my dear, for better or for worse." Mr. Cross placed a hand on hers and smiled. "You are better than him, have more empathy than he does. You worry because that is the core of your nature. Don't see it as a weakness. See it as a strength."

Chrysta sighed and nodded, a swirl of emotion still making it hard for her to leave. She grabbed her father's hand and placed her own on it, glowing gold for a moment until the cut in his palm disappeared. She replaced her father's hand on his chest.

"The start of any journey is hard, Chrysta," Mr. Cross said softly, watching as she worked. "It's scary to step into the unknown. And more frightening still that your father will not be there to help you. But he is an adult, and sometimes we make mistakes. You can't stop him from making them or keep him from suffering the consequences of his actions." Mr. Cross shrugged. "You have done all you can to help yourself and Tommy, and I, for one, am very proud of you."

Chrysta nodded again, not trusting her voice. She swiped at her eyes and slowly got up, placing Poe on her shoulder. "Let's go," she said.

Mr. Cross smiled but didn't move. "Well?" he asked. "Do you want to do the honors, or shall I?"

"Excuse me?"

"I do believe we promised a kick to the ribs of one Jozef York for Rosa, yes?"

Chrysta laughed and gave her father a kick to the ribs, probably lighter than Rosa would have liked. Mr. Cross nodded and gently guided Chrysta away.

They climbed the stairs and went into Chrysta's room. Julien had set up the circle and was placing the empty cauldron in the backpack. Chrysta went to the wardrobe, grabbed her dress, and joined the two men in the ring. Julien flashed Mr. Cross a thumbs up. "Fine job, my boy," Mr. Cross said. "Want to take us home?"

Julien nodded and started to sign. Blue light began to form around his hands, and the stones in the circle glowed. Chrysta held her breath as the pressure built, and then they were gone.

31

When they popped back into existence, there were so many things going on: Poe squawked and took flight, landing on a bookcase on the far side of the round room. Chrysta threw her stuff on a nearby couch and knelt beside Tommy. Kevin, Rimsha, Rosa, and Ichiro tackled Julien to the floor, all talking at once. Miss Normandy went up to Mr. Cross and hugged him, almost making him fall as well. When she leaned back, she had tears in her eyes that she wiped away. "Welcome back," she said.

"Cuffed to be back," Mr. Cross said with a smile. He reached into the backpack and brought out the vial of blood. "Is this what the doctor ordered?" he asked, and Miss Normandy snorted. All the teens stopped talking at once and rushed to gather around Chrysta and Tommy.

Miss Normandy took the vial and grabbed a bowl. She had already made a base of silver liquid that swirled and moved on its own. She poured the blood in, and the liquid started to move quicker. Chrysta looked up from the floor. "What do we do now?" Chrysta asked.

"Now we write the spell," Miss Normandy explained. Rimsha handed her a small paintbrush, and she gently mixed the fluid. "The book says to make a slave band, you have to take the two pieces of silver and write the spell to bind the slave on the inside with the slave's blood." The liquid turned black, and Miss Normandy smiled.

"To get the band off, you have to write the same spell on the outside with the master's blood."

Chrysta held Tommy's arm up, perpendicular to the floor, and Miss Normandy started to write on the band, the letters glowing slightly as the brush moved along. Miss Normandy filled as much of the space as she could, writing the same thing over and over. Chrysta squinted at the words when she rotated Tommy's arm. "Is that Latin?" she asked.

"Yes," Miss Normandy said. "'Use this silver to form a band. Use this blood to bind. Use this ring to hold steadfast. Let the blood of the one that possesses it all unmake them.'"

She continued to write, the teens holding their breaths. Finally, Miss Normandy filled the last free spot. All the words glowed brighter. The band itself started to redden like it was fresh from a forge, but Chrysta didn't feel any heat. The metal began to flow and melt, dripping off of Tommy's arm. Miss Normandy got an empty bowl, handed the bowl of magic ink to Rimsha, and started to collect the metal.

There were soft gasps around Chrysta, but she hardly noticed. The metal was slowly revealing Tommy's bare forearm, and cuts, burns, and scars covered every inch of exposed skin. The last of the silver dripped off Tommy's arm and started to cool into a twisted sculpture in the bowl. Miss Normandy placed the bowl to the side and put a hand to Tommy's chest.

Tommy took a deep breath, but otherwise, he didn't stir. Chrysta watched for any sign he was waking up. "Is he alright?" she asked Miss Normandy softly.

"Patience, dear," Miss Normandy said. "Give him a minute."

Finally, after several agonizing moments, Tommy started to move on his own, lip curling as he groaned. The room erupted into cheers and whoops, and Chrysta let out a laugh that almost turned into a sob. She leaned down to put her ear closer when Tommy started to talk, Miss Normandy trying to hush the others.

"M'head," Tommy moaned. "It's 'ounding." His nose twitched as he took a breath. "Beautiful? Is that you?"

"Yeah, it's me," she said.

His right hand reached up, groping the air, and Chrysta took it. Tommy started trying to sit up, Chrysta and Miss Normandy helping as gently as they could. "Congratulations, Mr. Cross," Chrysta heard Kevin say behind her. "Operation was a success."

"All praise goes to Chrysta," Mr. Cross confessed. "Welcome to the Disaster Club, Mr. Monroe," he said in a louder voice.

"Huh?" Tommy moaned. He finally cracked an eye open when he was sitting up and slowly looked around the room, taking in all the teens staring back. "Where?" he asked thickly.

"Somewhere safe," Miss Normandy said, and Tommy glanced at her, eyes blinking slowly. He turned to his other side and finally caught sight of Chrysta.

He growled deep in his throat, and Rimsha squeaked and backed up. Tommy reached with his right hand and lightly traced the bruise around Chrysta's eye with his fingers, tips of his nails lightly scratching her skin. "Who gave you this?" he grumbled.

"Long story," Chrysta said. She held Tommy's hand to her face, fighting back some tears. "I'm just glad you're okay. How do you feel?"

"Head hurts," he rumbled, "throat is dry. Can't feel my left arm, but at least it doesn't hur—" He had been turning to look at his arm and froze when he finally saw it. Tommy went still as stone, eyes wide and ears back on his head. He gently brought his left arm into his lap and cradled it close to his body.

"Tommy?" Miss Normandy asked when he didn't move for a full minute. "Are you okay?"

"It's gone?" Tommy asked, voice so quiet Chrysta barely heard him. He looked up and glanced between Chrysta and Miss Normandy. "Am I dreaming?"

"Told you I would get rid of it," Miss Normandy said. And Tommy chuckled, stopped, and sniffled when it started to sound like he was crying. Suddenly, Tommy's form shifted, becoming smaller, his skin turning brown, his hair growing back on his head, and his face returning to normal. But he stayed in his pose, just staring at his arm. He ran his right hand over the bare skin like he didn't believe it was real.

"How?" Tommy asked in that soft voice Chrysta didn't recognize.

"We found a spell to get rid of it," Miss Normandy explained. "And Chrysta got the main ingredient."

Tommy looked at Chrysta, tears in his eyes. "Is that how you got the black eye?"

Chrysta shrugged, trying to look unconcerned. "In a way."

Tommy looked back down at his arm, still rubbing it. "You were supposed to be safe, beautiful. We were getting you somewhere safe, and you were supposed to stay there."

"Well, I couldn't sit by and let you die," Chrysta said. She watched him for a moment, not able to see his face. "Are you okay?"

Tommy suddenly hugged her, right arm crushing her to him, face buried in her throat. She smiled and returned the hug, rubbing his back as he let out a sob. Miss Normandy got up and shooed everyone else away, ignoring the teens as they protested.

"Alright, everyone, let's give them a moment."

"What, you mean, go outside? In the cold?"

"Aw, but the show was just getting good."

"Hey! No pushing!"

"You too, Akrur, get moving."

"Doctor's orders? Ow! Don't hit me. I'm a hero, don't you know?"

And the Disaster Club filed out to give the two figures on the floor some privacy.

32

Chrysta slowly woke up. She was in a bed she didn't recognize, and it took a moment for her to remember what had happened. Something about seeing her father again. To help Tommy.

Tommy.

Chrysta quickly sat up. She noticed Miss Normandy sleeping on a couch across the room. That's right. She and Chrysta had guided Tommy into the guest room so that they could have some privacy. Other than saying his left arm was completely numb, Tommy didn't complain of any further pain. He wasn't himself, though. He kept rubbing at his arm in a daze, over and over again. At one point, he had grabbed Miss Normandy's arm. "Heal Chrysta, please," he asked, voice low and pleading. Miss Normandy just smiled and complied. Only then would Tommy let them tuck him into bed.

She had changed her clothes and then dragged a chair into the guest room to sleep by Tommy's side, wrapped up in a borrowed blanket. Poe sat on the back of the chair, tucking his head under his wing after Chrysta settled down. She must have fallen asleep while watching Tommy's chest move up and down as he slept, just glad to see him moving at all.

She checked the skylight and noticed the sky was pink and purple, winter sunset colors. Tommy probably got up at some point and put her in the bed.

But where was he?

She padded over to the couch. Poor Miss Normandy had gotten less sleep than she had for the last few days. Poe clicked his beak and landed on her shoulder. She made sure the older woman was covered before going into the main room. The door to the kitchen was open, and Chrysta went to investigate.

Everyone was there except for Mr. Cross and Tommy, eating at the table. They all flashed her big smiles and waved. "Well, look who's up," Kevin said. "Grab a plate, dinner is still hot."

"Where is Tommy?" Chrysta asked while she accepted a plate but didn't get any food. Poe hopped down to the table and started inspecting the food.

"With Mr. Cross," Rimsha explained. "They went to talk to Mr. Burke after they had lunch."

"Is that... is that safe?" Chrysta asked while she sat down. Kevin had given Poe a small plate of food, and Poe was pecking at some chicken. "I mean... Mr. Burke is a former hunter. And Nyla could try to hurt Tommy."

"I'm sure they will be okay," Ichiro said, putting food on Chrysta's plate without asking. "Mr. Burke gave you the book about slave bands to get rid of Tommy's. He helped to keep Hafeez away."

Chrysta nodded, still not sure if Tommy was protected or not. "Was Tommy okay when he woke up?"

"Oh, yeah, a perfect ray of sunshine," Rosa said sarcastically.

"Mr. Cross told him everything that happened the last few days. He wasn't happy about Mr. Cross letting you go back to your father," Rimsha explained. "But then Mr. Cross said, 'do you really think I could have stopped her from helping you if I tried?'"

Chrysta looked at her plate for a moment, not understanding why she felt a flush of shame. Did Tommy really think she would sit by and let him fade away? Not when she could do something about it.

"Is he going to stay?" Ichiro asked. "I mean, having a changeling around might be cool." Kevin, mouth full of food, nodded in agreement.

"I'm not sure," Chrysta confessed. "I didn't save him to force him to stay with me." She shrugged as she poked her food with a fork. "He's free now. He can choose to stay or go." She took a bite of her food. "I... I hope he stays, though."

.....

Tommy walked along the river bank, slow and lazy, with Mr. Cross by his side. There was no rush—such a weird feeling, to be free and master of where he went and what he did. He brought up his left arm and pulled down the jacket's sleeve to glance at his wrist for the hundredth time that day. No metal, just skin. Skin scarred and puckered, true. But bare skin all the same. They were reminders of a horrible thing done to him, but the fact that they were on display was a cause for celebration. He was free.

Although if he was going to keep his head was another question entirely.

Burke's meeting was not the most uncomfortable conversation he had ever had, but Tommy wouldn't say it was a walk in the park either. Burke, former hunter, one of the strongest magic users alive, with his black sword within reach, asking Tommy if he had killed a long list of people. Some were yes; some were no; most were murders that Tommy had been under orders to make. If Burke thought he was lying, he didn't say so or kill Tommy outright.

Burke paused after asking his questions. "There are rumors that you sometimes would attack people but not kill them. Why is that?"

Tommy shrugged. "After a few decades, I got tired of being their hitman. If they wanted people dead, let them be the ones to get blood on their hands. It got to the point that I was sent along to be a living shield since spells didn't work on me."

"Twenty-four years ago, a hunter was killed in his home. His name was Hafeez. Is that name familiar?"

Tommy winced. "Yeah. I remember that night."

"Who killed Hafeez?"

"York did."

Burke's eyebrows shot up. "Why?"

"Don't know. Hafeez opened some magic safe and got a magical item out of it. Then York slit his throat, even though he was helping."

"So, what did you do?"

"Pushed York, so he fell over a railing from the third story and broke his hip," Tommy confessed with a smirk.

Cross snorted, and Tommy swore he saw Burke's lip twitch. "So, you are the reason he limps?" Burke asked. "How do we know you're telling the truth?"

Tommy held up his arm and moved his borrowed sweater's sleeve to show the scars on his arm. "I wouldn't have gotten such lovely mementos if I listened like a good little slave."

Burke did smile this time, and he studied Tommy for several minutes, and Tommy tried not to shift or fidget. Finally, Burke sighed and got up from his desk. He placed the sword on a shelf and then turned around. "Hafeez's daughter, Nyla, was there that night. She saw you in your other form, standing over her father's body. She is convinced you killed him, so she became a hunter to kill you."

Tommy winced again. He did remember her, a young girl screaming for her father and calling Tommy a monster, hearing her cry while he and Guerra grabbed York and got out of there as fast as they could. "Maybe I should let her kill me. I couldn't stop York."

"That is not justice, though," Burke explained. "Miss York was right about that."

Tommy blinked but didn't respond.

"You are free to stay, Mr. Monroe," Burke said. "But if you harm anyone, you will have to answer for it."

"With my head?" Tommy asked dryly.

"Exactly. I will order Nyla to leave you alone, but I recommend that you don't go off on your own."

Tommy blinked again. "Thank you," he said. "I appreciate... I appreciate the chance to live without worrying if a hunter is going to put a sword in my back."

"Well, Mr. Monroe," Burke said as he sat down. "Just make sure you don't do anything that makes me unsheathe my sword."

. . . . .

They finally came to the collapsing bank with the tree with exposed roots, and Tommy found his backpack and guitar case. It felt like years since he hid them, never dreaming he would return for them. At best, he had hoped Chrysta would find them after he kicked the bucket, something to help her in her new life. But now he had them again. He checked that everything was dry and okay before they turned to walk back to the Disaster Club.

The two men walked side by side, not talking. Cross brought out a cigarette case and let one hang from his lips as he checked the many pockets of his jacket, grunting as his search dragged on. Tommy wordlessly found a lighter in one of his jacket pockets and lit it. Cross nodded in appreciation and got the cigarette lit. He took a deep breath and let it out. "So," he said almost too cheerfully. "What are your plans?"

Tommy gave the man a sour look. "Wondering if the changeling is moving on?" He almost regretted his harsh tone immediately. This man had helped him, after all.

"Not at all," Cross said. He picked a piece of tobacco off his tongue and flicked it away. "Chrysta needs to stay at the Academy and work on her abilities. If you leave, she will go with you." He took another drag off of the cigarette and blew the smoke into the sky. "And if you leave without telling her, she will be devastated."

Tommy felt a stab of guilt. "Yeah, well, I did think about it," he admitted. "She would be better off if I left, but... I will stay until she sends me away. I owe her that much."

Cross looked at him for a long moment, and then he snorted. "You have a meager opinion of yourself, Mr. Monroe."

"No, just a very honest one," Tommy said with a grin. Both men chuckled.

"Well, you are welcome at the Disaster Club as long as it is needed," Cross said. Tommy blinked at him in shock. "What?"

"You're letting me, a changeling, stay?"

"You may be a changeling, Mr. Monroe," Cross stated after taking another drag. "But the fact remains, you risked your life for Chrysta, and she risked hers for you."

"And?"

"Chrysta will be shunned, first for her name, second for her abilities. She will need allies, people she can trust. I think you have proven that you are such a person."

Tommy just slowly blinked at the man but didn't reply.

It was dusk when they got back. Chrysta and Normandy were sitting on the bench under the tree, waiting for them. Poe was in the tree and croaked a loud "Tommy!" in greeting. Chrysta had taken a shower and was wearing fresh clothes, hair down. Gods, she was beautiful. She smiled at both men when they got close. "What were you two up to?"

"Just boy talk," Mr. Cross joked. He took another drag on his cigarette. "How are you doing, by the way?"

"Tired," she admitted. "I feel like I could sleep for a few years after the last few days."

Cross nodded. "No wonder, with all the magic you performed."

Normandy scowled at Cross and gestured at the cigarette. "I thought you said you quit," she said.

Cross hummed and looked at his hand, looking in shock at the cigarette. "Goodness, how did that get there?"

"Mm-hmm," Normandy said. She looked at Tommy. "How are you feeling?"

"Good," he replied, glancing at Chrysta, trying to judge her mood. He took his jacket off and put it around Chrysta's shoulders, rolling up the sleeve of his borrowed sweater so Normandy could inspect it. "Arm is still numb, but I can move it now."

"Good," Normandy said, running her hands over the skin. "We will have to keep an eye on it."

Chrysta suddenly looked nervous and shuffled her feet. "Can I have a minute alone with Tommy?"

"Of course," Mr. Cross said and put out his cigarette. Tommy fought the urge to grab the man's arm to force him to stay. He had a feeling that being alone with Chrysta was the last thing he wanted.

Cross and Normandy made their way down the stairs, and Tommy sat down next to Chrysta. She coughed and fidgeted. Tommy just tried to keep his eyes forward. He just had to let her get her anger out. Let her tell him to get lost, and then he would do just that, and it would be over.

"You lied," she said. And she must have been really pissed because her voice came out even and not raised at all. That seemed worse. Tommy swallowed past the lump in his throat, mouth suddenly dry. "You said you were going to be okay, and you weren't," she continued.

She looked at his face then, smiling for some weird reason, but it died when she saw his expression. Her eyebrows furrowed. "What's wrong?"

"I... I know you're angry with me, beau—Chrysta. I can leave right now if you want. I do want to stay. I owe you my freedom, my life." He paused, looking at the ground. "But if you'd rather I leave, I will. Whatever you want."

There was a long silence, Tommy not tearing his eyes from the ground, although he wanted to. If he caused her so much pain, he should suck it up and look at her. Let her anger burn him if she wanted.

"Why would I make you leave? I just got you back."

He did look at her then, mouth opened in shock. She was smiling softly. She sighed and looked up at the sky. "Am I upset you kept the whole truth from me? Yes. But I do realize why you did. Why you had to." She looked back at him. "But you saved me, you didn't have to, but you did."

"Yeah, well," Tommy said and then coughed. "You didn't deserve what your father had planned for you. And you saved my life, so we're even."

They fell into an uncomfortable silence, Chrysta looking up as stars started appearing in the night sky. "You can leave," Chrysta started to say, "if you want to. I have to stay. I have to work on these... abilities. I don't know if I'm going to be as strong as everyone says I will be, but I need to control them." She shifted and tucked some hair behind her ear. "But you don't have to stay. I want you to, but it's up to you."

Tommy blinked at her. Freedom. Did she understand how much that meant to him? After wearing that fucking slave band for so long? But she was giving him a choice, something he hadn't had in a long time. "Well, beautiful," he said softly. "I warned you. You said you loved me. You're not getting rid of me now."

She laughed. "Good," she said, eyes dancing. She suddenly stood up and turned to him. "I think we need to start over. Start from the beginning. No more lies, no keeping secrets from each other." She stuck her hand out. "Chrysta York, daughter of Jozef York. I glow gold."

Tommy looked at her hand and then back at her face. A broad smile and dancing bright eyes, all for him. And he felt himself melting at the sight of her. He wanted to cup her face and kiss her deeply. But that is not what she was offering. She was offering something better. Not ending their relationship, but renewing it, restarting it, and trying again, the right way this time, with honesty and trust. And he couldn't be happier.

He smiled as he shook her hand. "Thomas Monroe, murderous changeling. Friends call me Tommy."

Her smile grew, and she laughed. "It's nice to meet you, Tommy. I have the feeling this is the beginning of a beautiful relationship."

He snorted and then chuckled when she looked up again. "You're acting like you have never seen stars before."

"I haven't," she said, flashing him a smile but then looking back up. "I have never been out of the city. I never imagined that the stars could look this beautiful."

Tommy got a fantastic idea and grinned. "Want to go stargazing?" he asked.

"Oh, can we?" she asked.

He grinned wider, and then he changed. He was towering over Chrysta with sharp teeth and claws, and she gasped and stepped back, but she was still smiling at him. Not afraid of him, even as strange as he looked. He held out his hand, and she put her hand in his palm.

The sound of the door opening made Tommy's ear twitch, and Miss Normandy came up the stairs. Her eyebrows rose, but she didn't comment on Tommy's form. "Everything okay up here?" she asked.

"Yeah, we are going stargazing," Chrysta said as if there was nothing weird about her talking to this giant creature in front of her.

"Think you can use your arm and not hurt it?" Miss Normandy asked.

Tommy rumbled and brought it up. He wiggled his fingers. "Yeah, I'll be careful."

"Alright, but I'm doing a full exam when you get back," Miss Normandy warned and then went back down the stairs.

Chrysta grinned and bounced up and down. "Can we go?" she asked.

Tommy chuckled again and gently picked her up. "Of course, beautiful."

Tommy moved her so that she hung off his back, her arms wrapped around his neck. Poe followed them, loudly cawing as Tommy weaved through the trees. He jogged deeper into the woods on the lookout for the best tree, finding it after several minutes of running. "Hang on," he said, and he started climbing, using claws to scramble up. When he was high enough, he gently placed Chrysta on a tree limb and sat in front of her. Her eyes were screwed shut, knuckles white as she clung to the branch underneath her. He leaned forward and whispered in her ear. "Look up, beautiful."

She looked up and opened her eyes and gasped, breathe fogging in the cold air. She grinned at the sight of thousands of twinkling lights strewn across the black.

He changed back, the branch creaking in the change in his weight. "Chrysta?" he said softly.

"Yeah, Tommy?" she replied with a smile.

"Thank you."

She cocked her head and carefully leaned forward to place her forehead on his. "Of course."

And then they both looked up, gazing at the stars.

Chrysta's and Tommy's story continue in…

HER MOST LOYAL SERVANTS

Now available wherever books are sold.

e PROLOGUE o

May 2003

The slave felt the summons, and he grumbled.

He had just bought a hotdog and was chewing his first bite when the summons caused the itch from his middle finger to his shoulder blade. Really, if they wanted him to come at their beck and call, they could at least let him enjoy his food first. He sighed and looked at the rest of his dinner, wondering if he should finish it or throw it out and get his butt in gear. He felt another bolt of pain in his left arm and decided to get to the mansion first. Food could wait.

Thomas Monroe threw away the hotdog and started walking. Warm weather had brought everyone out of their homes, and the streets were crowded even as the sky darkened. Late shoppers, diners heading out for supper, lovers on dates. And musicians. Tommy's people. Singing, dancing, playing any instrument they could find. Guitars and drums and saxes and violins. He grabbed a roll of money out of his pocket and made sure to tip every person he saw. No bill was under twenty dollars. Some people nodded and smiled at him; most ignored him, lost in their music. Tommy didn't mind.

When he arrived at the mansion, a servant ushered him into the study without a word, closing the door behind him. Wilkes was sitting at the desk, but Tommy was surprised to see someone sitting in a chair in from of him. Generally, Wilkes met with Tommy by himself and kept him away from the other acolytes.

"Ah, Thomas," Wilkes greeted the changeling with a grimace. Wilkes's smile seemed forced, and Tommy noticed the overweight man was sweating. Tommy blinked as he put his hands in his pockets. Something was wrong. "Thank you for joining us. Do you remember Jozef York?"

Tommy looked at the seated figure and broke out in a malicious smile when the name finally clicked. He had not seen the man in eight years, but his haughty expression was the same. York was glaring at Tommy over tented fingers. "Yeah, I remember," Tommy drawled. "Not every day I get to throw one of you assholes off a landing."

Wilkes cringed and glanced at York, but York didn't stir. "Now, I don't think we need to mention that unfortunate night," Wilkes said. York continued to frown at Tommy while Tommy smirked back. Wilkes turned to Tommy. "It has been decided, for the honor of our Lady, York will now be the leader of the acolytes. Your ring will pass to him, and you will serve him."

Tommy didn't say anything. They always acted like he had a choice and he should treat it as an honor when he literally had no option. Wilkes glanced at York and took the slave ring off of one fat pinkie. "Take off your jacket," Wilkes ordered, and Tommy complied. He had worn a sleeveless shirt that night and crossed his arms so both men could see the slave band.

Wilkes turned the ring in several directions, studying it. Tommy fought the urge to surge forward and try to snatch it. He didn't know why the magic of the ring worked on him, but it would stop him from getting close, just like it would block him from hurting whoever wore it. So he just had to wait while they went through their song and dance.

Wilkes brought out a short knife, made a small cut on his thumb, and smeared blood on the ring. "The blood makes you his master," Wilkes explained as he passed the ring to York. "He has to listen to you and only you. He can't harm you. But..." Wilkes trailed off as York took out a hidden knife from his cane to cut his palm. "He's been... stubborn for the last few decades. He doesn't always want to listen. Do with that information as you will."

York didn't comment as he watched the blood well from the fresh wound. He looked at Tommy as he smeared his blood on the ring. Both the ring and the band glowed for a moment, and Tommy tried not to grimace as it burned. Finally, both items stopped glowing, and York smiled as he put the ring on his pointer finger.

"Congratulations," Wilkes said with a smile as he stood up from the desk. "You are now the leader of the acolytes."

York kept his smug smile for a moment, examining the ring on his finger. Tommy waited to see what he would do. Some acolytes sent him away; others wanted him to stick close. There was no telling which category York would be in. York's smile died a little.

"Tell me, slave," York started in a tight tone, "The night you injured me..."

"The night you killed a man in cold blood," Tommy interrupted, and York glared at him.

"...what were your exact orders?" York continued without commenting on Tommy's interruption.

"Now, I don't see why we have to talk about that night," Wilkes said with a nervous chuckle.

"Shut up," York told him in a cold tone, and Wilkes's teeth clacked with how fast he closed his mouth. He kept his glare on Tommy. "What were your orders?"

"To keep you alive," Tommy said.

"No orders to keep me safe?"

"None."

"Now, wait just one minute—" Wilkes started to object.

"Silence him," York told Tommy, and Tommy actually felt a flush of glee at Wilkes's frightened expression.

"Thomas, don't you dare," Wilkes said as Tommy took a step towards him. Wilkes tried to slash the short knife at him, but Tommy dodged the poor defense and transformed. He growled as he grabbed Wilkes's head and slammed it onto the desk. The man cried out but quickly fell silent as Tommy let out a snarl and bared his teeth.

York smiled as he used his cane to stand up, and he leisurely walked behind the desk and sat down. He tented his fingers again and looked at Wilkes as the fat man whimpered. "Looks like the slave's loyalty does not extend to former masters," he drawled.

"I couldn't have known that he would hurt you!" Wilkes cried out. Tommy tightened his grip on the man's head, claws cutting into the skin, but Wilkes just kept babbling. "It's like what I said before! He doesn't always want to listen. You have to give him a direct order to follow!"

"And you neglected to order him to protect me," York said. He was looking at his palm, and with a wave of his hand, the wound started to close. "I have often wondered if that was pure stupidity or spite on your part."

Wilkes groaned. "You were an enforcer. Your role was to go on dangerous missions! The slave was there to keep you alive, not keep you safe!"

"It's true. I was one of the ones to go out and perform the missions that others declined to do. Meanwhile, you sat here and grew fat," York said. He was examining the ring again, comparing it to the gold band on his ring finger. He looked Tommy in the eyes. "Kill him."

"No."

York blinked, and even Wilkes stopped panting for a moment. York's shocked expression gave way to anger, and he glowered. "You have to listen to me. I am your master."

Tommy winced as the band started to burn, but he just rumbled and bared his teeth at York. "I made a promise a long time ago. I wasn't going to kill anyone for you assholes anymore." He nodded at the fat man he was still holding onto the table. "Even this bastard."

York's eyes narrowed. "You hate this man."

"Yep."

"But you won't kill him, as I've ordered you to."

"Nope," Tommy said. He gave York a toothy smile. "Ain't it a bitch?"

Wilkes started to laugh, a high and unhinged twitter. York scowled at the sound and looked like he was chewing on something sour. "You see?" Wilkes asked in that high tone. "He's stubborn."

York moved so fast that Tommy barely saw him, but he took out the hidden knife from his cane and drove it into Wilkes's neck, nicking Tommy's finger as it pinned Wilkes to the desk. Tommy let go and jumped back, watching Wilkes twitch as blood gushed from the wound. York didn't look at the man as he glared at Tommy, sitting back in his chair. "A slave who will not listen is a useless thing indeed," he drawled as Wilkes made a horrible gurgling sound.

Tommy looked between the dying man and the new leader of the acolytes and felt a cold finger of fear run up his back. For as long as he had known them, the acolytes always surprised him with how cruel they could be. The smell of blood filled the air, and Tommy felt his stomach clench in hunger. York called out, and someone opened the door of the study.

Two men came in but paused when they saw Wilkes's dead body and Tommy in his other form. The blonde man turned green, but the redhead just smirked at the body and the blood pooling on the rug.

"Wilkes fought the exchange of power," York lied. He pulled the knife out of Wilkes's neck, and the lifeless body fell to the floor. York wiped the blade on a handkerchief before putting it back into the cane. York tossed the cloth onto Wilkes's body with a dismissive hand wave. "Frost, have someone clean this up."

"Yes, sir," the redhead said and made a slight bow before leaving the room. The blonde was studying Tommy, and Tommy made him jump with a snarl.

"Stop that," York snapped, and Tommy straightened up. "You are not to harm any acolyte unless I say so. You only listen to me. I will be moving my wife and daughter into this mansion. You are not to show up here unless I summon you. Now leave."

"Fine by me," Tommy replied. He transformed into his human form and grabbed his jacket, putting it on. Tommy snapped his teeth at the blonde, making the man jump again. He just smirked as he strolled out of the study and out into the warm night.

Tommy studied the wound on his hand as he walked down the city streets, debating what he would eat. The smell of blood was still in his nose, and it was making his stomach flip in hunger. Meat. Red meat. As raw as he could get it. And booze. Lots of booze. He stretched his arms behind his head and studied the night sky.

So there was a new leader of the acolytes. It would take some time to see if that was a good or bad thing. The man was cold. That much was certain. And apparently, the guy was married. Tommy pitied his poor family.

But then, that wasn't his problem.

www.ingramcontent.com/pod-product-compliance
Lightning Source LLC
Chambersburg PA
CBHW060315260626
47160CB00007B/2624